John Hutton was born
Burnage Grammar Sch
North Wales, where h
various schools and co
North Wales and is no
North East Wales Instit

JOHN HUTTON

29, Herriott Street

TRIAD
PANTHER

Triad/Panther Books
Granada Publishing Ltd
8 Grafton Street, London W1X 3LA

Published by Triad/Panther Books 1983
Reprinted 1984

Triad Paperbacks Ltd is an imprint of
Chatto, Bodley Head & Jonathan Cape Ltd and
Granada Publishing Ltd

First published in Great Britain by
The Bodley Head Ltd 1979

ISBN 0-586-05573-8

Printed and bound in Great Britain by
Collins, Glasgow

Set in Plantin

For my father and mother

AUTHOR'S NOTE

Many readers of this story will recognize that the details of the murder outlined in the first chapter correspond closely (but not exactly) to the facts of the Wallace murder case of the early nineteen thirties. I had better say, therefore, that my novel is not intended as an 'explanation' of that case. My characters, their backgrounds, and all other details are invented and are not intended to bear any relation to actual people or events.

1

It was the evening of Tuesday, February the tenth, 1931. A man was standing outside the front door of his house, Number 29, Herriott Street, in a mean suburb of Manchester. He was rattling the knocker in a despairing way, pausing every so often to bend down and call the name 'Florence' hoarsely through the letter-box. It was a miserable, sodden evening. It had been raining since three o'clock that afternoon with a fine, relentless drizzle, as penetrative as mist. The man was saturated. It was about quarter past nine, and he had been out in this rain since shortly before seven. He looked bedraggled and worn. He was a rather slight man, with no chest to speak of and inadequate, sloping shoulders. He wore steel-rimmed spectacles which flashed occasionally in the dim street lighting, and under his arm he carried a small attaché case which the rain was steadily reducing to a cardboard pulp. When he got tired of shouting through the letter-box, he would huddle back in the doorway, trying to get what shelter he could from the small projection over it which the builder had optimistically called a porch and which served merely to channel water down the back of his neck. He varied this by stepping out on to the pavement and gazing up at the unlighted bedroom window, or occasionally by going down the narrow passage-way which separated his house from the one next door, so that he could rattle and bang on his back door instead of the front one.

He was returning from one of these visits when the light came on in the hall of Number 31, and his neighbours, Mr and Mrs Johnson, emerged. Whether he accosted them or they accosted him was a matter which was never satisfactorily cleared up. He steadfastly denied that he had spoken first; and they firmly maintained that, since they were in a hurry anyway, and had never been much in the habit of talking to their neighbour at the best of times, they were hardly likely to have spoken to him now. However, a conversation was, somehow, started. Mr Rimmer – that was the name of the bedraggled gentleman – explained that he had been locked out of his house, and that he could not get his wife to hear him. Mr and Mrs Johnson, with their hands on their front gate, sympathized perfunctorily, determined to lose as little time as possible.

'It is odd,' said Rimmer, 'very odd indeed, and most unlike Florence.'

'Perhaps she's gone out?' suggested Mrs Johnson. Rimmer considered this carefully and then shook his head.

'That would be very unusual. Florence never goes out; besides she knows I haven't got a key.'

'Is there a window open?' asked Mr Johnson. 'You could get in through that.'

'There's no window open. I've already looked.'

'We'd ask you in to our place to wait for her,' said Mrs Johnson, 'but we're on our way out.'

'It's very kind of you, but I'd rather get into my own house. I'm worried in case something has happened.'

'If you could smash the window of the back door, you could get your hand through and turn the key,' said Johnson. 'I had to do that once.'

'And a right mess you made of it,' said his wife. 'Blood all over the place. Had to have two stitches.'

'Glass can be very dangerous,' agreed Rimmer absently. 'I suppose you don't have a hammer that I could borrow?'

Johnson hurriedly whispered to his wife to go inside again and wait for him there. 'It'll not be long. It'll only take a minute.' Then he went to the coal-shed to fetch the coal hammer.

'It's very kind of you,' said Rimmer when Johnson got back. 'I'm not easy in my mind about things. As a matter of fact I've had a rather disturbing evening.'

'You look wet,' said Johnson. 'You been out in it a long time?'

'Do you know where Welfield Road East is?'

It seemed to Johnson to be an odd sort of thing to ask; it had come out so abruptly; it seemed to have so little to do with the business in hand.

'Never heard of it.' Johnson took stock of Rimmer's back door. 'I suppose you have tried opening it?' he asked. Rimmer smiled like a schoolteacher wearied by a stupid question and said that indeed he had.

'Well, you can do daft things sometimes,' said Johnson, meaning nothing personal by the 'you'. He rapped smartly at the glass in the pane nearest the door handle and nothing happened.

'You'll have to hit it harder than that,' said Rimmer. 'Take care, we don't want any more blood.'

Johnson hit the glass a sharp blow and it cracked in a star shape.

'Good,' said Rimmer. 'Now easy does it.'

Johnson tapped carefully and pieces of the glass fell into the kitchen. Finally he was able to get his hand through.

'The key's in the lock,' he said. 'We should be all right. It won't be bolted will it?'

'The bolt's just below the lock,' said Rimmer.

The bolt was stiff and, from his unusual angle, Johnson had some difficulty in freeing it, but at last he got the door open and he and Rimmer stepped into the kitchen, treading gingerly because of the glass which was all over the floor.

'Everything seems to be in order,' said Rimmer, staring round the room.

'I expect you'll find she's just slipped out somewhere for a few minutes,' said Johnson. He didn't go, although he had now done all that a good neighbour could be expected to. The fact was that he wanted to see what Rimmer said when he discovered that he had smashed his door in for nothing; he would have been mildly amused to see his neighbour discomfited. He followed Rimmer on an inspection of the ground floor – it was very quickly completed.

'Looks as though you're right,' said Rimmer. 'It's too bad of Florence, when she knows I haven't a key.'

He started to climb the stairs and Johnson, rather uncertainly, followed. Johnson did not go beyond the top of the staircase, and he waited there as Rimmer popped his head into each of the two bedrooms in turn.

'Looks all right,' said Rimmer. Johnson turned to go down while Rimmer went towards the bathroom. Johnson was at the foot of the stairs when he heard Rimmer's voice calling him.

'Johnson, she's here; come here, Johnson.'

Johnson went up the flight two steps at a time. Opposite the bathroom was a very small room, just large enough for a child's bedroom, and Rimmer was there. So too was his wife. She was lying on the floor. Fortunately it was not possible to see her distinctly. Rimmer had been lighting the gas jets as he had searched the house, but the only light here was the one on the landing, and that did not shine directly into the room. Rimmer was standing with a spent match in his hand, staring down with horror. Johnson got a blurred impression of the body sprawled on the floor, and of blood all over the place. The pathologists were to speak in detail, later, of the severity of Florence Rimmer's injuries. The attack, the newspapers said with relish, had been of an almost unbelievable ferocity. Fragments of bone had been driven into the skirtingboard, part of the brain had been pushed out through the skull, and blood had even bespattered the ceiling. Johnson took none of this in. It was quite clear, without any close examination, that Mrs Rimmer was dead; and Johnson kept his head, plucked Rimmer away from her, carefully shepherded him downstairs, took him next door, and then summoned the police.

It became a famous case. One of the 'Notable Trials', one of the 'Most Amazing Crimes' series. It was the sort of case that is argued over endlessly, possessing all those elements which recommend a murder to the crime-reading public. It had been ferocious, it was a domestic murder, it was a wee bit mysterious because no adequate motive was ever found for it, and there were some rather puzzling details. But most of all it caught public fancy because of the character of the murderer. Wilfred Rimmer was arrested commendably quickly – the whole investigation was regarded as a credit to the police – and was shown to be an assassin of exceptional talents. This insignificant little man had played his part with a callous coolness, a machiavellian subtlety, that placed him beside the Crippens, the George Joseph Smiths, the Landrus of the criminal world. His self-possession at the trial was astonishing, and ultimately damning. He stood up to an eight-hour cross-examination without flagging or faltering, without ever contradicting himself, and without for a moment losing his self-control. Indeed one of the commentators on the case had said that if Rimmer had shown himself to be a little more human in the witness box he would probably have been alive today.

There was a good deal of prejudice against Rimmer, and his unsympathetic character more than offset any difficulty posed by the absence of a tangible motive. To all outward appearances Wilfred and Florence Rimmer had lived together in complete peace and harmony for fifteen years. Their lives had been quiet and dull, their financial affairs were in perfect order, and no irregularities of any other sort were turned up by the most thorough investigation. Fortunately, in British law, as the prosecuting counsel and the judge in turn reminded the jury, one does not have to prove motive. It is usually rather cynically reckoned that in fifteen years of marriage most couples will find sufficient reasons for wanting to batter one another to death. The more Rimmer protested that his marriage had been ideally happy the more the jury, and the public they so ably represented, smiled their disbelief. The prosecuting counsel put the matter rather neatly when he said: 'These two people had cohabited together for nearly sixteen years. To the world they presented a face of domestic happiness. Neighbours had never heard voices raised or blows struck; in their public appearances they showed as a happy, united couple. But, members of the jury, I do not have to remind you that marriage is a very private thing. The real strains and stresses of married life develop behind doors and away from the public gaze. Who can possibly know the bitterness, the resentments, the disappointments which festered between these two people? Such matters, by their very nature, are carefully hidden away, not confided to strangers. They would be known only to two people, and one of them is dead, and the other in the dock before you.'

In this manner it was elegantly proved that Rimmer must have had a sufficient motive for killing his wife, and that it was impossible that this motive should be known.

The odd circumstances which contributed to the fascination of the case were as follows. Rimmer was an insurance collector who operated from one of the company's offices in the centre of Manchester. Nearly opposite this office was a public telephone box, and at lunch time on the day before the murder a call was made from this box to Rimmer's office. The caller gave the name Benson, J. T. Benson, and he asked to speak to Rimmer. After a brief enquiry the caller was told that Mr Rimmer had just left the building for lunch, so he left a message, which was given to Rimmer when he returned. The message was that Rimmer was to call at an address, 34, Welfield Road East, in a district on the other side of town from where Rimmer lived. He was to call there some time after seven-thirty on the following day, the day of the murder, to discuss some insurance business. When Rimmer was given this message he made a note of the address, asked two or three people if they knew where Welfield Road East was, and then went off to continue his day's routine.

This telephone call became the crux of the whole case. Whoever had made it had had some difficulty in dialling the number and had obtained it through the operator; it was because of this that the call could be traced at all. When it was discovered that the call had come from a telephone box which was actually within sight of the insurance office, it began to look decidedly fishy. Any person honestly intent on insurance business would have saved his twopence and walked across the road to conduct his business at first hand. It also became clear that Rimmer himself must have been very close to the box when the call was made. He had literally 'just gone out for lunch'. Either he was passing the box when the call was made, or he made it himself. So the jury were presented with two possibilities. According to one theory the murderer had waited in the box for Rimmer to emerge and then telephoned his message through, deliberately going through the operator so that the call could be traced and Rimmer incriminated. Obviously the caller would not have wished to speak to Rimmer himself because his voice would have been recognized. On the next evening, confident that Rimmer would be absent, the murderer had persuaded Mrs Rimmer to let him in to the house, done her to death, and then made his escape; all this while poor Rimmer combed Manchester for a non-existent address. According to the other theory Rimmer himself had telephoned the message, disguising his voice to do so, in order to give himself an alibi for the following evening. He had battered his wife to death, then he had gone off and spent a damp two and a half hours looking for Welfield Road East, which he knew did not exist, asking, in the process, an unreasonable number of people, so that the police would have no difficulty in establishing that he had in fact been where he said he had been. Then he had returned, collected a witness in the shape of Mr Johnson, and 'discovered' the body.

The trouble with the theory that somebody else had plotted against Rimmer was that, again, no motive for such an elaborate plot could be found. Rimmer's insurance collecting was on a very small scale. There was no money in the house, and no reason for anybody to expect any. The objection to the theory that Rimmer had done the deed was that he must have been very quick. Mrs Rimmer had been seen, alive and normal, just before half past six, and at ten to seven Rimmer was boarding the first of his trams and imprinting himself on the mind of the first of his witnesses. Fortunately, 'just before half past six' is an elastic term, which could be pulled back, after careful questioning by the police, to mean something nearer ten past. Perhaps a really quick murderer could have battered a woman to death, cleaned himself completely, for not a spot of anything incriminating was found on Rimmer or his clothes, and got to the tram in thirty-five minutes. There was a rather bizarre theory about this – that Rimmer had stripped before the murder so that he could the more easily wash away the blood. Most newspaper readers were delighted with the vision of the thin, cadaverous, bespectacled Rimmer, stark naked, pounding his wife to death. It was the sort of touch that helped to make the murder popular.

There were other things that counted against Wilfred Rimmer, who seemed to be a very odd sort of fish indeed for an insurance pedlar. He had a number of pursuits which could only be called 'intellectual'. He read philosophy, and a number of books on the subject were found in his house. He dabbled in science, and, at one time, had fitted up the little room in which his wife was done to death with a small bench on which he conducted experiments. This led at least one newspaper to christen the case 'Murder in the Laboratory'. He played the violin, and he and his wife, who was described as an accomplished pianist, had been known to go through a Beethoven sonata in the front room. All in all he created a very unfortunate impression, which was compounded by an air of disdain, which made him appear stand-offish. He dressed in an old-fashioned way, with a high wing collar, and appeared to put on airs, to consider himself better than anyone else, 'like a teacher', as one of the neighbours put it. He had prided himself on being a rational man, one controlling his emotions, and this made him seem heartless. Throughout his hours in the witness box he had striven to appear calm, lucid, controlled, fully in possession of himself, and it was this that finally damned him; if anyone could have concocted and carried through this remarkable crime it would be the sort of man Rimmer had shown himself to be. As one of the writers on the case, Mr Gervase Pleyel the well known crime novelist, said, 'The evidence was admittedly ambiguous but there could be no doubt about the character of the man. There in the witness box Rimmer gave a demonstration of callous indifference and inhuman self-possession which was more damning ultimately than the most direct evidence could have been. One knew as one saw Rimmer that he was the incarnation of evil: cold, calculating, merciless, and, above all, diabolically clever.'

The evidence, psychological and factual, seemed convincing enough to the jury, who took less that two hours to decide that Rimmer was guilty. He was sentenced, his appeal was dismissed, and in due course he was hanged.

The English have a weakness for a good murder, and this was a very good one. It was taken up by the 'connoisseurs of crime', people who make, or supplement, their living by writing about famous cases of the past. The study of Rimmer and his fate became a great game for such men and women, because it offered scope for psychologizing, and because it was always open to them to challenge the verdict and comment on the flimsiness of the evidence. So it became one of that small group of 'classic crimes' that are exhumed every so often to serve as newspaper articles, or television plays, or even full-length books. Nearly forty years after the trial Mr Charles Winnick, addressing himself to the task of writing the definitive account of the case, found himself preceded by nearly thirty writers, including one of the counsel who had been prominent in the case, one of the medical witnesses – a famous expert in his field – and one of the police officers. Most of these writers had confined themselves to brief sketches, essays or monographs, but there had been two full-length, and manifestly biased books. Charles Winnick was determined that his own book should supersede all the others. It would examine what the others had said and decide if they had been right to say it; it would investigate all those matters which the police ought to have investigated and had not; it would seek out the witnesses who were still alive and test the validity of their evidence; in short, it might even improve upon the trial as an examination of the case.

Winnick had already been round to the house at Number 29, Herriott Street, where the crime had taken place, measuring rooms and taking photographs, while the bewildered lady of the house watched and made him cups of tea. He had consulted all the official records. He had followed the route which Rimmer had taken in his search for Welfield Road East, knocking at the doors of Numbers 34, Welfield Roads North, South and West, and number 34, Welfield Crescent, all of which Rimmer had visited. He had examined the Post Office telephone procedures current at the time, had studied the methods of the insurance company for which Rimmer had worked, and had learned a good deal about Rimmer's own punctilious methods of dealing with the money that came into his hands.

This patient accumulation of detail had already brought its rewards. Winnick was able, for instance, to contradict the American criminologist, Mr Dwight K. Chambers, who, in a monograph on the case, had stated that Rimmer had rented the house in Herriott Street. In fact he had bought it, and after he was hanged the balance of the mortgage had had to be paid out of his estate. Another writer on the case, Miss Ursula Hope-Johnson, had published as a fact a statement that Rimmer had been an accomplished actor, prominent in local amateur theatricals. This, Winnick demonstrated, was probably based on a misreading of evidence given at the trial. Rimmer had once produced a play for an amateur group, and he had also contributed a criticism of a performance by another group to the local paper. Winnick was also able to state, categorically, that there were no poisons in Rimmer's 'laboratory', though it had often been said that there were, and that there were no books on 'black magic' on his shelves, though this too had been suggested.

The fly in the ointment, to be expected after so many years no doubt, but still deplorable, was the high death rate amongst the people who had been connected with the case. It was urgently necessary to hunt up the survivors while there was still time; and it was in this frame of mind that Winnick sat down to write begging for an interview with a person he had only just realized existed – Florence Rimmer's sister. The background of the victim in a murder case is often shadowy, inevitably attention is focused on the murderer. Winnick had a vague idea that Florence was a 'lady', socially superior to her husband, but he had discovered nothing about her family, and none of the books had said anything about a sister. It was quite a find, and Winnick rubbed his hands over his discovery. This sister was living with her husband in Bournemouth and, provided that she was still in possession of her senses – Winnick calculated that she must be in her late seventies – she would surely have something to tell about her sister's married life. Winnick sat down and wrote an exquisitely tactful letter, then went on with his investigation of the Manchester Tramways timetables for 1931 while he waited for a reply.

2

In writing to Beatrice Naismith, the sister of the murdered woman, Winnick had naturally expressed himself cautiously. A murder in the family is not something which, even after forty years, one wishes to be reminded of. What Winnick could not have known was that the memory was closely bound up in Beatrice's mind with a period of her life, and a set of recollections which were, independently of the murder, quite painful enough. She had been told of Florence's death when she was in hospital, and any mention of it brought vividly to her mind the scene in the private ward, with its cheery, flowery wall paper, the bottles and the antiseptic smell, and the reproduction of a Monet snow-scene, which hung on the wall opposite her bed. The operation, coming after a series of miscarriages, had finally ended Herbert's hopes of having a child. It had also, it seemed to Beatrice, finally ended the serious relationship between them. The strains had been evident for a long time, but there had always been the hope that a child would have made things right again. Now she lay in her hospital bed, weak, listless and irritable, trying to resign herself to the ending of that hope. Herbert visited her punctiliously, and she watched him with a morose particularity in case he betrayed the fact that he had finally rejected her.

Of course he didn't. His manner, as always, was impeccable. There was nobody better than Herbert at concealing his feelings. He allowed the world to see only what he chose, and at this time he chose that it should see an attentive, anxious, and kind husband. Every day he brought her a little gift, fruit, flowers, jewellery. He was pleasant and friendly with the hospital staff, but he had a quietly authoritative manner and made it quite clear that only the best was good enough for his wife. He played his part so flawlessly that Beatrice, when she was left alone again, found herself wondering why it was that it all seemed hollow. He had always protested that his feeling for her had not changed, that his infidelities were a mere concession to the animal side of his nature. And Beatrice had tried to persuade herself that her own physical feebleness and mental depression had tricked her into making a mistake about him, and that he really did love her still. But she knew that it was not so. He might smile, and say gentle things, and produce little gifts, but it was a façade, there was nothing behind it. Perhaps he was just hanging on until she was strong enough to be told the truth. She lay there wondering listlessly about the years ahead. Not, in a sense, that she had anything to worry about, she told herself. She wouldn't divorce Herbert, and he couldn't divorce her. Nor, with his business interests, could he simply walk out on her. No, they would simply have to rub along as best they could; a humdrum, commonplace fate, shared, she supposed, by many couples. Did they, she wondered, all find it as bitter as she did?

On 'that day' – as she came later to think of it – Herbert had visited later than usual. She had noticed straight away that he looked tired, under the weather, although he had done his best to appear normal.

'Better not kiss you,' he had said. 'I think I'm running one of my colds.'

He touched the tip of his finger with his lips and pressed it to her cheek. Beatrice saw that the doctor had come in with him and was keeping himself in the background, fiddling about with some bottles and pretending to examine her charts. Behind his back she made a little face at Herbert, but he took no notice. Evidently it had been arranged that the doctor should stay, and she began to wonder why.

'The fact is,' began Herbert, speaking slowly, 'I – er – there is something to tell you.'

Presumably because of his cold he was keeping his distance from her and stood, rather awkwardly, in the exact centre of the small carpet by the bed. He avoided looking at her, and she began to wonder what was coming. Was this it? Was he about to tell her that their life together was over? And had he asked the doctor to stand by in case she took it badly? He needn't have worried, thought Beatrice. In her terrible, dead weariness of spirit it seemed impossible that she would ever get worked up about anything again, even about this. She was able to look at him quite tranquilly, and to say 'Go on, Herbert,' in a perfectly steady voice, before gazing back at the ceiling again.

'The fact is, Bea, something has happened.'

She lay quite still and said nothing.

'It's about Florence.'

'Florence?' Now she did look at him; this was completely unexpected.

'She's – there's been an accident.'

Ideas seemed to rattle round for a long time in Beatrice's head before she was able to absorb them. She repeated the word 'accident' a couple of times in a slow, meditative voice, while the idea came into focus. Then, laboriously, she found the appropriate thing to say.

'What sort of an accident?'

'It's rather serious.'

It all reminded Beatrice of something, and then she remembered being told of her father's death just like this, a slow, painstaking build-up. She stirred a little, irritably.

'Do you mean she's dead?'

'Yes, Beatrice, she's dead.'

Even now, Beatrice noted, there was not a flutter in her heart.

'You'd better tell me about it. Get it over.'

She saw Herbert glance towards the doctor. Still he seemed to find it difficult to speak, and she wondered why.

'You're going to find this a bit of a shock, Bea. The fact is, it wasn't an ordinary sort of an accident.'

She stared at him.

'A burglar must have broken into the house. Florence must have disturbed him or something, and he must have hit her. That's what killed her.'

This was very difficult to grasp.

'What do you mean, Herbert?'

Herbert repeated what he had said, slowly and carefully. This time he used the word 'murdered'. Florence had been murdered, and Beatrice repeated it two or three times, wonderingly. The doctor began fussing round with something for her to drink, and she saw him make an imperious gesture towards Herbert. Soon after this everything grew even more confused, and she passed into unconsciousness. That was how she had heard the news of Florence's death.

Oddly, the murder drew her closer to Herbert than she had been for some years. Without him she would have been totally lost. She insisted on being told all the details of what had happened, and in the early days at least Herbert managed to make it all sound more or less like a bizarre accident. Getting in the way of some homicidal burglar is, in some respects at least, like getting in the way of a double-decker bus – a horrible, random misfortune. Beatrice wanted to know how Wilfred was, how he was bearing the loss, whether he was going to come down and see her. The fact that Herbert's replies were rather evasive did not surprise her because, naturally, he had never felt particularly drawn to Florence's husband, and he could not be expected to start gushing about him now. So Beatrice was completely unprepared for the second shock. She was not allowed to look at newspapers, and all her information about the case came through Herbert, and one day he came into the ward looking grey-faced and anxious.

'Bad news again,' he said, baldly, sitting on the side of her bed.

Beatrice did not say anything, though she could not imagine any additional bad thing that could have happened. But she had made a great point of the fact that she wanted to be told everything, assuring the doctors that she was strong enough to take it, so it was up to her to prove this strength. Herbert looked directly into her eyes.

'The police have arrested Wilfred.'

'Arrested Wilfred? What for?'

'For the murder. They seem to have got it into their heads that he was responsible in some way.'

Beatrice could make nothing of this.

'You said it was a man – someone who had broken in – a burglar.'

'That was what they thought at first, but they couldn't find any signs of a break-in.'

Herbert did his best to make light of it. Apparently the husband was always the first person to be suspected in a case of this sort. It was, Herbert tried to imply, a kind of amusing routine procedure, the husband being arrested while they looked about them and found out who had really done it. Beatrice was not quite so easily satisfied as that.

'They wouldn't arrest him unless they had some kind of proof. What is it? What have they found?'

And when Herbert answered that as far as he knew they had not found anything, Beatrice did not believe him. Like all respectable people she had been brought up to believe that the law and the police worked in a fair, just, and rational manner. Her father, in the old days, reading in his newspaper that a man had been arrested for some crime or other, would invariably greet the news with the words: 'They've got him, then'. It seemed to him such an inevitable step from the arrest to the conviction and sentence. All that Beatrice knew about Wilfred told her that it was absurd to think of him as a murderer, but this news that he had been arrested left her helplessly feeling that he must be. Herbert was very patient with her, and much later, when the whole thing was over and Beatrice was able to read about it and judge the evidence for herself, she was able to see that he had spoken the literal truth. But at this time, lying in her hospital bed, cut off from all other information, she convinced herself that Herbert must be concealing something in order to spare her feelings.

'There must be something more than that. Why ever would Wilfred want to kill Florence?' she would ask, and Herbert would carefully explain that nobody could suggest any reason at all, but that in British law that did not matter.

'That's silly, Herbert. That can't be right. Nobody murders anybody without having a reason for it. What sort of thing are they saying about Wilfred?'

Herbert gave up almost the whole of his time to the case, travelling repeatedly between Manchester, where he gave Wilfred what help he could, and his home and the hospital in London. He gave Beatrice a step by step account of what was going on, which made it quite plain that the prosecution was no frivolous mistake, but that it would be pressed to a trial. All the details about the telephone call, and Mr Benson and Welfield Road East, had perplexed Beatrice. They seemed rather thin and confusing evidence on which to support a charge of murder. There was some hope, so Herbert said, that the case would be thrown out at the committal proceedings, but this hope failed, and after that everything seemed to proceed with a horrible inevitability. Before the trial itself began Beatrice had been sent home from hospital and she was able to read the papers, which had angered her exceedingly. The picture which they presented of Wilfred was so monstrously distorted. Herbert had reported to her Wilfred's own steadfast assertion of his innocence, and of the idyllic nature of his life with Florence. When Beatrice sat down to think out her own attitude to all this she settled into a stubborn belief that a dreadful mistake was being made, that Wilfred had had nothing to do with the murder, and that his life with Florence had been as happy as he claimed. The real grounds for this belief of Beatrice's were emotional. The marriage between Wilfred and Florence had always seemed odd, sometimes odd in a romantic way and sometimes odd in a depressing way. Wilfred had been, according to some standards, a disappointment; it was a tribute to some quality in him that, latterly, Beatrice had begun to wonder whether, perhaps, it was these standards that were wrong; viewed in another light Wilfred could appear admirable.

Whatever his faults Wilfred had integrity. He was an honest man; he was a mild man; he carried self-effacement to the point of a vice, but he was kindly and generous. And he had been strictly true to his own principles. Wilfred had been a reminder to Beatrice that people can be decent and honest and sincere. His marriage to Florence had been fine precisely because it so pointedly ignored all the values which ordinary folk held so highly. If all this had been a sham, then everything was a sham, there were no values at all anywhere. And if Beatrice had misjudged Wilfred so completely then she could never trust in her own judgement again either. In short, it became a mental and moral necessity for Beatrice to believe in Wilfred. What sort of hatred could it be that festers as quietly as Wilfred's must have done for her never to have seen a glimpse of it, and then expresses itself in such a dreadfully savage piece of violence? What kind of life did it point to between her sister and Wilfred? Beatrice pushed these ideas away. They made no sense, they contradicted everything that Beatrice knew.

The official processes gave Beatrice no help at all. She seemed to be alone in her belief; Herbert loyally supported her, but she could not be quite sure of his sincerity. The rest of the world clamorously asserted Wilfred's guilt. Beatrice read all about the crowds booing Wilfred on his way to the court, she saw the hostile paragraphs and the unflattering photos. After the verdict was announced there was cheering, and the newspapers were able to be more specifically unkind. Herbert tried to be optimistic, holding out hopes of what the appeal court might do, but the appeal court did nothing. All these high legal authorities seemed to be just as certain of Wilfred's guilt as everybody else. Finally the last hope, of a reprieve, vanished. One morning they took him out, this person she had known and respected, and hanged him for murdering a sister she had loved very dearly. Herbert visited Wilfred for the last time on the day before the execution, and then hurried back to be with her. She remembered how worn he had looked, and how shattered. He never spoke very much about that last interview with the condemned man, except to say the Wilfred 'had taken it very well'. To the end Wilfred had maintained his innocence, and in the face of almost universal condemnation of him, Beatrice continued to believe him.

After it was all over Herbert took a strong line, forbade Beatrice to think about it, which was impossible, and refused to talk about it with her.

'It's over, it's done with. Nothing can help Wilfred now. You'll make yourself ill again if you go on like this.' This was the burden of what Herbert had to say; and, as far as the last point went at least, he had some justification. Beatrice had very nearly had a breakdown after the execution. It had been entirely owing to Herbert's care that she had pulled through, and she felt that she owed it to him not to let herself go again. Gradually the affair sank to the back of her mind. She surreptitiously read all the accounts of it that she could get hold of, like a person who indulges a horrid secret vice. And, like such a person, after every fresh indulgence, she regretted it bitterly. All the accounts were the same, ignorant and biased, false to the spirit of Wilfred's marriage as she had known it. Herbert was right. The damage was done and was not likely to be undone; the best thing was to put it out of her mind. It took nearly ten years before, in any sense, she could be said to have done this.

When Winnick's letter arrived a further thirty years had pretty well buried it out of sight. As far as it was possible ever to forget something like that Beatrice had forgotten it. It was always ready to be recalled, of course. References to the case could still raise disturbing memories, and Beatrice winced a little at Winnick's tactful request. She passed the letter across to Herbert without a word. He read it and set his jaw at an angle expressive of disgust.

'Put it at the back of the fire.'

She took the letter back and read it again. Then she carefully folded it and put it in its envelope.

'What are you going to do?' he asked.

'I'm going to think about it.'

'If you've got any sense you'll do as I say. Put it at the back of the fire.'

'I may do, but I'm going to think about it first.' And she went upstairs.

What had given her pause was a phrase which Winnick had used about 'setting the record straight'. He had only hoped by this to give an impression of his own impartiality, but to Beatrice the words conveyed a promise of redeeming Wilfred's character. This was not what Winnick had intended, and it would have surprised him. Naturally he imagined that Beatrice shared the general opinion of Wilfred's guilt. She carried the letter around with her for some days, reading it every so often and brooding over it. She knew very well what Herbert was worried about. He had intended to marry Florence himself, and the way Wilfred had cut him out with her had always been a sore point. Well, she would be tactful. He was entitled to every consideration on that score at least.

Herbert waylaid her a couple of times in the next few days to ask if she had decided what to do. At first she said that she had not, finally she told him that she had decided to write back and agree to see Winnick.

'Well,' he said after digesting this, 'I think you're very silly. It's all over, it's gone, it's dead and buried. What good do you imagine it'll do to rake it all up again?'

Beatrice pressed her lips together grimly. Naturally Herbert had never felt about Wilfred as she had.

'It might do some good. It's time somebody tried to do something about all those lies that were told.'

'What makes you think this fellow won't tell some lies of his own?'

'He talks about setting the record straight.'

'He'll talk about anything,' said Herbert heavily, 'that will get him into this house. Well, if you let him you're a bigger fool than I take you for, that's all I can say.'

Beatrice was not offended by this plain speaking, but it was bad tactics on Herbert's part. She merely smiled acidly and said that they would see about that.

'I'll write to the fellow,' Herbert offered. 'I'll send him a letter that'll tell him where to get off.'

But Beatrice refused this offer, and he did not care to press her any further. Her intelligence told her that Herbert was right, but she still felt that she ought to do what she could, that she would be failing Wilfred and Florence if she let this chance slip. She had a series of recollections of Wilfred as a kindly, likeable man, a man who had been gentle and honourable, and this opinion could be put on record. It ought to count for something. At least someone would have spoken up for him. Surely this writer, whoever he was, would be interested to hear her views and would give them publicity. This was Beatrice's state of mind when she sat down eventually and wrote to Winnick inviting him to visit her.

3

When Beatrice had got her letter off to Winnick she sat down and began to think about the past. This was partly an attempt to rehearse what she might, and might not, say to him, but it was also a piece of self-indulgence. She had always enjoyed going back to the days before the First World War, which had become, in her mind, a kind of golden age. She must make it clear to him what kind of home it was that Florence had come from. In those days their father, Mr Calderwood, had been pretty wealthy. Not any silly, showy wealthiness, but good, solid, comfortable affluence. Their house had been large, with servants to do all the unpleasant work, so the girls and their mother had been left free to lead graceful social lives, visiting and entertaining, cultivating their minds, reading the latest books, studying the piano (in Florence's case at least, Beatrice had had 'no ear for music'). Sometimes they had visited London, not that London has anything very sensational to offer your thoroughbred Mancunian, and, once, had even gone abroad, to Brussels. It was easy for people to forget, looking at photographs of the dingy house where Florence had spent her married life, that she had this kind of background. Winnick must be reminded of it and encouraged to place it fairly prominently before his readers.

The two families, the Calderwoods and the Naismiths, had lived close together and had been on terms of the greatest intimacy. Mr and Mrs Calderwood and Mr and Mrs Naismith had known one another long before the girls, or Herbert, had been born. Mr Calderwood was in cotton, he was the third generation of his family in that business. Mr Naismith's father had been in tobacco, but Mr Naismith had been farsighted enough to see the possibilities inherent in engineering, and he had branched out on his own, founding a firm which was to do quite well out of the coming of the motor car, and very well indeed out of the war. The young people, in 1913, had been the fortunate ones of the earth. Beatrice was twenty in that year, Florence was a little less than two years younger and Herbert was exactly six weeks older than Beatrice. In the summer of 1913, Herbert was at the end of his first year at Oxford and it was confidently expected that he and Florence would marry in two or three years' time. There was not a shadow of any sort on the horizon.

Florence envied Herbert his luck, as she called it, in being sent to Oxford. She imagined Herbert as being engaged twenty-four hours a day in a constant dialogue about political and social and religious thought, though he laughed at her and tried to tell her that it was not at all like that. Mr Naismith had thought that it would be a good idea for Herbert to go to Oxford, largely on social grounds. Herbert himself, while he had no pretensions to being a scholar, was certainly no fool, and Manchester Grammar School had given him an excellent education. He always had a dread of appearing to put on airs, so he made less of himself, in Beatrice's estimation at any rate, than he might have done. Oxford, to him, was stimulating and enjoyable, he took his studies fairly seriously and was far too sensible and cautious to get himself mixed up in any of the 'smarter sets' in the 'varsity', as his father insisted on calling it. He enjoyed the pleasant life of an undergraduate whose future is quite secure whatever he does, or fails to do, in his final examinations. Florence professed herself disappointed with his attitude. He was 'wasting his opportunities' she thought. Herbert asked what opportunities it was that he was wasting.

'Well, are you going to be quite satisfied just to go into your father's business? Don't you want to make something of yourself?'

He laughed pleasantly as Florence said this, and appealed to Beatrice for her support.

'What's wrong with making something of myself in Dad's business? What do you think, Bea? What's Florence got in mind for me? Do you see me as a big bug in politics or something?'

'There are many problems in the world,' said Florence solemnly, 'and great changes are on the way. Shouldn't you be involved in these changes?'

'I suppose I will be whether I like it or not. I don't see myself as a great intellect. Of course we talk about these things.'

To Beatrice this seemed a very sensible attitude and she would much rather hear from Herbert about the social life he was leading. Florence had always been intense about 'these things'. She used to talk in a rather daring way about politics and social problems and religious belief, repeating ideas from books which Beatrice was sure she had not properly understood. She was an ardent feminist, and her father used to tease her about this, saying how surprised he was that she had not broken anything, or chained herself to anything, or hit anybody over the head with an umbrella. He used, jokily, to ask her to choose something cheap to smash.

'I'll have to pay for it, you know, just let me off lightly.' This sort of chaff annoyed Florence. She would toss her head and look prim, and tell her father in her 'school-missy' voice not to be so silly. Fortunately Herbert was able to save some of his credit with her by telling her about the debates he had attended, and the notabilities who had come down to address them. She was happy to listen to him when he spoke like this.

It was almost by chance one day that he mentioned meeting in a second-hand bookshop near Deansgate a boy he had known at school. 'He's quite a bobby-dazzler, really,' he said. 'Rather in your line, Florence.' It was perilous to abbreviate Florence's name. Beatrice cheerfully answered to 'Bea', or even, though she didn't much like it, 'Beatty'; but Florence would give anyone a hard stare who called her 'Flo' or 'Flora', and 'Flossie' made her outspokenly indignant.

'What do you mean, in my line?' she asked now, suspecting some kind of jibe or dig.

'Oh, you know,' said Herbert, 'he's not like me. He hasn't got all the privileges that I've got. He's starting at the bottom of the ladder and all that sort of thing.'

It seemed to Beatrice that there was a certain amount of hurt pride in this speech, but Florence either did not notice this, or affected not to.

'What is he doing then?'

'He's working in a shipping office, clerking; but most nights he goes to night school, and he spends the rest of his time in the Central Library.'

'That's very fine,' said Florence gravely. 'I suppose he had not the money to go on to the varsity?'

'He hasn't any money at all. He got to M.G.S. on a scholarship – it takes some doing, that does. They don't give scholarships away. He was pretty clever at school.'

Florence was impressed.

'He sounds very interesting,' she said. 'You must bring him round to see us.'

Herbert laughed a little uncertainly.

'Oh, I don't know about that.'

'Nonsense, Herbert, you shouldn't be such a snob.'

This was unkind of Florence. Whatever one said about Herbert, he was not a snob. Beatrice was about to make an indignant protest when Herbert cut in.

'It's not that. It's just that I don't think Wilfred would like it himself. He's an independent sort of chap. When we were at school he would never come to our houses because he couldn't invite us back.'

Florence said that he sounded rather a fine sort of person, and Herbert said that he would not be surprised if old Wilfred did quite well for himself, and then the conversation dropped. Later, when the girls were alone together, Beatrice tackled her sister.

'You were a bit beastly to Herbert, Florence, saying that he was a snob.'

'Well, he annoys me sometimes. And I could see perfectly well that he only told me about this boy Wilfred in order to impress me.'

'Impress you with what?'

'Oh, you know. He expected me to say how wonderful it was of him to mention this Wilfred. Herbert always expects to be admired for being nice about people; he thinks that it wiil make people say how nice he is himself.'

Beatrice bit back her exasperation. There was enough truth in what Florence said to annoy her. She could only reply that she thought that Florence was very unfair.

'Herbert's all right,' said Florence, 'but he's wasting himself. He's simply content to take what comes. I think he needs shaking up a bit.'

Perhaps pursuing this idea of shaking Herbert up, Florence, a few days later, raised the question of Wilfred.

'Have you seen that friend of yours again, Herbert?'

'Friend of mine – ?'

'The one you were telling us about the other day – Wilfred – the one who goes to night school.'

'He's not really a friend of mine, Florence, I just happened to meet him. No, I haven't seen him. I don't suppose I ever shall.'

'That would be a pity. He sounds the sort of person who ought to be encouraged.'

'I don't think he would appreciate the idea that he was to be encouraged,' said Herbert bluntly. 'I think he might find it a bit patronizing.'

Florence thought about this carefully for a moment or two before replying. 'I meant that he sounded as though he might be an interesting friend to have, a worthwhile sort of friend. It would be a pity to lose touch with him. Aren't you going to try to see him again?'

Herbert did his best to explain that their previous meeting had been a matter of pure chance, and that the last thing that Wilfred would expect, or even perhaps want, would be for Herbert to start seeking him out.

'We didn't even know one another very well at school.'

'Didn't he say that he spent a lot of time in the Central Library? You could probably find him there.'

'I don't want to find him there,' Herbert laughed genially. 'And I don't suppose he wants me to either. He goes there to work.'

But Florence was not to be put off. She could be very pigheaded when fixed on an idea, as Beatrice well knew, and eventually Herbert had to promise that if he met Wilfred again by some chance then he would ask him for tea, and the girls would be invited too. Florence made it quite clear that she expected this chance to happen.

'I can't promise that he'll come, mind you,' said Herbert. 'I'll ask him but I can't promise.'

But Wilfred surprised Herbert by agreeing to come; indeed, Herbert said, he seemed quite pleased to have been asked. In this fortuitous way the girls got their first sight of Wilfred Rimmer.

Beatrice remembered the afternoon vividly. Herbert had warned them to keep everything as casual as possible, so as not to make Wilfred feel awkward, and they had arranged themselves with a careful negligence about the Naismiths' drawing room. Herbert had entered with a slightly artificial geniality, as though he had just that moment met Wilfred unexpectedly and decided to bring him in.

'Nice to find you here,' Herbert said, smirking at his own adroit pretence. 'This is Wilfred, I ran into him in the Central Library the other evening.'

Beatrice herself was chiefly aware of a contrast. Herbert was big, broad-shouldered, and carried himself well. He was always well dressed, his clothes carefully and expensively tailored, and he was perfectly relaxed, being on his own territory. Wilfred was shorter, very thin, with a narrow chest and sloping shoulders. He did not exactly stoop but his head poked forward. His clothes were, quite simply, terrible. Obviously they were the best he had and spent most of their time in moth-balls, but they were cheap and readymade out of some kind of shiny, dark-blue material. His shirtcollar was too large for his neck, and the sleeves of his shirt were too long for his jacket. Also he was obviously very ill at ease and did not know what to do with his hands. He looked what he was, a seedy little second-rate clerk.

Once or twice Beatrice looked covertly towards Florence to see whether she was disappointed by Herbert's friend, but Florence's manner was giving nothing away. She behaved charmingly, got Wilfred to sit next to her and did her best to draw him out. It was uphill work. Wilfred's voice was no more impressive than his appearance. It was rather flat and dreary, Beatrice thought, and a little bit common. His replies were laboured, and Florence's prattle began to sound desperate. It was at this moment that Mrs Naismith entered the room. Herbert would have preferred it if his mother had not come in at all, but it never crossed her mind to stay away. If Herbert brought a friend home for the first time, then it was her duty to meet him, and Mrs Naismith took this duty seriously. She was a formidable woman, even the girls were a little bit in awe of her, and poor Wilfred looked completely swamped. She was tall and large – physically Herbert took after her. She had a hard commanding voice, and a bright, incisive social manner; she saw at a glance that Wilfred was ill at ease and she set out to be as gracious as possible, an act of condescension which reduced her guest to a state of inarticulate twitching.

'You were one of Herbert's school chums, I believe, Wilfred?' she asked, pausing ever so slightly before the name. Wilfred made a complex movement with his right hand; possible intended to indicate agreement with the broad lines of this statement while modestly disclaiming quite such a close intimacy.

'I am very pleased that Herbert is keeping up his old

friendships,' said Mrs Naismith. 'All too often the old friends tend to be forgotten when a young man moves out into the world.'

Wilfred managed to say in a gravelly voice that he didn't think Herbert would do that, and Mrs Naismith sailed on: 'Herbert tells me that you are working very hard. You go to night school, I believe.'

Wilfred said that he did.

'Very meritorious,' said Mrs Naismith. 'I am glad to see a young man working so seriously to make his way in the world.'

Wilfred did not reply to this; he merely looked rather foolish.

It was a relief to Beatrice when the tea was over and Wilfred finally left. The whole thing had been an embarrassing failure, and when Wilfred's over-enthusiastic thanks had at last died away and he had shambled out of the room, she never expected to see him again. Herbert went with him to the bus stop, and the girls were left alone.

'Well,' said Beatrice, 'so that was Herbert's friend. What a disappointment.'

'I thought he was very nice,' said Florence. 'He was awfully nervous; he isn't used to mixing in circles like these. At least it's better than being one of those bumptious people who are at home anywhere.'

Beatrice agreed that nobody could have looked less at home. She saw what Florence was doing, she was covering up. She had been so insistent on Wilfred's coming that she wasn't going to admit that it had been a failure. She even said that Wilfred had a rather nice face and that his eyes were attractive which, to Beatrice, was just a piece of silliness. When Beatrice suggested that he was, perhaps, just a little bit common, Florence flared up and told her not to be such a snob.

'I suppose you mean the way he spoke. I don't see why he should be ashamed of it, there's nothing wrong with it.'

When Herbert returned he seemed to be in excellent spirits, though he felt bound to apologize for his friend.

'I didn't know he'd be like that. I don't know what was the matter with him. I expect Mother put him off.'

He stood in front of the empty grate looking down at the girls. He carried himself with a careless ease, his face was bland and full of self-confidence. He did not speak of Wilfred again, but his demeanour said as clearly as words, 'Well, there it is, I brought him. You wanted to see him, and I brought him. I hope you're satisfied.'

They did not see Wilfred again before Herbert returned to Oxford. In fact when they did meet it was by chance and Beatrice had almost forgotten his existence. It was nearly mid-day, the girls were in the city on a shopping expedition when, almost literally, they bumped into Wilfred, who told them that he was on an errand from the office. He used the word 'errand', Beatrice noticed, reducing himself, without any sense of shame, to the status of a schoolboy. She thought that he looked much better in his working clothes than he had in his Sunday best. He was carrying a large, black leather bag which he swung round his legs, as a schoolboy swings a satchel, while he spoke to them.

'I'm on my way to the bank,' he explained, 'to pay his in.' He indicated the bag. 'No, there's no particular hurry,' he said, in reply to a question from Beatrice, 'won't do old Burkinshaw any harm to have to wait. I'm glad I met you, I wanted to say how much I enjoyed meeting you.'

This seemed quite genuine, though thinking back to his embarrassment, thought Beatrice, it was hard to see what he had found so pleasant about it.

'We enjoyed it too,' said Florence. 'I hope to see you again at Herbert's. Are you still studying as hard?'

'Just the same,' smiled Wilfred. 'You've got to keep it up if you want to get anywhere. Of course, it's not all I do. I go out occasionally.'

He laughed as he said this as though he was speaking of a prisoner or some kind of wild beast that was allowed a taste of freedom every now and again.

'And what do you do when you go out?' asked Florence.

'Well – last night I went to the theatre.'

'The music-hall?' asked Beatrice. As soon as she had said it she realized that it was a mistake. Wilfred, who had been relaxed and expansive, suddenly grew wary, like a snail which has received a whack on its antenna. She must not, she saw, believe that he had the tastes of a common clerk simply because he looked like one.

'Oh, no,' he answered, 'it was at the theatre club, just an amateur performance, you know. It was Ibsen, Ibsen's *Ghosts*.'

Evidently he expected them to know this play, but Beatrice had never heard of Ibsen and she was pretty sure that Florence hadn't either. Florence, as usual, covered up. 'How interesting,' she said. 'Did you enjoy it?'

'It was magnificent, it was marvellous. I haven't been able to get it out of my head. Of course, I'd read it' – Florence nodded gravely – 'but you only get the full effect in the theatre, don't you think? That scene when Mrs Alving tells Pastor Manders the truth about her life with her husband, it – it was just terrific.'

The black bag circled more and more wildly round his legs and it suddenly struck Beatrice why he had been so glad to see them. He must have been positively bursting to talk about this play, whatever it was. He had been walking about the centre of Manchester in a state of suppressed excitement, longing for a chance to get his feelings off his chest, and then, providentially, these two girls had come his way.

'Everything was so inevitable and so right,' he said, 'a coming together of these tremendous, suppressed forces; Mrs Alving's protest against a lifetime's suppression. As a matter of fact,' he looked directly at Florence as he said this, 'I half thought that you might be there, but I suppose it's not really – '

'I wish I had been,' Florence hastened to say. 'As a matter of fact we hadn't heard about the performance, had we, Beatrice?'

This was certainly true; Beatrice could nod with a clear conscience.

'If we had we would certainly have made an effort.'

'You mean your father would have let you?' Wilfred's voice betrayed his surprise. Beatrice began to grow cautious. She wished she knew a little more about this play that he was talking of.

'You are advanced. I know a lot of people think it not – er – not quite the thing for ladies.'

'I can never see,' said Florence eagerly, 'why people should think that women are less able than men to face unpleasant facts. After all, we bear the children.'

'That's exactly what I think,' agreed Wilfred, delicately pink. 'In fact that is just what Ibsen is saying, isn't it?'

Beatrice had been making surreptitious signs to Florence for some minutes and now she came right out into the open and said that she thought that they had better be getting along. Wilfred suddenly recollected that he was supposed to be working, and they parted rather hurriedly, much to Beatrice's relief. She was used to Florence and the startling things she was capable of coming out with, but Wilfred had surprised her. There was no telling what they might have been talking about next.

'Well,' said Beatrice, 'what a change. He was quite a different person.'

'He is a very remarkable young man,' said Florence solemnly, almost reverentially. 'How wonderful it is to find somebody who really takes an interest in things of the mind.'

Beatrice eyed her sister narrowly. Florence's eyes were gleaming, and her mouth was set in a determined little line. Beatrice recognized the signs. Florence was busy making plans of some kind.

4

Winnick, sitting talking to Beatrice and her husband, and trying to balance a cup of tea, a cream cake, and a clipboard, was bemused. In the first place he had been taken by surprise by the Naismiths' house which, while not particularly large, positively breathed wealth. He had had no idea that Florence Rimmer's sister had been as well-to-do as this. In the second place he was rather put off by Herbert's attitude to him. Herbert Naismith was a large man, not fat by any means, but tall, with a good physique, imposing. He had the sort of face which was not easy to read, but his eyes watched you very intelligently, even warily, Winnick noticed, and he was looking at his visitor with a hostility which was only very barely veiled by common politeness. He took it that, for some reason, Herbert Naismith regarded his presence as an intrusion. In the third place Beatrice Naismith herself had come as a surprise. He had expected that she would be either senile, and therefore useless as a source of information, or else a figure of brooding tragedy, who would wince away from any mention of the murder and would have to be carefully coaxed. Instead he discovered that she was a gay old bird, quite anxious to prattle away about the family history and, most surprising of all, by no means hostile to Wilfred Rimmer. Fortunately Winnick was a discreet man, careful always to adapt his attitude to the opinions of whomever he happened to be talking to, and he had not committed himself on the subject of Rimmer before Beatrice had allowed him to judge what her own feelings were. Quite soon in the conversation she had begun talking about 'poor Wilfred', and how nobody had understood him.

'You don't think that he did it, then?' Winnick asked.

'No, no, never,' Beatrice replied with a great deal of

decision. 'You don't mean that you think that he did, do you?'

Winnick answered that he was totally impartial, that, as a deliberate policy, he had completely cleared his mind of prejudice or bias one way or the other. He gave her to understand that a researcher like himself, before beginning a project of the sort on which he was now launched, undergoes a process of purgation, of cleansing, in which the mind is freed of the merely human dross of opinion.

'It is necessary to bring a scientific judgement to bear on the problem, so that one can dispassionately weigh up all sides of the case.'

He hoped that she was impressed by this, certainly she was a little nonplussed. Out of the corner of his eye Winnick saw Herbert watching him. There was nothing so crude as a sneer on his face, but Winnick received in full a sense of his scorn.

'I was hoping that you would be able to do something for poor Wilfred,' said Beatrice.

'Do something in what way?'

'None of the books have told the truth about him. They all make out that he was a horrible man, a sort of monster. Well, he wasn't like that at all. I think it's about time people knew what he was really like.'

Winnick hoped that he would have no difficulty in reassuring her on this score. The manifold deficiencies in the books that had been written about the case was a subject in which he was an expert. Heartily he agreed that so far there had been nothing but trash written about it. In fact he saw that as the justification for his presence.

'What I am interested in is the truth. If you can give me the true picture of Rim – Wilfred Rimmer – that is what I want, and that is what I'll use. I entirely agree with you. The man descibed in the other books isn't even a human being, he's just a monster.'

Beatrice seemed to be reassured by this reply, either that or she had made up her mind to speak anyway and could not keep it bottled up any longer. Certainly her reminiscences appeared to gush from her. It was always Winnick's policy to ask as few questions as possible on these occasions, so that he would get the undirected thoughts of the person he was interviewing. Afterwards would come the job of sifting and sorting and extracting the bright nugget that would illuminate the narrative he intended to tell. So he was content to let Beatrice prattle on about, in particular, their life before the First World War. She told him about the family, Uncle this and Aunt that, the picnics they had had, their trips, the little naughtinesses the two girls had got up to. Herbert figured frequently and prominently in most of these stories, and occasionally confirmed, with a dour nod of the head, some fact which Beatrice wanted verified. 'Wasn't it in 1912 that we went to Matlock, Herbert? When Uncle Jim came with us and brought his camera?'

Herbert agreed that it was 1912.

'Of course, a camera in those days was quite a thing. It's not like today, is it, Herbert? Do you remember Uncle Jim's camera?'

Herbert remembered it.

'Father had to help him carry it, it was so heavy, with the tripod and everything; and it used to take him about three-quarters of an hour to get it set up. Do you remember, Herbert, there were those labourers working in the field? They were reaping the corn, Mr Winnick, and stacking the stooks, and then a cart was coming round to pick the stooks up. Well, it looked very pretty and Uncle Jim wanted to take it. "I'll have that," he said, "it'll make a fine print that will, for the exhibition." So he started to get the camera out, and the tripod, and get everything set up, and he kept looking up at the workmen in the field. They were working so fast that he could see that they were going to spoil his picture. He kept calling out to them not to go so fast, but of course they didn't take any notice of him. And by the time he'd got the camera arranged and the sun was in the right position the field was completely clear, and there wasn't anything to photograph at all. "Damn the men," he said, "they could have waited, damn the men." It was very funny. We did laugh.'

Winnick agreed that it must have been very amusing. Beatrice gave a spirited account, imitating her uncle's rather harsh and deep voice as she said 'damn the men'; Winnick could see that it was one of those family jokes that must have been retold scores of times. Herbert did not laugh, he remained impassive and watchful.

Winnick did not think much of this was likely to be directly useful to him, but he began to get a picture of a pleasant, ordinary, rather jolly family. If Beatrice's account was to be relied on the girls had spent most of their childhood giggling, so many of the tales ended with the words 'we did laugh'. It was also clear, and perhaps very significant indeed, that Florence's childhood had not prepared her very well for the sort of life she must have led as Wilfred's wife. Also he began to wonder when Wilfred was going to put in an appearance.

'How did you come to meet Wilfred?' he asked, at last, feeling that otherwise this could go on indefinitely.

'That was quite an accident, really, wasn't it, Herbert? Herbert ran into him one day when he was in town.'

'Ran into him?' asked Winnick.

'In a second-hand bookshop.'

'Had Mr Naismith known him earlier then?'

'They were at school together, I ought to have told you. You knew him at school, didn't you, Herbert?'

'M.G.S.,' said Herbert, and then, seeing Winnick's puzzled face, translated, 'Manchester Grammar School.'

'R – Wilfred was at Manchester Grammar School?' Winnick was surprised, perhaps Rimmer's background was better than he had thought. He also wished that he could get used to calling him 'Wilfred' instead of 'Rimmer'. 'I didn't know that he had been there.'

'He was a scholarship boy,' explained Herbert. He spoke rather unwillingly, with a side-long glance at Beatrice, as though he only opened his mouth because she expected him to.

'Wilfred was very clever, very clever indeed,' said Beatrice. 'That was something that people didn't realize.'

Winnick bent his head to make a note. He thought that in this matter at any rate, Beatrice was wrong. Whatever else people may have thought about Rimmer at least they had given him credit for being clever; that was the trouble, he had been too clever for his own good. Winnick seized the chance of drawing Herbert further into the conversation.

'So you and Wilfred Rimmer were friends at school then, sir?'

'I wouldn't say that we were friends.'

'But you knew one another.'

'We were in the same class, yes.'

Herbert said each of his sentences in the tone of voice used to close conversations. There was no invitation to Winnick to continue talking. Winnick was familiar with the type. Herbert had determined in advance that this writer feller was not going to get anything out of him. It quite often happened. The correct procedure was to ignore the hostility, keep being bright and friendly, and gradually the suspicion and diffidence would disappear. Winnick was confident that he could do it, but it would take time. In fact it was becoming obvious that these two people would have to be coaxed into giving him several interviews. Beatrice at least seemed willing enough.

She went on to describe how Herbert had brought Wilfred home and how, later, quite by chance, she and Florence had run into him – Wilfred was a one for being run into – when they were in town.

'So it was pure chance?' asked Winnick. 'Pure chance that your sister met Wilfred Rimmer at all?'

'Yes, we often thought about it later, how such an accidental meeting could be so important.' Winnick naturally imagined that Beatrice was referring to a time after the murder. In fact it would make a rather good point to stress in his book. Winnick had the habit of composing fine-sounding paragraphs in his head. On this occasion he thought that a good passage could be woven round the chance meeting that had started the whole thing. 'No one could have imagined, when these two girls set off for the centre of Manchester one fine morning in – whenever it was – that the seed was being sown that would be reaped – eighteen years later – ' That was the sort of thing, it would need polishing, and checking.

Winnick had time to arrange these sentences in his head because Beatrice's flow of reminiscence had momentarily stopped. She was remembering that the fortuitous nature of the meeting with Wilfred had been the subject of some comment by Herbert in the days after Wilfred and Florence had become 'sort of' engaged. This was an aspect that could hardly be followed up in front of this man. Beatrice gave herself a little shake and addressed herself to the task of describing Wilfred, of trying to give this Mr Winnick some idea of Wilfred's charm.

Not that it was charm exactly. Beatrice had always had difficulty in putting her finger on what it was about Wilfred that she had liked. Certainly he had not been attractive in any obvious way, in any sexual way, that is. At first he had been very quiet, diffident even, until the conversation turned to ideas, and then he seemed to light up. It was this that attracted Florence to him, and when she said, as she did once or twice, that it was his mind that she admired, Beatrice's scorn was a little modified by the thought that this could, just possibly, be true. Beatrice had always been convinced that to begin with Florence had used Wilfred as a means of teasing Herbert. As soon as Herbert came home for Christmas Florence was at him to invite Wilfred round.

'Wilfred?'

'I told you in one of my letters, that we'd met him in town.'

'Yes – but – why do you want him to come round again? You remember what happened last time.'

'He was so different then. I'm sure he must be a remarkable person. You said yourself that he had great powers.'

'I didn't say that. I think Wilfred's a pretty clever chap, but I don't know about "great powers".'

'Anyway, Beatrice and I would like to see more of him,' said Florence. She would shamelessly use Beatrice's name on occasions like this to help her get her own way. Beatrice immediately protested that, for herself, she would find life quite tolerable without Wilfred, but it was no good. Florence could twist Herbert round her little finger, and she knew it.

So Wilfred duly came round again. He wore the same terrible blue suit, but he seemed to be more at his ease, and this time Mrs Naismith contented herself with greeting him in her customarily queen-like manner, and then leaving the young people alone together. Florence made a considerable fuss of Wilfred, trying to draw him out and, when she had succeeded, hanging on to his words in a way that astonished Beatrice. Normally, if Florence felt any reverence for anybody, she took the greatest pains to conceal it. Beatrice supposed that this was Florence's way of demonstrating to Herbert and her sister that she could appreciate real worth wherever she found it. She managed to start Wilfred off on the subject of religion.

'Herbert tells us that you never go to church. Don't you believe in Christianity, then?'

'No, do you?'

'Of course,' Florence replied uneasily; she was not used to a direct, frontal question like this.

'Isn't that the trouble – "of course"? You believe in it because it's the ordinary thing to do. It's less trouble to believe in it than it is to think about it.'

'Well, we do think about it, of course. I mean, you are supposed to think very deeply about religious matters.'

'I don't think so,' answered Wilfred. 'When the church has said that it wants people to think about religion, what it has meant is that it wants people to accept whatever the priests have told them.'

The argument had gone on from this point, as it seemed to Beatrice, who was not particularly interested in abstract ideas, interminably. Wilfred had mentioned all sorts of books, from which, apparently, he had got these notions of his. Florence had quickly found that her own attitudes were disappointingly conventional. Herbert had made gallant attempts to keep his end up by insisting that they had been into all this pretty thoroughly at Oxford. And Wilfred had kept talking about some book in which a cobbler had compared the accounts of the Crucifixion in the four gospels and found them inconsistent; he seemed to think that this was rather significant.

'But look here, Wilfred,' said Herbert. 'Naturally we have discussed this amongst ourselves, and we pretty well agreed that if you compared any four accounts of the same incident you would get inconsistencies. I mean, look how witnesses in a court of law contradict themselves and one another.'

Beatrice had rather admired Herbert for thinking of this. She thought that Florence always underrated Herbert's intelligence.

'Oh, quite,' said Wilfred, coolly. 'But of course that puts a totally different complexion on it. If you are simply going to reduce the Bible to the level of ordinary history then there is nothing more to be said. But surely the Bible owes it position to its being regarded as the revealed word of God, and the revealed word of God oughtn't to be inconsistent.'

Beatrice was quite anxious that Herbert should be able to reply to this. She did not like the idea that he could be worsted in argument in front of Florence. Triumphantly he rose to the occasion.

'Well, it's revealed through men, and men are fallible.'

Wilfred laughed at this reply.

'Now, that's what I call having it both ways,' he said. 'When it suits you you consider that the Bible is the word of

God Himself, and as soon as it gets inconvenient then it's just an ordinary, fallible mortal's idea of the word of God. I don't think you can get out of it so easily.'

The argument went on and on. Florence soon dropped out altogether and the two young men were left to enjoy a kind of single combat. Beatrice knew that this was all a piece of intellectual showing off on their part, that they were quite keenly aware of their audience. What surprised her about Wilfred was his good-humoured coolness. All his shyness had disappeared; Herbert's Oxford reputation in no way daunted him. He was confident that he could argue rings round his old school friend any time he liked, whatever the ancient university had done for him. Wilfred did not get heated, or raise his voice, or take refuge in bluster or feeble jokes, all of which sins against the rules of debating Herbert sooner or later committed. Gradually it dawned on Beatrice that Wilfred had a complete reliance on the power of human reason. He would gently chide Herbert.

'It's no good arguing like that, Herbert. I've given you my reasons, perfectly logical reasons it seems to me, and unless you can show me where I am wrong you'll not convince me.' Or again, 'You can't get out of it by making a joke, Herbert, the argument remains unanswered.'

He had been talking about the guilt of the church, and Herbert had tried to unsettle him with a feeble joke about taking the gilt off the gingerbread. Wilfred went serenely on.

'You only have to consider things like the Inquisition, the persecution of the Catholics under Elizabeth, what Cromwell did in Ireland, the witch-hunting trials – all these things in the name of religion. You can't name any cruelty – torturing, racking, thumbscrewing, hanging, burning at the stake – that hasn't been practised in the name of so-called religion. And it is this same religion,' he continued, turning to Florence, 'that you, "of course", believe in.'

It was undeniably impressive. He stopped talking and sat

there with his eyes downcast. He had transcended his cheap suit and his slightly common accent. He had spoken very quietly, very evenly, very precisely, and made his points with a lethal efficiency that left them with nothing at all to say. There was a short pause, and then Florence, shaking herself slightly as though waking herself out of a spell of some kind, turned the talk to other matters. Beatrice cast a swift look at Herbert. He was doing his best to preserve his usual affability, but she could tell that he was displeased. His nose had been put out of joint, and Beatrice felt a little pang for him.

When the girls were alone together later, Florence was triumphant.

'What do you think of Herbert's friend now?' she asked.

'He came out of his shell a bit, didn't he?' was the best Beatrice could manage.

'I knew he was a remarkable young man. Even when he first came I knew there was something about him. When you think of the poor start he's had in life and what he's made of himself. The reading he's done, the things that he knows. I think he puts Herbert to shame.'

'I thought Herbert stood up for himself very well,' said Beatrice.

'Herbert is a university man, Wilfred is a clerk in a shipping office, and you talk about Herbert standing up for himself. You know, I really do think that Wilfred is some kind of genius. I've never heard anybody talk so well, he could be a politician, anything.'

In justice to Wilfred, Beatrice had to admit that he had done very well indeed, but it made her unhappy to hear Florence running down Herbert like this. She seemed to have fallen out with him. Beatrice wondered whether they had had words earlier in the evening. Herbert had got Florence on her own for a short time, while Beatrice had entertained Wilfred. Perhaps there had been some sort of quarrel and this was Florence's way of getting back at him.

When Herbert saw them again it was clear to Beatrice

that he had decided to play the part of the jolly good sport paying full and fulsome tribute to the man who had bested him.

'I told you there was something in old Wilfred, didn't I? He was always a clever chap at school, used to put the rest of us to shame. He's the one who ought to be at the varsity, not me.' He said more in the same strain and even Florence had to admit that he had come somewhere near to doing justice to Wilfred.

'Florence thinks that he ought to be a politician,' said Beatrice.

'He's got the gift of the gab,' admitted Herbert, 'always had it.'

Then he said that Wilfred could surprise them all. He had his reward for these generous speeches when Florence gave him her almost undivided attention for the rest of the day.

In the succeeding weeks it became necessary for Florence to see Wilfred quite frequently. At least she asked Herbert about him often enough to make him protest a little.

'He's pretty busy, you know. You don't want him round here all the time.'

'I only said,' replied Florence, 'that it would be nice to see him again. I didn't say anything about 'all the time".'

'No, but you say it so often.'

'I simply feel that by asking him here we can help him, we can enlarge his social circle. You said yourself what a narrow life he leads.'

Herbert made the mistake, at this point, of muttering something about wanting Florence to himself sometimes, and about his having to go back to Oxford soon. Putting on his plaintive voice never worked with Florence.

'You shouldn't say it as though it was a penance,' Florence said sharply. 'Just think what Wilfred would give to have your chance.'

It seemed to Beatrice as though Herbert was on the point of damning and blasting Wilfred to hell, but he managed to restrain himself.

In fact Wilfred visited them another two times during that vacation, and was brought round to the Calderwoods' house, causing Mrs Calderwood to speak to her elder daughter when they were alone together one day.

'That young man seems to be coming round here quite a lot these days. What do you know about him?'

'Only what you know,' said Beatrice. 'That he's a friend of Herbert's. Why, don't you like him?'

Mrs Calderwood was a tall, thin, rather vague lady, and she shied away from this directness.

'Oh, he seems all right. I just wondered why we hadn't seen him before if he's an old school friend of Herbert's. All his other friends have been round often enough.'

Beatrice tried to explain that they had just resumed the acquaintance. She was anxious not to mention Florence's part in the reunion if she could help it.

'He seems a funny sort of friend for Herbert to have,' said Mrs Calderwood.

'He's very clever,' said Beatrice, 'and he talks well.'

'Does he?' said Mrs Calderwood. She was not in the habit of listening to the conversation of these young people. 'Arnold thinks he talks too much.' Arnold was Mrs Calderwood's husband. This did not surprise Beatrice. Her father was a perfectly amiable man, but he was apt to consider any young person who had strong opinions, and voiced them freely, as being 'cheeky'.

'Anyway, Mother,' said Beatrice, 'Herbert will be going back to Oxford soon, and then we won't see Wilfred again for some time.'

'I don't mind seeing him. I've no objection to him, I don't want you to think that. I just wanted to know something about him, that's all, and I wish he could do something about his clothes.'

Beatrice told Florence about this conversation, as she knew she was expected to.

'Mamma was wondering why we are seeing so much of Wilfred these days.'

'Did she say that? What did she mean, "so much", he's only been here twice.'

Florence brooded for a few minutes.

'What did she say about him? Doesn't she like him? Doesn't she want him to come any more?'

'She didn't say that. She just wanted to know who he was. She wondered why we hadn't seen him before.'

Florence had no difficulty in interpreting this.

'I suppose she thinks that he's not quite our class, not quite out of the top drawer.' She said these last words in a passable imitation of her mother's voice; it was a favourite phrase of hers. Beatrice said nothing.

'I do think it's a pity,' Florence continued, 'that people have to be so unkind. Just because Wilfred's origins are not what Mamma would like them to be we're supposed to turn our backs on him.'

'She never said anything of the sort,' said Beatrice, reasonably. 'She just asked who he was.'

'It all comes to the same thing. What else did she say?'

'She said that Dad thinks he talks too much.'

'Yes, well, he would, wouldn't he? Wilfred's got ideas of his own. He can see that society is due for a shake-up; Father wouldn't like that.'

Beatrice tried to question how far, in fact, Wilfred's ideas were really his own. She suggested that perhaps he owed most of them to books; and she was surprised when Florence, instead of flaring up at this, replied quite coolly that of course they were.

'Wilfred would tell you himself that there is no such thing as a genuinely original idea. All ideas come from other people; the merit is not in thinking of the idea, but in seeing its importance.'

It was a sign, Beatrice thought, of how deeply impressed Florence had been by Wilfred, that she was beginning to copy him. This was the sort of thing he would have said; he had a knack of disarmingly agreeing with some point you had made in order to turn it against you later.

After Herbert had returned to Oxford, of course, Wilfred ceased to come to the house. Nothing was said to order this; it was simply that Wilfred was quite clearly Herbert's friend, so that, equally clearly, when Herbert was not there there was no point in Wilfred's dropping in. Florence talked about him from time to time, and it dawned on Beatrice that she must be carrying on some kind of correspondence with him. She mentioned one day his reaction to some event which had been in the newspapers recently, and Beatrice was prompted to ask her how she knew. Florence coloured a little and confessed, if that is the word for a statement accompanied by a defiant toss of the head and a remark about its being none of Beatrice's business, that she had had a letter from him.

'I asked him to send me the details of some books he'd been talking about, so of course he wrote to me.'

Beatrice was a little perplexed. There was nothing exactly wrong with this, the girls were free to write to whom they pleased, but it seemed to her that something a little underhand had been going on.

'Have you told Mamma?'

'Of course not, why should I?'

'I think you ought to. I think it's a bit deceitful writing to Wilfred without telling anybody.'

'She wouldn't mind.'

'Then why not tell her?'

'It's so absurd,' complained Florence. 'Why do you have to make a big thing of it like that? If I go to Mamma and say, "Can I write letters to Wilfred?" she'll immediately start thinking of all sorts of things that aren't true.'

'Why don't you just mention, casually, that you've had a letter from Wilfred?'

But Florence scoffed at this idea as too artificial and clumsy for words. Beatrice did not know what to do, but she revolted at the thought of being a tell-tale and so did nothing.

When Herbert was next home, of course they expected to

see Wilfred again, but Herbert neither mentioned him nor brought him to visit, and at last Florence was forced to ask about him.

'Wilfred?' said Herbert, affecting to have a slight difficulty in remembering who he was. 'No, I haven't heard of him for some time.'

'Aren't you going to look him up?' asked Florence.

'I wasn't thinking of doing. He's not exactly the first person I think of when I come down.'

He said this with a meaningful look at Florence, but Beatrice could have told him that he was wasting his time. Florence was in no mood to notice sentimental hints.

'You haven't had a quarrel, have you?' she asked.

'A quarrel? What an absurd idea. No, the fact is that Wilfred was never what you might call one of my bosom pals. I just bumped into him one day and found him interesting.'

'And now you're going to drop him?'

'It's not a case of dropping him. I daresay I'll get in touch some time.'

'I'd like to see him again, Herbert,' said Florence frankly. 'I thought we had some very interesting talks during your last vacation.'

Herbert seemed to be at something of a loss. After a short pause, and in a changed tone, he said, 'The fact is, Florence, I don't think your parents are very fond of him.'

'Have they said so?' Florence flared up.

'Not in so many words. I mean, they haven't ordered me not to bring him round or anything like that, but there are ways of telling, you know.'

'And that's why you haven't brought him here?'

'Well,' said Herbert, with the air of one who has a clinching argument, 'I couldn't bring him into the house if I felt that he wasn't really welcome, could I?'

Florence did not say anything, and Herbert went about for the rest of the day looking rather cheerful. Beatrice, however, did not expect the matter to rest there, she knew

Florence. Sure enough, that evening, Florence tackled Mrs Calderwood. Beatrice was not present but from the account which Florence gave her afterwards it had been a pretty easy victory. Florence came into the room where Beatrice was doing some embroidery.

'I can tell Herbert that he needn't be afraid to bring Wilfred round,' she said.

'What do you mean?' asked Beatrice.

'I've just had it out with Mamma. It all seems to have been a misunderstanding; she has no objection to Wilfred at all, really.'

'What did she say?' asked Beatrice, intrigued.

'Nothing much. She asked me one or two questions about him, that was all.'

The news did not really surprise Beatrice. Her mother usually capitulated to a frontal attack. She could well imagine her, in self-righteous tones, saying that no, she had nothing against Wilfred, and whatever had given Florence that idea? When she spoke to her mother this view was confirmed.

'Well, whatever could I say? I don't know anything against Wilfred; all that studying and so on, I suppose he's a perfectly nice boy really. If she sees enough of him she'll probably get tired of him. You don't suppose there's any nonsense between them, do you?'

Beatrice didn't think there was and Mrs Calderwood looked a bit happier. Herbert, on the other hand, when the news was broken to him, looked decidedly glum.

5

It seemed to Winnick that a pattern was beginning to emerge. It was always the way. Beatrice had been chattering on about Wilfred, and about the girl's first meeting with him and his constant attendance at their house, and it was as much, Winnick thought, what she had not said as her actual words which had painted the picture for him. Winnick had got a clear idea of their social circle and standing. They had been a well-to-do, comfortable, easy-going family group for whom the present had been most agreeable and the future assured. Herbert, equally well provided for, had been a constant member of this group, and Winnick could quite see how, probably from early childhood, he would have been picked out as a future husband for Beatrice. The two of them had grown up together and in their marriage the fortunes of the two families would be united; quite a romantic notion. And then, into this idyllic domestic situation had come the serpent, admitted first of all by the mistaken kindness of Herbert; perhaps it was this which accounted for Herbert's moroseness now; no doubt for years he had been blaming himself. Winnick could imagine the real situation. Herbert accidentally meets this boy whom he has known at school. He does not wish to appear stand-offish and he offers Wilfred hospitality and a kind of friendship. He discovers that Wilfred is by no means a fool, that he is making praiseworthy attempts to better himself, and he feels bound to do something to help and encourage him. Winnick made a resolve to investigate further, if he could, the reality of these studies that Wilfred was making. Possibly the whole thing had been simply a device to attract sympathy. At any rate Wilfred was taken to Herbert's home, received kindly, and in the natural course of things introduced to the girls; introduced to that problem girl, Florence.

Winnick was beginning to see Florence with a gratifying clarity. Obviously Beatrice had been the pretty one of the two sisters. She was the one Herbert was destined for, her future was secure enough.

Florence, on the other hand, had been, he supposed, a bit of a worry. He fancied that she was plain. All the books on the Rimmer case contained one photograph of Florence. It had been taken with her, apparently, staring into the sun. Her eyes were screwed up, and there was a bad-tempered droop about her mouth. She was wearing a moth-eaten fur and a cloche hat, and she looked like a charwoman out on a spree. He noticed that the account which Beatrice had been giving left Florence in a rather negative role. She seemed to be the quiet one, overshadowed by her brilliant and attractive sister. An occasional waspish remark of hers had been recorded, and that too was characteristic. It was, Winnick recognized, a classical case of the mousy, frumpish girl trying to compensate by saying unkind things. What, Winnick wondered, had been going on in her mind as she saw the courtship between her sister and this handsome, rich, agreeable young man? How much bitterness and resentment had built up over the years? What young man would be interested in taking a girl like Florence off her parents' hands? Beatrice had mentioned Florence's piano-playing, and this gave Winnick a telling glimpse of her desperately and pathetically working at her accomplishments in order to catch a husband.

It was easy to see what the unexpected arrival of Wilfred must have meant to Florence. What had quite probably happened was something like this. One or two totally unsuitable, ghastly suitors had been proposed for her by her anxious parents and rejected by the poor girl, who would have been deeply offended by their assumption that she was not able to make a choice of her own with any chance of success. Florence must have felt that she had something pretty solid and worthwhile to offer Wilfred, and in her mind she had worked to invest him with various more or less imaginary qualities, not only with a view to making him more acceptable to her family, but because some saving illusions were necessary for her own pride. So Wilfred's brilliance must be worked for all it was worth. Presumably all that he really had was a certain glibness. Later on he had been an insurance salesman, a job which, Winnick considered, required a ready tongue and a scant regard for truth. This glibness had given Florence the opportunity to create the romantic picture of a young scholar fighting against poverty, magnetic, eloquent, capable of the Lord knew what great destiny; and Florence would be in this picture, the only one perceptive enough to realize, in his days of poverty and struggle, the true merits of this apparently insignificant little man. She would make the supreme assertion of her faith and devotion by marrying him, a kind of King Cophetua and the beggar maid situation in reverse. No doubt she had had her dreams of a future in which Wilfred was Prime Minister or a Master of a college at Herbert's old university, or something equally dazzling.

From Wilfred's point of view things were even more simple. He must have stood in the drawing room of the Calderwoods' house like Aladdin in his magic cave practising the words he needed to say in order to make this wealth his own. He had simply had to play a certain part and, it must be admitted, he had played it very well. Winnick judged this from the fact that he had deceived Beatrice as well as Florence. It was odd, Winnick continued to think, that Beatrice even now liked Wilfred as well as she did. He couldn't quite make it out, nothing that Beatrice had yet said about Wilfred seemed sufficient to account for it. The person whose views would have been most valuable was Herbert.

One thing was quite clear. If Wilfred had expected to get any money out of marrying Florence Calderwood then he had been disappointed. 29, Herriott Street had never been the address of a man of means. And that meant that Florence herself had been in effect, disinherited. There must have been scenes of the 'never darken my door again' variety. Florence's parents had rebelled. Wilfred must have settled in Herriott Street with this dowdy little girl and brooded over his situation. Tied up for life, and nothing to show for it. No extravagant flights of imagination were needed to reconstruct the consequences. In time his resentment would have been transferred from Florence's parents to Florence herself. The claustrophobic rooms in that unspeakable hole of a house provided a perfect setting for a kind of Sartrean hell: two people hating one another and brooding over lost opportunities. In this atmosphere the murder began to seem not so much possible as inevitable. Inwardly Winnick began purring. More digging was needed. Some of these tensions must have been apparent to an observer as close as Beatrice had been. She must have known all about the family row, for instance. Probably she knew more that she had ever let on about her sister's domestic misery.

He decided to start with the question of Beatrice's own attitude to Wilfred. He could think of no reason at all why she should deceive him about this. If she had not liked Wilfred there was nothing, after all these years, to stop her saying so, but she persisted in saying that he was 'nice'. There was another thing about it. When Beatrice spoke of Wilfred she kept using the word 'later'. At first she had not thought much of him, she had said so, and it was 'later' that she had begun to see his merits. Now this was odd. By Winnick's reckoning 'later' was when she should have begun to see through him. A plausible rogue like Rimmer usually makes an immediate impression which is favourable; as one gets to know him better one begins to see his essential falsity. Winnick decided that he would start probing here, delicately, like a surgeon manipulating sensitive tissues. His questions perplexed Beatrice. It is not easy to say what it is that you like about a person, or to pin down, in words, a person's individual quality.

'He was very straight,' she said. Winnick blinked and repeated the word wonderingly.

'He hated any sort of pretence, he didn't put on any airs.'

Beatrice tried to explain. It had been a part of Wilfred's pride. As soon as he had come into the Calderwoods' house, which was so different from his own, he had been anxious that there should be no mistake about his social position. 'No, no,' he said one day, in reply to an uncle of Beatrice's who had spoken of him as a secretary. 'I'm not a secretary, I'm just an ordinary clerk, about the lowest form of office life.' She remembered Wilfred once, when he had got to know Herbert's mother, Mrs Naismith, rather better, explaining to her that they had no bathroom in their house.

'It's more of a struggle for us to keep clean than it is for you people,' he explained, lumping all the wealthy together with a single wave of his hand. 'We have to use a tin bath in front of the kitchen fire, and lock the back door to keep the neighbours out.'

Beatrice began to understand that it amused him to shock his superiors by this sort of bluntness. Florence had once or twice made the error of trying to put a slightly flattering gloss on Wilfred, and been firmly put right. Once she spoke of his father as a 'railway employee'.

'He's a porter,' said Wilfred. 'He's a porter on London Road Station.'

'That's a railway employee, Wilfred.'

'I know it is, so's the Station Master. You may as well be exact and say what he really is. "Railway employee" gives the wrong impression.'

Beatrice tried to explain this to Winnick, and Winnick was impressed. There was no doubt about it. Wilfred had been superbly clever. The ploy of the blunt, honest, take-me-as-I-am, Northern boy had been superbly well judged tactically.

'Was Mrs Naismith put out when he talked in this way?' asked Winnick.

'I think she rather admired him for it, didn't she, Herbert?'

'We weren't snobs.' Herbert shot the words out. Winnick was encouraged to hear his voice at all but disappointed by what he said, which seemed to him merely a conventional disclaimer. Beatrice understood it more fully.

Both the Calderwoods and the Naismiths had liked to think that they were above silly snobberies. The girls would have been severely taken to task if they had ever turned their backs on an acquaintance because of some fancied social superiority. One incident from Beatrice's youth had bitten deep into her soul; it had happened when she was about thirteen. There was a woman who used to do the washing for the Calderwoods and who often brought her daughter, a girl of Beatrice's age, with her because she did not like to leave her at home. Naturally Beatrice and she played together. One day when she was going to the shops with her mother Beatrice passed this girl without acknowledging her. She had, she insisted later, genuinely failed to see her. Well, she had been made to feel very mean indeed.

'You should just think how she must have felt when you walked past her like that. If she's good enough for you to play with then she's good enough for you to speak to her in the street. You've no call to put on any high and mighty airs.' There had been tears from Beatrice and she had had to take the girl a little gift and say that she was sorry. It had all been very distressing and, Beatrice felt, unjust, and the two girls had, for some odd reason, not played again together after that. But the affair was symptomatic of the way they had been expected to behave towards people 'less fortunate' than themselves. Herbert seemed to Beatrice to be speaking no more than simple truth in saying that they had not been snobs. Herbert had had the same kind of training. He would play with the sons of his father's work people and not be expected to put on 'side' about his position. Mrs Naismith's greeting to Wilfred and her expressed pleasure at the fact that Herbert was keeping up his old friendships, had been perfectly genuine. In fact both sets of parents had applauded Herbert for the spirit he had shown in resuming the friendship, and they had been equally appreciative of Wilfred's sturdy assertion of his own position.

'We wouldn't have like Wilfred so much if he hadn't stood up for himself,' she explained to Winnick.

'Of course not,' said Winnick.

Winnick thought of the figure who had stood up to that grilling in the witness box at the trial and assented silently. It could not be denied that he had shown spirit.

'Wilfred had quite a good sense of humour,' said Beatrice. Winnick expressed surprise at this; this was a side of him that had had little scope at the trial.

'He used to tease people. When he said that about the bathroom to Herbert's mother he was teasing her, you know.'

Mrs Naismith's solemn and deliberate manner had provoked Wilfred more than once. And sometimes, when Herbert was being pompous and heavy, Wilfred would tease him too, and tease him by referring to his mother. Beatrice remembered an argument between Florence and Herbert about women and the vote, when Herbert started talking in a rather grandiose way, and she had seen Wilfred eyeing him sideways.

'All I'm saying, Florence, is that I take the ordinary, commonsense view of things. There are certain departments in life where women shouldn't meddle, just as there are other departments where men shouldn't meddle.'

When Florence asked indignantly why women were not supposed to meddle in politics, Herbert had replied in a clinching sort of voice, 'Because they don't know anything about it.' Herbert was pleased with this reply and could not resist asking Wilfred's approval of it.

'Isn't that a good enough reason, Wilfred?'

'No,' said Wilfred, 'I don't think that it is.'

'That sounds rather silly to me, Wilfred. You're not suggesting that people should meddle in things even when they don't know anything about them?'

'I rather think I am,' said Wilfred. 'Look at your mother,

for instance.' Herbert stiffened at this. Who, after all, was this clerk to criticize his mother?

'She is immensely active in all sorts of ways, she acts on committees of all kinds, she's busy in the church. Would it be better if she stopped to ask herself what she knows about these things?'

Herbert became tremendously pompous and icy, and Beatrice felt a sense of unease. Surely Wilfred was going rather too far.

'Aren't you being rather personal, Wilfred, talking about my mother like that? After all, you have been to my house – '

'I'm not saying anything against your mother,' said Wilfred in a perfectly tranquil voice, 'you are. Look at that man over there.'

They were walking down the main street of the local shopping centre late on a Sunday afternoon. On the other side of the street, in the gutter, was a human derelict, a drifter, appallingly filthy, shambling along in a hopeless way with his eyes fixed on his boots.

'Now, he's a man. Do you think that just because of that he's better fitted to meddle with political matters than your mother?'

Herbert reddened slightly but did not speak.

'The trouble with your argument, Herbert, is that it cuts us all out. If you limit the vote to people who really know about matters then no one will vote at all. What do you or I know about foreign affairs, about high finance, about agriculture, about nine-tenths of the things politicians have to decide? If you want to get things done in this world you do what your mother does, go ahead and do them, and don't hang round trying to find out whether you know what you're talking about or not.'

Herbert still did not reply, though Florence gave the tiniest of giggles at this last remark. Beatrice spoke rather quickly, as she was afraid of leaving a silence hanging in the air.

'You make it sound as though nobody ought to vote, Wilfred.'

'Well, you see, you can't have that either,' he answered. His voice still level and unemotional and good-humoured. 'That would mean leaving everything in the hands of a small gang of men who might do anything they wished. No, I suppose what I'm really saying is that you might as well give women the vote because they can't possibly be more ignorant than most of the men. Does that satisfy you, Florence?'

Beatrice was certain that Wilfred had enjoyed this complicated tease, but she could not have said who was the victim of it, Mrs Naismith, Herbert, or Florence herself. Beatrice wondered what Florence had thought about it, but when she asked her later all that Florence said was that of course Wilfred was quite right. None of this was easy to explain to Winnick, who sat there poker-faced making careful notes of everything Beatrice told him without seeming terribly amused by it, and who merely asked, 'Did he speak of nothing but politics and religion and things like that?'

It puzzled him. It was not exactly the sort of chatter calculated to ingratiate Wilfred with these people, if that was his aim. He was beginning to sound, to Winnick, like the sort of prize bore most people run a mile from. Possibly the explanation was simply that if that sort of thing would impress Florence then he did not care about the others.

'Oh, no,' said Beatrice, 'he was very interested in books; and he used to go to the Hallé concerts and talk about them; and there was the theatre, of course, when he could afford it.'

Winnick bent his head over his notebook in case his expression should betray what he was thinking. Every allowance must be made for the difference in social climate; all this was before the First World War when moral earnestness was in fashion, but it really did sound as though Wilfred had overdone it a bit.

'He sounds a rather intense young man,' Winnick ventured to say.

'We all were in those days,' Beatrice chuckled. 'I think young people always take themselves very seriously, don't they? But we used to have fun as well. Do you remember that time, Herbert, when Wilfred got us all to climb on a rock, just to prove something about land?'

It had occurred, Beatrice suddenly recollected, after Wilfred had made one of his characteristically provocative remarks. He enjoyed throwing off some outrageous statement, which everybody would immediately denounce as preposterous, and then demonstrating that it was, in fact, a rather obvious truth. On this occasion he had repeated a remark which he had read somewhere about all property being theft. Even Florence, who normally gave unquestioning assent to everything Wilfred said, found this a little far-fetched.

'You mean that I'm not even supposed to own my gloves or the clothes I stand up in?' she asked.

'Wilfred wouldn't have you own anything,' said Herbert. 'He's a diehard socialist; he thinks the state should own everything and dole it out to you as it thinks fit. Isn't that it, Wilfred?'

'Not quite,' said Wilfred, smiling, letting them have a little rope so that they would hang themselves.

'Well, what on earth do you mean, then?' asked Florence.

'Things like gloves and clothes,' explained Wilfred, 'are what is called personal property. Socialists have no objection to personal property, they know perfectly well that it is necessary and useful.'

'Very good of them,' said Herbert, to be sternly shushed by Florence. Beatrice thought that Florence was wrong. She thought that Wilfred was a bit tiresome and that Herbert was quite right to make fun of him.

'The point about personal property,' continued Wilfred inexorably, 'is that it is controlled by the law. I mean, you're allowed to own a carving knife, but you aren't allowed to stab your next-door neighbour with it.'

'Is that so?' said Herbert. 'I never knew that.'

But Wilfred was impervious to this sort of treatment and he continued in the same calm tones. 'The other sort of property is what is called real property – that is, property in land. You're allowed to own land – Herbert is about to tell us that he never knew that either – but has he ever thought that there are no controls over what you can do with the land that you own?'

Florence obligingly asked him what he meant by that.

'Well, if you own a bit of land you can do, literally, what you like with it. You can put a sick woman and her starving children out in the street if you think you can get more money from cattle than from her rent. If the community wants food and you want rough shooting, then the community can go to blazes as long as you get your sport. These things may be a lot more damaging than stabbing your neighbour with a carving knife, but the law allows you to do them. Land-ownership is simply a nonsense. You do realize that theoretically one single person could own all the land in the British Isles and order everyone off it.'

The three others contemplated this undeniably dramatic picture, then Herbert spoke.

'The trouble with these socialist ideas of you fellows is that you don't know when to stop. Up to a point there's a bit of sense in them perhaps, and then you push them to a silly, footling conclusion.'

'It's not quite silly and footling, Herbert.'

Beatrice noticed yet again how wonderfully Wilfred preserved his calm. Whatever he said his voice remained quiet, rather flat even. When he had spoken about putting a starving woman and her children on the street he had deliberately avoided any emotional, rabble-rousing inflections but had said the words in a dry, almost sardonic way. Herbert was the one who had sounded heated and angry.

'It's not quite silly and footling,' said Wilfred. 'In fact it has happened. The enclosures in the eighteenth and nineteenth centuries were examples of precisely this. Whole populations were turned off their land, deprived of their livelihood, reduced to starvation at the whim of the landowners. That shows what can happen if you give individuals control of the country's land.'

'You're side-tracking us,' said Herbert unexpectedly. 'It's an old trick of yours. A few minutes ago you said that to own anything was theft. Now, all of a sudden, you're talking about land enclosures. Just come back to it and explain what you meant about theft.'

They were walking through a field when Herbert said this, and by way of answer Wilfred suddenly called out, 'Follow me' and sprinted for a large flat rock. He reached it first because he had had a start on the others and jumped on it, panting hard. Herbert arrived just after him and scrambled up in time to help the two girls on.

'Well, what was all that about?' asked Herbert when he had caught his breath. The rock was not large and it was necessary for the young people to hold on to one another to prevent themselves falling off. Beatrice found this rather enjoyable. Herbert's arm was round her waist and he was holding her harder than was strictly necessary. His other arm encircled Florence.

'I declare this rock mine,' said Wilfred firmly.

'As far as I'm concerned, you can have it,' said Herbert amiably, 'and I'll keep these two. Mind you, we're three to one. We could pitch you off neck and crop if we wanted to.'

He pulled the two girls closer to him as he spoke about keeping them. Beatrice was quite breathless from the strength of his hug and Florence gave a sudden subdued exclamation of anger and tried to pull away from him.

'Even if you did you'd prove my point,' Wilfred persisted, unaware as far as Beatrice could see of the game Herbert was playing under his nose. 'When I say that I claim it as mine, I simply mean that I got here first, and because I got here first I have been able to steal the land from you three. If you are strong enough to take it from me then you are stealing it in turn. Either way it's theft. And once I've stolen the land then I've stolen the means of life from you. Either you get off my land into the sea – this grass is the sea – or you must work for me, serve me, be my vassals. That's what people really mean when they say that property is theft.'

'Actually I'm beginning to like it here,' said Herbert, still pulling the girls firmly to him and allowing his head to loll against Beatrice's cheek. Florence had averted her face when he had tried it with her. 'I like it as long as I've got these other slaves to keep me company.'

Florence snorted, there is no other way to express the sound she made, and indignantly pushed herself free. Herbert, to save himself from overbalancing, clutched at Beatrice, and the pair of them tottered for a moment on the edge of the rock and then fell sprawling in the grass. Florence clambered down and stood looking at them.

'Get up, you two,' she said, 'it's disgusting rolling about on the ground like that. You're not children now.'

Herbert got to his feet and bent forward to help Beatrice up.

'I think it's very nice, don't you, Beatrice? Besides, if you're pushed off into the sea you've got to swim for it.'

Wilfred jumped down also and, sensing a slightly prickly atmosphere, tried to relieve it by making amateurish swimming movements with his arms.

'It's a funny thing,' he said, 'but this is the nearest I've ever been to the sea.'

'Why is it a funny thing?' Herbert was bending over brushing bits of grass off his trousers, and when he looked up to say these words his face was flushed and red, and his tone sounded snappy.

'I work in a shipping office,' said Wilfred reasonably. 'All day long I'm dealing with all sorts of things connected with the sea, and I've never seen so much as a rowing boat, except on the Manchester Ship Canal, which doesn't count.

I suggested to Mr Greenhalgh in the office one day that I ought to be sent somewhere to get a look at the ocean. I said I felt a bit of an imposter. But he wasn't very much amused. He didn't seem to realize that I was making a joke.'

'It's not easy to tell, Wilfred,' said Herbert slowly. 'You ought to put a flag up or something to give people a hint.'

'Have you really never seen the sea, Wilfred?' asked Florence, deliberately turning away from Herbert.

'Never once. In fact I've never been further from Manchester than you can get on foot in a day. I've been out into Derbyshire. I take the tram beyond Stockport – New Mills way – you can get up into the hills quite quickly from there. I can walk thirty miles in a day.'

The girls were deeply impressed by this information, and even Herbert had to admit, grudgingly, when pressed by Florence, that thirty miles a day was good going. The talk gradually drifted to other matters as they returned home. Florence became very quiet, and Beatrice could see that she was thinking something out. This mood of abstraction continued when the girls were alone together and Beatrice tried to tease her out of it.

'Thinking of Wilfred's eyes again?'

Florence looked up with an expression of polite incomprehension which Beatrice was quite sure was assumed.

'I beg your pardon?' she said.

'I asked if you were thinking about Wilfred's eyes again. You haven't had a word to say for yourself since he left us.'

'I was thinking about Wilfred, yes. Not of his eyes particularly; what are you suggesting?'

'I'm not suggesting anything, only you've got quite a far-away look in your own eyes.'

'You are silly, Beatrice,' said Florence, without any great heat. 'You're as bad as Mother. If I mention a young man's name twice she starts hinting at all sorts of things. I just happen to think that Wilfred is a very fine sort of person, but I'm not looking at him in the silly, spoony sort of way you seem to suggest.'

'I'm sorry,' she said. 'I must have misunderstood you.'

Florence did not say anything more, but Beatrice was convinced that she was up to something, and her suspicions were confirmed two or three days later when Herbert came round in a state of agitation. Beatrice was alone, sorting out some clothes for a jumble sale, and without any greeting at all he blurted out what was on his mind.

'I say, Beatrice, what's all this about Wilfred and the Lake District?'

Beatrice looked at him blankly. Every year the two families went for a holiday in the Lake District; it had been a long tradition with them, but how Wilfred could be connected with this she was at a loss to say. She asked him what on earth he was talking about.

'Father's just been speaking to me. He seems to think that we all want Wilfred to go with us this year. Your father had a word with him about it.'

'You mean he's taking Wilfred?'

'What could I say? The way he put it, he thought I wanted it. I suppose Florence is behind it. The trouble is that if I say that I don't want Wilfred then that makes me out to be awfully mean.'

Beatrice nodded. She could quite see his dilemma; Florence would never forgive him.

'Can't you do anything about it?' he asked piteously.

'I don't see what. It's no good talking to Florence, you know what she is. I'll have a word with Dad if you like.'

Herbert was not sure that that would be much good either.

'I could kick myself for bringing Wilfred back home in the first place. I should never even have mentioned him.'

He went on in this vein for some time; Beatrice was surprised at the strength and bitterness of his feelings and did her best to console him. It was a role she was good at. Herbert was accustomed to unburden his heart to her and to accept comfort from her, and she was not surprised that he remained despondent, it was almost a point of honour with him on these occasions not to cheer up. She did speak to her father later about it.

'Herbert tells me that Wilfred may be coming to the Lakes with us.'

Mr Calderwood immediately looked guilty and tried to appear bland.

'Yes, yes. Just for a week, mind you. I didn't want him there the whole time.'

'I'm surprised you wanted him there at all. I didn't think you liked him all that much.'

'There's nothing wrong with the lad that I know of. He's a bit fond of airing his own opinions, but I suppose he'll grow out of that. In any case it's Naismith who's taking him, not me. He's Herbert's friend.'

'Did Herbert ask for him to go?'

'I thought you all liked him. I thought you were all friends of his.'

'I think Wilfred's a very nice boy, but I don't think Herbert's very keen on his going, even if he is his friend.'

Mr Calderwood looked at Beatrice shrewdly. He got on very well with both his daughters. Florence was perhaps his favourite, but he and Beatrice were very confidential together, and he respected her judgement as he might have respected his wife's, if she had been a little more sensible.

'You tell Herbert from me that if he's got any sense he'll keep quiet about this. I don't suppose I need to tell you that this is all Florence's idea.'

Beatrice shook her head.

'There hasn't been anything going on between Wilfred and Florence has there? Anything I should know about?'

'No,' said Beatrice instantly, 'I'm sure there hasn't. Wilfred's a very nice boy.'

Mr Calderwood looked a little relieved.

'I didn't think so. In my opinion this is just one of Florence's fads. The worst thing any of us could do would be to make a fuss. If Herbert takes my advice he'll just look pleasant about it.'

Beatrice recognized the soundness of this and so, when she told him, did Herbert but, as he said, it wasn't so damned easy, and in fact he signally failed to look anything but sulky and aggrieved.

It was curious, Beatrice thought, going over these memories in her mind and editing out those part unfavourable to Herbert, how one idea led to another. Until she had started describing to Winnick that scene on the rock she had quite forgotten how it had led on directly to Wilfred's getting invited to the Lakes.

'It was his saying that he'd never been away from Manchester that did it,' she explained. 'It really brought it home to Florence how few opportunities he had had. And then it was something that she could actually do. It wasn't easy to help Wilfred in any other way but it was quite natural for Herbert to offer him a holiday just out of friendship. Of course, Father paid his expenses.'

Winnick nodded. Of course he would have. Poor Mr Calderwood. He couldn't have known which way to turn. There was no doubt about it: Wilfred Rimmer had been an artful beggar. One had to admire the way he had played his cards.

6

When Winnick's first visit was over Beatrice sat down to make up her mind about him. On the whole she was pleased, and a little inclined to crow over Herbert, whose sour remarks had made her nervous about what kind of person this writer might be. She had braced herself to meet someone brash and insensitive, and instead she had found Winnick polite, with a scholarly manner and a pleasingly open mind. He had been flatteringly attentive to her, commenting on the accuracy and detail of her memory and scribbling away whenever she opened her mouth. It began to seem possible that, at last, her version of the affair would get into print and Wilfred's memory be cleared, or partly cleared. Beatrice did not expect Herbert to endorse this view of their visitor entirely, but he did admit that the fellow might have been worse, and he took the trouble to warn his wife that Winnick was a pretty sharp sort of chap and that she had better mind what she said. Beatrice assured him that he had nothing to worry about, she would not let slip anything that she shouldn't, and in fact she was looking forward to Winnick's next visit. She had suddenly realized what a relief it was to talk openly about Wilfred and Florence and the early days. It was understandable that Herbert should have placed an embargo on discussion of the case, but nonetheless regrettable. It is not easy simply to sponge from your mind all the memories of a time which, while it was being lived, had given so much pleasure. Happy memories of the past are a legitimate source of enjoyment, and her memories of Wilfred were inseparably bound up with the happiest scenes of family life, holidays, walks, tea-parties, everything that makes life worth living. You could not simply pretend that these things had never existed. It would have been a lot better, not that she was in any way blaming Herbert, if she had been able to chat about them without receiving discouraging grunts. Winnick had been a delightful audience, and under his promptings she had remembered things which she had not thought of for years. It had even given Beatrice some malicious amusement to see how uneasy Herbert became when the talk veered in certain directions. Perhaps his prohibition had not been solely on her account. Even after all this time he was sensitive on the subject of Florence, and he still resented the way Wilfred had, quite simply, cut him out. That was why he was like a cat on hot bricks: he was afraid that Winnick would get on to that old story and publish his humiliation to the world. Of course he was quite safe, but his uncertainty made Beatrice smile.

Herbert had never forgiven Wilfred, she knew that. This husband of hers had a curious psychology, owing, she supposed, to the way he had been brought up. Not that he had been spoiled, the reverse in fact. His parents had had a strong sense that he must be trained to be responsible, that he must not be led to expect to get anything for nothing. He had been allowed a fixed, and moderate, amount of pocket money and was expected to account for it. He had not been given expensive toys, and the presents that he was given were often linked to the successful, or at least conscientious, performance of work. An unsatisfactory school report, for example, was likely to be followed by a period of privation. Beatrice remembered one occasion when Herbert was fourteen when he had been promised a bicycle if he came in the first five in his class at the end of term. Herbert had come sixth, and the bicycle had gone back to the shop. Mr Naismith expected his son to see the fairness of this, and Herbert did see it. He had sat there, in his short trousers, tightlipped, kicking at the carpet, while the girls commiserated with him, and Beatrice had said that she thought his father might have stretched a point.

'He was quite right,' said Herbert. 'He said the first five; that's what he said, the first five; well, I only came sixth. I'll just have to try to do better next time.'

Mr Naismith was proud of the way Herbert had taken his disappointment. He thought that it showed that there was good stuff in him. Beatrice could remember many such incidents which could be used to prove that Herbert had not been spoiled; and yet, in spite of it all, he had grown up believing ultimately everything would come to him. His training had been like the training of a prince, who has to be taught to be natural with people and set them at their ease because he is so infinitely their superior. Herbert knew that one day he would be wealthy, that he would take over his father's company, that he would belong to a social élite. There was no merit in this; it did not mean that he was superior in point of any personal qualities; Herbert had had his own personal limitations kept well before his eyes, but these things would be his as of right. All that he really wanted he expected, in the fullness of time, to get; and in only one respect did he fail: he failed to get Florence.

And it had all been his own fault. Beatrice was sure of that. If he had only had the sense to take her father's advice and look pleasant about Wilfred, and not make a fuss, nothing would have happened. The first part of the holiday had gone absolutely beautifully; Wilfred was not to join them until their last week, so Herbert had had Florence to himself. It is not surprising that a holiday taken in July, 1914, should, in retrospect, have acquired the quality of an idyll. This annual visit which the two families made to the Lakes had acquired, over the years, a certain ritual element. There was a routine of visits, excursions, picnics, and walks which had to be performed, and if one of them was omitted there was a sense that the holiday had been somehow incomplete. In this way all that they did gained an extra charge from the number of times they had done it before in previous years, and the air would be heavy with reminiscence: 'Do you remember Uncle Charlie fell in that stream over there?' or 'That was the field your Aunt Mabel wouldn't cross in '01 because she stuck us out that a cow was a bull. Philip said something very rude to her.' And all those who remembered what it was that Philip had said had a good laugh about it, and for some years the girls had pestered the adults to know what it was and been told that they were not old enough to understand it. By 1914, of course, they had heard Uncle Philip's daring quip and considered themselves, and were treated, very much as adults. Indeed it was one of the pleasantest features of this holiday that the three young people were no longer expected simply to tag along with the 'old folk', as they called their parents. They could go on the lake in a boat by themselves – they always hired a rowing boat for the duration of the holiday – and Herbert frequently took Florence for short excursions and the two of them could be seen floating idyllically far from the shore. Herbert was now twenty-one. His allowance, which he had long since ceased to refer to accidentally as pocket money, had been increased and he was smoking and drinking quite on equal terms with the other men, learnedly talking about pipes and tobacco and giving his views on the vintage of wines. It was he as well as they, now, who would stride into an hotel and order the meal, giving very precise and detailed instructions about its preparation.

This raised Herbert's prestige in the eyes of the two girls, and part of the enchantment of this particular holiday was the feeling which they shared of being on the threshold of a new and exciting kind of life, emancipated from the old family ties. Herbert was at his best, sunnily self-confident, utterly charming, and Florence gave him every encouragement. It began to seem to Beatrice that when Wilfred arrived it would be her job to entertain him, and she made a private resolution that she was not going to allow all of that work to fall on her shoulders; that would not be quite fair, she had not particularly wanted him to come. Neither Herbert nor Florence mentioned his name at all, an omission which was understandable on Herbert's part but which, for Florence, smacked of calculation. Beatrice thought that she had better say a word or two herself before he came, so she ventured a comment to Herbert one day that it was a pity that Wilfred's arrival would spoil things for him.

'Spoil things? How?'

'Well, you won't have so much time alone with Florence, will you?'

'We'll see about that,' Herbert answered easily. 'I don't see why he should make much difference.'

'I hope you don't think that I'm going to look after him on my own,' said Beatrice.

'He'll be part of the group,' said Herbert, 'don't worry about him.'

'I won't,' Beatrice assured him, 'and I'm glad to see that you're not worried.'

Herbert looked at her sharply and then became more confidential. 'I'm not bothered about Wilfred any more. Florence hasn't mentioned him at all. I'm beginning to think that you were right in the first place.'

'I was right?'

'You know, when you said that she was just feeling sorry for him. I think that is all it was. All we've got to do is to give him a good time and then pack him off back to that office of his. I don't think we'll be seeing much more of Wilfred after this holiday.'

He spoke very confidently and Beatrice began to think that there must be some kind of an agreement between him and her sister. He certainly seemed to have forgotten that he had ever regarded Wilfred as being a rival.

Wilfred arrived on the Thursday. Herbert and the two girls went to the station to meet him and he stepped off the train looking rather frail and a trifle second-rate in a summer outfit that was new without being particularly smart.

'We've got a programme worked out for you,' said Florence producing a piece of paper. 'I hope you're feeling pretty fit.'

They were sitting in a taxi which Herbert had generously

provided, and Herbert, seated rather uncomfortably with his legs round Wilfred's suitcase, seized the paper and read it.

'I don't wonder she hopes that you're fit, Wilf; you'll need to be a real champion to get through this.' He showed it to Beatrice. It appeared to her that Florence had tried to condense into Wilfred's short visit all the expeditions that the family usually accomplished in their whole holiday.

'I just want Wilfred to do the things that we do ourselves,' explained Florence. 'We've talked about them often enough, now he'll be able to see for himself. Oh, and I've put in that walk that you said you'd take us on, Herbert.'

This offer had originated in a joke of Herbert's, a kind of mocking challenge to Wilfred of a walk of about twenty-five miles, a challenge issued when Herbert was still smarting under Wilfred's boast of his prowess as a pedestrian. Florence had insisted on cutting this down so that she and Beatrice could go with the boys, and it had finally emerged as an actual proposal for a walk of about twelve miles. Beatrice was not quite sure that she could manage twelve miles, but Florence insisted that she could, easily. And she also managed to incorporate in her scheme another offer of Herbert's to provide lunch at a hostelry famous for its work in that line. It was understood that the girls themselves would provide the tea at a farmhouse recommended by their parents. This was to be the high spot of Wilfred's visit, and Florence launched into an enthusiastic description of the itinerary while Wilfred beamed his grateful pleasure and Herbert curled disconsolately round his luggage and listened in silence.

It was an odd little comedy that developed under Beatrice's gaze in the next day or so. The first morning after Wilfred's arrival the two young men strolled over to have breakfast with the girls and Herbert suggested to Florence that they should have a little row on the lake, as had been their custom every day at this time for the last week. The invitation was expressed confidentially, Herbert simply saying, 'Shall we?' and jerking his head in the direction of the water. He was standing behind Wilfred at the time and he contorted his face into an elaborate expression of enquiry and secrecy. Florence rose very briskly.

'I'd love to,' she said. 'Wilfred, Herbert suggests that we might have a little row on the lake. Would you like that?'

It was fortunate that Wilfred could not see Herbert's face, although it would certainly have given him the cue for his reply. As it was he said that he would love to and what a fine idea it was, and that they really knew how to live he must say.

'Are you coming, Beatrice?' asked Herbert dully, accepting defeat.

'Yes, I think I'll come this morning,' said Beatrice. 'You must let Wilfred do some of the rowing today, Herbert.'

'Don't worry,' said Herbert, 'Wilfred will do some of the rowing.'

'Yes, I'd like that,' said Wilfred, eager to please, 'I've never done any rowing before.'

In the middle of the lake Wilfred had his first lesson in oarsmanship. He made his first mistake when the moment came to change seats. He simply stood up and the boat gave a violent lurch, nearly capsized, and Wilfred was sent sprawling among the thwarts.

'That was very silly of you, Wilfred,' said Herbert venomously. 'I thought you'd have understood that in a small boat like this you have to keep the weight low.'

'It's the first time Wilfred's ever been in a boat, Herbert,' said Florence.

'I know all about that. There are some things that are too obvious to need explaining at all, it's a matter of simple common sense.'

'There's no need to be unpleasant about it,' said Florence.

'There's every need to be unpleasant. He nearly had us all in the water. A lot of silly fools we'd have looked if we'd all got back soaking wet. After all, I am supposed to be responsible for you.'

Florence pressed her lips together petulantly and then said that she had not realized that she was supposed to be Herbert's responsibility.

'I am the oldest, naturally the old folk expect me to see that we all behave in a sensible manner. There is nothing very sensible about falling into the lake.'

Wilfred, looking very embarrassed, was bleating his apologies, convicting himself of abominable carelessness and inexcusable thoughtlessness.

'Herbert's quite right, you know. You can't be too careful with water. A boat's a very dangerous thing, it's really not something just to play about with. Particularly if you can't swim.'

'Can't you swim?' asked Herbert.

'No, I've never been near the water before.'

This last revelation of Wilfred's incompetence actually cheered Herbert up. He rolled his eyes and lifted his hands in the air in a mocking despair. It was one of the strictest rules of the old folk that no one was to go near a boat until he could swim at least fifty yards unaided. So he called Wilfred a duffer and told him that he shouldn't really be there at all by rights.

'The point is, Wilfred, that when you get up to move about in a boat of this size you keep your centre of gravity as low as possible.'

'And how do you do that, Herbert?' asked Wilfred, keeping firmly in his seat.

'You keep your legs bent and your – er – hips down as much as possible. Look I'll show you.'

Herbert rose an inch or two from his thwart and took a couple of tiny steps with his legs bent and body stooping.

'You see, Wilfred, if you keep in this position it is quite safe. You can turn round and move about without danger.' The boat gave a sudden lurch and Herbert sat down very quickly.

'I see, yes,' said Wilfred. 'Doesn't he do it well?'

'The great thing is,' said Herbert, as Wilfred rose in a parody of the movement he had just made, 'not to get too near the side. Keep to the centre as much as possible.'

'I'll have to get to the side to pass you,' said Wilfred.

'That's all right; my weight will counterbalance yours. Easy does it – just wriggle past – keep your weight down – there. That wasn't difficult, was it?'

Florence raised her eyebrows a little, set her mouth in a certain line, and remarked that it was colder than she had expected. Wilfred took the oars and Herbert began to instruct him in their use, but after about five minutes, and after Wilfred had shot a pint of water into Beatrice's lap, he decided that they had better return.

'It'll take some time to make a sailor out of you, Wilfred,' he said. 'Perhaps we'd better carry on another day.'

Wilfred was apologetic. 'I'm awfully sorry, Beatrice, it was very stupid of me. Herbert explained what I was supposed to do.'

'It doesn't matter, Wilfred, everybody does that when they start. Herbert was just as bad.'

On the way back Herbert pulled a very strong, steady stroke. 'The great thing, Wilfred,' he said, 'is to get the full weight of water behind your blade before you start the pull. Otherwise the oar skids and you catch a crab or chuck water over someone, see?' He gave a pretty demonstration, sending some drops of water first near Beatrice and then near Florence, who was not much amused. Wilfred made appreciative noises and asked Herbert about the rowing at Oxford, and Herbert entertained them with stories of this until they reached the shore again.

Whatever happened in the next few days, and Beatrice was never quite clear about what did happen, one thing was certain – it was not Wilfred's fault. His behaviour was impeccable. Florence seemed to make a point of teasing and frustrating Herbert. Whatever he suggested, more or less transparently, as a way of securing a few moments alone with her she eagerly agreed to, and then as a matter of course invited Wilfred as well. Beatrice wondered how far Wilfred was aware of the situation and finally decided that he knew nothing. His manner was completely normal, polite and grateful. Everything that was shown to him was magnificent, every walk proposed was first-class, every picnic was really memorable. As Mr Calderwood remarked to Beatrice, nobody could accuse him of not being appreciative. Herbert's behaviour, on the other hand, was beginning to cause comment.

'I don't know why he's got to go glowering about like that,' said Mrs Calderwood.

'Florence is behaving abominably,' said Beatrice.

'Well, if he doesn't know Florence by now he never will. Besides, if he's going to marry her he'd better get used to her.'

'Is he going to marry her?' asked Beatrice.

'Now why ask me that?' said Mrs Calderwood. 'Florence is the only one who can tell you.'

'And she won't, I asked her the other day.'

'Won't tell you, or won't marry him.'

'Won't tell. She says it's her business.'

'Well, I suppose it is, dear.' Mrs Calderwood twisted her head to see if the others were following. They were on their way back from church, Florence was walking arm in arm with Herbert on one side and Wilfred on the other.

'Isn't it yours and Daddy's business as well?' asked Beatrice.

'I stopped worrying my head about Florence years ago. She's got a mind of her own, that one; she takes after your grandmother.'

The grandmother referred to was Mr Calderwood's mother, a grim, iron-faced lady, of whom Mrs Calderwood had some unhappy memories.

They walked on in silence for a few minutes, then Beatrice spoke again. 'Suppose Florence's plans included marrying Wilfred, wouldn't that be your business?'

'I don't think she's got any idea of marrying him. Has she said anything to you about it?'

Beatrice shook her head.

'Florence knows which side her bread's buttered. For all her talk, she's fond of nice things and an easy life. Wilfred's got nothing to give her, nothing at all. What sort of life would she have if she married Wilfred?'

Beatrice did not reply, but privately she thought that her mother was wrong. Behind them the three young people were talking and laughing in an animated fashion. Florence's voice could be heard clearly above the other two. Mrs Calderwood was evidently turning things over in her mind because she suddenly spoke.

'If anything did come up about Wilfred your father would have something to say.'

They waited by the gate for the others to join them.

'What have you three been talking about?' asked Mrs Calderwood. 'You seemed to be having a good time.'

'We've been talking about religion,' said Florence gaily. 'Wilfred's been explaining his beliefs.'

'There you are, Beatrice,' said Mrs Calderwood, 'they were talking about religion, that was all. Did you like the sermon, Wilfred?'

'It was most interesting,' said Wilfred politely, measuring out his words carefully. Florence suppressed a giggle.

'The vicar always sets a very high standard in the holiday season,' said Mrs Calderwood. 'Everybody says so.'

Wilfred looked down at the ground without speaking and Florence stifled her merriment. Herbert seemed to be on the verge of saying something but turned away instead.

'I don't think Wilfred would have cared for the sermon, somehow,' said Mrs Calderwood to Beatrice as they went in.

Most of Florence's itinerary for Wilfred had been quietly dropped, but the big walk remained, in spite of incredulous opposition from the parents.

'You'll never do it,' said Mr Calderwood bluntly when it was explained to him. 'It's not far short of twelve miles, and it's right over the fell.'

'We're not the weak little things you think us,' said Florence. 'Twelve miles isn't far.'

'It's further than you've ever done, my girl.' Mr Calderwood always called Florence 'my girl' when he was trying to be jocular and firm at the same time. 'Why not just let the boys do it, and we'll drive to meet them.'

'There wouldn't be much fun in that. Wilfred and I aren't particularly keen to go walking by ourselves, are we, Wilf?' Herbert said in alarm. This unfortunately provoked Mr Calderwood into offering to come himself.

'Naismith and I will come with you. I wouldn't mind a decent walk myself.'

And Florence made it worse by suggesting that perhaps twelve miles was beyond his present capacity.

'When I was your age I was doing twenty-five to thirty miles in a day. There's many a time I've done twenty miles pushing a pram with you in it.' Fortunately Mr Naismith was less certain of the pleasures of a long walk, and Florence briskly settled the matter.

'We'll go by ourselves, we're perfectly capable. Good heavens, we're going to take the day over it. And we're stopping for lunch at the Pack Horse.'

'You see, that takes you out of your way,' said Mr Calderwood.

'It's worth it, they do you a very good lunch at the Pack Horse,' said Herbert.

'I know they do. I've had more lunches at the Pack Horse, my boy, than you've dreamed of. Have you got a good pair of stout boots?'

This was directed at Wilfred.

'Oh yes, Mr Calderwood, I brought them specially. Florence warned me there'd be some hiking.'

'You need a good pair of stout boots up there. And you'll need to start early. Make a good start. Get the back of the day's work broken before the sun is up, and then you can enjoy yourselves. Dawdle about and you find yourself with half the work still to do and too little time to do it in.'

In this way Mr Calderwood finally gave his blessing to the enterprise.

7

Fortunately they had a fine day for their walk. The boys came over to have an early breakfast with Beatrice and Florence, intending to set off shortly after eight o'clock. At ten past eight Mr Calderwood came downstairs to see them off, to wish that he was coming himself, and to offer any last-minute advice that seemed to be needed.

'No need to take our coats,' said Herbert.

Mr Calderwood squinted up at the sky and then said that he thought it would be all right.

'It's better to travel light,' he said. 'You want to keep your hands free to keep a good, steady pace going.'

He produced a map and made a great display of checking the route with Herbert. At last, it seemed, they were ready to go, but there was a short delay while Florence went to change her blouse for a lighter one, as it seemed likely to be hot, and another delay while Beatrice went for a heavier pair of shoes, because Mr Calderwood said the going would be rough. He then asked Herbert if he had plenty of money. Herbert said that he had, but the question reminded Beatrice that she and Florence were supposed to be providing the tea, so she had to go in for her purse; and then Mr Calderwood slipped her something extra to put into it. At last, with stern injunctions not to overdo it and orders to Herbert to look after the girls, they were ready to set off, and by five to nine they were actually on the road.

It was a pleasant morning and the sun was not yet hot enough to be a nuisance.

'Poor Daddy,' said Florence, turning from waving to him, 'I'm sure he would have loved to come with us.'

'I don't think he really believes that you can manage an expedition of this complexity on your own,' said Wilfred with a smile.

'I suppose that it is natural for a father to be anxious about his daughters,' said Herbert heavily. His tone was rather peevish and it struck Beatrice that Wilfred was beginning to get on his nerves.

'Very natural,' said Wilfred, still speaking quite lightly, 'but nothing very terrible can go wrong, can it now?'

'You think he was rather fussy and foolish?' asked Herbert.

'I didn't say he was foolish, of course not – ' Wilfred floundered a little. He had not expected a harmless remark to be greeted in this way.

'I don't think you quite realize, Wilfred, how kind it is of Mr Calderwood to allow us to go off like this on our own.'

Wilfred was at a loss once more. Of course he realized how kind Mr Calderwood was, nobody could be more appreciative than he of the kindness of all their parents – Florence cut him short in the middle of a rather complicated answer by asking Herbert what was the matter with him.

'There's nothing the matter with me, Florence. It just struck me that Wilfred was taking your father's concern in rather the wrong way, that's all. Particularly as it is largely on Wilfred's account that he has to be so careful.'

'What do you mean by that?' asked Florence, flaring up.

'Isn't it obvious? Wilfred is the one who is the stranger. I'm a part of the family, there's no objection to my taking a walk with you, we've done it often enough.'

'I hadn't thought of it like that,' said Wilfred, still trying to preserve a light tone. 'I suppose I am a rather dangerous beast, don't you think so, Beatrice?'

'I think you're a very dangerous beast indeed, Wilfred. I wonder that Daddy allowed you near us at all.'

'Herbert's quite right really,' said Wilfred, 'and of course I see that it's very kind of Mr and Mrs Calderwood to show their trust in me like this. It is different with Herbert, he's more like a brother than anything else.'

For the life of her, Beatrice could not make up her mind whether this speech was the result of accident or calculation on Wilfred's part, but the word 'brother' stopped Herbert in his tracks and made Florence give an instantly checked giggle. After a few minutes Herbert said something about making up for lost time and set a speed that made conversation impossible. By half past ten the day was really hot and both girls began to grumble to Herbert about the pace he was setting.

'It's no good complaining to me. If we'd got off a bit earlier we could have taken it more steadily. How's it going, Wilfred?'

Wilfred was looking rather pale but he was matching Herbert stride for stride and insisted that he was feeling fine, absolutely fine.

'You're not beginning to slacken already, are you, Florence?' said Herbert. 'It was your idea to come in the first place.'

'I was thinking of a walk, not a race,' said Florence, 'but if you insist on going at this ridiculous speed I can keep up with you.' And she set her jaw in a firm line and strode out. Beatrice really did not know how she got through the morning. Herbert was the only one who did not seem to find the walk an effort. Wilfred's brow was beaded with sweat and his face seemed to get paler and paler, Florence looked grim and silent, and Beatrice felt herself getting hotter and stickier all the time, but Herbert was gaining in joviality. By the time the inn came into view he was able to eye his companions with some complacency.

'Only half past twelve,' he said, looking at his watch. 'They reckoned we'd be making good time if we got here by one. I enjoyed that, that's what I call a proper walk.'

He stood with his legs astride and his arms folded looking at Wilfred who had immediately propped himself against a wall.

'Now that we've broken some kind of record,' said Wilfred, 'perhaps we can take it a bit easier this afternoon. Take the views in, you know.'

'If Herbert imagines that I'm going to keep up this pace all day,' said Beatrice, 'he's got another think coming. I'll take it easier with you, Wilfred.'

'So will I,' said Florence. 'Herbert's been setting a ridiculous speed.'

'We've made up the time. Now we can have a nice leisurely lunch and enjoy ourselves this afternoon. This was the whole point. You people don't understand,' Herbert protested.

'He was just showing off,' said Florence to Beatrice, 'he wanted to show how much stronger he is than the rest of us.'

'He wants to be able to tell the old folk about it when we get back,' said Wilfred. 'He'll ask them when they used to get here and tell them that we did it by half past twelve.'

'I'm not really sure that I like you calling my father and mother the "old folk", Wilfred,' said Herbert, and disappeared into the inn. The girls looked at one another and at Wilfred. His face remained carefully expressionless, and Beatrice noticed that he did not, by pulling a face or making some slight gesture, enter himself into a league with them against Herbert. She suddenly realized how carefully, all the time, he was measuring his attitude towards all of them. He knew that he was the outsider and he did not care to risk inviting a rebuff by presuming to be too familiar, too much a member of their close inner circle. He had momentarily forgotten this when he had referred to the 'old folk' and Herbert had given him a rebuke. Wilfred was not going to risk it again, and so he stood there unwilling to make a move or a comment. Florence was the first to speak. She went to Wilfred and took his hand. 'Never mind, Wilfred,' she said. 'Herbert is being rather horrid today, I don't know what's the matter with him.'

Wilfred muttered something about it being his own fault.

'Of course it isn't,' said Florence. 'We all call our parents "the old folk", they don't mind, there's nothing rude about it. He knows you didn't mean anything by it.'

Wilfred thawed a little. Beatrice was almost sure that he gave Florence's hand a slight squeeze before he let it go.

'Well, I'll apologize anyway,' he said cheerfully. 'We mustn't let a little thing like this spoil our day.'

'It isn't being as gay as I'd hoped, so far,' said Beatrice as, after a few minutes, they followed Wilfred into the inn.

Wilfred had evidently made some kind of apology to Herbert, for the two of them were chatting together quite amicably when the girls appeared, and throughout the meal Herbert made a great effort to be charming and friendly. It was a very good meal, Herbert had obviously given a lot of thought to it, and a bottle of wine was kept circling throughout. At last the expedition began to live up to their hopes of it.

'I say,' said Wilfred, helping Beatrice to wine and filling up his own glass again, 'this is really going it.'

'I think that you need a bottle or two of wine to make a meal complete,' said Herbert.

'I hope you're not turning into a drinker, Herbert,' said Beatrice giggling.

'Isn't that like a woman all over! You have a bottle of wine with a meal and straight away they say you're turning into a drinker. On the Continent they don't understand how we manage to do without it. They regard it as a civilized accompaniment to food.'

'I wonder what Father and Mother would say if they could see us now,' said Beatrice.

'They'd say we were very naughty girls,' said Florence, 'and they'd say that Herbert was leading us astray.' She seemed to Beatrice to be getting a little merry and Beatrice hoped that the wine was not going to her head.

'What do you think of it, Wilfred?' asked Herbert, indicating the bottle.

'The wine? It tastes very good to me, very good indeed. Mind you, I haven't had your experience in these matters, you're the connoisseur, but it'll do me very nicely. I entirely agree with you, Herbert, this is the only civilized way to eat. I must start having it for breakfast.'

Florence laughed.

'You are silly, Wilfred; did you hear what he said, Beatrice, he said he was going to start having wine for breakfast.'

Herbert smiled indulgently.

'Wilfred makes a joke of everything he doesn't understand,' and Herbert filled all the glasses again.

They had coffee on the terrace and Wilfred and Herbert, after asking the girls' permission, smoked some cheroots which Herbert had brought with him. In Herbert's opinion this was the only civilized way to end a meal.

'This is a change from my usual mid-day grub,' said Wilfred.

'Why, what do you usually have?' asked Florence.

'A couple of sandwiches and a glass of ale in the pub round the corner from the office.'

'Poor Wilfred,' said Florence.

'Poor Wilfred be blowed,' said Herbert. 'It's a good meal, that. Bread and cheese and a pint of ale makes a very good lunch. It's what I often have myself.'

'I will say this, Herbert,' said Wilfred, 'it's nice to be able to take our time like this. It makes this morning worthwhile.'

Herbert accepted the tribute with a modest raising of his hands, scorning to rub in the fact that he had been right all along. 'Now we can take it easily,' he said. 'It doesn't do to exert yourself too much when you've just had a big meal.' This was another part of the family lore. There was a whole range of things that one was not supposed to do after a heavy meal, and taking exercise was one of them. So the young people moved off in a strolling, dawdling fashion, loitering through the afternoon. When they left the roads and took to the footpaths Beatrice noticed that Herbert was tending to saunter with Florence, and she thought that it was owing to him to give some assistance, so she did her best to entertain Wilfred.

'Are you enjoying your first sight of the Lakes?' she asked.

'Marvellous, I'll never forget it. It's been a revelation to me. Of course I've read about it, Wordsworth and all that, but you really can't get an idea of its beauty from books, can you?' He was watching, as he spoke, Herbert and Florence walking side by side about thirty yards ahead of them. Herbert had his arm round Florence's shoulder and was whispering something in her ear.

'Just look at the lake down there,' Beatrice stopped and turned and pointed, and of course, Wilfred stopped too.

'Your family and Herbert's are very close, aren't they?' he said.

'We've known Herbert since we were children together. Mummy and Daddy have known Mr and Mrs Naismith since before they were married.'

'It must have been very pleasant,' said Wilfred, 'like one big family together. I am the only one. It's different being on your own.'

'Herbert,' said Beatrice, 'gets the best of both worlds. He's an only one, so he gets made a lot of, but he has us as well.'

'Herbert has the knack of getting the best of all worlds,' said Wilfred. Beatrice looked at him in surprise. This was the first time she had heard him say anything in the remotest degree critical of Herbert. He did not follow his remark up, and Beatrice did not ask him to explain it. Herbert and Florence had stopped to wait for the others. Florence had moved away from Herbert and turned as Beatrice and Wilfred came up with them.

'Come along, you two,' she said, brightly, 'we were wondering where you'd got to.'

'We stopped to look at the view over the lake,' said Beatrice. 'Wilfred said it reminded him of Wordsworth.'

Herbert laughed a short, snappish laugh.

'Isn't that typical? He looks at a pretty view and it makes him think of a book. He'd be just as well off in a library, it's a waste of time bringing him away on holiday.'

'As a matter of fact,' said Wilfred, 'I said the opposite, didn't I, Beatrice? I said that books did not give you a real idea of it at all.'

'My word,' said Herbert, 'we are coming on. It's not

wasted after all.' He set off at a rather faster pace and for a time the four of them kept together. As they marched on, the day became hotter and hotter and something of the discomfort of the morning began to return.

'The next time we find some shade,' said Beatrice, 'I'm going to sit down for a few minutes.'

'We've quite a way to go,' warned Herbert.

'I shall melt, that's all, if we don't. I shall melt to nothing. You wouldn't want me melting away, would you, Herbert?'

'I don't think there's much danger of that, Beatrice.'

She called him a beast, and seized some grass to stuff down his neck. He galloped away, keeping just out of reach, and then turned on her and caught her wrists and they tussled for a little while. Wilfred and Florence stood watching them, like indulgent parents looking on as their children frolicked.

'You'll make yourselves hotter than ever,' said Wilfred. Beatrice was panting and laughing, and brushing away wisps of grass. Herbert had succeeded in getting most of her own handful down the neck of her blouse.

'You're horrid, Herbert,' she said, 'you cheated. Just because you're stronger than I am.'

'Don't Wilfred and Florence look prim and proper,' he said.

Beatrice tore out another handful of grass and advanced upon Wilfred, who took flight. As she set off in pursuit Beatrice heard Florence telling her not to be so silly.

Wilfred frolicked more awkwardly and self-consciously than Herbert. He put up a good show, like a studious uncle playing uneasily with the children. Beatrice's tussle with Herbert had been a rousing, uninhibited affair of encircling arms and warm contact. His touch had been firm and manly, with an almost caressing, lingering quality. Wilfred was slightly panic-stricken because he did not quite know what he was expected to do. So he laughed a good deal, and grasped Beatrice's wrists tightly, and submitted to having grass pushed down his neck and contented himself with throwing his own handful over her hair. At the other side of the field, as Beatrice was dimly aware, Herbert was struggling with Florence. Suddenly there was a sharp cry of pain, and Beatrice heard Herbert's voice. 'There was no need to do that, Florence.'

He was standing a little way from her examining the side of his hand. Florence, her face a little flushed and trembling slightly, said, in a composed voice, 'You hurt me, Herbert, you were a bit too rough.'

Herbert was suddenly aware of Beatrice and Wilfred looking at them. He was obviously in a black temper, angry with Florence, and angry with himself for having given himself away with his cry of pain. He tried to cover up by making a joke of it.

'You were a bit rough yourself, Florence.' He sucked the side of his hand. 'Look what she did to me.'

He exhibited his hand to the others; Florence appeared to have bitten it.

'Oh, Florence,' said Beatrice.

'It's your fault,' said Florence, 'you started it. That's the trouble with these silly games. People go further than they intended.' She was fastening the buttons at the top of her blouse.

Herbert looked at Florence with a baffled anger. He seemed to be on the point of saying something to her but changed his mind and, instead, abruptly started off down the path, grinding out the words, 'Come along then,' from between his teeth. Beatrice, after a moment's pause, ran to overtake him.

'Wait for me, Herbert, you're going too fast.'

'We'd better get on,' he said, without slackening his pace, 'we wasted too much time over our silly games.'

'Florence is always like that, you should know her by now.'

'Oh, I know her, I know her all right.' Herbert's voice had a juvenile, plaintive, whining note, which ruined the effect of withering irony which he seemed to intend.

'Don't let it spoil things, Herbert.'

'What things? What is there to spoil? She can't spoil anything for me. This whole day has just been one long disaster from start to finish.'

'The holiday, Herbert, everything. It was all going so well. Even today, this afternoon and the lunch and everything, was being lovely.'

But Herbert was not to be comforted. He had these moods occasionally, and Beatrice set herself, as she always did, to soothe him into a better opinion of himself and the world. She thought that he looked like a bad-tempered baby, and she had an impulse to take him on her knee and dandle him and kiss him into a better humour. Gradually, as Beatrice went on talking, Herbert's pace eased and he began to answer her in something more than monosyllables. She talked of how nice the meal had been, she reminded him of the easy chatter at the beginning of the afternoon, she brushed some remnants of grass off his shoulder and spoke of how much she had enjoyed the romp with him. 'You should have seen Wilfred's face when I went towards him, he didn't know what to do, he was simply scared stiff of me. He was afraid to touch me. It's a funny thing about Wilfred, he doesn't seem to be able to do anything except talk, have you noticed, Herbert?'

Herbert said that he had noticed and added that Wilfred seemed to him to be gravely deficient as a personality.

'You've got to remember, Beatrice, that I have to put up with him twenty-four hours a day, we're even sharing the same room, you know.'

Beatrice said that it was a bit thick.

'It is a bit thick. I didn't even want him to come in the first place. You've no idea what a dreary chap he is. He goes on and on about his bally ideas, he can't talk about normal things at all, he's the most boring person.'

In this way Beatrice coaxed Herbert into a better frame of mind. In quite a short time she was able to draw his attention to the view and obtain from him an admission that it was not bad. A little later still and she had persuaded him to tell her about Oxford and his life there and the friends he had made. This was a topic of which he did not easily tire, and it lasted them until they came within sight of the farmhouse where they had arranged to have tea. Beatrice suggested that they should wait by a stile for the others. This suggestion brought on a return of Herbert's earlier mood, he didn't see why they should have to wait, let them look out for themselves, it was just like them to do this. Beatrice sat on the stile and Herbert leaned against it, and they looked back the way they had come. The last part of the walk had been down a slight incline so the path back was visible for nearly a mile to the top of the hill. Florence and Wilfred were nowhere to be seen, and for about ten minutes Beatrice and Herbert chatted and waited but the two did not appear.

'I hope they haven't got lost,' said Beatrice at last.

'Their own silly fault if they have.'

Beatrice felt a great desire to giggle but she knew that it would have a disastrous effect on Herbert if she did, so she suppressed it. It really began to seem as if they would have to go back and look for them.

'I don't think either of them knows the way,' she said.

'All the more reason why they should have kept up. I've no patience with them.'

Herbert was beginning to look black again. Beatrice could sympathize with him. In his present state of mind the less he had to do with them the better, and he obviously had a strong impulse just to leave them to stew in their own juice. On the other hand, as he had told them himself earlier, he was, in a way, reponsible for the party. If Florence and Wilfred had got lost and were wandering all over the fells, and if local shepherds had to be recruited to go out to look for them, Beatrice knew whom the old folk would blame for it. After another five minutes she rather timidly suggested going back. 'I really think we'd better, just in case anything has happened to them.'

Herbert's manner suggested a man too full of righteous indignation for words. He uttered a kind of shuddering groan of exasperation and flung off along the path, with Beatrice again in pursuit. As she came up with him she heard him muttering something to the effect that it was like taking a parcel of children out. She did not reply. Keeping up with him was using most of her breath, and in any case for the time being she had exhausted all her resources for conciliation.

Eventually after a long, panting, toilsome climb to the summit of the hill, they were able to look down into the hollow beyond. There were Florence and Wilfred. They were sitting in the shade of a tree, they looked very comfortable and relaxed, they were not actually touching, though their heads were close together, and they were in earnest conversation. Herbert paused, exhausted, and gazed at this spectacle. It roused him to a fury, his face twitched with the effort of trying to control himself, and he ran a few steps towards them as though he was going to swoop down on them and exact a terrible revenge. Instead he yelled at them, in a voice, which, in his passionate anger came out thin and cracked and incoherent.

'Hi, there, you two, you two down there, what the blazes do you think you're up to? What do you think you're doing?' He turned to Beatrice and leaned against a rock, wiping the sweat off his face. 'Look at them, they weren't coming at all, they were just sitting there enjoying themselves, we could have waited all day like a pair of bloody idiots.' It was the first time that Beatrice had ever heard him swear. His outburst would have been comic but that his face expressed so strongly an agony of jealous despair. Florence and Wilfred started and looked round. It occurred to Beatrice that to them Herbert's voice must have been quite faint and unimpressive. Florence said something to Wilfred at which he appeared to smile and then, with a truly maddening slowness, she gathered herself together, gave her arm to Wilfred, and they moved off up the slope to where Beatrice and Herbert were standing. Beatrice thought that Herbert looked rather forlorn and pathetic. He was obviously striving to appear commanding and impressive and stern, but his face was pale and his eyes glittered wildly, his hands were clenching and unclenching without his seeming to be aware of it, and he was constantly turning and twisting about as he spoke.

'Wherever have you been? What on earth do you think you're playing at? Do you know what time it is? Beatrice and I have been waiting nearly an hour down at that farm there.'

'Really, Herbert,' said Florence, 'you sound just like your mother when she's in one of her moods.'

'I suppose you think you're very clever, Florence,' Herbert had dropped his voice and was speaking very rapidly, 'but I'd like to know exactly what you two have been doing while our backs have been turned.'

Florence and Wilfred both exclaimed at once in protest against this, but Herbert swept on. 'Beatrice and I came up here and saw the two of you sitting together like that. How long have you been there, that's what I'd like to know, while Beatrice and I waited like a couple of silly fools.'

'Just a minute, Herbert, just a minute – ' Florence tried to interrupt Herbert but he would not listen.

'Wilfred's supposed to be my guest, I'd have thought he had more manners than to do a thing like that – he's being paid for and everything. Just you wait until the old folk hear about all this, that's all.'

By now Florence was in a passion and was starting to shout at Herbert, and Wilfred, a deadly white, was trying to make himself heard as well. Beatrice could hear Florence's voice saying things like, 'No right to say such things, absolutely disgusting, not fair to poor Wilfred,' mingled with Wilfred's tones, calmer but intense, 'I say, Herbert, that's a disgusting thing to say to Florence – I'll repay you, every penny of it – nothing I'm ashamed of.'

'Stop it!' Beatrice shouted suddenly. She had a loud voice

and was supported by an old tradition of asserting herself in their children's quarrels, which this, essentially, was. 'Stop it at once, all of you, this has gone far enough.' There was a moment's silence. Florence began to speak but Beatrice cut her short imperiously. 'Not another word, Florence. You are like a lot of children, all of you.'

'But didn't you hear what Herbert was suggesting?'

'I heard everything, and I'm deeply ashamed of you. I think our parents were right when they thought we couldn't be trusted on our own.'

'If Herbert's got anything to say about Wilfred and me then there are one or two things I could tell them about him,' said Florence stoutly.

'Nobody is going to say anything about anyone,' answered Beatrice. 'Let's get that straight. We're going to go home and tell everyone what a nice day we've all had. The less said about the way you've behaved this afternoon the better.'

This brought the quarrel to a stop. Herbert was standing looking away from the others over the valley, Florence was biting her lip. Beatrice knew that she would have said more if Wilfred had not been there. Wilfred himself had drawn a little apart and was watching the three of them. Outwardly he seemed to be the calmest of the party and he was thinking deeply.

'Now we'll go down to the farmhouse and have tea,' said Beatrice.

'I don't want any tea,' said Florence.

'Neither do I,' said Herbert.

'We'll all go down together and have tea,' said Beatrice, in her best 'no nonsense' voice. 'We've still got quite a long way to walk, and if we all get home fagged out and famished, Mother will want to know why, and then there'll be a row.'

So they all went down to the farmhouse and had the special afternoon tea.

8

It was fortunate, Beatrice thought, that when they arrived back from their marathon all four of them were so tired that if the old folk noticed that they were rather silent, or inclined to peevishness, they put this down to fatigue. They all insisted that they had had a wonderful day, they spoke of the views in glowing terms, described the meal, and then relapsed into silence. The old folk exchanged knowing smiles and glances and suggested an early night, 'So that you'll be fresh for tomorrow', and they were glad to escape to bed. Beatrice congratulated herself, as she climbed the stairs rather stiffly, that she had brought them through a crisis without disaster. Neither she nor Florence said very much as they undressed and washed themselves and cleaned their teeth. It seemed to Beatrice that Florence avoided even looking in her direction. Beatrice fell asleep very quickly and slept right through until half past eight the next morning. At breakfast matters seemed to have returned to normal. The boys appeared as usual. Beatrice watched them coming up the road and saw that they were not talking, but when they came through the door they were smiling, and Herbert called out a cheery welcome. Wilfred asked if the girls were stiff after their walk, and they all talked energetically about the state of their calf muscles for several minutes.

'I gave you fair warning,' said Mr Calderwood, who, for once in a while, had got up to have breakfast with them; Mrs Calderwood was breakfasting in bed.

'I think we surprised you though, sir,' said Herbert. 'And don't forget, we were at the Pack Horse by half past twelve, weren't we?'

The others energetically agreed.

'You all looked jiggered last night,' said Mr Calderwood.

'It was a very hot day,' admitted Herbert, 'and I think that took it out of us.'

'It was a hard walk,' said Wilfred, 'there was so much uphill work in it.'

Mr Calderwood observed that since they had arrived back at the place they had started from there must have been as much downhill as up, and Wilfred said that he supposed that this must be true but that it had not felt like it. Beatrice said that she thought that coming down, if the slope was steep, was just as bad as going up, and they argued the point for a short while. On the whole they were making a pretty good show, Beatrice thought, particularly the boys; Florence was sitting there saying nothing and looking 'pudding-faced', but there was nothing too unusual about that. In fact all appeared to be quite normal when Wilfred suddenly dropped his bombshell. Mr Calderwood had raised the question of the day's activities. 'You girls had better take it easy today,' he said. 'I suggest that we hire a launch and go out on the lake, make a day of it.'

There was enthusiastic support for this idea. It was one of Mr Calderwood's favourite expeditions; they would go off with a great hamper of food and spend a thoroughly lazy day, swimming when they felt like it and idling when they didn't. Then Wilfred said, 'It all sounds marvellous, Mr Calderwood, and I wish that I could come, but I'm afraid you'd better not include me.'

'Not include you? Why not, Wilfred?'

Beatrice was aware that Florence, on her left, had suspended all activity, including, apparently, breathing. Wilfred's tone was perfectly level and controlled.

'The fact is, I've had a telegram from home this morning, it arrived just before we left.'

He produced the telegram from his pocket. 'It's an uncle of mine, taken ill,' he explained. 'My mother will be rather upset and I think, in the circumstances, I ought to get back to her.'

Everyone was most sympathetic, and Mrs Calderwood got up a full half hour before she normally would have done. It would obviously have been indelicate to try to persuade Wilfred not to go back, and everyone said how much of a loss his departure would be. Mr Calderwood produced railway timetables and discovered that the best train for Wilfred's purpose was the one which left at two-thirty.

'You get your packing done quickly, Wilfred, and then you'll be able to get the morning in with us.'

So Herbert and Wilfred went off to do this as speedily as possible.

'What a pity,' said Mrs Calderwood, summing it up, 'when everything was going so nicely.'

Florence left the breakfast table abruptly; she had not spoken a word. Mr and Mrs Calderwood exchanged glances. Beatrice followed her soon after and found her sitting in the little bedroom which the girls shared. She was weeping, and Beatrice sat down next to her on the bed and put her arms round her.

'What a beastly mean thing to do,' sobbed Florence, when she was able to speak.

'What do you mean, Florence? Wilfred's uncle can't help getting ill.'

Florence shook herself fiercely and pulled away from her sister.

'Don't be silly. You don't suppose I believed that, do you?'

'But Wilfred had the telegram, you saw it.'

'He must have sent it himself. Herbert must have made him. It's all Herbert's fault, Herbert must have done something to him.'

'Oh, Florence, what could Herbert have done?'

'I don't know. You know how beastly he was yesterday, he must have told Wilfred he wouldn't have him any longer. Perhaps he said something to his father.'

'But what was there to say?' Beatrice was seized by a momentary doubt. 'You and Wilfred didn't do anything yesterday, did you?'

Florence flared up again at this; of course they had not done anything and how dared Beatrice make such a suggestion.

'I'm not suggesting anything,' said Beatrice, 'it's you. You keep on about Herbert saying something, well what is there for him to say?'

'Oh, I don't know. All I know is that he's been so beastly to Wilfred that Wilfred has had to go back to that horrid little house of his. Just because he's too mean, he grudges poor Wilfred even this much holiday, he couldn't even let him have his last four days.'

Beatrice did her best to console her but gave up after a while.

'Be careful not to waste time,' she said, getting up to go downstairs again, 'Wilfred's sure to have finished his packing soon and there's the rest of the morning to go.'

As she went downstairs, Beatrice pondered on what had happened. It was certainly an odd coincidence, but she was not convinced that the telegram had been sent by Wilfred himself, or even, perish the thought, by Herbert. Beatrice had caught a glimpse of Herbert's face immediately after Wilfred had made his announcement and Herbert had looked astonished. Beatrice did not think that he was that good an actor. A quarter of an hour later Florence set off for the Naismiths' house.

Beatrice found her parents in the sitting room.

'How's Florence?' asked her father.

'A bit weepy. It's a pity that Wilfred has to go.'

'A great pity.'

'So unexpected,' said Mrs Calderwood.

'Wilfred was very cool about it,' said Mr Calderwood. 'He must have been sitting there all through breakfast with that telegram in his pocket and he didn't say a word about it. Odd that.'

'I wonder what is the matter with his uncle,' said Beatrice.

Mr Calderwood said he wondered too.

'I hope it's nothing serious.'

Mr Calderwood said that he hoped it was nothing serious as well. There was a short pause in the conversation and then Mr Calderwood said, 'What happened yesterday, Beatrice?'

Beatrice darted away from this one like a fish in a tank.

'Oh, nothing.'

'Funny sort of nothing,' said her mother.

'Give us credit for a bit of sense,' said Mr Calderwood. He was an easy, amiable father, but he did not like it that his children should think him an absolute fool. 'You should have seen yourselves when you came in last night.'

'Herbert looked as if he'd swallowed a lemon,' said Mrs Calderwood, 'and Florence was worse. The only one of you that was like normal was Wilfred.'

'Herbert and Florence had a bit of a quarrel,' said Beatrice.

'What was it about?'

'Oh, nothing much.'

Beatrice looked down at her shoes. She felt that she was in a rather delicate position because she could not say much without making either Herbert or Florence out to have misbehaved rather badly, and she did not want to put ideas into her parents' heads.

'Was it anything to do with Wilfred?' asked her father.

'Why do you ask?'

'Because of what's happened this morning. Why is Wilfred leaving? Did he and Herbert have a row?'

'It wasn't a row. I think that Herbert felt that Florence spent more time with Wilfred than she did with him.'

'I thought the idea was that you were all to stay together,' said Mrs Calderwood in a rather injured tone.

'Well, we were together really. I mean we didn't separate or anything like that but it was just that Herbert wanted to talk with Florence and she preferred to talk with Wilfred.'

'I see,' said her father. 'You must have had a jolly walk yourself. What did you do while all this was going on?'

Beatrice laughed. 'You're making it all sound worse than it was. We had a jolly day really, it was just that – well, Herbert behaved a bit childishly.'

She thought this was fair; either Florence or Herbert would have to be sacrificed, and it had been mainly Herbert's fault.

Mr Calderwood did not pursue the matter any further. He knew that he had got as much out of Beatrice as he was likely to, she could give a good imitation of a clam when she chose.

It was another beautiful day, and later that morning Beatrice went into the garden of their house and sat on the seat under the trees in one corner and did some sewing which she had brought with her as a holiday task. At about half past eleven, Florence, with Wilfred as it seemed to Beatrice rather explicitly 'in tow', came through the gate. She called out to them but they simply waved to her and marched with an air of determined purpose into the house. Five minutes later Florence came out alone and joined Beatrice on her garden seat.

'Wilfred is in with Father now,' she announced.

'What do you mean?' asked Beatrice. There was only one thing as far as she could see, that Florence's words could mean, but she wanted to have it properly confirmed and not to be left to guess at it.

'Wilfred and I had a long talk this morning about our future,' said Florence.

'You don't mean you're going to get married?' asked Beatrice.

'Eventually, yes. But we both realize that that won't be possible for many years yet.'

Florence sat there quite composed as she said this, and Beatrice perceived that the matter had been not so much discussed with Wilfred as rehearsed, and that Florence was word perfect and, so to speak, fresh from a performance. Beatrice felt duty bound to play her own part.

'Aren't you both rather young?'

'You sound just like Father.'

'I suppose I do, but it's a natural thing to say. After all, you're only nineteen, and nineteen is a bit young to be talking about getting married.'

'It's not too young to start thinking seriously about one's life.'

How appallingly priggish she sounded, thought Beatrice – the fruit, no doubt of all those hours of solemn conversation with Wilfred. And how accurately she had caught his tone of calm, unanswerable reason. Their line was clearly to place the actual wedding so remotely in the future as to be beyond the reach of criticism. Beatrice did point out that, nevertheless, Florence was, in a way, already committing herself to Wilfred, and that from henceforth she would be tied just as much as if they had actually got married.

'We thought about that,' said Florence, 'and Wilfred said that it would not be fair to tie me down in any way. We both agreed that if either of us began to feel differently then he or she would be able to call it off.'

This had the true ring of Wilfred about it. It was in line with many of the things he was in the habit of saying about individual freedom and equality between the sexes, and the artificiality of the marriage tie, and the monstrous state of the divorce laws. Beatrice supposed that they should all be glad that the young couple had not gone the whole hog and simply decided to live in sin. Her father had been rather scathing about some of these notions when he had heard them expounded as abstract theory; what would he think now that they were translated into the terms of an affair between his own daughter and this odd young man?

'You're not getting engaged then?' Beatrice asked. Florence shook her head.

'Not formally, we want to leave the arrangement quite free.'

Beatrice marvelled at how muddle-headed a clever person like Wilfred could be. What sort of proposal, exactly, was he laying before Mr Calderwood at this moment? Either there was a definite engagement of some kind between him and Florence or there wasn't, and if there wasn't – Beatrice wondered how her father, who had a fine tone of impatience with what he considered nonsense, was taking it.

'What did Father say to all this?'

'He didn't say very much. I left Wilfred explaining it to him.'

Beatrice felt rather dejected. She did not like to see Florence tying herself down so soon and, she could not help thinking, so unsuitably. Florence was so young, and confident, and assured, and about her everyone had had such hopes of a brilliant sort of future. When one spoke of Wilfred's making his way in the world one was speaking of a steady rise to a more or less meritorious position. Whatever he got he would have to earn it by slow, plodding, conscientious toil, and his wife would have to plod with him. Beatrice had never thought Florence cut out to be a plodder. Florence's future seemed grey and dull, and it all seemed very sad to Beatrice.

'I haven't congratulated you yet,' she said, 'though I'm not at all sure what it is that I'm congratulating you on.'

'You're not supposed to congratulate me,' said Florence, 'you're supposed to wish me happiness. You do, don't you?'

'Of course I do,' said Beatrice, 'you know I do.'

Florence turned and looked directly at her.

'But you don't think I'm going to be happy, do you?'

Beatrice found herself floundering, and chose her words very carefully. 'Wilfred is a very nice boy. I think he's very clever and – and a very fine person in all sorts of ways, all the work he does to improve himself and all that. It's just that you're not used to the sort of life you'll have to lead if you marry him. It'll be years before he starts to make his way – you've got to consider these things.'

'Wilfred may surprise you all,' answered Florence solemnly. 'I don't think you really appreciate what sort of a person he is for all that you say about him. Why do you suppose I don't want to get married straight away?'

'I suppose it's because Wilfred couldn't really support you yet,' said Beatrice.

'I expect that's what everybody will think, but that isn't the reason at all. The real reason is that I don't want to be a handicap to Wilfred. He's got his way to make in the world, and he's best making it alone at present. I know very well how a woman can pull a man back.'

Beatrice wondered how on earth her sister could fancy that she knew anything of the sort. All these books that Wilfred had been recommending to her, she supposed. It made quite a pleasantly romantic attitude for her. She would be the lady staying at home while Wilfred went out and won his spurs. Beatrice did not say anything but she began to feel better. If Florence stayed at home long enough, and Wilfred found the spurs difficult to come by, who knew what would happen?

'That's very fine of you, Florence,' said Beatrice in a rather matter-of-fact voice, 'but in that case I don't quite see why you have to do anything at all. I mean, if you're not going to get married, and you're not going to get engaged, then you're not going to do anything at all. What is Wilfred seeing Father about then?'

'So that we can go on meeting,' answered Florence simply. 'Herbert won't be much use for bringing us together from now on. We could have kept meeting in secret, but we decided that it would be more honest this way. Wilfred wants everything to be absolutely above board.'

They were children, of course, Beatrice thought. All this striking of attitudes and fine talk.

'Well, Wilfred is a very nice, clever boy, and if you do get married I hope you'll be very happy, both of you.'

A short time after this Wilfred emerged from his interview with Mr Calderwood looking remarkably calm, even tranquil. Beatrice stood up, feeling that this meeting called for a certain formality.

'Your father was very kind,' said Wilfred, 'very kind indeed. He quite saw our point of view.'

Beatrice offered him her hand, feeling rather foolish and

hearing herself say something about believing that congratulations were in order. Wilfred blushed a little, grasped her fingers, leaned forward, and kissed her on the cheek. Beatrice managed to check an instinctive jerk away from his contact. She was more sharply aware than she had been before of the cheapness of his suit and the pasty sallowness of his complexion; his breath was not quite as sweet as it might have been. She tried to suppress these snobbish reflections, but they confused her and made it difficult for her to speak naturally. Fortunately, after a few minutes Florence and Wilfred said they must be off to make the most of Wilfred's last morning.

'You're still going, then?' she asked.

'You didn't believe in the uncle?' said Wilfred. Again Beatrice was confused.

'The uncle?'

'If he was ill at breakfast time then he must be ill now.' Wilfred was smiling.

'Oh, of course. No, at least – well, I thought it was rather odd.'

"I think I'd better go back all the same,' said Wilfred. 'I can't very well be beholden to Herbert now, can I?'

Beatrice said that she supposed not and the two lovers left and sauntered down the road. Beatrice went indoors to find her father, who was standing in the dining-room looking out of the window.

'It's you, Beatrice,' he said as she came in. 'I suppose you've heard the news?'

'I came to ask you about it.'

'I couldn't do anything,' he waved a hand irritably. It was as though he was rehearsing what he was going to say to Mrs Calderwood. 'You know what Florence is like. Besides, Wilfred is a worthy enough lad.' He looked very unhappy and very weary.

'They weren't actually asking for anything. I said, straight away, that marriage was out of the question and Wilfred said, straight away, that of course it was. He said that they were not even asking for a definite engagement. They just wanted the situation regularized.' Mr Calderwood spoke the last six words in a kind of singsong parody, as though adding the words 'the damn fools' to them. 'It put me in a very difficult situation.' He seemed irritated by appearing, in his opposition, merely to be falling in with their own wishes. 'Wilfred assured me that he was entirely honourable. Well I never thought that he was anything else.' Again Mr Calderwood's tone was rather savage, and suggested that he would have thought better of Wilfred if he had thought something else. 'I couldn't very well deny him the house.' Mr Calderwood stared moodily out of the window again. 'I don't know what your mother will say,' he muttered.

'She hasn't heard yet?'

'She's gone back to bed. She's got one of her headaches. I'll tell her when she gets up.'

'I don't think anything will come out of it,' said Beatrice. 'I've just been talking with Florence. She knows that she'll have to wait years and years.'

Mr Calderwood brightened a little.

'That's what I think,' he said. If we make difficulties it'll only make Florence more obstinate. If she has to wait any length of time she'll start getting tired of him.'

They talked on these lines for some minutes until they were both in a more cheerful frame of mind and then they separated, Mr Calderwood to attend to some correspondence and Beatrice to return to her seat under the trees. This time she took a book because she felt that after all these excitements she would be rather clumsy with her needlework. She had been settled there for about a quarter of an hour when Herbert entered the garden.

'Hullo,' he called out cheerily, 'seen Wilf anywhere?'

'He's gone for a walk with Florence.'

'Ah, making the most of his last morning.' Herbert crossed the lawn and sat down beside Beatrice. He was in excellent spirits again.

'You haven't heard?' asked Beatrice.

'Heard? Heard what? I haven't heard anything. I've just been for a swim in the lake.'

He looked brimful of health and happiness. Beatrice could imagine him cavorting in the water while these momentous things had been taking place.

'About Florence and Wilfred?'

It was as though, in the middle of his frolics, a monster had risen in his path from the depths of the lake.

'What about them?'

What about them indeed? What could be said about them?

'They're – they're sort of engaged.'

'Engaged?'

'Sort of engaged. Father won't allow an official engagement yet.'

Herbert studied his boots.

'I see.'

'They won't be able to get married for years and years.'

'No,' said Herbert. 'I don't suppose they will.'

He stood up suddenly. 'I think, if you don't mind, I'll be getting along.'

9

When Beatrice reflected, as she often did after the murder, and as she now did again under the pressure of Winnick's questions, on what sort of a man Wilfred had been, and on the nature of his relationship with Florence, she was always struck by the fact that her acquaintance with him had been short and intermittent. After his engagement, or whatever one was supposed to call it, he was a regular visitor at the Calderwoods' house. He used to pop in, as he expressed it, every Sunday afternoon, but on these occasions Florence very naturally and properly monopolized him. He appeared to be educating her. At least, she was always reading books which he had recommended, and they would spend most of his visits pacing about the garden in deep and serious discussion. The rest of Wilfred's spare time was spent in the Central Library, for he was now more conscious than ever that he had a way to make in the world, and that he must win his lady-love in the lists of examination successes. It did not seem a very satisfying courtship to Beatrice, but Florence made no complaint. Herbert contrived matters so that he did not meet Wilfred. Not that he ever said anything against him; he remained officially of the opinion that Wilf was a very good chap, and that he would go far. During this period Florence was very sweet to Herbert.

Then the war came, and this placid, comfortable, leisurely existence became like the memory of those old, graceful civilizations which are dug up from time to time in the sands of the desert. Herbert, predictably, enlisted straight away. He had been in some kind of cadet corps at Oxford, and the father of one of his Oxford friends pulled some strings. In a surprisingly short time he appeared at the house in his uniform, looking absolutely gorgeous. Wilfred's enlisting was more unexpected. He disapproved of the war and of the rather hysterical talk, he called it, which he heard going round. He even made remarks about the politicians having let the country down, and being manipulated by big business. Mr Calderwood had become very cross with him, and it had begun to look as though he did not intend to join up at all. Then, one Thursday, he arrived at the house and had a long and serious talk with Florence. Afterwards he came into the room where Beatrice and Mr Calderwood were sitting.

'I've decided,' he said very solemnly, 'that I must go.'

The expression on his face left no doubt about what he meant and Mr Calderwood bounded to his feet and seized Wilfred's hand.

'I'm very glad, Wilfred,' he said, 'very glad to hear it. It does you credit. It's a fine thing for a young fellow to do.'

Wilfred continued to look solemn and said that he had reached his decision only after much painful heart-searching.

'It's a serious step, Wilfred,' said Mr Calderwood, rummaging in the sideboard for his whisky and a box of cigars, 'nobody doubts that. But you won't regret it. I wish I was a few years younger, I'd be off like a shot.'

Beatrice took Wilfred's hand and kissed him, and said that she was very proud of him. Then Florence came in from the garden, a bit weepy and red about the eyes, and her father made a fuss of her and said that she must have courage, and that women had to make their sacrifices as well as the men.

Wilfred did not take as naturally or easily to military life as Herbert had done. Dressed in his uniform Herbert looked a born soldier, but when Wilfred first came back wearing his he looked like somebody dressed up, rather unconvincingly, for amateur theatricals. He paraded self-consciously for Beatrice and the others to see him.

'They don't exactly suit me, do they?' he said, making a little parody of standing to attention. 'The trouble is that I think they know that I don't really approve of them.'

Beatrice was not much amused. It seemed to her that Wilfred was being flippant about essentially serious matters. When he joined his squad it was just the same. There was a shortage of rifles, which meant that some of the men had to drill with walking sticks, and Wilfred wrote a long and satirical account of this, imagining the effect of them all rushing into battle waving their sticks in the air. Florence thought it was all very droll but Beatrice and her father were doubtful about it. When Wilfred reached the front line they no longer needed to worry that he was not taking matters seriously enough.

It was the fashion of the time for these young men to speak and write in a wryly humorous vein about the discomforts of trench life. It was a tone of cheerful insouciance and careful understatement which was popularized by a number of professional writers and journalists. It was felt to be eminently British and fine. Herbert caught the note rather well in the letters he wrote to Beatrice, and she was in the habit of reading extracts to the members of the family and friends. The general opinion was that they were good enough for *Punch* and reflected great credit on the writer.

Nobody suggested sending Wilfred's letters to *Punch*. He had never regarded the war as a lark or spree, it was a serious business. At first it wasn't as bad as he had expected; later on it became as bad as he had expected; and later still it became a good deal worse. His old, rather perky manner of handling life's problems dropped from him. He said once that theory seemed a bit silly when you were actually out there. He seemed to grow grey and worn and old. He was mentioned in despatches for his behaviour at Ypres (Herbert got the M.C. later for conspicuous gallantry) and this was recorded on a large, imposing document. Florence showed it to her family, and there was serious talk of having it framed. When he heard of this Wilfred, back in the front line, laconically advised them to stick it at the back of the fire – if they had any fires, that was.

Wilfred and Florence were married in 1916. Florence had gone down to London to work in a hospital there because, she explained, it made her feel nearer to Wilfred and gave her something useful to do. So, in February, 1916, Beatrice received a telegram asking her to come straight away as Wilfred was due on leave in a couple of days and they intended to get married.

'It was my idea,' explained Florence when Beatrice arrived. 'Wilfred didn't want to. He's afraid of leaving me a lone, lorn, widow woman, but I say we ought to take the chance.'

Beatrice had not seen Wilfred for over a year, and she was rather shocked at the change that had come over him. He seemed to be spiritless, without any sparkle of any kind. He quite lacked the cheerfulness that ought to characterize a young bridegroom. Beatrice compared him unfavourably with Herbert. When Herbert came back on leave he was full of fun and gaiety.

It was an unimpressive ceremony. There was a queue at the registry office, so the proceedings were kept simple, not to say terse. A man gabbled a few words without looking up from his book, asked the appropriate questions in a perfunctory manner and did not listen to the answers, and Wilfred and Florence were joined together for life. Then they adjourned to Claridges, where Mr Calderwood had instructed Beatrice the party was to be entertained. There were only four of them altogether, but Beatrice tried to make as much ceremony as possible by insisting on the telegrams being read out and toasts proposed. There was a telegram from Herbert wishing the couple 'Good Luck'. Beatrice wondered how he had managed to get it sent in time, but she learnt later that he had left instructions with his father to send such a message whenever the wedding was to take place. Wilfred had produced a rather awful person, with slicked-down hair and a slightly common manner, to act as best man, explaining that he was 'one of the chaps from the front'. Apparently they happened to have got leave at the same time and he had very decently offered to see Wilfred through his ordeal. Wilfred explained all this in a very apologetic voice, trying to convince Beatrice what a sacrifice it was for a chap to use up precious leave time in this way, but she found it difficult to like him. He insisted on kissing both of the girls at every opportunity, excusing himself each time with the words, 'Best man's perks'. He kept indulging in rather vulgar horseplay and making remarks whose only wit depended on their double meaning. When the young couple had finally left for their brief honeymoon he took it for granted that he and Beatrice were to spend the evening together, and she had some difficulty in getting rid of him. To excuse herself she was forced into a series of falsehoods, each one more transparent than the last, until finally he took offence and became sarcastic and abusive, apologizing with embarrassingly crude irony for 'presuming to disturb her ladyship', and regretting that he 'was not good enough for the likes of her'. Then he left in a temper. Three months later she heard that he had been killed when a shell struck his dug-out, and she felt miserable and guilty.

'You must remember,' Beatrice tried to explain to Winnick, 'that I didn't see all that much of Wilfred while the war was on, particularly after they were married. I often used to go down to keep Florence company, but I naturally kept away when Wilfred was on leave. That was her time.'

'Of course,' agreed Winnick, 'but I suppose Florence talked about him with you, showed you his letters, perhaps?'

'She certainly never showed me his letters,' said Beatrice, 'but she talked about him. Nearly every day we would go through the casualty lists in the newspapers, columns and columns of them, and every time you saw a name that you recognized your heart gave a jump in case it was somebody you knew. It was a dreadful time for those with men at the front.'

'It must have been,' said Winnick, 'but Wilfred seems to have come through all right. He wasn't wounded at all, was he?'

'He was gassed, very slightly, at Lens. He was very lucky. He was in a raised part of the dug-out. Several men below him died. That was all. Both Herbert and Wilfred got through without a scratch.

Winnick was not very concerned about Herbert's military career, but this about Wilfred was interesting. It confirmed what he had learnt from the army records, and it enabled him to contradict, categorically, the tale that had so often been circulated about Rimmer's personality having been changed as the result of a head wound sustained in the war. Winnick scribbled a note and then turned to Beatrice again. It was what had happened after the war that was important. Something, obviously, had gone badly wrong. Consider the picture. Here was Rimmer, all set to screw himself up to enlist, little as he wants to, because if he doesn't then Mr Calderwood will have nothing more to do with him. Beatrice has hinted as much. Then he has to get married, and in the circumstances of war-time it is not too difficult to push Florence into a hasty ceremony. Winnick did not believe what Beatrice had told him about Rimmer actually not wanting to get married. All that that meant was that he had been clever enough to let Florence make most of the running. Now he returns unscathed, a war hero, having, let us be fair to him, acquitted himself quite well. He must have looked to gain his reward – what had happened?

'What did Wilfred do after the war?' he asked.

'He went back to his old job; they'd kept it open for him, you know.'

'And resumed his studies?'

Winnick had asked the question without any malicious intent, but he observed immediately that he appeared to have touched Beatrice on a raw spot and that she began to make excuses for him.

'No, as a matter of fact we all felt, at least I felt, that it was expecting a bit too much to think he would start up again as if nothing had happened. He needed time. He needed rest.'

Winnick could walk through an open door as easily as the next man.

'Did your father think this?'

'There were difficulties,' said Beatrice. 'Naturally he wanted to see Wilfred making his way again.'

It was more complicated than this. Mr Calderwood was quite prepared to allow that it would not be easy for Wilfred, that it would take him some time to get into his stride, but he was confident that he would manage it. He even resolved, in private conversation with his wife and Beatrice, to see if he could help the couple, though his own affairs were far from rosy. Wilfred, however, did not fall in with these ideas. He and Florence took lodgings near his office and he settled down behind his old desk, but his enthusiasm for accountancy seemed to have abated.

'You're back in harness again?' Mr Calderwood would enquire, on their occasional visits to Florence's old home.

'Shaking down,' agreed Wilfred. It amused him to fall in with his father-in-law's conversational styles.

'Takes a bit of time to get back into the swing of things,' said Mr Calderwood. 'How are the evening classes going?'

'Well, they're not going at all at the moment,' said Wilfred calmly. 'I haven't started again.'

'Plenty of time,' said Mr Calderwood. 'You fellows have earned a rest if anybody has. When do you plan to start them?'

'As a matter of fact, I'm not planning to start them at all,' said Wilfred, with the same easy smile on his face.

Beatrice could remember her father walking up and down the room after this conversation was over and Wilfred and Florence had gone.

'I couldn't make Wilfred out. I'd like to know what it is that he intends to do with his life. Surely he doesn't want to remain a tinpot clerk for the rest of his days?'

'I shouldn't worry, Father,' said Beatrice. 'After what Wilfred's been through he probably needs a rest or something.'

'Oh, I know all about that,' replied Mr Calderwood. 'I don't expect miracles, but he hasn't time to waste. He's lost four years already, and if he really wants to get on he'll have to get cracking. I think the next time he comes I'll have to have it out with him.'

But Wilfred had developed a way of dealing with people who wished to have anything out with him. He would smile, he would be perfectly pleasant and courteous; as in the old days he never lost his temper or allowed himself to become ruffled, but at a certain point he would say, simply and sweetly, that he thought that the topic being touched upon was his business. If Mr Calderwood tried to force the conversation past this point then Wilfred would look a little cold and refuse to answer, or just turn away.

'Florence and I have discussed all that,' he would say and begin speaking on some other topic. In desperation Mr Calderwood actually approached Florence herself.

'I've just been talking to Wilfred, Florence. I can't seem to get any sense out of him about his future.'

'Can't you, Father?' said Florence.

'What is it he intends to do? He tells me he hasn't started his classes again.'

'He isn't as keen on accountancy as he used to be.'

'Well now, look here.' Mr Calderwood allowed himself a little indignation. He began to feel that he was being imposed upon. 'What does he intend to do with himself then? I can understand him wanting a bit of a rest after the trenches – '

Florence cut him short. 'What do you mean, "a bit of a rest", Father? Wilfred is working, you know. He goes to the office very day.'

'And he is going to do that for the rest of his life? Does he just see himself as a twopenny-halfpenny clerk? That wasn't what he was saying when he first asked me if you could marry him.'

'Oh, Father, all that was a long time ago. Everything is very different nowadays.'

'I'll tell you one thing that isn't so different, Florence. Rubbing along on twopence a week isn't any different from what it used to be. You've never had to do it, I have, and I know what I'm talking about. I didn't bring up one of my daughters to that sort of life.'

'If I don't mind, Father, I don't see why you should.'

It developed into quite a row between the two of them. Mr Calderwood was all hurt indignation, Florence was rebellious and defiant. She pointed out, quite rightly, that she was no longer a child, she reminded her father that Wilfred had spent four years of his life in appalling conditions and constant danger defending his country, she insisted on their right to lead their own lives as they thought fit without interference from anybody. Beatrice thought that her father had rather overstepped the mark in some of the things he had said about Wilfred and that this had incensed Florence. Of course, she had heard of the affair from both sides because each of the parties had afterwards turned to her for support. It ended in a considerable coolness between Florence and her father, which grieved him unspeakably. Wilfred was presumably told about this row, but his behaviour was typical of him. It made not the slightest difference to his manner when he next met his father-in-law. He chatted to him easily and naturally; it was Mr Calderwood who was embarrassed and awkward.

Beatrice did not really want to explain all this to Winnick. It had been a private matter which had nothing at all to do with his enquiry, but he persisted in asking the most penetrating questions. 'Did you father resent the fact that Wilfred did not resume his studies?'

Beatrice floundered. They did not have a quarrel about it, if that was what Mr Winnick meant. Of course Father would have been pleased to see him get back to his accountancy course but – Winnick smiled and scribbled, and saw the whole thing as clear as daylight. There must have been a really serious row. Beatrice's face had given her away when she denied it. The old man must have been very angry indeed, and he must have made his feelings known. In all probability – it was easy to reconstruct such a scene as that – Wilfred had lost his temper as well and said things which in cooler moments he would have kept to himself. The rest would follow as the night the day. Florence would take her husband's part, and the two of them would be cast out into the darkness of Herriott Street. No, wait a moment, not Herriott Street – Winnick recalled that they had not taken that house yet. Or had they?

'It was about this time that they moved into Herriott Street, wasn't it?' asked Winnick, smiling at Beatrice. She was relieved to get away from this thorny point and answered eagerly and promptly.

'It was in nineteen twenty, March, nineteen twenty. I can remember it so well because they moved into their house just at the time Herbert and I were getting our own place ready for after our wedding, and that was in July.'

Winnick gave a thoughtful nod. It fitted nicely. The move to Herriott Street he saw as a decisive step. If Wilfred had still hoped to get something out of his father-in-law he would hardly have committed himself to the purchase of a rathole like that. It was a clear sign that he had given up hope and decided to make the best of a bad job.

'Did they consult you, or your family, about choosing the house?'

Beatrice gave a little laugh. 'Oh, I don't think that any of us would have advised it. Quite the opposite, I assure you. No, it was a great secret, we had no idea about it. Of course, we were very much taken up with the house we were preparing for ourselves out at Wilmslow.'

Winnick was not desperately interested in the house they were preparing for themselves at Wilmslow, wherever that was, but he composed his face into an expression of eager anticipation.

'It was the contrast that struck me later. Our Wilmslow house wasn't a mansion or anything like that, but it was quite big, the rooms were large and it had some nice grounds round it. Wilmslow was right out in the country in those days.'

Winnick said that it must have been a rather fine sort of place.

'Well, it was, really, by the time we had finished with it. We had it absolutely gutted, and refitted throughout. It was an awful mess while the builders were doing it, they were knocking walls down, and laying drains and I don't know what. Well, in the middle of all this Florence and Wilfred came to see what was being done, and Herbert and I showed them round and explained what it was going to be like. And then a fortnight later they invited us round to see this house they had just bought, and we went and found them in that dreadful little place in Herriott Street. Then it struck me. All the time they had been looking over Stone Gables they had already bought this one of their own. I don't know what on earth could have been going on in their minds.'

Winnick agreed that it must have been rather a piquant contrast. The thought seemed to give him genuine pleasure.

10

Beatrice was not quite as contented with Winnick as she had been at first. The way he had pounced on the question of Wilfred's not going on with his course had been ominous, distinctly hostile to Wilfred, and Beatrice had caught Herbert looking at her with a triumphant 'I told you so' expression which had been hard to bear. Winnick seemed to want Beatrice to say that there had been some resentment on Wilfred's part, but this was simply not true. In any case Beatrice could not for the life of her see how, even if it were true, it made Wilfred out to be a murderer. The problem was that it was so difficult to explain things without suggesting more than you intended. Certainly Father had been annoyed, but as soon as you said that then someone like Winnick would jump to the conclusion that Wilfred had been annoyed too, and that there had been some kind of quarrel.

It was the same with this business of the visit to the house. It would be very natural for Winnick, who had never known Wilfred, to assume that Wilfred had been madly jealous of the Wilmslow house. But it was not in Wilfred's nature to be jealous like that. He was one of the last people in the world to bother himself about another person's possessions. He had paid the same kind of attention to it that a man would give to the Crown Jewels if he was being shown over the Tower of London. He would look at them, ask about them, wonder at them, but it would not occur to him to be jealous of the monarch for owning them, or to wish he had a set like that himself. That was Wilfred's frame of mind when he looked at Herbert's house, or his motor car, or the boat which he bought later, on Windermere.

'That's jolly fine, Herbert,' he would say, peering into the bonnet, or the bilge, as the case might be. And he would want to know how it worked, or how it was made, or how you navigated it, and he would enjoy being taken for a drive, or a sail, in it, but then he would go happily back to his own pursuits, which he found even more absorbing. That was why he had no jealousy. He was quite satisfied with the life which he had made for himself, and did not hanker after anything different. Beatrice knew this was so, but had no idea how she could get it across to this stranger. He would misunderstand it, as everyone had done. Even more, if he heard about them, would he misunderstand the dry little remarks which Wilfred used to make to deflate Herbert. This matter of the visit to Wilmslow was a case in point.

Wilmslow lies to the south of Manchester and, in those days, was a small rural town. Its attraction, to Herbert and Beatrice, had been twofold: it was out in the country and they wanted to live in the country, and it was on the main railway line to Manchester, and they wanted a place convenient to Manchester. By an odd coincidence this line, raised high on an embankment, ran through the dingy district where Herriott Street was situated. Beatrice and Herbert had not known of it at the time, but the train that carried Florence and Wilfred to see the fine house out at Wilmslow took them past their own recent purchase. They must have looked out of the window to catch a glimpse of it, and the contrast must have been with them throughout their visit.

Herbert and Beatrice met them at the station.

'We didn't bring the car,' said Beatrice. 'It's only a short way and we thought you'd like the walk.'

This was a calculated effect. The car was a new purchase and was intended, mentioned in this casual way, as a staggering surprise.

'The car?' said Wilfred. 'My word, did you hear that, Florence? Did you notice how nonchantly she said it? The car – just like that, as though they'd had it for years. And which of the cars is it, modom?'

'Herbert been indulging himself again?' asked Florence. 'You're getting too grand to walk.'

Herbert smiled tolerantly. 'Hardly an indulgence these days. Everybody will have one before long. Even Wilfred, I shouldn't wonder. It's just in his line. He'd simply love taking it to pieces. He wouldn't drive it anywhere, but he'd love taking it to pieces.'

Wilfred chuckled, and acknowledged a hit.

They walked a short way down the main road and then turned along a leafy lane which led them in about ten minutes to the house itself. There were two large stone pillars, supporting a pair of ornate wrought-iron gates, and beyond them a drive curved away to the left. There were banks of rhododendron bushes on either side of this drive, and behind them trees, through which the house itself could be indistinctly glimpsed. As Herbert opened the gates Wilfred said, 'Shouldn't you have a man to do that, Herbert? I'm disappointed. I expected an old fellow to dash out tugging at his forelock, with his apple-cheeked wife dropping curtsies in the background.'

'I don't allow them to work on Sunday,' said Herbert, smiling bleakly. 'I'm one of those masters who are very strict about the servants observing the Sabbath.'

Wilfred grinned, and Florence told him to behave himself.

'As a matter of fact,' said Herbert, 'if you think the house looks imposing from here you'd better make the most of it. When we turn that next corner there'll be an anti-climax.'

It did indeed look a bit of a mess. Half the window frames had been taken out and deposited in a heap on what had been the front lawn. Holes had been punched in some of the walls and others had been removed completely. The ground had been made hazardous with trenches, dug to accommodate new drains, and the garden near the house obliterated with piles of bricks, heaps of sand, bags of cement, and a litter of drain pipes and discarded plumbing. One could nevertheless see that the house itself was large, and would probably be very handsome when all the work was finished.

'I like it,' said Wilfred, 'this is the best time to see a house. It's at its most interesting when you can see all its guts.'

So they clambered about, and entered half finished, or scarcely begun rooms, while Herbert explained how this wall had been taken down, and that doorway opened up, and such and such a window reconstructed.

'We had to do away with the staircase, it was taking too much room where it was, so we moved it to the other end of the corridor. Then we took down the dividing wall between the dining-room and the small breakfast room, and we were left with this.'

'I'm glad something was left,' said Wilfred staring round at the commodious cavern which these alterations had provided.

'It gives us more room.'

'It certainly does.' Wilfred made an elaborate pantomime of speaking behind his hand to Beatrice. 'What do you want this room for?'

'We'll be doing some entertaining, Wilfred; it's big enough for us to have a dance here if we want it,' she explained.

'It's big enough for a cavalry regiment if you want it. It's fine, most impressive, Herbert.'

When Wilfred had done teasing Herbert he was genuinely fascinated by it all. He wandered off to look at the new drains and examine the walls that had been put up. Beatrice joined him in a short while to show him the garden.

'Have you ever thought,' he waved his hand at the hideous mess all around them, 'of the skill and organization needed for a job like this? You tend to think of these people as common workmen, ignorant louts, mere clowns, but if you consider what it is that they're doing you've got to agree it's very clever. All these drains have got to run right and fall at the proper levels, and link up with one another. The walls have got to be the right length and direction, and to keep vertical, and at the right places gaps have got to be left for the doors and windows, and these gaps have got to be exactly the right size – it's no good being two inches out and then finding that your frame doesn't fit. And these common workmen get all these things right as a matter of course, and we take it for granted, and don't think that they're clever at all.'

Beatrice said that she supposed that it was their job, and they certainly managed to leave a fearful mess everywhere. Eventually she got him away from the drains and began to show him where the plants were to go.

'We'll have a lawn here, and the lily-pond will be in this corner, then beyond it, so that it can be seen from the sitting-room, we'll have a herbaceous border against that wall there.'

Wilfred thought that this would look very nice.

'You're lucky that you've got the trees and shrubs there already.'

'Only just,' said Beatrice indignantly. 'Do you know the builders were going to cut all the shrubs over there down, just so that they could get their lorries through. Herbert came along one day, quite by chance, to see what they were doing, and stopped them just in time.'

'What did they do with their lorries?'

'Herbert made them leave them at the gate and carry the stuff across.'

'Of course.'

They made the complete circuit of the garden, two and a half acres Beatrice explained it was, and then returned to the house.

'I don't know where Florence and Herbert have got to,' said Beatrice. 'He was showing her the rest of the house.'

They went into the large entrance hall, and Beatrice called Herbert's name. There was a distant noise from somewhere near the top of the house, and a few minutes later Florence appeared, followed by Herbert.

'We've just been looking at the servants' quarters, Wilfred,' Florence said.

'Did you approve of them?' asked Wilfred.

'They'll be very comfortable; I could live there myself.'

'I suppose Herbert thinks that a happy servant is a good servant.'

'I think it's a good idea to treat them well,' said Herbert. 'I know you don't approve of servants, but you must agree that if you're going to have them at all you should look after them properly.'

'I can't quarrel with that,' said Wilfred, 'and, of course, you get your reward – they tend to stay with you.'

'Quite, we both benefit,' said Herbert urbanely. He was not in the least ruffled by Wilfred's sniping – indeed he was looking rather pleased with himself.

Finally Florence and Wilfred had to be shown the new car before being driven back in it to Mr and Mrs Calderwood's house for tea. Herbert displayed all the fittings for them. There were little tables that could be swung out over one's knees if one wished to eat, and there were concealed ashtrays and tiny cupboards to hold bottles and sandwich boxes. Everything that wasn't leather was walnut. Wilfred sat in the driver's seat and tooted the horn and asked Herbert if he had a peaked cap and goggles. Herbert replied placidly that you did not need goggles in a saloon car. Then they drove off.

In telling Winnick about the sort of person Wilfred had been, Beatrice was careful to play down these little jokes of Wilfred's, not only because Winnick might get the wrong idea about them but also because it was rather unfair to bring them up in Herbert's presence. Not that he had ever minded very much. He regarded Wilfred, at this time, as a footling little fellow who had landed himself in a dead-end job and presumably tried to find compensation by sneering at those who were doing better for themselves. After their visit to Wilmslow, for instance, when Wilfred had settled himself down in the back of the car, he had remarked that it was just like a funeral.

'I haven't travelled like this since we buried Uncle Fred.'

Beatrice, in the front seat, had shot a glance at Herbert to see if the jest had wounded him, but he just smiled tolerantly. This was the kind of joke that would be misunderstood by a man like Winnick, who would also be incapable of understanding Herbert's tolerant acceptance of it. So all that she said was that Wilfred had been very interested in their new house and that you couldn't possibly have guessed, either from him or Florence, that they had just bought a house of their own.

'They weren't the least bit jealous. In fact Wilfred seemed to be very full of himself that afternoon and kept making jokes about everything. We realized later why it was, when he told us, right out of the blue, that he and Florence had bought a house as well. He put it in a rather funny way. He said that they had capitulated to the capitalistic ethic. Mother didn't understand what he meant and had to have it explained to her.'

Winnick thought rather sourly that if that was Wilfred's idea of a joke he must have been a hilarious companion to have around. Frankly, he did not give a damn about this house at Wilmslow, or about Herbert's motor car, and he seized this chance of getting the talk back to the issues that mattered. 'He didn't tell you until he had completed the deal?'

'No, he never breathed a word of it. We were all quite staggered, especially when we heard where it was.'

'He hadn't, for instance, asked your father for financial help in buying it?'

Beatrice looked at Winnick with a sudden understanding. At last she began to see what it was that he had been driving at. 'Good heavens no. Wilfred would never do a thing like that. If you knew the first thing about Wilfred, you wouldn't even ask such a question.'

She was not speaking angrily, or defensively. Her tone conveyed a sort of hearty, good-humoured, 'what a silly-billy you are'. Winnick felt bound to defend his view.

'It's a fairly natural thing to think, isn't it? Wilfred might well have expected his father-in-law to make some sort of financial contribution.'

Beatrice leaned forward and prodded at him.

'You haven't been thinking that Wilfred married Florence for her money, have you?'

'Not only for that, I mean, I'm not – ' Winnick's voice trailed away. It was his turn to be on the defensive now.

'I don't blame you. Nobody could understand Wilfred who didn't know him but he wasn't like that at all. He would never have taken money from Father, or anybody else. As a matter of fact, Father offered to help with the house, but Wilfred wouldn't accept.'

His manner of refusing had been typical of him. He had been full of gratitude to Mr Calderwood; it was all of a piece, he said, with the kindness he had always received from his parents-in-law. But he must make his own home for his wife without help from anybody, he owed it to his self-respect. He was sure that Mr Calderwood would understand.

'You've always provided for your wife and family on your own without being beholden to anybody and you'll understand me when I say I must do the same.'

Mr Calderwood had tried to say something about Florence, but Wilfred had cut him short. Florence, he knew, was quite happy to live the life that he, her husband, was able to give her, and wanted nothing else. Had she ever said that she wanted anything else? No, Mr Calderwood hastily assured him, Florence had never said anything of the sort. Well then, Wilfred beamed at him, the question of Florence did not arise, did it?

As Mr Calderwood said afterwards, 'You can't quarrel with him. I can see his point of view, and he's absolutely right. In a way I like him for taking that stand.'

He finally managed, with a great deal of difficulty, to give Florence fifty pounds to help towards the furniture. Wilfred was not happy about this, but Mr Calderwood felt, and told Wilfred, that he had a perfect right to give his own daughter a present occasionally, and Wilfred, always reasonable, had to agree that this was so.

'The whole point about Wilfred,' Beatrice explained to Winnick, 'was that he was so independent. He would never be beholden to anybody, and he would never be ashamed of what he was himself or what he was able to offer. The first time he showed us his house, for instance – '

Winnick allowed his attention to wander. All this was rather awkward. If what Beatrice said was true then the theory that he had been carefully constructing would have to be abandoned. If only he could get some independent testimony, if Herbert would break his monastic silence, for instance. He would value Herbert's views. Beatrice's assessment seemed to him suspect, though she undoubtedly believed it herself; the character of Wilfred as she described it hardly made sense.

'What happened on your first visit to Herriott Street?' he asked.

'Nothing happened. We saw the house, that was all, and we had tea.'

They had gone by train. Wilfred had met them at the station and showed them the way.

'It's not quite such a pleasant walk as we had at Wilmslow,' he said, shepherding them off the platform, 'but it has its own graces.' And he pointed out the landmarks. 'Over there you can see the chimneys of the factory, and in a moment we are about to pass one of the warehouses of the London and North Eastern Railway.' He kept looking at them in a slightly amused way as though he was challenging them to turn up their noses at the district. But Herbert could play him at that game well enough and he said that he thought that the chimneys looked rather distinguished, and that the warehouse looked a noble building. When they came to Herriott Street Wilfred stopped to give them time to drink in the vista.

'The houses have a certain quality in their simplicity and design. The motif is repeated from terrace to terrace and from street to street. You get the best effect from some distance away.'

When they got to Number 29 it was exactly the same. It had not taken them very long to see the house. Wilfred opened each door in turn with great éclat, and gave the rooms names. The kitchen was the 'blue room' because there was blue distemper on the walls. The front bedroom was the 'rose room' because the wallpaper had a pattern of roses on it. 'I think they're roses,' said Wilfred, peering at the design, 'species unknown. Anyway it'll have to do for some time. We've got to decorate downstairs first.'

Wilfred also relieved them of the embarrassment of finding something nice to say about the house by quoting to them from the comments in the house-agent's description. 'Compact, that's what the kitchen is, compact. All the conveniences are close to hand. It reduces walking to the minimum.' And he told them that, by the standards of Herriott Street, the front bedroom was spacious.

'Spacious, that's what this room is. A spacious front bedroom. And the other one is "convenient", it doesn't say what it's convenient for.'

'It's not a bad house at all, Wilfred,' said Herbert. 'It's quite big enough for you and Florence, and it'll be easy to keep clean and so forth.'

'It should suit us very well, I know. And I haven't shown you the best room yet. Florence doesn't think it's the best one but I do.' The room he led them to was at the back of the house, next to the second-best bedroom. Its door was opposite the door of the bathroom, and he swung it open with a flourish and invited them to step inside. It was a tiny box of a room. At one side the ceiling sloped down at an acute angle so that it was impossible to stand upright. A very small window let in a rather dim light. There was nothing in the room at all except some boxes and a suitcase. Beatrice looked round her, glanced at Herbert, and said,

'Well.'

'You don't like it,' said Wilfred, 'you don't see the beauty of it.'

'Oh, I do, Wilfred, it's a lovely room.' Herbert chimed in that they could both see that it was very fine indeed, they had never seen a better room.

'It's mine,' said Wilfred, 'my very own room. Florence has let me have it; she's abandoned all claim to it.'

'What are you going to do with it?' asked Beatrice doubtfully.

'All sorts of things, anything. I can use it as a workroom, or make a laboratory out of it, or a study – anything. I haven't decided yet. Do you know, this is the first time in my life that I've ever had a room that was entirely my own, where I could really do the things I wanted to do.'

Beatrice saw that he was quite serious when he said this. This room did mean a lot to him, and Beatrice, who had spent her life in spacious surroundings, got a glimpse of what it must have been like to have been perpetually cramped for space. Wilfred grinned at them as he closed the door again and ushered them downstairs.

Beatrice used this as an example, to Winnick, of what she had meant when she spoke of Wilfred's joky style.

'He was laughing at himself, really. I mean, he showed us the room with such a flourish and it was such a miserable little cupboard of a place. You've got to remember that he had just been out to Wilmslow looking at rooms that really were big. It was a sort of skit on the way we had shown off our house to him.'

Winnick nodded rapidly to indicate that he had grasped the point of the jest. 'That was the room where – er – where it took place?'

'The murder you mean? Yes, that was the room. The laboratory, all the newspapers called it. That was Wilfred's name for it, but of course when Wilfred called it that it was intended as a joke, just as he sometimes called the kitchen the refectory.'

Winnick made a quick note. This would be a striking scene for his book. Three or four ironical paragraphs could be made out of Wilfred's pride in this little den of his where eleven years later he was to do his wife to death. 'What are you going to do with it?' Beatrice had asked: 'Oh, anything,' he had replied. 'Little did Beatrice think what that "anything" was to encompass.' Winnick smiled as he wrote, and Beatrice asked him what he was smiling at.

'Wilfred seems to have been a curious fellow. Almost everything he said was a kind of joke.'

'Yes,' said Beatrice. 'It was his way of looking after himself. If he thought that you might take him down a peg he'd get in a comment first, then you couldn't. He was terribly pleased with the whole house really. But he knew what we were thinking of it, he knew what was going on in our minds, so he made his jokes to leave us nothing to laugh at.'

Winnick was struck once again with the reflection that Beatrice was not quite as feather-brained as her meanderings occasionally made her appear. That was a perceptive piece of character analysis, and he showed her his sincere appreciation of it. It began to seem as if he had misjudged Wilfred somewhat. Just suppose that Wilfred had not been after Florence's money, suppose that he had not been disappointed, what alternative theory could be concocted? Beatrice was chattering on about this visit of theirs, and Winnick allowed his mind to wander. It came down to a question of how Florence had taken it. Perhaps this was the nub of the thing. Consider the matter – Wilfred was leading the life he would have led anyway. As far as he was concerned he had lost nothing. Florence, on the other hand, had lost a good deal. She was the one who would be likely to find Herriott Street oppressive and unpleasant. Beatrice had shown clearly enough what she had thought about it, and Florence was her sister, with the same background and upbringing. It was Florence who must have thought with dread of the chances of spending the rest of her life in a semi-slum. It was here that the strains must have come. Wilfred, lazy, easy-going, hiding behind his little jokes, a maddening Micawber figure; and Florence, strained and neurotic, resenting her husband's indolence, constantly nagging at him to better himself. It would build up over the years and result in an explosion of blind anger on Wilfred's part. Winnick tested his theory in his mind, and it looked good. Wilfred's refusal of Mr Calderwood's money must have been especially galling to Florence; it was significant that she herself had accepted the fifty pounds. Winnick came to with a jerk and spoke to Beatrice.

'What was Florence's feeling about the house?'

'Well, I was just telling you. You were far away, weren't you?'

Winnick blushed and looked foolish and apologized.

'I could see from your eyes that you were far away. I was just saying that I had a little talk with Florence on her own after tea in the kitchen, when we were washing up.'

'And she was happy with the house?'

'Perfectly happy, in fact she was very excited about it. We were talking about the furniture they were planning to get. Of course, when we visited them it was hardly furnished at all – there were only two chairs for us to sit on at table, so Wilfred and Herbert had to sit on boxes with cushions on them. Wilfred said it was rather fun, like a picnic without the wasps.'

Winnick was getting a bit tired of Wilfred's jokes. He must have been a tedious person to live with. In time, no doubt, it would have got on Florence's nerves as well. He listened to the rest of what Beatrice had to say without expecting any illumination. Florence would hardly have given herself away, and perhaps on this first visit she was still thinking of Herriott Street as a temporary lodging.

Beatrice was irritated by Winnick. It was really not worthwhile talking to the man. In the kitchen, after the meal, she had asked Florence straight out about how things were.

'They are very well,' Florence had replied. 'I'm glad to get out of those depressing digs at last.'

'You don't find this depressing?'

'It's our own, nobody can interfere with us here. In the flat you always had old Partlett or his wife poking their noses in.'

'How long are you going to stay here?' asked Beatrice.

'I don't know,' Florence laughed at the question. 'How long are you going to stay in Wilmslow? I suppose it depends how things turn out.'

'But isn't Wilfred ever going to do anything else, is he going to stay stuck in that same dead-end job all his life?'

At this Florence had stopped washing the glass dishes they had had jelly in and turned to face her sister.

'Now look here, Beatrice, don't you start. I've had quite enough of this sort of thing from Father and Mother without you joining in. Wilfred has got a perfectly respectable job – I'm not ashamed of it even if the rest of you are. He works very hard and he makes enough money to keep me properly, and now he's even saved enough to buy a house for us to live in. What do you want me to do? Insult him by telling him that I'm not satisfied with what he does for me? Not everybody wants to live like you and Herbert, you know. I'm quite satisfied with Wilfred as he is, and I wouldn't try to change him for anything.'

Beatrice had apologized immediately. She had not intended to criticize Wilfred by saying what she had said. It was just – just – she found it awfully difficult to say what it was just. That was the problem, and for Beatrice it remained the problem. You couldn't say anything against Wilfred. Any review of his character could be nothing else than a catalogue of virtues. It just seemed a pity that he represented a kind of cul-de-sac where Florence had come to a dead stop. It did not seem possible to Beatrice that her sister could really be content with this, and she cast a glance round the cramped little kitchen, and looked out of the window at the blank walls of the yard.

'Yes,' Beatrice repeated to Winnick, 'she told me that she was perfectly happy.'

11

Shortly after this visit Beatrice and Herbert were married and went to the South of France for their honeymoon. When they came back they settled into the house at Wilmslow and began entertaining on a lavish scale. Not for Herbert his father's caution and prudence; his father was almost dismayed by the prodigality of Herbert's style, and Herbert laughed at him.

'Get on with you, there's nothing wrong with it, the business can stand it. What's the good of keeping it? You make money to spend. Enjoy yourself while you can, I learnt that in the trenches.'

And his father shook his head and talked about rainy days. But he was also proud of his son and his social magnificence. Occasionally Florence and Wilfred would be invited, and Wilfred was able to hold his own surprisingly well by using his old trick of displaying an embarrassing frankness about his own humble origins. He was introduced one day to a man who told him that he was in shipping.

'I'm in shipping myself,' said Wilfred, and in reply to the question as to which company added, 'Manning and Wilson. I'm the second desk from the left in the outer office.' He delighted to tell people where he lived.

'Longsight. It's a two-up and a two-down in Longsight. I'm not used to fancy places like this, you know,' and he would dismiss, with a sweep of his hand, the house, the grounds, and the whole of Wilmslow, as being beyond his social ken. In this way he would trap them into despising him, and then engage them in argument about politics, or literature, or the latest Hallé concert, for Herbert liked to think that his friends represented a cultural élite as well as being well-to-do, and absolutely demolish them, because he was always careful to know more than they did.

'Well, the movement is marked *molto allegro*, you know, and of course you remember what Richter used to say about it?'

All in all Wilfred got the name, amongst Herbert's friends, of a bit of a character. Herbert himself used to swear to Beatrice that he was in the habit of thickening his Manchester accent just to show them how much he despised them.

Leading this very full social life it was not surprising that they should take little account of what was happening at Herriott Street. They paid a duty visit there every three or four months, and that was that. Florence used to come out to Wilmslow quite often, but she usually came in the daytime when Wilfred was at work. Winnick asked about life at Herriott Street, and Beatrice had to confess to him that it had been as featureless as had been suggested at the trial.

'It seemed to me,' Winnick said, 'from what everyone said, that Wilfred and Florence did absolutely nothing at all. Surely it couldn't have been quite like that?'

'I'm afraid it was,' said Beatrice. 'The only exciting thing I can remember was when Wilfred changed his job. Florence told me when she came over to Wilmslow once. Of course I was interested because we'd all been wanting Wilfred to give up that dreadful shipping office for long enough; and do you know why he'd given it up?'

'No,' said Winnick.

'Because they wanted to promote him.'

'He gave up his job because they wanted to promote him?'

'That's what Florence said. Do you remember, Herbert?'

'But it doesn't make sense,' said Winnick.

'That was what we thought but, you see, Wilfred felt differently about these things from other people. He said that he didn't want to command, that he'd seen enough of that sort of thing in the army. Herbert was awfully annoyed, weren't you, Herbert?'

Herbert once again drew on his repertoire of conversational noises and thus avoided committing himself to words.

'Anyway,' Beatrice continued, 'that was when Wilfred took the insurance job.'

'And what did Florence think about it?' asked Winnick.

'She felt that it was Wilfred's decision, not hers. I don't think she minded, there was no reason why she should.'

No reason my eye, thought Winnick. Florence must have minded, unless the insurance job brought in more money. He asked about this.

'I think it was about the same,' said Beatrice, 'there wasn't much in it, anyway. I think Wilfred got a commission on any extra policies he sold, but he worked in such a poor district that I don't think that amounted to much. No, Wilfred said that he preferred it because he was more his own master and it got him out in the fresh air.'

'He preferred fresh air to promotion?' asked Winnick. The phrase had just occurred to him and he thought it sounded rather good and made a note of it. Beatrice supposed, rather doubtfully, that that was it.

'And nothing else happened at Herriott Street?'

Beatrice did her best to explain. The visits which she and Herbert made all conformed to the same pattern. They would arrive and have tea; then she and Florence would do the washing up; then Wilfred would take them upstairs to his laboratory, or show them his latest hobby, or talk about his recent reading, whatever that had been. Then there would be a little general conversation, they would have supper and then they would go home. But nobody who had known Wilfred could have truly said that his life was vacuous. The high spot of their visits, as far as Wilfred was concerned, was the moment when, once the tea things had been cleared away, he was free to take the visitors upstairs to his den, or to produce his latest book. His spectacles would glitter, his face would become animated, he would often pace up and down a little as he got into the stride of his explanations. This was the time when Herbert would poke Beatrice surreptitiously in the side and roll his eyes, and do his comic yawns behind Wilfred's back.

'I've just been reading this remarkable book,' Wilfred might say, waving the volume in the air at them. 'It's called *The History of the Conquest of Peru*, it's a wonderful book, truly wonderful. It's the sort of book that really opens your eyes to the way that other people live, or have lived.' And he would describe some of the more colourful incidents, even going so far as to read selected passages to them.

Often he wanted to show them something that he had made, or some experiment that he was engaged in, so off they would troop to his tiny laboratory, where he would stand behind the table and perform his demonstrations.

'Come on upstairs, both of you, I've been making a Wimshurst machine, you ought to see this, you'll find it quite impressive.'

A Wimshurst machine, Beatrice discovered, was something to do with electricity. It consisted of two circular glass plates, which were spun round with a handle. If you could spin them fast enough, apparently, remarkable things happened.

'Watch the feather, there,' said Wilfred, panting a good deal and winding away at the handle. 'When the static begins to collect you can see it stiffen.'

Herbert made an exceedingly rude comment in Beatrice's ear, and she dug him smartly in the ribs with her elbow.

'There, did you see that spark?' asked Wilfred, but they had not seen it. After a little while he gave up.

'It's the evening,' he explained. 'It's too damp. The dampness dissipates the static. Ideally everything has to be quite clean and dry and rather warm; then you really do see something.'

Herbert remarked, jocularly, that at least Wilfred was rather warm. Beatrice asked what the machine was supposed to do. Would he be able, for instance, to light the house from it?

'Well, hardly, Beatrice. I mean, it's only a very small experimental model. But you can collect the static in these Leyden jars and produce quite large sparks. Of course, the principle behind it is as old as the hills. In a way it's remarkable that it took mankind so long to develop it.' Then he gave them a lecture on static electricity, and rubbed pieces of amber for them, and combed Beatrice's hair and showed how the comb picked up little bits of torn paper.

Once he and Florence went on a camping tour in Scotland, living in a tent and, as he proudly told them afterwards, not seeing another living soul for days. He had collected all the tufts of wool left by sheep on the barbed wire fences and put them in a bag. When they had got home he had cleaned the wool, spun it on a spinning-wheel which he had constructed out of bits of an old bicycle, dyed it in dyes which he had prepared from wild plants, and woven it into a scarf on a loom, which he had made out of some old picture frames.

'We're getting far too industrialized,' he told them when he exhibited this dingy garment. 'What we urgently need is to get back to being more self-sufficient. It seems remarkable now that one man should have controlled all the processes that produced that,' and he waved the scarf in the air at them, 'but a peasant in Shakespeare's time would have thought nothing of it.'

Herbert said, pleasantly, that he was inclined to agree with the peasant, and tried to put the case for dividing the work so that it was more expertly done. Wilfred laughed.

'I know it's not very much to look at, but at least it does show what is possible. Of course, if you divide the work you get each process done quicker. Don't forget, Herbert, that in the industrialist's eyes it's the quickness that matters, not the expertness. But you are driving the soul out of the work, you are making men into machines.' And he was away, happily arguing about the evils of the production line.

He had taken up the violin. In fact this became one of his

steady hobbies. Florence had been quite a good pianist when she was a girl, and when they had set up house in Herriott Street one of the luxuries she allowed herself was the piano from her old home. It had struck Wilfred that it would be pleasant if they could play duets together.

'I always wanted to learn the violin. It's the prince of instruments. So tiny, so simple, and all that glorious sound coming out of it.'

Wilfred took lessons with a violinist who had at one time played in the Hallé orchestra, and this Mr Grein became his oracle on matters musical. His conversation became full of snippets of information which Mr Grein had given him about the correct interpretation of Brahms, and technicalities of bowing in the Beethoven Concerto, and how Richter used to conduct Mozart. One or twice he and Florence actually gave them a little concert.

'Of course, it's a very difficult instrument,' he warned them as he took the violin out of its case, and went on to explain that the chief value of learning to play was the insight it gave you into the music. 'Until you've wrestled with the technical difficulties yourself, you know, you've never really got below the surface of the music,' and he and Florence wrestled with a Mozart sonata.

'He's very deceptive is Mozart,' Wilfred said afterwards as he was putting his instrument away. 'His music always sounds very simple, but it isn't, it's really profound.'

Herbert assured him that he made it sound very difficult indeed. 'I think you got a bit too far below the surface of the music there, Wilf old boy,' he said, genially.

'You should hear old Grein play that movement,' answered Wilfred, 'it's truly beautiful. It always gives me an odd feeling. He's a shabby little man with snuff all over his waistcoat, but when he starts to play it's absolutely lovely. He really makes that fiddle sing. The problem comes about the fifth bar,' and he took the music down from the stand and showed them what the difficulties of the piece were.

Winnick listened attentively.

'All this is quite fascinating, Mrs Naismith, and marvellous material for me. But there's one thing I don't quite understand. It's obvious that you had a great liking for Wilfred, even perhaps a respect for him. But as you describe him like this he seems to me to have been rather a pathetic little failure of a chap.'

'Oh no,' Beatrice spoke slowly, she did not rush out with her denial, 'I never thought that Wilfred was pathetic. He was always quite happy, quite content. I don't think I've ever known a more truly contented person than Wilfred.'

'Was he a bit selfish, perhaps?' Winnick asked. 'I mean, how did he justify spending all his time doing footling things like the ones you've told me about?

Beatrice stared at Winnick rather distantly. As he said that he had sounded exactly like Herbert. That was just the sort of thing Herbert used to say about Wilfred and, for quite a long time, Beatrice had agreed with him. It was Herbert who had described Wilfred as bone selfish, he had even used the very word 'footling' that Winnick had just used.

'I don't care a damn about Wilfred,' Herbert had said, 'but he's no right to make Florence live like that just so that he can amuse himself with bits of frog-spawn.' Wilfred was, at that time, engaged on a course of nature study. This had represented Beatrice's own feelings as well, and though she had changed her mind since, the change had been a gradual one, forced upon her in part by Herbert's own conduct. She tried to reply to Winnick. 'It depends what you mean by "selfish". I suppose Wilfred was entitled to amuse himself in any way he liked.'

'It doesn't seem to have been very cheerful for Florence,' Winnick suggested.

'I don't think Florence minded. She never said anything. Herbert spoke to him once. Wilfred had got interested in nature study and he was showing us a collection of plants and twigs and leaves. I remember he had a little aquarium, not for fish, for pond life, and it was full of water-beetles and things. Well, he was showing us this and talking about all the things in it, and suddenly Herbert said that it was a pity that Wilfred didn't find some more adult interests – something like that.'

'That must have made Wilfred a bit angry,' said Winnick. 'What did he say?'

Beatrice again directed a look at Winnick that made him feel that he must have said the wrong thing.

'Wilfred was never angry,' she said. 'When you say that you show that you still don't really understand him. In all the time I knew him never once did I see him angry.'

Winnick drew his lower lip in between his teeth and chewed it gently. This was very interesting. He thought of some of the descriptions he had read of Wilfred Rimmer attributing to him an almost inhuman self-control. He thought of the figure he had presented at his trial, surviving with unimpaired coolness and fortitude a gruelling five-hour cross-examination. A man who never, never once lost his temper – what sort of a monster could this be?

Beatrice was beginning to feel a sense of defeat. Probably it was not Winnick's fault, probably it was just that she had expressed herself badly, but he seemed as far away as ever from really understanding what Wilfred had been like. What Winnick had suggested would have been natural enough as far as most people were concerned. Most people, faced with the criticism that Herbert had made, would have been angry or taken a huff, but not Wilfred. He had paused, turning the idea over in his mind, before speaking.

'Well, that's a rather interesting question, Herbert. I suppose it depends on what you mean by an adult interest.'

Wilfred collected together some drawings he had been doing of plant stems and put them back in their folder.

'These are my leisure pursuits; now what are the leisure pursuits of the average grown man? He spends his time going to the pub, or watching a set of trained dogs running round a circular track, or yelling himself hoarse while twenty-two muddied oafs boot a ball about a football field.

Now, if you are telling me that these interests of mine are less adult than that, it seems to me that it's up to you to make the case out.'

Wilfred was enjoying it all. That was what you couldn't get someone like this Mr Winnick to see. An argument was meat and drink to him.

Herbert had been a bit tight-lipped on the way home, but all he had said about it was that it had been his own fault.

'I should have had more sense than to start the argument in the first place. The best thing to do with Wilfred is to leave him severely alone.' And he concluded, as he so often did, by saying that it was Florence that he felt sorry for.

Beatrice tried once more to explain to Winnick what sort of a man Wilfred had been. 'He enjoyed arguing about things like that. He believed that he was right. He thought that the sorts of things he was doing were interesting, and that anybody who didn't find them interesting was only showing his own limitations. He used to quote Chesterton – something about never finding anything boring. And, you know, the things that he was doing were quite interesting.'

Winnick considered this carefully. These oddities of Rimmer's had not, in themselves, been significant. The question was in what way, if at all, they had contributed to the murder. Beatrice had described a harmless sort of crank, and the real answer to his problem must lie, as he had thought, in the way Florence had taken his crankiness.

'Yes,' he said. 'It does seem as if life at Herriott Street was pretty quiet. What friends did they have?'

'I don't know. We never met any of their friends, in fact I don't think Wilfred made many close friends.'

'And Florence?'

'She never spoke about any.'

'Some of the neighbours said, in newspaper interviews, that they were rather stand-offish. Do you think that was so?'

'Perhaps they were a bit,' Beatrice answered slowly. She had not liked the question much. 'I don't think they had much in common with the people round them. Of course, until you got to know Wilfred he was always very quiet and that made people think that he was not very friendly. You must remember that I rather lost touch with them after a bit. I was ill, I had a series of illnesses, and we stopped going round there. I used to see Florence, she used to come over to keep me company, but I didn't see Wilfred very often after that.'

Having said this Beatrice fell silent. That was all she intended to say about that. She wasn't going to go into the details of these illnesses with this man. It had nothing to do with him. Herbert had been pressingly anxious to have a child. She had not been quite so keen herself but she recognized that it was her duty to co-operate, and she had done her best. Unfortunately she had had a series of miscarriages, and that had been that. It was a time she preferred not to think about too often. Herbert had been bitterly disappointed but had never in any way reproached her. In fact everyone said how well he had taken his disappointment. Of course he had not lost heart straight away. After the first miscarriage he had had long talks with the doctor and had emerged quite restored in confidence.

'He says it's nothing at all to worry about. It's quite normal, it often happens, it doesn't mean a thing. He says there is no reason why we shouldn't be successful next time.'

Beatrice stiffened under the bedclothes and thought sourly that these men had got it all worked out. She was going to have to go through all this again. Their tone of easy unconcern jarred on her. If men had to have the babies they would talk in a different way.

Beatrice kept having the feeling, at this period of her life, that she was like some prize animal that a farmer is keeping for breeding purposes. She was cosseted, rested, fed carefully, jealously guarded, weighed and examined at regular intervals, and all this so that when the time seemed ripe Herbert could impregnate her again. It became clear to her that her value in Herbert's eyes depended on her qualities as breeding stock, and unfortunately, when the second attempt was well under way and everything seemed to be going smoothly, fate stepped in. Mr Calderwood's affairs had been for some time in difficulty, Beatrice knew, but she had imagined that there was nothing very seriously wrong and she had thought very little about it. Consequently Beatrice only learnt that matters were serious when, one day, Herbert had an urgent message to go round to his father's house. He did his best to keep quiet about what had happened, but Beatrice fretted and worried him and he was afraid that in her condition this might be bad for her, so he had to explain that her father was on the verge of bankruptcy. He had called on his old friend to ask for help, but it seemed that he had left it too late.

'If he had come to us six months ago we might have been able to stop the rot. I'm afraid, Beatrice, that he has been committing the shareholders' money in a very unwise way. I don't think any of the other directors know what he's been up to.'

Herbert did what he could. The most important thing, as he explained, was to save as many of Mr Calderwood's assets as possible from the inevitable catastrophe. He managed to transfer some of them to Mrs Calderwood and some of them to Beatrice. He tried to put some in Florence's name, but Wilfred objected. There had been quite a scene, Beatrice heard later. Apparently Wilfred had demanded that the reasons for the transaction should be explained to him. 'What you are really trying to do, Herbert, is to get these assets away from the creditors. If you settle them on Mrs Calderwood, and Florence and Beatrice, they can't be touched – is that it?' Herbert had said that that was it exactly.

'I'm sorry, Herbert, but I can't agree. I know it's probably normal business practice, you'd say that it was just common sense, but I can't quite see it in that light. It seems to me that the money ought to go to pay the debts.'

Wilfred had gone even further than this and insisted on repaying the fifty pounds Mr Calderwood had given Florence to buy furniture. Herbert had been very annoyed with him indeed, and there had been a lot of bad feeling about it.

It had been shocking to Beatrice to see how her father changed during this period. The failure shattered him completely, he seemed to become senile over night. When Beatrice went to visit her parents she found that her mother was upstairs, prostrate on her bed, and her father was sitting in the living-room, in the dark, in front of a small fire. He hardly moved when she went in and put her arm round his neck and kissed him, and when he spoke she noticed that he avoided looking at her. 'Well, Bea,' he said, 'it's a bad business.'

She began trying to console him, but he put his hand on her lips and stopped her.

'Don't say anything. It's no good saying anything. Go upstairs to your mother. She's very upset. She'll be glad to see you.'

His uselessness was made savagely clear to him at this time. All the real work was taken out of his hands. Sometimes the Chief Clerk from his office would come round bringing a sheaf of documents, and Mr Calderwood would try to greet him in the old way and behave as though he was still an important man and scan the papers with an air of authority, but it was all play-acting, and the clerk knew it, and so did Mr Calderwood. Beatrice found him sitting one day with a set of bills in front of him, entering figures in a little book.

'I'm no use, really,' he said, looking up as she came in, 'they've taken everything out of my hands, they don't think I'm capable.'

She tried to cheer him up by telling him that Herbert would put matters right, but this was the wrong thing to say. Time was when her father had put things right for himself without having to call in his son-in-law's help. Now, the only time when he did anything which had an actual, practical effect, was when Herbert pushed some documents in front of him and showed him where to sign his name.

Beatrice could not keep away from her parents' house although it was a great strain to her to be there. She felt that she was needed. Her mother had collapsed utterly and was of no use at all, and her father would have been almost entirely alone if she had not been there. Florence came round, of course, but since the quarrel with her father about Wilfred all those years ago, she had never been on comfortable terms with him again, and he had heard about Wilfred's refusal to allow Florence to accept the transfer of money and returning the fifty pounds, and this had hurt him deeply. So Beatrice did what she considered her duty and in due course she paid for it by losing her child once more. The strain had been too much. She always blamed her father's bankruptcy, later on, for robbing her of her child and wrecking her marriage.

12

Winnick began to feel that he ought to take his leave. Beatrice had probably told him all that she could, and she seemed, doubtless because she was getting tired, to have fallen into a dour silence. On the other hand he did not want to go unless he had some kind of guarantee that he would be readmitted. He wanted to get that husband of hers talking. There must be all sorts of things that Herbert could tell him, if only he had a mind to. Unfortunately, if Winnick was any judge at all, what Herbert's mind was actually made up to do was to get rid of him as quickly as possible and never, under any circumstances, to allow him back. At least he was there in the room, and could hardly be ejected by force, and he did not want to surrender that positive advantage.

'I believe, sir,' he turned to Herbert, 'that you were present throughout the trial?'

Herbert inclined his head.

'I would find it enormously valuable, sir, if you would tell me some things about it, from your point of view.'

'But you must have all that,' Herbert spoke testily, 'there are plenty of accounts of it, why don't you read those?'

'I have done. I may say,' added Winnick modestly, 'that I've read every word that has been written about the case. But written reports are not the same as an eye-witness account, particularly if the eyewitness knew the defendant personally. Have you read the accounts yourself, sir?'

Herbert agreed that he had seen some of them.

'And what did you think of them? Were they accurate, did they give a true idea of what actually went on?'

Herbert's head moved restlessly from side to side.

'No, not really, no they didn't.'

'Well, there you are, you see, sir. I need your help to try to correct them.'

Herbert was silent, and Winnick held his breath. The fatal thing to do would be to try to hurry him or force his hand, and then, suddenly, help came from Beatrice.

'I'm sure Herbert will tell you what you want to know, won't you, Herbert?' Her tone was the tone of a schoolmistress telling a little boy to take his hands out of his pockets and sit up straight and get on with his work. It was a surprise to Winnick, who had thought that Herbert was very much the master in his home. Evidently she kept a pretty firm hand on him. Herbert at once agreed to tell Winnick what he wanted. He did not agree very graciously, but Winnick had got what he wanted and had too much sense to outstay his welcome, if you could call it that. He took his leave immediately.

When he had gone Herbert went straight off to his room without speaking to Beatrice, who sat, silent and brooding, in front of the fire. He knew why she was brooding. He had known all along that this meddling with the past would eventually lead to this. She was remembering his own treachery, and how she had discovered it. It had taken Herbert a very long time to live all that down, and it was a bit thick if this meddlesome writer fellow had started it all up again. He just hoped that she would get over it pretty quickly, and in the meantime the dignified thing to do was to have as little contact with her as possible, to retire to his den and smoke his pipe and put his feet up and try to forget the whole damned business.

Beatrice was remembering the first moment of disillusionment. It was at breakfast one morning. She was alone because Herbert was making one of his trips to London, trips which had become almost weekly events. She quite enjoyed being alone; she was free to get up when she wanted, and do what she wanted, and take her own time about things. She was beginning to feel normal again after the last of her miscarriages, and she was enjoying a lazy tranquillity. She was just buttering her second piece of toast when the maid came in with the morning's mail. She picked up a brown, business envelope with her name and address typed on it and slit it open, expecting to see a bill or a catalogue. Inside there was a single sheet of paper which bore the following words: 'Have you ever wondered what your husband gets up to when he goes to London?'

Beatrice read the words four or five times without really taking them in. It was such a crude assault, a terse question from an unknown person, dropping on her breakfast table like that and destroying her peace of mind. No, she had never wondered what her husband got up to. It had never occurred to her to wonder because she had trusted him absolutely; and it never would have occurred to her if this abominable person had not asked this poisonous question.

Of course, she knew, from her reading, what was the proper thing to do with an anonymous letter. You tore it into small pieces and threw it into the fire and then you put it right out of your mind. Well, she managed the first part of the operation well enough, but the second part proved more difficult. These letters, she understood, were always written by frustrated spinsters whose minds had been distorted by years of sexual deprivation, and there was no reason at all why the unsupported assertion of such a person, who had not even the courage to sign her own name, should have the power to make her doubt her own husband. She had been with Herbert once or twice on these London trips of his, and very boring she had found them. All that Herbert did was to work the whole time and leave her on her own in the hotel all day, while in the evening, as likely as not, she had had to help him entertain some business connection, or go with him when he visited an important client. Herbert was working very hard at this time. His father was not in good health, and he had all the responsibility for the Manchester end of the business as well as for this new venture in London. Many a night he would be sitting over his papers until two o'clock in the morning. And besides, he had never given her the slightest anxiety in this way. There were husbands who could not see a pretty girl without slobbering over her, pawing her, putting their arms round her waist, and paying her silly compliments. And she had heard stories about the way some of these men treated the young girls who were unfortunate enough to be in their employment. But Herbert was not like this. He was openly contemptuous of such behaviour. No, the accusation was a silly lie and should be dismissed from her mind.

Herbert was not due back for another three days, so she had plenty of time to forget it. But it would not be forgotten. She found herself wondering, at odd moments, what Herbert was doing, who he was talking to, where he was going, and when he got back from London she looked at him very closely for tell-tale signs of misbehaviour, but he appeared to be perfectly normal, tired and rather quiet, but that was usual these days. Beatrice began to be thoroughly ashamed of herself for these suspicions of hers, but she found that she could not control them. She even looked in the drawers of Herbert's desk, and went through his pockets in case he had left incriminating evidence there, and of course she found nothing. She excused herself by claiming that all that she wanted was positive proof that he was innocent, so that her mind would be at rest again, but it gradually dawned on her that the only proof that she would get would be proof of guilt. Every time she ransacked his possessions and found nothing, this did not prove that there had been nothing to find, and so it was never finally effective in setting her mind at rest. She took to asking artless little questions about what Herbert did with himself, and whether he was lonely in the evenings, questions which surprised Herbert, for Beatrice did not usually bother her head about such things.

'There isn't much time to be lonely. Do you know what that damn fool in Ilford did?' and he launched into a story about the misdeeds of one of his suppliers. From what he said to her it seemed that his life there was the same as it had always been. 'I go round to the Donaldsons' quite a lot, and I see old Markovitch occasionally.' Donaldson was one of his managers. Beatrice remembered Mrs Donaldson as a stout, dull, middle-aged woman who could talk about nothing at all except her children; Markovitch was an old business friend of Herbert's father. Certainly there was nothing there to alarm her. She covered up for these questions by telling him that she got rather lonely herself sometimes and wondered if he were too.

'Well, it's not very jolly for either of us,' Herbert's tone was peevish, 'but it's got to be done. The thing won't run itself in London, you know.'

'I'm not complaining, Herbert. I'm glad to have you back, and I miss you. Don't you like to feel that I miss you?' She snuggled up to him – they were sitting together on the sofa – and nuzzled her face into his shoulder.

'Why don't you come down with me again? I know it's not much fun for you in the day-time, but you could look round the shops. I could see if Mrs Donaldson would keep you company.'

Beatrice declined Mrs Donaldson, but agreed to come. Herbert promised to leave at least one evening free so that they could 'do a show'.

Beatrice went with him several times, with the same result as before. She became completely bored, found herself sitting in her hotel room for hours on end twiddling her thumbs, and discovered that she much preferred her own house in Wilmslow. She had wondered whether she would catch the hotel staff out, but she saw nothing. And she baulked at the idea of actually questioning them, that would really be inexcusable. And so her London trips were discontinued; but she still could not rid her mind of the suspicion that had been planted there. She had one quite bright idea. One week Herbert left in his study at home some papers. Beatrice was pretty sure that they were of no importance at all but it was just possible for her to think that they might be necessary for what he was doing in London.

At least it gave her an excuse to telephone him one evening. She worked out carefully what was the best time for her to ring. If he was really 'up to something', as the letter had suggested, then probably he would be 'up to' it later rather than earlier in the evening. She decided that nine o'clock would be about right and put a call through to his hotel at that time. He answered immediately. 'Hullo, Beatrice, is anything wrong?'

She assured him that there was nothing wrong.

'It's just that I found a file of yours in your study and thought that it might be important. Do you want me to send it down after you?'

Her voice sounded false to herself. She had addressed Herbert as 'darling' because she wanted to sound affectionate and concerned, but it was not a term she normally used to him, some of the rather silly wives they knew used to 'darling' everybody. Herbert, at any rate, seemed perfectly natural. He expressed just the right degree of gratitude for her trouble, and assured her that the file was not important. No, he had not been disturbed, he was working in his room on some estimates he had been sent and would soon go to bed. They chatted for a few more minutes and then she hung up. Beatrice realized that she was precisely where she had been before. Even if Herbert had been out there would have been a dozen innocent and respectable explanations for it. She was ashamed of herself and her suspicions, and Herbert heaped coals of fire on her head by returning on Friday with a small, expensive piece of jewellery, to thank her for her thoughtfulness.

'I think I wanted to hear your voice as much as anything else,' she said, in explanation of her call, 'it was lovely to hear you.'

In the course of the weekend she managed to establish that it would be quite normal for her to ring Herbert at odd times when he was in London, just for the pleasure of chatting with him, and he agreed that it would be a fine idea.

Later on she felt that she ought to have seen that Herbert's behaviour was a little too perfect to be absolutely true. He expressed not the least surprise at this sudden access of interest on her part in all his activities in London. He answered all her questions patiently and convincingly, like an obsequious book-keeper presenting his accounts for an unexpected audit, anxious to prove that everything is above board. But it was only in retrospect that this seemed odd. At the time Beatrice accepted it in good faith as evidence that he was what he seemed. She had inspected Herbert's books, and they balanced to a halfpenny, and he was entitled to be considered an honest book-keeper.

It was Beatrice's misfortune that she was completely alone. The only person she had even considered taking into her confidence was Florence, but finally she could not bring herself to do so. It would have been too great a confession of failure. Beatrice had always regarded herself as the matrimonially successful sister, and Florence as – well – not so successful. She had occasionally thought that Florence had been a little jealous of her happiness, that she had grudged it her. She remembered the time when she told Florence that she was going to marry Herbert. Florence had compressed her lips and turned a little away. The good wishes she had offered had sounded insincere and strained. Florence, for some reason, had disapproved of the marriage; perhaps even now she felt some proprietorial interest in Herbert. It had given Beatrice pleasure to show her sister how happy she and Herbert were together and now, when it came to the pinch, she preferred to keep her secret. If she had jumped to quite unjustified conclusions about Herbert on the strength of a single anonymous letter, what would Florence think about her trust in him? So she said nothing to anybody.

After a few months she had begun to forget it, and then the second letter arrived. It looked, as far as she could remember, exactly like the first. It was a brown, foolscap envelope containing a single sheet of paper with a brief, typed message: 'Find out what your husband does with himself on Thursday nights.'

Beatrice began to think very hard. She must try to get some certainty one way or the other. It was now Tuesday; the letter, she noticed, had arrived on the same day of the week as the previous one. She would follow him on Thursday, without saying a word to anybody, and arrange to stay in a different hotel. Then she would watch, on Thursday evening, and see if her husband went anywhere or did anything. It was a simple plan, but in the two days she had to brood on it it began to seem more and more difficult. Keeping a watch on an hotel, and following people in the street, were specialist activities. One would have a cab, of course, and say, 'follow that vehicle in front', and if the quarry walked, well, one walked behind him and looked in shop windows whenever he stopped. That was about the limit of her knowledge. One thing she was quite clear about. Herbert must not see her; if he did the cat would be out of the bag with a vengeance.

Sometimes she had a vision of a gross anti-climax, of herself toiling up to London and spending a hideous day lurking and spying, only to track Herbert to a decorous, dull evening with the Donaldsons. Perhaps that was the truth of it. Perhaps her anonymous well-wisher had simply misinterpreted some innocent social habit. Beatrice had no suspicion at all that Mrs Donaldson might be the lady in question; she would have trusted Herbert to any degree with Mrs Donaldson.

When she reached London she installed herself in an hotel not too far from Herbert's, and spent the afternoon resting on the bed and making her plans. The taxi-cab idea was the best. She would sit in a taxi and watch the entrance of Herbert's hotel, then if Herbert came out she would be in a position to follow him. The first step was the hardest, explaining herself to the taxi driver. She commandeered a vehicle and gave him the name of Herbert's hotel.

'I want you,' she said, 'to take me there and then stop

somewhere where I can watch the entrance. Can you do that?'

The driver was a heavily-built, elderly man, and he swivelled round in his seat and surveyed her steadily.

'It'll cost a bit,' he said.

She fumbled in her handbag and exhibited a sheaf of bank notes.

'I don't care how much it costs. A man may come out of the hotel, and then I shall want you to follow him.'

The driver digested this idea slowly. Beatrice noticed that he showed no curiosity, no surprise, nor any other emotion; his response was entirely practical.

'How do you mean, follow him, is he going to be in another cab?'

'He may be. I don't know.'

The driver brooded for another fifteen seconds.

'If he walks I'll get out and follow him myself,' said Beatrice.

'All right,' said the driver at last, 'but you'd better let me have something on account. I don't want you just jumping out after him and forgetting to pay, do I?'

Beatrice conquered an impulse to rise haughtily and seek another cab; she could not go through all this again, and probably they would all be just as bad. She passed three one pound notes across without speaking, and the driver tucked them away in his costume somewhere and let in the clutch. It was a miserable evening. A light drizzle was falling and the streets were shining in the wet. People huddled past under umbrellas or with their coat collars turned up. Her driver appeared to be thoroughly experienced in this sort of thing, for he placed his cab in a perfect position for her to watch the front entrance of the hotel. He did not speak at all except to discourage people who thought that he was on hire and tried to climb in, and he did not look round at Beatrice, although once or twice she caught him eyeing her through the mirror. Beatrice fixed her gaze on the hotel steps and waited. The rain had cleared the streets and this made it easier for her.

It was extraordinarily difficult, she found, to keep a steady watch. After a short time the street and the hotel entrance began to dance about in front of her eyes. She had to keep blinking, or looking away, and every time she did this she looked back in a panic in case Herbert had chosen that exact moment to emerge. Being a novice at the game she at first sat rigidly to attention with all her muscles tensed, and after ten minutes of this various pains and cramps began to develop themselves. There were one or two false starts. Men appeared who were vaguely Herbertesque in appearance, and there was a bad moment when a group of men came out of the hotel together and Herbert might, just possibly, have been the figure in the middle. Then the hotel porter appeared and hailed a cab, and Herbert himself came out and stood on the top step contemplating the street. He looked relaxed and at his ease. He was pulling on his gloves, and he descended the steps slowly and spoke a word or two to the porter who was holding open the cab door for him. Beatrice had responded to this sight by leaning forward and clawing at the handle of the window with a view to pulling it down. Her heart was pounding and her hands trembled. The driver spoke.

'That him, then?'

She could not say anything, she swallowed rapidly and made agitated gestures and nodded several times. Her driver needed no more instruction than this. She had had the presence of mind a short time earlier to take another two pounds out of her purse and hold it in her hand ready for an emergency, and this acted on him like the scent of a fox on a fox-hound. He drove expertly and methodically, and Beatrice saw the tail light of the other cab constantly before her. Near the entrance of one of the underground stations Herbert's cab stopped, and a young woman who had been standing in the shadows of the entrance hurried forward and climbed in. Beatrice's agitation became extreme, she was shaking all over and her teeth began to chatter slightly until she exerted herself to check them. She found that she was gasping or sobbing in air rather than breathing in any normal way. Finally, Herbert's cab drew up in front of a depressingly seedy-looking establishment. A strip of coloured glass illuminated over the door announced its name to passers-by, The Belgravia Hotel. With this Beatrice's last hope died. Even after the arrival of the young woman in Herbert's cab she had been concocting innocent explanations for his conduct. Perhaps he had an evening conference and had had to pick up one of the secretaries who was to take notes; or the young woman might be the daughter of some business friend whom Herbert had arranged to meet. But for what she saw now she could invent no explanation at all except the obvious, sordid one. Her cab drew up at the kerb, in a patch of darkness between two street lamps, about twenty yards behind Herbert's. She got out quickly and shakily, thrusting the two pounds towards the driver. 'Want me to wait?' he asked.

She shook her head. Herbert was paying off his own vehicle in front and the girl was standing on the pavement beside him. She began to walk rather unsteadily towards them, and at that moment Herbert turned towards the girl and caught sight of her as she walked into the pool of light cast by the next lamp. It remained a source of astonishment to see how calmly Herbert behaved in this crisis. She had known that he was a cool hand, there was a medal in a drawer at home that testified to his behaving well in trying circumstances, but it was surprising to see it in action. He caught the girl's arm and whispered something in her ear. Then, in a continuation of the same movement he guided her towards the door of the cab and opened it for her. She got in, and he said something to the driver and handed over a note. The cab drove away instantly, and she and Herbert were left facing one another in the empty street. He walked towards her.

'Hullo, Beatrice,' he said, 'been following me?'

His tone was completely normal, he appeared to be absolutely calm.

Beatrice was not able to speak, so she nodded instead.

'We'd better find a taxi,' he said. 'We should get one at the main road.' He took his place by her side and offered her his arm and, in a daze, not thinking what she was doing, Beatrice took it, and they strolled side by side towards the main road, like any husband and wife out for an evening together. They were lucky. They found a cab almost as soon as they reached the corner, and Herbert gave the address of his hotel and settled himself down beside her.

'You came down on purpose for this?' he asked in a matter-of-fact tone.

'Yes,' said Beatrice, finding her voice at last. Herbert's calmness had had the odd effect of calming her down also.

'What put you on to me?'

She took the anonymous letter out of her handbag and gave it to him. He screwed up his face a little as he took it and read it.

'I see – this isn't the first you've had?'

'No – last June.'

'Last June?' Herbert's face was not expressive, but Beatrice knew him very well and she was sure that he was remembering her sudden flurry of interest in his affairs and her expression of love and loneliness.

'Have you still got that one?'

'No, I burnt it.'

It was infuriating that Beatrice actually found herself saying this with a spark of pride. Herbert's wrinkling of his nose, his expression of distaste as he read the letter, had managed to suggest that it was unclean, and that it was unworthy of Beatrice to have bothered with it, so it was almost proudly that she said she had burnt the first of them. Herbert looked at the letter again.

'I wonder who sent it?' he said.

'What does it matter who sent it?' Beatrice managed to regain some of her composure and with it her temper. 'Obviously it was true.'

'Suppose,' said Herbert, fractionally inclining his head

towards the driver, 'we postpone discussing that until we're back in the hotel.' They both sat mute for the rest of the journey.

When they reached the hotel Herbert, as was natural, took complete control. Beatrice did not know what she looked like, or how much she was giving the game away, but nobody could have judged from Herbert's manner that anything was wrong at all. He sent the cab driver to pick up her luggage from the other hotel and bring it over. He explained that madam had arrived unexpectedly, and chambermaids were packed off to prepare her bed. Beatrice had wanted to make some protest about these arrangements that were being made without reference to her. Did they really expect her to sleep in the same room as Herbert? But she could not make a scene in public. She had neither the strength nor the wit to do anything about it. All she wanted was to get on her own away from all of them.

Finally they reached Herbert's room. He ordered two brandies to be sent up, made arrangements for receiving Beatrice's luggage when it arrived, and then closed the door. At last Beatrice was able to give way to her feelings and she sat in a chair and wept silently and without control. Her teeth were chattering again and she was once more experiencing difficulty with her breathing, gasping in short, rather hurtful, gulps of air. Herbert prowled round the room and kept looking at her sideways as though trying to assess his problem. Now that there was no longer any positive action for him to take he began to lose his ironclad composure. He made a number of abortive attempts to say something, and when he finally succeeded what he said was not very conclusive or satisfactory. He tried to be reasonable, to be persuasive, to make light of the matter. He reminded her he was not a hermit. 'You couldn't expect me just to cut sex and that sort of thing out. I mean – I'm not blaming you' – he was emphatic, irritatingly often, that he in no way blamed Beatrice, ' – but did you never look at it from my angle?' Again and again he pressed upon her, as the supremely important thing, his own point of view. Calmly, reasonably, he reminded her that he was a normal man with normal appetites; in fact he carried calmness and reasonableness to such lengths that he fell into the trap of taking the thing rather too easily. It was surely the most reasonable thing in the world that he should find some kind of outlet for these instincts. Was this so terrible or so important? Wasn't it really a rather trivial matter to make so much fuss about? And at this point came the slight smile, the self-deprecating little laugh; but Beatrice could not quite meet him on that plane. She was not capable of thinking coherently or productively, but she still knew what was trivial and what was important. And Herbert made one bad slip. Beatrice asked him how long all this had been going on, and he replied, 'You mean with the girl this evening?'

'How many other girls have there been, then?'

'Oh really, Beatrice. You mix up the sort of feeling that I have for you with the sort of use I make of these girls, but the two are totally distinct.'

'I don't see,' said Beatrice, 'that you can have any feelings for me at all if you behave like this.'

The talk circled interminably, drearily, about the same points, and finally came to an end not because they reached any conclusion but because the futility of repetition finally silenced them. Beatrice announced that she was going to bed: 'I might be able to think more clearly in the morning.' There was one point on which she had made up her mind. Herbert must sleep in a different room that night. He started to argue, but she stopped him instantly. Where he slept, how he arranged it, she did not care. It was of no interest to her what the hotel staff thought about it. All she knew was that he was not going to sleep in the same room with her, not when he had prepared himself to sleep with that – that dreadful, common looking little shop-girl. Beatrice dissolved into tears again as she thought of the dowdy little creature in the shoddy-looking coat with its artificial fur collar, who had hurried from the shadows of the underground station to her husband's arms. How could he possibly have preferred that to her?

13

Upstairs, in his den, Herbert stretched his legs and puffed at his pipe, and pondered on Winnick. Since one could not actually take him by the scruff of the neck and throw him out of the house, what the devil did one do with the fellow? He had watched him as he listened to Beatrice's meanderings and wondered, a trifle grimly, what he was making of it all. He had this mania for facts, as though a mere accumulation of trivia would solve the problem. As soon as Beatrice mentioned a name, or a date, out would come the little notebook, and he would be jotting away. And he had a positively astonishing belief in the retentiveness of human memory. Did he really expect them to recall the name of that Polish chap that Wilfred had started his game of postal chess with? And even if they had remembered, what on earth would be the use of the information to him? Was he going to go all the way to Poland to ask the man for his impressions of the great murderer? What, Herbert wondered, had they made of the notorious Rimmer case from the distance of Cracow? At least it would explain to that chap why his game was unfinished, why Comrade Rimmer was so long meditating over his next move. Fortunately Beatrice had said nothing important that was not already public property, and she was blessedly consistent in her attitudes, any implied slur on either Florence or Wilfred set her on the defensive immediately, but she was happy to chatter away about things that had no bearing on the case at all, and Winnick's pencil was kept busy. He collected names. The name of the hotel where they had stayed in Llandudno, the name of the hospital Florence had worked in, the name of the man who had taught Wilfred the violin – Beatrice trotted them out and Winnick wrote them down. There was one flaw, Herbert noted with glee: Beatrice usually got the names wrong. Herbert remembered these details very well himself. He had an accurate memory, an astonishing memory for his age, only he was not such a fool as to make a boast of it. That violin teacher's name – it was Weiner, a German name, one of those Germans who had settled in Manchester, half the musicians in Manchester were German Jews. Weiner, Gerhardt Weiner, that was it; but he was not idiot enough to say anything to that fellow. The trouble was that all this rummaging about, although it seemed aimless enough, was potentially dangerous. Once a man started rooting about like this there was no knowing what he would turn up.

Herbert knew the sort of book he was going to write. It would be just like all the other books that had been written about the case, completely worthless. They tried to pry into the secret lives of a couple like Florence and Wilfred, and all they could come up with were guesses – Freudian, he supposed. You could see the way the fellow's mind was working, suspecting Wilfred of all sorts of devious motives; they were all of them almost exclusively interested in Wilfred. Florence, now, they never gave a mention to her. If Wilfred was unrecognizable in the accounts they wrote, then Florence was almost totally invisible. A little mouse of a woman, created to be battered to death. The absurdity of this idea had often moved Herbert to silent, helpless fury, even though he recognized the utility of it.

Herbert remembered Florence as she was before the war, rather tall and graceful, with a wonderful skin. She had very open, blue eyes, that could hold you in a grave, steady gaze as she questioned you passionately about some point of your beliefs. He had fallen quite suddenly and helplessly in love with her. For her sake he had joined debating societies and read serious books. To impress her, he had taken Wilfred to his house. Here's an amusing chap, you see, different from the usual run; quite in your line, Florence, clever as you like, reads the latest poetry, advanced ideas. Oh, yes, he's poor, poor as a church mouse, but I don't mind that, I'm a cut above that sort of thing; after all he's a worthwhile human being. Later Herbert realized the trap he had set for himself. There had been the agony of that business in the Lake District. After it was all over Herbert could not believe it of himself that he had handled things so ineptly. He had known the quality of Florence, and he could have foretold what the result of behaviour such as this would be. When Florence had announced that she and Wilfred were engaged, and that old fool of a father of hers had actually acquiesced in it, Herbert had gone through a period of deep self-disgust. And he had resolved on a process of slow re-establishment, for surely the affair with Wilfred would not last. If he was patient and prudent Florence would come to her senses again. Even as a boy Herbert had always been capable, when he wanted a thing sufficiently, of immense, watchful, prudent patience. And he had known how to ingratiate himself with people. He was very sensitive to the way people felt towards him, and he could turn this feeling to his advantage. He could be pleasantly unassuming and self-mocking, and he could fall in with their moods. He knew how he should have behaved in the Lake District. He should have put up with Wilfred, he should have welcomed his company on their boating trips, he should have acted as an enthusiastic elder brother, doing his best to see that Wilfred had a good time. Florence would have responded to this generosity, Wilfred would have acknowledged to her what a decent chap Herbert was. It would only have been a matter of a week, and then he would have had her to himself again and Wilfred would have been gone, and he would have taken jolly good care that he did not come back in a hurry.

It was Florence that had unsettled him and spoiled his judgement. She had a provocative coolness, a way of holding you at arm's length that was very disturbing. One would long, sometimes, to unsettle her self-possession, and this longing could thrust one into unwise action. He remembered a time when he was about sixteen, and he and Florence had been playing together in a game of sardines. They had got themselves closeted in a cupboard, and she had allowed herself to lean against him, had pressed her cheek and hair against his face, and he had felt the warmth of her breasts through her dress as she snuggled up to him. But when he had made a clumsy but positive response she had sprung away and made a public display of her anger with him. What a fuss there had been over that. He had had an interview with his mother at her most formidable, reminding him of the need to be a gentleman at all times.

'You are allowed a good deal of freedom with these girls, Herbert. We believed that we could trust you not to abuse that freedom, and I hope you are not going to prove us wrong.'

He had tried to excuse himself, but his excuses had the unfortunate effect of seeming to put the blame on Florence, and his mother had rejected this fiercely.

'No, Herbert, I don't want to hear any talk like that. It is a particularly mean thing for a gentleman to try to put the blame on a lady, remember that, Herbert. Now it will be best if we all try to forget that it ever happened. Perhaps, in time . . .' Et cetera. He would remember scenes like this in later years and suddenly grow hot and clench his fingers.

When he was unsettled he had a tendency to sulk, this was his abiding weakness. He had read somewhere that sulking is a call for attention, because your successful sulker wishes to be caressed and made a fuss of. If that was true then he was not a successful sulker. He did not sulk because he wanted attention, but because, for the time being at least, he hated the entire world and everybody in it, and wanted to damage them as deeply as possible. When he was in a sulk he wanted to hurt people, to reject them, to storm out of their lives. In a mood like this he would say and do extraordinary things, and when he came to his senses again would see how damaging to himself they had been. Remorse and regret would follow, with resolutions to control himself better in future. In the grip of this kind of mood he had lost Florence, and the loss was retrievable only if he was allowed time. It was the war that spoiled his chances. Even that old ass of a father of hers would not have allowed them to get married before Wilfred had established himself, which was a very long shot indeed, Herbert had always reckoned. But the war had made everything different. There was a silly, hysterical atmosphere about. Florence had been able to appeal on such nonsensical grounds as that Wilfred was fighting for his country, or that the future was so uncertain, or that they had a right to a little happiness, and old Calderwood, instead of seeing in this uncertainty fresh reason for delay, had weakly given in. Not that he had much chance to do otherwise. Once he had allowed Florence to go off to London on her own he had lost her; after that she was quite capable of getting married whether he liked it or not.

Herbert had not abandoned hope, even yet. Naturally he saw a good deal of Florence when he managed to get back on leave. He was gradually re-establishing the old, confidential intimacy which had subsisted between them before Wilfred had made his appearance. He managed to play the part of the dashing young officer rather well. He adopted a light, bantering tone about the war itself, and the dangers and discomforts of the front line. He was becomingly modest about his decoration, pointing out that there were many deeds of courage that went unnoticed, and preferring not to speak about it at all unless he was forced to. Back on leave in London he knew that he cut rather a fine figure, and it was by no means a punishment for Florence to be seen out with him, leaning on his arm as he escorted her to theatres and restaurants. Oddly enough, after her marriage she was even more responsive than she had been before it. It was as though she felt that she could now trust him not to be trying to cut Wilfred out; before her marriage she had always been a little wary, afraid perhaps to give him too much encouragement. When she was married and established in her flat things became very cosily domestic. Usually Beatrice would come down when she knew that Herbert was coming on leave, and the two girls would share one bedroom and Herbert would sleep in the other one. Then the three of them would go out to enjoy the brief time Herbert had away from the trenches.

On one occasion Herbert came back a day earlier than he had expected, and arrived at the flat at about four o'clock in the afternoon. Florence opened the door to him and, more or less, fell into his arms. She had had a wretched day; something very distressing had happened in the hospital. She was about to tell him about it but he stopped her. He gently pressed her lips together with his fingers and then kissed them.

'No more,' he said, sternly. 'Don't think about it, put it right out of your mind. Believe me, it's the only way, I know.' He had his arm round her and he hugged her and kissed her again. 'Once you start turning these things over in your mind you're on the way to going crackers. Forget it, put it right away from you. I'm here, a whole day early. I've got an extra eighteen hours that I didn't expect to have, and I'm going to enjoy them.'

Florence drew away from him and smoothed her dress down.

'How did you manage it? We weren't expecting you until tomorrow, Beatrice won't be here until then. She'll be disappointed.'

'Yes, it's a pity. But I got myself put on escort duty, a prisoner had to be brought back; it was too good a chance to miss.'

The routine was always the same. First, one had a bath, a marvellous luxury this, and then a sit down in front of the gas fire with a cup of tea, and then out for dinner, followed by entertainment of some kind. Herbert made a special effort over his appearance this time; he was a little excited at the prospect of an evening alone with Florence, and he was quickly aware that he was having an unusual effect on her. Possibly because of the low state of mind she had been in when he arrived, she seemed to be very responsive. She touched him a good deal, she had kissed him with unexpected warmth when she had first seen him on the doorstep, she straightened his tie for him and patted his cheek, and when she took his arm she clung to him very closely. Normally Florence was reticent physically, she was not one of those people who are forever touching and caressing. And Herbert did not think that she was quite aware of what she was doing; these attentions were natural, spontaneous and unconscious, produced by an unusual excitement of the mind. Years later, after the war, Beatrice told him of an occasion when Florence had seen the name Naismith in a list of soldiers reported dead, and had thought for a moment that it was him. She had been extremely distressed by this incident. Herbert had wondered whether something like that had happened on this occasion to account for her mood. For his part he was careful to accept all this quite naturally, so as not to break the spell and startle her into self-consciousness and reserve.

They had a first-class meal, after which they went to a theatre and saw a silly, frothy, vapid comedy which made them both laugh a good deal. Afterwards they told one another how silly it had been, quite beneath any serious person's notice. Then they went to a club, of which Herbert was a member, and danced and had a few drinks. Florence was exceedingly gay, laughed and chatted animatedly, and danced with enthusiasm. Usually she was rather solemn and serious-minded, and turned up her nose at frivolous pleasures. Herbert had often teased her about this in the past, but this evening all these principles of hers seemed to have been abandoned. She even smoked, a thing she had never done before.

'Do you really want one?' asked Herbert.

She nodded vigorously, and he lit it for her.

'You won't like it. It'll make you cough.'

She tossed her head at him defiantly and drew in the smoke deeply into her lungs. Then she suffered a frightful paroxysm of coughing, and her back had to be pummelled and she had to be given water, and her eyes streamed, and she was laughing at herself quite helplessly.

'You are an idiot,' said Herbert, 'I told you what would happen.'

She insisted on finishing the cigarette, stopping every so often to pick little flecks of tobacco off her tongue and breathing in cautious, shallow little puffs of air. It was quite a relief when it was over.

'There,' she said, when she had finished, 'I've wanted to try that for a long time. Now I can say that I've smoked.'

After they left the club they strolled through the London streets, arm in arm, talking confidentially and intimately about themselves and their hopes. Herbert had never felt so near to Florence, and in his heart he cursed Wilfred bitterly for having intruded. This was how it should have been, the two of them were cut out for one another. He thrust out of his mind the thought that this was the briefest of interludes, and forced himself to concentrate on what she was saying. She had made some remark about what they would do after the war. 'I don't let myself think about that,' he said in reply. 'I'll bother about that when I get to it. Out there, you know, we think that it's tempting Providence to make plans.' He entertained her with some stories of how superstitious some of the men in the front line were. One of his fellow officers always insisted on doing everything in the morning in exactly the same order every day. One morning he shaved twice just because he'd got the sequence wrong the first time. Some men hated anybody wishing them good luck before they went on patrol or went into battle. And, of course, lots of men carried Bibles.

'I don't suppose they'd ever read them in their lives,' said Herbert, 'in fact I don't think some of them could read, but they carried them just the same. Every other man you meet has got some tale about having had his life saved by a Bible. It's one of the first things you fish out when you are collecting a dead man's effects to send home to his next of kin. You always get the Bible and put that in with the other things, then you can say in your letter how much strength he drew from his religion, and what a true Christian he was. The truth, of course, is probably something else.'

'What letter?' asked Florence.

'The letter you write. That's one of my jobs, the officers have to do it. When a man is killed we write to his wife or his parents, telling them that he died bravely and all that. Of course we could hardly say he didn't. Sometimes it doesn't do to be too honest.'

Florence was silent and clung to his arm more closely than before. If it had been Beatrice that he had said this to, she would have answered by saying that he sounded very bitter and cynical, or something like that. Florence understood and made no such commonplace rejoinder.

Herbert was rather pleased with the note he had struck. It projected the right picture of the man burdened with responsibilities beyond his years, wearing them lightly, but nonetheless touched and worn down by them. Then he quickly turned the talk to the lighter side of life out there, and was really quite amusing about the habits and tricks of some of his fellow officers. They arrived back at the flat in the early hours of the morning and sat side by side, sipping coffee, to which Herbert added brandy from a little flask he carried.

Herbert knew that now was his chance, perhaps his last chance, and he also knew that if he had misinterpreted Florence's mood by even a fraction, then he would dish himself for ever. Throughout the evening he had been reckoning up her state of mind. She was fond of him, always had been, and the only time this fondness had been broken was during the early days of her engagement. After that, until quite recently, her manner towards him had been rather formal. The question was – did tonight mark a return to her previous feelings? They had been chattering, and laughing, and holding hands like an engaged couple. He had seen other people looking at them, and had known what was in their minds. He was a gallant soldier lad, out with his sweetheart, and good luck to them. Surely she must feel it, she must feel something much deeper for him than ordinary affection. Yet he was afraid to make the last unequivocal move that might shatter this intimacy which he had, with so much patience, created. Herbert stroked Florence's arm and Florence leaned drowsily on his shoulder; and very gently, very circumspectly, proceeding by tiny steps, Herbert acted, and Florence did not object.

It was the atmosphere of the night. Florence told him this the next morning as he lay in bed, luxuriating in the warmth of the blankets and the softness of the mattress, and she sat on the side of it pulling on her stockings. She had been in a depressed state, something had happened, again she failed to specify further what it had been which had affected her so badly. She had been overwhelmed by the loneliness of her position, London was a large, unfriendly place, and when she had seen him on the doorstep she had been so grateful for the sight of a friendly face that she had lost her balance. He had taken her when she had been in a state of shock, at the lowest depth of her feelings. This was the gist of what she said. Her tone was angular and strident. She had betrayed Wilfred. She said this several times, as though repeatedly confessing it would in some way make it better. He was defending his country, braving untold dangers, and she had betrayed him, thus becoming one of the meanest figures known to womanhood. Herbert lay back drowsing contentedly while this welter of reproach and self-justification passed over his head. He said very little, and what he did say was neither apologetic nor regretful. He told her that he had reached an intensity of joy last night that he would not have believed possible. She had known all about his feelings for her, he had never pretended that they had changed. If he could do it all again he would. He lay back between the sheets, massively calm and unmoved, and flexed his toes lazily, and clasped his hands behind his head, and gazed straight at her as he spoke.

'If I go back and get killed next week I'll be able to feel that life was worth it.'

She was avoiding his gaze, but he saw her flinch as he spoke about getting killed.

'You don't expect me to say "sorry", do you? Why should I be sorry about the most glorious thing that I've done yet? I'm not ashamed of my feelings for you, I'm proud of them. I haven't done anything mean or dishonourable.'

At this she spoke, in a small voice, still looking away from him, out of the window.

'Not even to Wilfred?' she asked.

'Let Wilfred look after himself, did he think about me?'

'That was different, I wasn't married to you.'

'It wasn't different as far as I was concerned. We ought to have married.'

Florence had started crying again. Herbert hoped that she was shedding tears of regret that she had not married him, but when she spoke it was to disabuse him of this idea.

'Don't say anything against Wilfred, Herbert. Don't think, because of what happened, that anything has changed. I'm very glad I married Wilfred, and now I feel that I've let him down.' She was speaking slowly, in a quite controlled way, as she finished her dressing. She seemed much more composed again. 'I'm not blaming you, Herbert, or reproaching you. It was my fault, I shouldn't have let you do it. I'll just have to be careful in future.' Herbert began to say something but she stopped him.

'I don't want to say anything more about it. We'd better behave as though nothing had happened.' And this Florence, marvellously, proceeded to do. She went into the little kitchen and began preparing breakfast, while Herbert got dressed. He was feeling enormously pleased with himself and contented with the world and had to check a tendency to grin like an idiot. She made him porridge and scrambled him some eggs, and made a pot of coffee, and he ate everything with relish. One savoured the small comforts during the few hours one had them to enjoy. And Florence's manner seemed quite normal, she behaved as though everything was exactly as it had been the last time he was on leave. He started to make a reference to the events of the previous evening but she stopped him straight away and returned the conversation to the subject of Beatrice.

'You'd better go and meet her train, she's due in at five to twelve. She'll get a surprise when she sees you.'

'Aren't you coming?'

'I've got my work to do, I'm due at the hospital in half an hour.'

Herbert was rather hurt, he had hoped that, while he was on leave, she would be able to get time off.

'I'm afraid life doesn't stop just because you're on leave, Herbert. I altered my shift once, so that I'd be back at the end of the afternoon, that's when you're supposed to have come back, you know. I'm not going to alter it again now.'

She was cool, almost distant, but there was nothing he could actually object to in her tone. He had been about to suggest that the two of them should go off somewhere for the day. Beatrice would arrive as usual and go to the flat, Florence could return as though she had been in hospital all day and he would arrive as though his leave had just started. He had worked it all out lying in bed, but now he did not even propose it. He could see clearly how Florence would receive such a proposal; she would regard it as a betrayal of Beatrice, though he had never, at any time, in any way, committed himself to Beatrice, and she would regard it as an invitation to her to betray Wilfred still further. And Herbert could not deny to himself that this was true. Still, he had hoped. An expression of real affection, made to him by Florence now, immediately afterwards, would have been of the greatest value, but she took care that she was not in such proximity to him that any such expression was even possible. She went out immediately to the hospital and did not return until after Beatrice had arrived. And after that everything was quite normal for the duration of his leave. Beatrice was affectionate and Florence was sisterly, except that she carefully and discreetly avoided being alone with him.

So Herbert was denied any opportunity of putting her feelings to the test, and had to console himself with the hope that she was afraid of the strength of her feelings for him, and wished to avoid further temptation. He gained one kiss from her when he said goodbye, and tried to believe that it had been given with extra warmth.

Then he returned to France pondering on the situation.

14

After this episode Florence did her best to arrange things so that Beatrice was already in London when Herbert came on leave. It struck him as funny that, while the parents in Manchester, and Beatrice herself, presumably regarded Florence as the chaperon, who made it respectable for Beatrice and him to meet, in truth it was Beatrice who was the chaperon, and Florence who needed the protection. This system failed only once, when Beatrice was held up by fog and was unable to get to London at the right time. Herbert had been surprised not to see her waiting for him at the station and had hurried to the flat, hoping that nothing was wrong. He found a message pinned to the door, telling him what had happened and referring him to Mrs Barraclough, the landlady, for the key.

He had a leisurely soak in the bath and made himself a pot of tea, and he was sitting in his pyjamas and a dressing-down, yawning over a newspaper, when Florence got back from the hospital. She entered abruptly, taking him by surprise.

'You got my note, then?' she said, taking full measure of the extent to which he had made himself comfortable. She seemed a little on edge. He sprang to his feet and embraced her; after a fraction of a hesitation she returned his embrace, then she pushed him away.

'It's good to see you again, Herbert.'

'Have some tea, it's fresh.'

'No, thanks, I'll change first.' She hesitated before passing into the bedroom. 'It's a pity about Beatrice.'

'A great pity.'

'But she'll be here tomorrow.'

'Yes, if the fog lifts.'

'Oh, I should think it will lift,' she still hesitated, 'it doesn't usually last as long as that.'

'Anyway, she'll be here as soon as she can.'

'Yes,' said Florence.

'Well, you go and change. I've left you enough water for a bath.'

'Good,' said Florence, 'good, I'll have one, then.'

She hesitated another moment and then, without saying anything more, went through to the bedroom, and Herbert sat down and poured himself another cup of tea.

They went out to dinner, and then saw a play. Florence said that if Herbert did not mind she would rather not go on to the club this time, so they returned to the flat. Florence made coffee, and they sat side by side on the sofa. Herbert put his arm about her shoulders but she removed it firmly.

'No, Herbert, please. It's been a lovely evening. Don't spoil it.'

'You mean, like I did before?'

'I didn't mean that. At least, I didn't mean quite that. I'm not blaming you for what happened before, but I mustn't let it happen again, must I?'

She spoke slowly. She was not looking at him, she was looking down at the gas fire. In taking his arm from round her shoulders she had seized his hand, and now she retained her grasp upon it and held it in her lap, gently stroking it. She continued speaking.

'I'm rather glad, in a way, that Beatrice didn't come, it gives us the chance of clearing things up. I know that last time was my fault. Well, I've got to feel that I can trust myself. Beatrice hasn't been able to get here, so we're on our own, and if we can get through this normally then I'll feel all right again, I'll feel that I've been fair to Wilfred.'

'What do you mean by "normally"?' Herbert asked, trying to put his arm round her shoulder again, but she drew away and flared up.

'Don't, Herbert. You mustn't make things more difficult for me. I want you to help me, Herbert.'

Herbert folded his arms, leaned back on the sofa and silently took Florence's measure. She had drawn away from him a little, and was leaning forward over the fire clasping her knees. She had said everything very artlessly and simply, as though she had rehearsed it for a long time. Her whole body was tense with the effort of resisting an advance which he could hardly be said to have positively made. He knew that a firm, decisive action on his part would probably meet with little resistance, but he calculated his long-term advantage and held back. He answered her quietly and firmly. He respected her decision. Of course she could trust him, and of course he would not cause her any pain. He even managed to insert a half sentence about fairness to Wilfred, which cost him something of an effort. His voice was very soft and caressing and sincere, and as she listened Florence relaxed and leaned back on the sofa. Herbert spoke of his feelings for her and she stroked his arm, and when he said that he would not take advantage of his position her eyes filled with tears. In quite a short time his arm was round her and she made no objection to this at all. In bidding her goodnight, Herbert kissed her affectionately and warmly, and she responded with equal warmth. But he most properly then went into the spare bedroom and slept on his own there. Lying in bed he was well satisfied with the night's work.

Sitting in his den, puffing on his pipe, meditating on these scenes from the past, Herbert wondered what a chap like Winnick would make of such an episode as this last one – if he ever heard of it. Incredulity, probably, that would be his reaction. He could understand coarse motives and coarse actions, and that was all. Herbert had had his reward in Florence's complete trust, and he had reaped the fruits of that reward later. And it had only been sheer, miserable chance that had robbed him of the ultimate reward. What Herbert had been counting on was that Wilfred would not survive the war. If this had happened then Herbert would have been waiting and Florence would already have been won over. This was the chance that Herbert was unwilling to jeopardize by a too hasty action. If he had forced himself on Florence, she would never have forgiven him. But his generosity, his consideration, his forbearance won her gratitude. He was completely redeemed, the episode in the Lake District was forgotten, Florence's opinion of him was higher than it had ever been. If only – It was a curious thing. Death on the Western Front was absolutely commonplace, and Wilfred lived obstinately on until the Armistice released them all.

'Release' was the appropriate word. Probably when a fellow like Winnick thought of the Armistice he would automatically think of crowds of people getting drunk and merrymaking in the streets, and loud hosannahs of joy. It hadn't been like that – at least, not in Herbert's experience. In some ways it had almost been a let-down. They had suddenly had to adjust from a life in which they existed from day to day, in which there was constant danger and excitement, and there was no point in making plans beyond the next weekend, to the rather drab routine of a garrison army, and the change had not been easy. He could remember an intense weariness and despondency, a grotesque sense of anti-climax. People had actually started talking to him about going back to Oxford and resuming his studies. He tried to think of himself as a student again and failed completely. There was no point in wasting any more time. He was going to take over his father's firm, and the sooner he started the better. Herbert had returned from the war somewhat joylessly and settled himself in an office next to his father's.

It also became impossible for him to postpone making a decision about Beatrice any longer. It was curious, looking back, to see how he had drifted, that was the only word for it, into one of the most important acts of his life. He had married Beatrice not because he particularly wanted to, but because there was no very strong reason why he shouldn't. He liked Beatrice, in fact he was very fond of her, but he was not in love with her. Everybody expected that they were going to get married. He had spent every one of his leaves with her, she had been in the habit of going down to London to meet him; it was clear to everybody that there was an understanding between them. True he had refused to tie himself down during the uncertainties of war, but this was regarded as a prudent and even generous act on his part. Now he was home, mercifully unharmed, and his love was waiting for him. He could see it in her face as he stepped off the train, he could see it in the behaviour of Mr and Mrs Calderwood, all his friends and relatives accepted the fact. He could not have been more securely tied to her if they had gone and sworn the most solemn oaths of fidelity in Westminster Abbey. Not that the marriage had been disagreeable to him. The most positive thing which Herbert held against Beatrice was that she was not Florence, but then, very few girls were. There was no one else he was interested in. Later on Herbert used to wonder whether he had married Beatrice in order to keep in touch with Florence, but if he did, this was not a motive that he was conscious of at the time. No, Beatrice was a very nice person. She was a good friend, she had a pleasant nature, she was pretty, and she was very much in love with him. What more could a man ask? As for Florence. Their relationship changed. Wilfred was now home for good, though there was precious little good about it that Herbert could see. Herbert had not seen him since that afternoon in the Lake District, when he had watched his train steaming out of sight and silently blasted him to hell for his interference. He had almost trained himself to think that Wilfred did not exist, but now there he was, oppressively present, and Herbert's meetings with Florence were limited to formal little family gatherings, with Wilfred hovering round handing out the blancmange and chattering interminably. Herbert was expected to give his future sister-in-law a dutiful peck on the cheek, which Florence received as inscrutably as ever.

Only once was this formality broken in the months before his marriage. This was on the occasion when Florence and Wilfred came out to look at the house they were preparing in Wilmslow. Herbert had listened sardonically to the account which Beatrice had given Winnick of this visit. He appreciated the fact that she made light of his attitude to Wilfred, because after they had got back he had expressed himself very forcibly about it. Wilfred, frankly, had been beginning to get on his nerves. He seemed to have come back from the war exactly the same half-baked, callow, superficial person that he had been when it started, and the pretence of bettering himself had been dropped, as Herbert had always known it would be. He was just a nothing, a nobody, a shabby clerk in a shabby office, and he would never be anything else. But he still talked in the same silly way, always speaking for effect, saying clever-clever things, making his adolescent debating points. Herbert could congratulate himself that he had grown out of this sort of thing, but it was irritating to have to listen to it. Wilfred had been particularly trying that day, and it had cost Herbert an effort to keep his temper. Eventually he had managed to pack him off with Beatrice to be shown the garden, while Herbert took Florence over the house. He was proud of the house. It was going to be magnificent, and he had talked for hours with the architect to ensure that it should be magnificent in the way that he wanted; he intended the house to express his personality, not merely to have been made for him by someone else. So he went into great detail in showing Florence over it, describing the colour schemes he had in mind, and pointing out the decorative features which he had taken so much trouble over.

Every so often Florence said that it was beautiful, varying this occasionally by saying that something was 'very nice' or 'striking'. Her tone was slightly unconvincing; Herbert felt; uneasily, that he was being pandered to.

'You're not really struck?' he said.

'I think it's going to be very nice, Herbert. I'm sure

Beatrice will be pleased with it.'

'Beatrice is delighted. It's giving Beatrice a lot of pleasure.'

'Well, that's what matters, then,' said Florence briskly. 'It'll be quite soon now. Are you getting excited about it?'

Herbert had been staring out of the window. They were standing in one of the bedrooms, one of the few rooms that had been almost completed, and he had been looking at Beatrice and Wilfred in the garden. Wilfred was showing her a drain and talking about it very energetically. He had not quite got the thread of Florence's remark.

'The wedding,' she explained, 'are you getting excited about it?'

'Oh, of course.' He kept his tone drab.

'You don't sound very excited. Are you very fond of Beatrice, Herbert?'

'Very fond,' his tone still colourless. Florence hesitated; Herbert saw, with satisfaction, that he had knocked her off course.

'Is anything the matter, Herbert?'

'Nothing at all, what should be?'

'You sound a bit odd, considering that you are going to get married in a couple of months. Are you in love with Beatrice?'

'Not really.' It was the chance he had been looking for, and he concentrated on keeping his voice matter-of-fact, off-hand.

'Shouldn't you be?'

'I really don't think, Florence, that you have any right to ask me that. I'm not in love with Beatrice by the only standard that I've got to compare my feelings with.'

'Why are you marrying her, then?'

'What am I supposed to do? The person I'm in love with is you. I don't suppose that I'll ever find anyone else as I feel about you. Do you expect me not to get married at all, then?'

It gave Herbert immense satisfaction to say this. He had

sat down on a packing-case in the middle of the room, and was playing with some wood shavings that he had picked up off the floor. He was carefully not looking at Florence, and studiously keeping his tone dreary. He felt that he was making exactly the impression that he wished. He was putting himself forward as a man whose life had been made meaningless, and who was rather drably going through the formalities of living it out. Florence betrayed her exasperation with a sharp intake of breath.

'Oh, Herbert, all that's over and done with. I know it sounds very romantic, but I think it's rather silly. I don't think that sort of Byron figure suits you.'

'I don't care whether it suits me or not. It's not a pose, I'm not pretending, I'm just stating a fact.'

'Suppose Beatrice knew?'

'Tell her.' Herbert looked directly at Florence as he said this. 'Tell her, and find out.'

He carefully split a shaving down the exact centre and dropped the pieces on the floor. The strength of his position was that he meant it, he was not bluffing. It genuinely would not have worried him if Florence had spoken to Beatrice, and she knew it.

'I think that's a rather terrible thing to say. If you feel like that about Beatrice you have no right to be marrying her.'

'I'm very fond of Beatrice. I'll give her everything she wants. I haven't deceived her. I haven't told her anything about my feelings for her that is not absolutely true.'

'But you are letting her think all sorts of things.'

'I suppose most people think all sorts of things when they get married. At least I'm going into it with my eyes open. There is no reason why we shouldn't be happy. But I'm glad I've had the chance of speaking to you like this. You asked me if I was excited, and I'm trying to give you an honest answer.'

Florence looked as though she was on the verge of tears, though she was not a weepy person.

'I think it's dreadful. I don't know what I ought to do.'

Herbert stood up and brushed fragments of shavings off the knees of his trousers.

'You'll have to make up your own mind about that. You don't need to worry about Beatrice. I'm very fond of her, I think I'll make her happy. I'd just like to feel that there will be one person who understands my true feelings.'

He could have touched her, but he did not. He had moved towards her and was standing very close, but he paused only fractionally and then went on towards the door. He held it open for her and they both went downstairs.

This conversation had given Herbert great pleasure. He thought that he had shown in a rather fine light. Principally he had wanted to make Florence feel uncomfortable and guilty. He had been stung by her attitude towards the house. There had been an inflection in those words of hers about Beatrice being delighted with it that he had not liked. They had implied, to his ear, that Beatrice had rather commonplace tastes, that of course she would be delighted with this sort of thing, and that he, Herbert, was commonplace enough to satisfy these tastes. He had wanted to make her wince a bit, and he had succeeded. He knew how fond she was of Beatrice. He had put her in an awkward position. She would be unhappy about letting the marriage go ahead, and she would be even more unhappy about the idea of stopping it. It would not have suited Herbert's book to have the marriage stopped. He was fonder of Beatrice than he had acknowledged to Florence, and he thought that she would suit him very well. It is not easy to resist the flattery of being thoroughly adored. What he had said to Florence was true enough, however sentimental or melodramatic it might have sounded. He did not think that he would ever feel about anybody else what he had felt about her, but he would do his best to make his marriage a success. If anything went wrong with it – well – Florence had had fair warning, she would know whom to blame.

Everybody agreed that they made a most attractive couple at the wedding. Beatrice was radiantly happy and her happiness made the ceremony and the honeymoon an unalloyed delight. They appeared to be the perfect partnership, completely contented, totally wrapped up in themselves. For a time Herbert genuinely managed to put the image of Florence out of his head. Their friends all said how sweet it was that two such nice people should have made such a perfect love-match. They visited Florence and Wilfred in their new home at Herriott Street, and their happiness communicated itself. Wilfred commented on it.

'I must say, marriage seems to suit you two. Don't they look well on it, Florence?'

'Very well,' said Florence.

'We didn't make the mistake of rushing into it like you,' said Herbert, 'we took our time, and now we are reaping the reward.'

'Oh, we had our moments,' said Wilfred. 'Of course we couldn't linger over the honeymoon like you two. How long did we have, Florence?'

'Two days.'

'Two days, just think, and then back to the trenches. That was living on the heights and in the depths for you. One thing about it, it made the heights seem higher.'

'And the depths lower,' added Herbert.

'They couldn't have seemed lower. No,' said Wilfred, 'all the emotions in those days were heightened somehow. It's a funny thing, I hated every minute of it, but life hasn't had quite the same flavour since.'

It struck Herbert that life has the sort of flavour that you choose to give it, and that Wilfred should not be surprised if an insipid life was flavourless, but he did not say anything. An argument with Wilfred would have bored him. Later he was alone with Florence for a few minutes.

'Well,' she said, 'according to Beatrice, marriage is a very satisfactory state.'

'Very satisfactory.'

'You certainly look very happy, both of you.'

'We are very happy, very happy indeed.'

'You're settling down as an obedient and dutiful husband.'

Herbert bowed mockingly from the hips and answered, 'I hope that Beatrice will have no cause for complaint.'

'I'm glad to hear it.'

She did not say any more, and Wilfred came in a moment afterwards.

Herbert could guess what was going on in her mind. She was not entirely pleased that he was happy with Beatrice. She was pleased that Beatrice was happy with him, but that was a different thing. 'I am glad to hear it,' she had said. Just so might a schoolmaster speak to a boy who has assured him that he was paying attention all the time.

In fact he was extremely happy. His marriage was suiting him very well, and he was quite content to let Florence stew in her own juice. She was married to a boring little husband, who inflicted his boring conversation on everybody who came near, well – so be it. She had made her own bed and she must lie on it. What added spice to the situation was that Herbert was convinced that she knew the mistake she had made. Not that she would admit it in a hundred years, she was too proud for that. It was not only that she had lost the chance of an enjoyable, stimulating social life in marrying Wilfred, though no doubt she was beginning to regret that. There was something else. She had grown quieter since the war. She was less self-assertive. At times she had a slightly pinched, frustrated look. She was missing something, Herbert was sure. Wilfred was a sexually timid man. Between the sheets, where a marriage is made or lost, what kind of performance would Wilfred give? Herbert recalled her words earlier: 'According to Beatrice marriage is a very satisfactory state.' Was it only his imagination that had lent the word 'satisfactory' a certain inflexion? Had these two sisters – sisters will talk – been comparing notes? Had Beatrice been describing the joys of the marriage bed? Herbert smirked to himself. If she had, he was sure that her account had not disgraced him.

15

One afternoon in late November, about four and a half years after his marriage, Herbert met Beatrice and Florence in the centre of Manchester, and they all had tea together before going out to Wilmslow. The girls had been doing some Christmas shopping, and the seat of the car beside Herbert was stacked with parcels, while the girls chattered and laughed in the back. They had then spent an exciting evening trying on frocks and waltzing downstairs to ask Herbert's opinion of them and then rushing upstairs again to giggle together. It had seemed to him that Florence was behaving in a rather unusual manner, and in the intervals between their appearances he had had time to ponder it. In the old days there had always been one or two expressions which Florence could put on, which Herbert had found irresistible. He had once tackled her about this, and she had absolutely and indignantly denied using any such stratagems.

'What do you mean, expressions?' she had said. 'What are these marvellous expressions of mine?' and pulled various grotesque faces and challenged him to define the exact way of looking that he had in mind so that she could make herself irresistible to all and sundry. But of course he had not been able to define them. It was not simply that they made her more beautiful, or anything like that, but they served perfectly to express her, or to express his idea of her – whenever she looked at him in that way his blood stirred, he knew that for a fact. Well, he had caught that expression once or twice that evening, as she and Beatrice pirouetted before him and made the skirts of the gowns swirl. He knew no better now than he had in the past whether the look was deliberate or accidental, but when the time came to drive Florence home he was in a state of some excitement himself, though he was careful to conceal it. There was a well-defined routine to these trips. Florence would invite him inside for a cup of coffee, and his reply would depend on how anxious he was to have a boring little chat with old Wilf. If he decided that he could not stand the idea then he would explain that he had a busy day ahead of him and drive straight back. Florence understood perfectly well the real reason for his refusal, but it was a condition of their relationship that never must he criticize Wilfred. This evening he was about to make a polite excuse when Florence added artlessly, 'I'm afraid that Wilfred's out at the chess club. He won't be back till late. They've got a visiting grand-master or something, and he's playing twelve games simultaneously blindfolded.'

'Sounds interesting,' said Herbert absently, eyeing Florence. And, of course, he followed her into the house.

'Wilfred wanted to analyse his technique,' explained Florence.

'Naturally,' said Herbert.

Florence made them coffee, and they sat side by side on the sofa drinking it. Herbert felt his customary sensation of dry-throatedness at the proximity of Florence. Gradually she relaxed against him and he put his arm about her shoulder and she rested her head against his. He stroked her neck and slipped his hand inside her blouse. Neither of them said anything. She slowly turned her head towards him, her eyes half-closed, and they kissed. His fingers were busy with buttons, and hooks, and press-studs. She threw herself on him fiercely, and they discovered the discomforts of the sofa, which was too short and covered in a hard, cold, rexine material. As she nuzzled her face into the side of his neck she whispered the word 'upstairs'. Even at the time Herbert thought what foolishly undignified figures they must have looked to anyone watching as they made the short trip to the bedroom. They were both clutching unbuttoned garments that threatened to slip off at any moment, Herbert had to keep pulling his trousers up because they were falling about his knees and threatening to trip him, and Florence was carrying her skirt in her hand. Afterwards they both giggled together remembering the figures of fun they must have appeared.

When they had finished they dressed slowly and came downstairs, and Herbert sat in Wilfred's easy chair in front of the fire, while Florence prepared his supper. Neither of them spoke very much, and what they said was quite trivial. Herbert was experiencing a sense of satiation, and he stared into the fire feeling rather sleepy and pleased with himself.

Florence appeared quite normal. Herbert noticed that she avoided looking at him and when he once spoke of what had just occurred, she turned the conversation immediately.

Wilfred returned just after ten o'clock, and seemed surprised to see Herbert. He was bubbling over with enthusiasm for the exhibition he had witnessed at the chess club.

'You should have been there,' he said to Herbert, 'it was an experience not to be missed. It was an astonishing display, absolutely astonishing.'

'A Russian grand-master, Florence said?'

'Twelve separate games he played, with twelve different people.'

'Blindfold, Florence said.'

'No, he wasn't blindfold, but there were screens round the tables, and in any case he didn't look at any of the boards, he didn't need to. He just paced up and down in the middle and the moves were called out to him. You really should have been there, Herbert, you missed something special tonight. It was a revelation of the powers of the human mind. The move would be called out to him and he would sometimes call out his reply before they had finished. It was as though he knew the move they were going to make.'

'How many did he win?'

'All of them, every single one.'

'Of course,' said Herbert, 'the opposition must have been pretty easy by his standards.'

'Oh, I don't know about that. It wasn't only our club, you know, there were people there from all over. They were some of the best players in South Lancashire. It makes you realize,' Wilfred continued solemnly, 'that if you take your mind and train it rigorously for long enough, it is capable of doing things which look like sheer magic to the ordinary person. His concentration was absolute. You could have gone up to him and smacked him across the face and he would never have noticed.'

'Don't let your supper get cold,' said Florence. Wilfred, who was pacing up and down, just like the grand-master, stopped abruptly, as though he had been smacked across the face himself, and then sat down to eat his supper. Shortly afterwards, Herbert took his leave.

He drove rather fast on the way back to Wilmslow. He was exultant, triumphant. He had completely displayed his powers. He laughed aloud, and even shouted, as the car sped through the darkness. It was an intoxicating sensation. At long last he had asserted himself over Wilfred. He grinned and laughed again and again as he remembered the scene after Wilfred had returned, and wondered how he had managed to play his part so perfectly. His face had worn just the right expression of polite, slightly bored interest: how, how, how had he managed to avoid laughing in the little bore's face? If only he had known! What a dupe! What a cuckold! The hardest part had been not looking at Florence. Herbert knew that this would have been fatal. Any attempt to involve Florence behind Wilfred's back, in a mocking conspiracy against him would have made her seriously angry. But he could not avoid catching her eye sometimes, and then he had to discipline himself so that there would not be the slightest suggestion of a twitching at the corners of his mouth or a puckering of the forehead. Even this was questionable, for in some circumstances to avoid a particular gesture or look is itself a kind of offence. It had been hard, too, to take his leave of Florence and give her the routine peck on the cheek that it would seem so odd to

Wilfred to have omitted. He wondered what they were talking about and what they were doing. Were they going to bed? How would Florence manage to sleep with him that night? What was she feeling inside herself? Herbert parked the car and let himself in. Beatrice was waiting for him.

'You've been a long time.'

'I waited to see Wilfred. He'd been to watch some kind of demonstration at the chess club, a Russian grand-master, he was full of it. You know what Wilfred is.' Beatrice laughed.

'Did he bore you to death? It was good of you to wait and listen to him. He must have loved telling you about it.'

Herbert put his arm about Beatrice's waist and led her back to the fireside.

'According to Wilfred, it was an astonishing demonstration of the power of the mind.' He produced a fair imitation of Wilfred's voice and made Beatrice giggle by giving a parody of some of the things he had said. He dropped into the easy chair and Beatrice sat on his knee and stroked his moustache and fondled him. He nibbled at her ear and nuzzled her neck.

'You seem to be in a naughty mood,' she said, lovingly. It was part of their code. The word 'naughty' had a precise meaning in their vocabulary, it was their term for sex. 'Do you want to be naughty?' 'Are you feeling naughty?' 'Shall we be really naughty?' were verbal counters in their love play. They had the advantage that they gave either partner the opportunity to retreat if he, or more usually, she, was not in the mood. Beatrice could reply apologetically that, no, she was not feeling particularly naughty tonight, or that she did not want Herbert to be naughty, not just now. There were even degrees of naughtiness. They might just be rather naughty, or they might be really naughty, or they might even be very naughty. The code had come into being gradually, most of it had been developed by Beatrice. On this evening Herbert agreed that he was in a rather naughty mood, and began proving it so thoroughly that she told him to stop – suppose one of the servants came in and found them?

So they adjourned to the bedroom, where it was possible to be as naughty as one wished without fear of disturbance. To tell the truth, Herbert was finding it very difficult to control himself. He was in a state of considerable sexual excitement. He almost frightened Beatrice, though she had seen him in this mood before. As soon as he was through the door he began pulling and tearing at her clothes. She warned him to be careful, but he whispered that, hang it, she could buy as many more as she liked. Fortunately she was feeling really naughty herself and had no difficulty in responding. It was an especially fierce pleasure to Herbert. Memories of the scene a few hours before combined with the immediate pleasure of coupling with Beatrice to make a peculiarly satisfying sensation. He wondered, if Florence could know, what she would think of him: and as he pressed down on Beatrice, he wondered what she would think and do if she knew about Florence. The sense of triumphing over everybody was still with him, he was superior to all of them. As he lay beside Beatrice afterwards he had the insane desire to whisper his secret in her ear. She was so blissfully unconscious of it all. He stifled a laugh at the thought, and she asked him what he was laughing at.

'Just happiness. I'm just happy, that's all. Didn't you enjoy it? Didn't you think it was marvellous?'

'Marvellous,' she said, and thought how inexpressibly sweet he was.

The affair with Florence had taken some odd turns. Herbert wondered what Winnick would think if he knew some of the turns it had taken. Probably he would start thinking that it had all been planned, but there had been no conscious design on his part; later he had been able to see that it had followed a course which he, and perhaps she also, had unconsciously willed. One of the odd things about it had been the complete refusal of Florence, between their bouts of sexual activity, to allow the slightest indication that this activity ever happened at all. If Herbert made a reference to it when they were alone together, she would become stonily indifferent, refuse to answer, refuse even to notice that he had spoken. If he persisted she would simply walk away. In all other respects her behaviour to him was exactly what it had always been since the end of the war.

Wilfred and Beatrice could have seen nothing in her behaviour to betray what was going on between them. Even he, and he was watching her like a hawk, could see nothing; it puzzled and depressed him profoundly, it seemed unnatural, almost sinister. It was also odd that Herbert could never be sure when Florence was ready for another bout. He certainly could not presume that, whenever fate threw them together and gave them the promise of undisturbed privacy, he could just take her in his arms and she would respond immediately. What was quite likely to happen was that she would shrug him off, or simply stiffen into an unmanageable, resisting lump, and he could do nothing with her. On these occasions she never said much: 'Don't, Herbert,' or 'Not now,' or simply 'No' rather as one might say, 'Down, sir,' to a dog that was making a nuisance of itself by jumping up. Sometimes Herbert would lose his temper. He would be all keyed up, expecting and hoping so much, and the disappointment, which was always increased by the realization that these opportunities were rare and had to be left to chance, would drive him to make a scene. But this never did him any good. Florence would look at him with contempt. When he spoke of never seeing her again she would demonstrate her complete indifference to the idea, she might even say that perhaps it would be best if he never did. He waited in vain for any expression from her that it would give her pain not to see him. He used to swear to himself that he was finished with her, that she was not worth it, but it was not an easy vow to keep. He could not get her out of his mind, however hard he tried to root it out sooner or later the memory of her would creep back. And, in any case, he was bound to meet her from time to time, and as soon as he saw her he had to start forgetting her all over again.

The other curious aspect of their affair was something that they drifted into quite accidentally, although again, looking back on it later, Herbert could see this as an element that fitted in very well with Florence's reticence. It had happened in this way. One week he had taken both Florence and Beatrice with him when he went down to London. Beatrice quite often complained about being lonely, left on her own in Wilmslow, but if he took her down by herself she said that she was bored. The opportunity to take Florence came because Wilfred's father was taken ill and Wilfred thought it would be a good idea for him to go home to help his mother. Florence had offered to go as well but he pressed her to go down to London; it would please his parents to have him on his own for a week. When they returned, as was natural, Herbert drove Florence back to Herriott Street. The moment they were in the car together he sensed that she was in the mood, and he began fishing.

'Glad to get back to old Wilf?' he asked.

'Very glad, although, as a matter of fact, Wilfred won't be back until tomorrow.'

'Why didn't you say? You could have stayed the night with us.'

'Oh, I'd rather be home. There are some things I have to do.'

Herbert turned this over in his mind. The omens looked favourable.

When they drove into Herriott Street it was already dark.

'I'll take the car to the Grapes, shall I?'

This was a way of sounding her mood. If he was likely to stay at the house for any length of time he was in the habit of leaving his car at a small hotel, about a quarter of a mile away. It was safer there, and it prevented his visits being too conspicuous.

'Yes,' she said, 'that will be the best thing.'

Herbert left the car at the hotel and, as he walked back, a feeling of pleasurable anticipation began to grow within him. He let himself in, he had his own key to the house, which Florence had given him, and he found Florence in the kitchen making the coffee. As they sipped it he sensed again a suppressed excitement in her. She was all worked up, there was going to be no question of a rejection this evening, he was sure of that. Since they had plenty of time they both enjoyed prolonging the pleasure, and they dallied over the drink. Then they sat side by side on the sofa and the preliminaries began. Neither spoke a word, Florence's eyes were closed and she seemed almost in a trance. At last Herbert could wait no longer and, as an act of bravado he took her in his arms and carried her upstairs to the bedroom and placed her on the bed. Then he turned to light the gas, while Florence lay back languorously. When it was lit he turned, and such a curious sight met his eye that he cried out in astonishment, 'What the devil is it?'

In a corner of the little bedroom a small tent had been erected, its guy-ropes attached to various pieces of furniture, and it swayed about drunkenly. The mood had been abruptly shattered.

'Oh, good heavens.' Florence sat up and gazed in dismay at the tent, and a general clutter of clothing, old sheets, and camping equipment that lay about the floor. 'I thought he would have taken it down again. It's Wilfred. He got the tent out to see if it is still all right. He's talking about going camping in Scotland.'

'Well, I'll be damned.' Herbert stared at the tent fascinated. He sat down on the bed by Florence and was caressing her absently. Out of the corner of his eye he could see that she had started to undress but he made no move himself.

'Do you remember that tent we had when we were children?' It had been an Indian wigwam belonging to Herbert. He and the girls had kept house in it, used it as a den, made it the focus for all sorts of adventures. In that tent he had made some early, and innocent, advances towards Florence. 'We had some fun in that tent,' he said.

Florence completed her undressing and stood in front of him, naked.

'You are a slow-coach tonight,' she said, nuzzling his neck. Herbert drew her to him and sat her on his knee. He began almost mechanically stroking her breasts, kissing her body. Deliberately he had slowed down. The unexpected sight of the tent had broken his stride, and he decided that he would take his time. Florence was hot and keen, all to the good, let her wait a little. Just for a change he would call the tune. He kissed her belly and ran his lips up between her breasts, up her neck to her face, very slowly. Then he pulled away from her.

'What's all the litter?' he asked, with deliberate inappropriateness.

She responded to this teasing, slipping off his knee out of his grasp and stood in front of him stroking her breasts and thighs, watching him out of the corner of her eyes. She had a good figure. He made a sudden dart at her and she evaded him and ran round to the other side of the bed.

'I suppose Wilfred must have been looking through some old holiday things.' She pretended to have lost interest in Herbert and knelt before the pile on the floor and began rummaging about. 'I'd forgotten I'd kept these. Oh look, do you remember this frock? I wore it in the Lake District, that last summer.'

She held the frock provocatively in front of her. Herbert remembered it very vividly indeed. Suddenly she slipped it over her head and pulled it on.

'It still fits, you see.' She looked absurdly young. It was a thin, cotton, flowered dress, that came down to her ankles, in the style popular before the war. She looked like a peasant girl, a peasant girl in a play, not in real life, innocent, demure. The knowledge that she was quite naked underneath it was particularly arousing to Herbert.

'My word,' he said. 'The simple English rose – the delicate lass from the country vicarage.' He stood up and bowed and extended his hand, and she took it and curtsied and said, 'Lah,' and wafted an imaginary fan. Herbert looked around him and caught sight of the tent and the sheets on the floor and suddenly thought of a film which had recently had a somewhat scandalous success.

'Close your eyes,' he said. 'I've had an idea. I know what I am.'

She obediently covered her eyes with her hands, and Herbert quickly undressed and took one of the sheets from the floor and wrapped it round him. Then he stood before her in a commanding posture.

'There,' he said, 'you can open them now.' She opened her eyes and gave a yelp of surprise. 'I'm the desert sheik, you are the noble English lady. I've kidnapped you and carried you off to my desert encampment.' He took her in his arms and, stooping, carried her into the tent, which promptly fell on top of them. With shrieks of laughter they struggled free, and Herbert nearly lost his sheet. Then he stood over her menacingly.

'Now, with one swift movement I tear off your flimsy garment, fling you to the ground, and ravish you.' He seized the neck of her dress but she stopped him.

'No, no, Herbert. Not this one. It's got sentimental value. Here,' she took the dress off, picked up another one which was faded and moth-eaten, and put it on instead. 'There now, you can tear that one to your heart's content.'

Herbert took a turn or two about the bedroom.

'That's not the sort of thing that happened to Valentino. Now I've got to work myself up again. Remember, you are supposed to be a terrified maiden.'

His sheet was dropping off again and he hitched it up and threw the corner over his shoulder and advanced on her. Florence gave a most creditable performance, cowering away, covering her face, falling on her knees in supplication. Herbert threw himself into his own part with equal abandon, and in the same spirit of sheer fun. He forced kisses on her reluctant face, and gave a splendid pantomime of striking her when she resisted. And then something rather odd happened. He began to feel that it would give him pleasure to act the part in earnest, to make the blows reality and the rape a real rape. He knew that he wanted to hurt her and he had to make a strong effort not to do so. When he gripped her arms to throw her on the bed she winced with sudden pain and the sexual climax gave him a savage pleasure. When it was over he lay back completely exhausted, like one stunned. His heart was pounding, and he was breathing heavily, and he avoided looking at Florence. He hoped that she had not noticed what had happened to him because he was ashamed and almost frightened of it. A really savage side of his nature had taken over and it was not pleasant to find how much he had enjoyed expressing it – because he had enjoyed it, he had felt a wonderful sensation of release.

It was Florence who made the first move, and Herbert eyed her furtively as she dressed herself. As always on these occasions she had reverted very quickly to her normal self, and there was no telling, as she sat at the dressing-table brushing her hair, what her feelings were. Herbert got up and dressed and then they both set about tidying up the mess on the floor.

'There's not much of that dress left,' said Herbert.

'It doesn't matter. It was only fit for dusters anyway. You put the tent and camping stuff in Wilfred's room, I'll see to the rest.'

Very sedately they put everything away, and then stood in the middle of the bedroom looking at one another.

'Well, we were idiots tonight,' said Herbert.

'I suppose we were.'

'A good job nobody could see us.'

'A very good job.'

'It was good fun, though?' he said, anxiously. Florence returned no answer to this. She gave a final look round the room and then moved towards the door. Herbert felt the old sensation of anger, bitterness, resentment. It was only Florence who ever made him feel like this, and the show of rage that she provoked him to was always unwise. It was that business of the Lake District all over again. He was not able to stop himself expressing his disappointment.

'You won't admit it, will you?'

'Admit what?' Florence paused and turned. She seemed genuinely surprised by his words and the tone he used.

'You won't say that you enjoyed it. You never do, do you? As soon as it's over you've always got to pretend that it didn't mean a thing to you.'

'Oh, really, Herbert.'

'You wanted it tonight, didn't you? You could hardly wait for it.'

The colour began to mount in Florence's cheeks.

'That's a very coarse and vulgar thing to say to me.'

'I don't see what's coarse and vulgar about it. I wanted it. I'm not ashamed to admit it.'

'Perhaps you ought to be, then.'

'What do you mean?'

'I haven't forgotten that I'm married, even if you have. We've neither of us got any right to carry on like that.'

'Well, why did you carry on like that, as you call it, if you didn't want it?'

'Oh, for heaven's sake, Herbert, do you have to go on and on about it? It's over and done with now. Even if I did want it, as you keep on saying, I've got it out of my system now for a bit. I'm not exactly proud of it, so let's not talk about it. Now I'm going downstairs, unless you've got anything else you want to say to me.'

But Herbert found that he had not got anything else to say to her, so she went down and left him sitting on the bed.

On the whole he felt victorious. She had chosen a funny way of doing it but she had, after all, expressed a pretty strong feeling for him. He could hear her in the kitchen downstairs, she seemed to be banging the pots about with some vigour. After a few minutes he went down and stuck his head round the door. She was washing a pile of dishes that Wilfred had left. Herbert could only see her back, but he could tell, by looking at that, that her lips were compressed and her eyes were smouldering.

'I – I think I'd better get back to Wilmslow,' he said.

She did not look round.

'You don't want any supper, then?'

'No, I'll have something when I get in.'

'All right.'

'Well, goodbye, then.' He paused. Florence lifted a dish that had once contained rice pudding and began scraping at the ring of skin baked black round the rim.

'Goodbye,' she said. She still did not look round. Herbert went to the front door and let himself out.

After this he tried to put Florence out of his mind. He decided that it would be better for both of them. In a way he had achieved what he wanted, or nearly so. She had virtually acknowledged that she regretted marrying Wilfred and not marrying him. Her words had been a kind of appeal to him not to tempt her further. If he put out his powers she could not resist the lure of his attraction – that, more or less, was what she had said, though she had not expressed it like that. The question was, what did he, Herbert, want to do next? Beatrice complicated the issue. If it had not been for Beatrice everything would have been plain sailing, if whatever wife he had had not been Florence's sister, then it would have been easy. He would have got a divorce, and Florence would have got a divorce, and then they would have got married, as they should have done in the first place. As it was, that course was impossible – so what had he, Herbert Naismith, been up to? Oh yes, he could quite see why Florence had been glooming over the sink and banging away so ferociously at the pots and pans. Put like that it seemed that he had simply been doing his best to make her uncomfortable and dissatisfied with Wilfred, and rousing feelings that he was just not in a position to satisfy himself. He had been so proud of the constancy of his feelings for Florence. At that painful interview he had had with her in the Lake District after she had announced her 'sort of' engagement to Wilfred, she had assured him that he would soon get over it, and he had promised her that he would not. Well, he had amply redeemed that promise. He could see now that his broken heart had been a luxury to him, he had wallowed in his feelings. Over all those years the romance of his yearning for Florence hugged to his bosom, revealed to nobody but her, had added a grace to his life, and it had been spiced by his determination that sooner or later she should admit her fault. And now that he had got his way the only honourable thing was to withdraw, to trouble her no more.

For a time Herbert was gripped by a puritanical aversion to self-indulgence of any kind. He attended fiercely to his work, and with the London development growing more important every day there was plenty to see to. He reminded himself that he was a happily married man, with the comforts of a wife and a home and still the hope, though alas a diminishing one, of children. He managed to be exceedingly rational about the whole thing and made the most admirable resolutions. It was a pity that he did not get a little help from Beatrice, who was going through one of her difficult spells. They slept in separate rooms, of course, and he was allowed into her bed only occasionally, as a little treat. Even so, it was a treat rather grudgingly given. He had to be careful how he touched her because she was extraordinarily sensitive in all sorts of peculiar places. Then, as soon as he got in bed with her she got very hot, and had to keep asking him to move over to the other side of the bed so that she could cool down. Attempts to make love to her seriously were usually disastrous. Everything he did seemed to hurt her, and even if she did not actually complain he had the sense of her crouching there in the darkness, clenching her teeth and steeling herself to put up with it and hoping it would soon be over. Fortunately these treats were rare, and Herbert never wished to prolong them, but he was left with a problem. He used to argue the matter out with himself at the wheel of his car, or sitting morosely at his office desk. He had never actually set himself up to be a Trappist monk, he would tell himself. He was not an animal, in fact he was a good deal more fastidious than most men that he knew, but he had certain neeeds. He had no taste for casual sex. He remembered vividly the brothels he had seen in France, behind the lines, with queues of men waiting outside for their turn. It seemed to be a speedy operation, and the sight of the weary, middle-aged women who provided these blisses was not exactly enlivening either. It had not been an excessive prudery on Herbert's part that had kept him aloof from this, he was just surprised how easily satisfied most men were. Some of his business friends, Herbert knew, made free with the girls in their employment. Frankly, he considered that they were damn fools. Business and pleasure did not mix.

As a matter of fact he was rather proud of the way he treated his workpeople; when he was in the army he reckoned he had known how to treat his men. Probably it was because he came from the North. Northerners had their feet more firmly on the ground than Southerners. He felt that he knew his father's workpeople, he had played with their sons, he had never been encouraged to be snobbish. It was a cardinal sin to put on 'side', to be stuck up or condescending. You had to know your job. They would not respect someone who didn't know what he was talking about, and they were by no means stupid, they were very sharp chaps, some of them. Herbert had spent time making himself familiar with the various processes that were used in his workshops, and knew how to handle most of the machines. He fancied that he made rather a good impression, and he went among the men with the affable ease of a prince among his adoring subjects. If they complained that a machine was difficult to handle then he would go along himself and try it. He would step back, wiping the oil off his hands, disregarding the soiling of his cuffs or stains on his waistcoat, and say, 'There you are, you're not going to let an amateur like me beat you, are you?' Or he might agree that it needed a new bearing, or had not been mounted properly. There was the time in Shed Six, when they complained about the constant cold. He took off his jacket, borrowed a set of overalls and went down and worked there with them himself. After two hours, during which they rather sulkily laboured away, shooting discontented glances at him, he stopped, rubbed his hands together vigorously and said, 'I tell you what, lads, it's bloody cold in here, we must do something about that.' And he had new heaters installed before the end of the week. It had caused quite a sensation, that had. You wouldn't get away with that today, not with the unions being what they were. They'd down tools as soon as he appeared in the workshop.

No, he reckoned that he had known how to handle them. He thought they respected him, and he was not going to jeopardize it by playing fast and loose with their women-folk. He had some good-looking girls working for him, he could have fancied some of them, bonnie lasses they were, but he put the temptation firmly aside. You couldn't do that sort of thing and expect that it would not get about. He would not care to think that his workpeople would be talking behind his back about what he had been up to with Jessie from Accounts, or Alice from the typists' room. As for the wives who visited his house, well, he never contemplated making the most innocent advance to any of them. Their bodies were singularly unattractive and their minds were non-existent. They chattered, chattered, stupidly, vacuously; it took him all his time to be even civil to them. No, he occasionally caught himself eyeing Jessie or Alice but never these, he was quite safe there. And that left him with the problem, the problem of not being a Trappist monk. Inevitably his thoughts wandered back to Florence and the pleasure he had in her company. Was what they were doing so very terrible? If nobody knew about it then nobody would be hurt by it. It would be nice just to have one more go. He wondered what Florence was thinking. Had she any regrets? It would not be fair to ask her, but it would be nice to know. At this stage in his meditations Herbert would pull himself together and immerse himself in the latest trade journal, but the image of Florence's face would be floating somewhere just beyond the page he was staring at.

16

It was very annoying, but as the time came near for his next meeting with Florence, Herbert found his spirits rising. He was like a young boy in the throes of calf-love who discovers that he is going to meet the girl he is dreaming of at a party. He tried to rationalize it by telling himself that he was merely curious to see how she would behave but he knew that this was false. She would be perfectly normal. No, the truth was that he simply wanted to see her again, to be in the same room with her, to talk to her. He became angry with himself and tried to argue himself out of this desire, but he could not. He had to wait almost two months before their next visit to Herriott Street was fixed to take place, and the last fortnight positively dragged. And then, two days beforehand, Beatrice began to get one of her moods, and to imagine herself ill again, and she actually spoke of putting it off.

'I don't really think I can go to Florence's. I don't feel up to it.'

'That would be a pity, dear; Florence would be awfully disappointed.'

'It's my back, I've been in agony with my back these last few days.'

'Why not get some more of those tablets from the doctor? They did you a lot of good last time.'

'I didn't like those tablets, they had a terrible taste, and I think they upset my stomach.'

'Perhaps he could give you something else. I'm sure Florence would be disappointed if you didn't go, I don't think she ever sees anybody apart from you.'

Finally Beatrice decided that she would go. Probably she had always intended to; she was fond of Florence, and had merely wished to be made a fuss of, but Herbert was surprised at the depth of his own disappointment.

As he had expected, Florence's manner gave no clue at all as to what she was thinking. She said, 'Hullo, Herbert' in a neutrally friendly way, looked at him quite steadily in the eye, and presented her cheek to be pecked without a tremor. It wounded him that, even when they were alone together, or she knew that they were not observed and it would have been quite safe to do so, she never made even a slight gesture to indicate complicity with him. She could hardly expect him to be deceived by this pretence that she was quite indifferent to him. He had no chance immediately of a private talk with her, though he had come intending, in some way if possible, to 'have it out' with her. Wilfred was there fussing round like a dog with a new bone waiting to be taken notice of and sure enough Florence soon directed their attention to him.

'Wilfred's got something to show you,' she said, 'you'd better go up with him straight away and then we can all settle down.'

Beatrice began to say something about her back, but Florence soon scotched that nonsense, nobody was going to escape this.

'It'll only take a minute, Beatrice, don't be mean. Wilfred's been longing to demonstrate it to someone, haven't you, Wilfred?'

'Well, I think you will find it rather fascinating. Mind you, I expect Herbert knows all about it already.'

'It' was a wireless, a crystal set, which he had rigged up in the boxroom. They all had to crowd in, clutching monstrous headphones to their ears, while Wilfred scratched about with his cat's whisker trying to locate the spot that would give them a good signal. Finally, to the accompaniment of grotesque crackling noises, they were able to make out the semblance of a man's voice.

'Isn't it truly remarkable?' said Wilfred. 'In a few years' time this apparatus will rule the world.'

'It makes my head ache,' said Beatrice peevishly, pulling the headphones off and flinging them down on the bench.

'It's in the early days yet, of course,' said Wilfred, 'but even so it is astonishing to think of the power it puts into man's hand.'

A curious thing about Wilfred, Herbert reflected, was a kind of deliberate naïvety. That was something else that this Winnick fellow would never be able to understand. All this talk about him as a kind of frustrated genius didn't really get you anywhere. What had he ever done to justify this kind of claim? Granted that he was clever, his cleverness had taken some very odd turns. For some reason this evening had stuck in Herbert's mind. In the normal way he paid very little attention to Wilfred's enthusiasms, but he remembered quite vividly this silly little crystal set and Wilfred staring over the top of it, his spectacles gleaming, looking like a child's comic version of the crazy scientist. And the apparatus itself illustrated perfectly the perversity of Wilfred's pursuits. It appeared to be a kind of rule with him to do things in the most amateurish and inefficient way. He was the sort of chap who, in an age of scientifically corrected lenses, did his photography with a pinhole camera. He appeared to have taken the design for his wireless set from the *Boy's Own Paper*, and to have constructed it, on principles approved by that publication, from odds and ends found in his own attic. He was not interested in technical perfection; it was the very fact that it was possible to get results from such crudely assembled apparatus that made, for Wilfred, the fascination of doing it. He had said so more than once when Herbert had tackled him about it.

'It's the concept that fascinates me, Herbert, I leave refinements to the experts.'

'But you'd get better results if you used better equipment.'

'I'm not interested in the results. Of course somebody else can make me a machine that will work a lot better than one I can make for myself, but I've had the satisfaction of making it. It always seems marvellous to me that you can get any results at all in this way.' And he waved his hand at the bench on which his improbable looking contraption was set up, and Herbert had to admit that it was marvellous that he got any results at all.

Herbert's chance of a quiet word with Florence came after the meal. Beatrice was resting her back on the sofa, and Herbert insisted that he would help with the washing up.

'No, no, Wilfred. You stay and entertain Beatrice. You're entitled to a rest on a Sunday evening; I'll give Florence a hand.'

His appearance in the kitchen caused Florence to raise her eyebrows and to ask, in a sarcastic tone, what had got into him.

'You're very domesticated all of a sudden.'

'I didn't want Beatrice to come, she needs a rest with that back of hers.'

Florence smiled enigmatically and pressed a tea-towel into his hand.

'It gives us a chance to have a bit of a chat,' said Herbert.

'It does, doesn't it? I rather thought that might be in your mind.'

'Don't you want to have a bit of a chat?'

'Well,' said Florence, 'that depends on what you want to chat about.'

'I've been thinking about the last time we met.'

Florence placed a cut-glass fruit bowl on the draining board and warned him to be careful with it.

'Have you been thinking about it?' he asked.

Florence admitted that it had crossed her mind once or twice.

'And what have you decided?'

'I didn't know there was anything to decide. I said my say last time.'

'But we can't leave it like that. You know how I feel about you.'

'You've told me often enough,' said Florence with some bitterness. She was fishing about in the dirty water for the spoons and forks. Herbert gazed at her and thought what a marvellous face she had: grave, serious eyes, a beautiful skin; rather a long face with a lovely, straight nose. Her hair was tied back from her ears and fell down her back in a beautiful sort of cascade. She washed the knives, being very careful with the bone handles, and working the hardened grease off the blades with her fingers. Herbert cursed, for the thousandth time, his lost opportunity.

'I wish, just once,' he said, 'you would say what you think about me.'

Florence stopped her work for a moment and turned to face him. 'I'll say one thing for you, Herbert, you're a trier, you don't give up.'

'Don't you think I'm entitled to know?'

'You're not entitled to anything. I just wish you'd leave me alone instead of making it so hard for me.'

She turned back to the sink and Herbert began polishing the knives. 'That must mean that you care something for me,' he said. 'If you didn't care at all then it wouldn't be hard for you.'

'You're very clever this evening, Herbert.'

'Well, I don't see that we are doing any harm to anybody else as long as we're careful.' Florence started to say something but he stopped her.

'No, no, listen to me for a moment. I've been thinking a lot about this. After the last time I made a really serious effort to forget all about you, and I couldn't do it. I don't think I can manage if I don't see you sometimes. I just can't get you out of my head.'

Florence bent over the sink and wiped the plates clean of gravy. She didn't reply, and he could not see her face.

'Just an occasional meeting,' said Herbert. 'We don't plan them, nobody can know anything about them. Wouldn't you enjoy it?'

She did not say anything. She went on scraping, and

rinsing, and then laying the plates and cups and saucers carefully on the draining board for him to take. He continued mechanically wiping them with the same part of the damp towel he was holding in his hand.

'I know you did enjoy it,' he said stubbornly, 'though you won't bring yourself to admit it. I know that part of you would like to do it again. You said last time that you were ashamed of it, well I don't see what there is to be ashamed of. If they are your true feelings, what's wrong with them? Do you remember how you used to speak, before the war? In those days you were all for showing your true feelings, you were awfully contemptuous about the people who just lived artificial lives, as you called them. Well, I'm more honest than you are. I know you don't think very highly of me, but at least I'm true to my own feelings, and I always have been. I've always told you what I've felt for you, and I've never changed. I don't think I could stand it if you threw me off, Florence, and it's partly because when you tell me that I don't mean anything to you I don't believe it.'

The whole of this speech was addressed to the back of Florence's head, which she kept studiously bent over the sink; she uttered no sound and she made no gesture to indicate any kind of response. Herbert went doggedly on. 'There's a part of you that wants me just as much as I want you. I found it out last time. You managed to forget that you were Florence. For a time you were that other girl, that Rose. Don't you remember Rose? In that tent? Wouldn't you like to be Rose again?'

She had finished the washing and finished cleaning out the sink, and she began to untie her pinafore, but Herbert seized her fingers gently and undid the knot himself. Then he slid it over her head and ran his hands caressingly down her bare arms. She did not pull away from him. 'Oh, Herbert,' she said. Her tone was curious, a mixture of anguish and despair and dismay.

'I want to meet her again,' repeated Herbert. Florence still had her back to him, and he placed his hands on her breasts very gently. She made a sudden effort and pulled away from him.

'We must get back to the others,' she said. She did not look at him still, and she marched back to join Beatrice and Wilfred.

That was the evening that Wilfred began talking about Marcus Aurelius. Herbert remembered very vividly, because it seemed to him that his relations with Florence had reached an important turning point. Wilfred was in full flow when they got back to the parlour, waving a copy of *The Thoughts of Marcus Aurelius* about and telling Beatrice, who was lying at full length on the sofa with her eyes shut, how important it had been to him.

'It was the very first book I bought with the first money I ever earned. I'd seen it on this second-hand bookstall, and as soon as I was paid my first week's wages I went straight along and bought it in my lunch break. Have you ever read it, Herbert?'

'Not exactly read it, no, Wilfred. I've heard of it, of course.'

'I'd forgotten how fine it was. I used to carry it with me in the trenches and argue about it with the chaplain.'

'I suppose it made a change from the Bible,' said Herbert, 'but probably not as good at stopping bullets.'

'It's curious how much it has in common with Christianity,' said Wilfred. 'I could never get the chaplain to see that. It seemed to me to show that the really important ideas have nothing to do with any superstition about a particular God, or nonsense of that sort, but he used to get quite wild when I said it. Just listen to this, for instance.'

He rifled through the pages and began to read: '"Think what revolting creatures men are in eating, sleeping, sexual intercourse, and all the other operations of nature." I used to read that bit to him and then quote from St Paul's *Epistle to the Corinthians*, all that part about "better to marry than burn" you know. There was a time when I knew it all by heart: "Neither fornicators, nor idolators, nor adulterers, nor effeminate, nor abusers of themselves with mankind, nor thieves, nor covetors, nor drunkards, nor revilers, nor extortioners, shall inherit the kingdom of God." I think it's a terrible sentiment, but it's got a wonderful sound to it.'

'Why a terrible sentiment, Wilfred?' asked Herbert.

'Well, it's such a denial of ordinary human feeling. I mean, if you say that it's better to marry than burn, what you are really saying is that sex is something disgusting and shameful, and if you must indulge yourself in that way then you must get a licence from the church and be disgusting in a way that God can bring himself to approve of.'

Wilfred beamed at the assembled company as he said this, but Florence had found herself some darning to do and was intent on this – at any rate, Herbert was amused to notice, she made no response. Beatrice appeared to be asleep. Herbert exerted himself to say something.

'What I can't understand, Wilfred, is that you obviously don't like St Paul, and you say that Marcus Aurelius is saying the same thing as St Paul, and yet you like Marcus Aurelius.'

Wilfred was happy. He had got what he wanted, a discussion, an argument. He beamed again and bent his energies to the task of answering Herbert. 'I don't think I said that they were the same thing, Herbert. What I said was that they had something in common. Marcus Aurelius is talking about achieving an inward perfection, that is what I find so fascinating about him. To him the bodily things are a nuisance because they interfere with our effort to rise above mere bodily needs. St Paul offers us a sort of bogey-man called God, and it is this bogey-man who says that sex is sinful. It seems to me that there is a lot of merit in giving up, say, sex, because you want to make yourself better; but there is no merit at all in having sex in a half-ashamed way, under certain conditions, just because a bogey-man says that that is the only way you can have it.'

And then Wilfred launched into an exposition of the ideas of Marcus Aurelius and the problem of achieving perfection. Herbert listened rather imperfectly, he felt that he had done his duty as a guest by asking his question. From what he could gather, the achieving of perfection was a rather difficult trick, to be accomplished only by a man who had trained himself not to care about anybody or anything. If you succeeded, then whatever happened did not matter to you because you did not care much about it. This appeared to Wilfred to be a highly desirable state of mind, and he preached its cultivation with a fanatical enthusiasm.

'Basically, what Marcus Aurelius is talking about, it seems to me, is self-control. A man who gives way to his feelings becomes sentimental or maudlin or passionate or something like that, and he loses his own dignity. According to Marcus Aurelius, it's not what happens to us that matters, but how we meet it. We must train ourselves to meet all the misfortunes of life with dignity and calm.'

As he listened to Wilfred's voice droning on, Herbert suddenly realized what he should have been – a curate. It would have suited him down to the ground. Herbert could imagine him perfectly, down-at-heel, out-at-elbow, prosing and platitudinizing in the pulpit, having slippers made for him by the elderly ladies in his congregation, forcing his advice on the more defenceless inhabitants of the parish. It was a pity that such a trifling matter as not believing in God should get in the way of this.

'"Look on every man who evinces pain or dissatisfaction at any event as on a level with the pig that is led out to sacrifice kicking and squealing."' Wilfred intoned the words from the book he was holding with great relish. 'You see, Herbert, that is it exactly. We ought to value ourselves at least higher than the mere animals. We must follow the light of reason to reach this higher perfection.'

Herbert had cause to remember these words later, when they acquired a different colouring, but at the time they appeared simply preposterous. Wilfred seemed such an odd candidate for perfection. He was a shabby little undernourished, narrow-chested nonentity, with stooping shoulders, who peered short-sightedly through his steel-rimmed glasses. It was ridiculous of him to stand there prating about the ideal. Herbert had to curb a strong impulse to make funny remarks about him. There was one thing about Wilfred that those women had never really understood: he had a pretty good conceit of himself. Beatrice, for instance, never realized this. When she had been talking to Winnick about the reasons why Wilfred had refused promotion she had showed that she had not understood him at all. She had suggested that he had refused because he had thought himself not fit to be another man's master. What rubbish. In Wilfred's own estimation he was fit for anything at all.

Wilfred was in a constant state of marvelling at his own brilliance and superiority. He had refused the offer of promotion for the same reason that, during the war, he had refused the chance of a commission; because he thought that he was so important, and because he attached such tremendous significance to his own actions. He said that he would rather be an innocent victim than a guilty leader. If you had no part in making the decisions, then you could not be blamed for their consequences. Like so much of what Wilfred said, there was an irritating core of truth in this, but only a man with a rare sense of his own importance would have pushed it to such absurd lengths. To him, being made a corporal was, apparently, the same as being made a general. To avoid being contaminated by the guilt of the capitalist system he refused to allow himself to be promoted to the senior desk in the clerk's room. He peddled insurance policies in the poorest districts of Manchester so that nobody could accuse him of being the cause of all the misery in the world. That, as far as Herbert could make it out, was his reason. He was like an elderly spinster who is forever talking about her virtue and suspecting everybody of having designs on it, though nobody has remotely offered to attack it. It was all nonsense. It aroused in Herbert an angry derision, and it irked him that nobody else seemed to see through it. Beatrice, for instance, constantly spoke of

Wilfred as though he was some kind of saint. What Florence thought God alone knew, but she allowed no criticism of him, and if she was becoming aware that she had made some kind of mistake, she was not going to admit it. Wilfred went on about human dignity and self-control, and the unimportance of material things – it became a favourite and recurrent theme of his – while, it seemed to Herbert, Florence wilted in the background. There was nothing in Wilfred's arid, selfish philosophy to nourish her particular needs. Occasionally she would be driven to cry for help, that was how Herbert interpreted it, and it was then that the utility of the idea of a kind of *alter ego*, the fictitious 'Rose' became apparent.

Herbert had had no design in mind when he had spoken of 'Rose' in the kitchen that evening. It had occurred to him on the spur of the moment, and all that he had been trying to do was to express his belief that Florence, with part of her mind, really cared for him, and that she had shown it too openly to deny the fact, when she had surrendered as 'Rose'. It was Florence herself who returned to the device. This had happened, not the next time Herbert and she were alone together, but the time after that. He had taken her back to Herriott Street knowing that Wilfred would not be there to greet them. Over tea Florence had told Beatrice and Herbert rather pointedly that Wilfred had gone to a political meeting in Bolton. Not that he was interested in politics, or had any belief in it, but because Lloyd George was speaking there, and he wished to hear one of the acknowledged masters of modern oratory. Florence explained all this at great length, unnecessary length, it seemed to Herbert. He would not be back until well after midnight, she made a point of this, but when pressed to stay later than usual, she said no thanks, she would rather get off, if Herbert did not mind, so that she could get a fire going in good time to warm the house. Herbert did not mind, he was at her service, so they returned, if anything, rather earlier than usual. As he drove, Herbert was in high spirits; the omens looked favourable. It was in the car that Florence came out with it. 'I think Rose would like to meet you tonight, Herbert.'

'Good, I've been looking forward to seeing her again.' He managed to appear quite calm and matter-of-fact, though his spirits jumped. 'What sort of a mood will Rose be in?' he asked, steering the car carefully between a lorry he was overtaking and an approaching bus.

'A responsive mood, I should think.'

'I wondered if she would be like last time I've got this friend of mine that I'd like her to meet. He's a bit stern, he's a bit of a bully.'

'What sort of a bully is he? Will he be too cruel? Rose wouldn't like him to be too cruel.'

'He's harmless really. He doesn't do anything too bad. He's a bit like that chap she met last time.'

They were speeding through the suburbs of Manchester. Herbert was speaking quite coolly, with a slight humorous overtone, and Florence's responses were pitched in the same key. She began to question him about the nature of this friend and his tastes. What sort of things did he do? What sort of girls did he like? Herbert began to embroider an answer for her out of his fancies, attending carefully to her responses. This friend of his enjoyed dominating his women-folk, he belonged, perhaps, to an older age. He had something in common with those wicked aristocrats of romance who would carry helpless maidens off to their castles and keep them there bound to pillars, or subject them to cruel inquisitions. And yet, withal, he was capable of chivalry, even tenderness on occasion. He had something of the wild impulse of the barbarian chieftain, or the relentless cruelty of the pirate king.

'He sounds a terrible figure,' said Florence, demurely.

'Very terrible indeed,' agreed Herbert equably, 'but as I say, he's harmless really. I rather think that she'll like him.'

'We'll have to wait and see,' said Florence.

It was in this way that a form for their meetings became established. It was a convenient fiction which pretended that neither Florence nor Herbert was personally involved. It became easy, for instance, for Florence to announce that she was not in the mood for dalliance; all that she had to do was to say that 'Rose' was not available; there was never an occasion when Sir Roger or Sir Charles, as Herbert's friends came to be called, failed to appear. If 'Rose' was available then the fiction was equally convenient for planning the form which the meeting should take, and custom made the negotiations more confident and more audacious. Herbert would drop hints, make suggestions, tentative at first but becoming more precise as Florence, on behalf of 'Rose', gave her approval. Gradually the scene proposed, and the characters the two were to play would become clear; later the more successful of these scenes would be repeated and improved upon. In time, too, more of the suggestions came from Florence. Speaking as 'Rose', Florence could be quite bold because, after all, what 'Rose' enjoyed was nothing to do with her. Afterwards she could shrug off responsibility for 'Rose's' behaviour. Herbert soon learnt that he must be careful not to discuss 'Rose' with Florence, that he must respect the division between the two. The rules of this complicated game developed gradually as the two of them, becoming more and more absorbed in their play-acting, took it ever more seriously. At first they protected themselves with the pretence that it was just a sort of game, a charade. They were a couple of asses, but it was nice to be thoroughly childish once in a while. It was all something to giggle over. But they discovered that there was more to be gained if they acted their parts with the utmost conviction. The more they could feel the passions which they simulated the more pleasure they found in releasing them, and the more the sexual climax, which was the consummation of each scene, satisfied them. In between his meetings with Florence, Herbert spent much time planning the next game. He would remember scenes from novels and films, episodes from the newspapers, and the chance suggestions of his own imagination. They also built up a collection of 'props' which they could use, mostly innocent objects which would not betray them to anyone who found them accidentally. There was the cord of an old dressing gown of Herbert's. It was heavy and ornate, and served perfectly as a rope for tying 'Rose's' hands together. He bought an old hunting crop in a second-hand shop, and there was a variety of scarves and silks. Wilfred's amateur theatricals came in handy, to Herbert's great, secret joy. Props would often be left at Number 29, and these props were given some quite unorthodox uses. A theatrical sword and a duelling pistol suggested a pirate scene and a highwayman scene respectively, which both wonderfully lent themselves to variations of many kinds.

After playing scenes like this to the end they would both of them sink back, replete, exhausted, enervated, to resume their ordinary identities.

17

Sitting in his study reviewing the past Herbert heard steps coming up the stairs. When they reached the landing they turned past the door of his room and went steadily on to the end of the corridor. It was Beatrice going to bed. She did not call out to him or acknowledge him in any way. He heard her bedroom door shut with a decided slam. He guessed that she had been doing some brooding on her own account, and he knew what it had all been about. She had been harking back to the Janet episode; a demonstration of unreasonableness if ever there was one. Whose fault was it that he had strayed? She had been quite content to turn him out of her bedroom amd make sex into an occasional treat. She was perfectly happy to be left alone in the house when he went down to London because it meant that he made fewer 'demands' on her. She ignored the fact that he was half-killing himself setting up the new enterprise, spending his life in railway carriages and hotel rooms. She was ill, as she constantly told him, and this excused everything. He must make allowances for her, be very kind. Well, he had made allowances, been kind. What about her making allowances for him? When he had taken the obvious course and found himself a bit of consolation she had behaved as though he was guilty of the ultimate betrayal.

Beatrice had always attached more importance to that Janet business that it had warranted. She always believed, whatever he might say, that it had lasted longer than it had. From his very first meeting with the girl, which had been innocuous enough in all conscience, to the moment, on that November evening in 1928, when she had confronted them in the London street, had been little over two and a half years. And he had been driven, in a manner, to Janet by the attitude of Florence, not that he could explain this to Beatrice. Florence had thought, or affected to think, that while Beatrice was so ill he had no right to be making advances in the guise of Sir Roger or anyone else.

'Have you no feelings at all, Herbert?' she kept asking, 'carrying on like this when Beatrice is in such a state?' She said that he was downright selfish, that he had no sympathy for anybody else. In truth Herbert did not have a great deal of patience with sick people. They made demands on him that he was not prepared to meet, they spoiled the pleasantness of life for him. Florence considered that he was callous, and she continued this hostility for over a year. Janet had been the result. In a real sense she did not count. She was evidence, in fact, of the low state of his mind when he had first met her.

He was sitting in his office in London, checking some letters that his secretary had brought in for him to sign. Suddenly he rang the bell to summon her.

'Miss Fellowes,' he asked peevishly, 'can you tell me who prepared this schedule of figures for Baring and Watson?'

She came round to his side of the desk and peered over his shoulder. She was big-boned and on the plump side. She liked to hold herself near him and press her bosom into his shoulder and breathe hard into his ear. Her neck was scrawny, and Herbert felt a spasm of bilious irritation.

'Oh dear,' she said, trying to make her tones sound girlish, 'that won't do at all, will it? I don't recognize the initials, I'll have to find out for you. Do you want me to take it and get it redone?'

'No, I'd like to see the girl myself. She'd better understand what it is she's doing. Ask her to come in to see me will you, when you've found out who it is.'

Miss Fellowes returned about ten minutes later.

'I've found out who did that typing, Mr Naismith. I've got the girl here. The fact is that Miss Rodgers had no right to ask her to do it in the first place. She was a temporary, a replacement. They've had quite a number off with the influenza and they've had to get a lot of temporaries in.' Miss Fellowes went to the door and summoned the culprit. It all reminded Herbert powerfully of his officer days and of the sergeant bringing the malefactors before him for judgement. He half expected to hear her call the wretch to attention.

'This is Miss Watson, Mr Naismith.'

She was rather sweet, thin and pale, looking as if she was on the point of bursting into tears.

'Thank you, Miss Fellowes,' said Herbert. He was not going to give her the satisfaction of hearing him rebuke this little thing.

'Please take a seat, Miss Wilson,' he said – he believed in extending every courtesy to his employees. 'I believe that you typed this document, did you?' He exhibited the schedule, which consisted of eleven pages of figures. She swallowed hard and spoke finally with difficulty.

'Y-yes, Mr Naismith. I'm awfully sorry, Mr Naismith. I know I didn't do it very well.'

'It's not your fault entirely, it's a rather difficult job to give to someone who is new here. Do you know what this document is, Miss Wilson? It's a tender. We are offering to do a job for these people, and all these figures show the prices we are charging and the specifications we are prepared to meet. Obviously it is very important indeed that the figures should be accurately typed. You understand that?'

The girl swallowed again and nodded her head as if she could not trust herself to speak. Her fingers were clenching and unclenching themselves in her lap, and she was biting hard on her lower lip. Herbert was rather proud of himself so far; he felt that he had hit just the right note, firm but kindly.

'Unfortunately there are a good many mistakes, and it is not a matter of correcting the odd figure here and there, all these lists are going to have to be retyped.

She found words at last. 'Yes, Mr Naismith, of course,

Mr Naismith, I'll do it right away, Mr Naismith, and I'll really do my best to get it right this time.'

'I don't know how fast you work,' said Herbert, 'but I'm afraid it may mean you staying on at the end of the afternoon. I'm off to Brussels first thing in the morning and I must have this schedule with me.'

'I'll do it, Mr Naismith, honestly, I don't mind staying. I'm awfully sorry, I know I've made a mess of it.'

Her eyes were appealing, and her lips were trembling. Clearly this job meant quite a lot to her. Herbert rather enjoyed the feeling of power that this gave him.

'Well,' he said, 'I shall be working late tonight myself. I have some important papers to go over, so I shall be in my room, but I don't want to be disturbed, do you understand?'

She indicated that she had grasped this point.

'When you have finished I want you to put the schedule in the tray in Miss Fellowes' room out there; I'll pick it up when I'm ready. Now, please check very carefully that every figure is correct.'

She nodded again and sat gazing at him like a hypnotized rabbit.

'Well, that will be all, Miss Wilson; you'd better start straight away, hadn't you?'

She blushed and jumped to her feet and stammered out a few more words of apology before, somehow, she got herself out of the room. Herbert was rather amused. She looked a nice little thing and obviously she held him in considerable awe. Probably she had been expecting to be cursed unmercifully, perhaps even sacked on the spot. Herbert would have bet a fair sum that those bitches out there had given her a pretty bad time. Now, no doubt, she was telling herself how unexpectedly nice he had been, strict but fair and considerate.

At five o'clock Miss Fellowes put her head through the door to ask if there was any mail for the post, and he heard the clatter of the rest of the staff preparing to go home.

Within five minutes they had all gone and he was alone in the building except for the cleaners and, presumably, that nice little thing. He yawned and stretched himself. He liked this time of the day when he had the place to himself so that he could get on with his own work without constant interruptions. He checked through some material that he had to take with him the next day and then decided that he would go to a corner café which he often frequented to get a bite to eat. As he went down the corridor he peered through the window into the typists' room. Sure enough she was there, sitting at the desk in the corner, typing very slowly and peering at the copy in a rather short-sighted way, as though determined to be absolutely accurate. Herbert smiled and hurried on.

In the café he had a light snack and read the evening paper. Once or twice he thought of the little girl in the office pecking away at her typewriter, and for some reason the thought cheered him up. He had an idea that she was doing it as a kind of personal offering to him; she was grateful for the chance of redeeming herself and because he had been kind to her, and so she was determined to make a creditable job of the work this time. Then an idea struck him and he summoned the waiter.

'Do you think you could make me up a packet of sandwiches?'

The waiter was certain that they could.

'And I don't suppose that you have a thermos flask that you could lend me?'

The waiter smiled. He believed that a thermos flask could be found. Herbert gave his order and then went on reading his paper while it was prepared. When he finally started back for the office he had a flask of coffee in one hand and a packet of sandwiches in the other. He reached the typists' room and knocked punctiliously before letting himself in. She was still there, pecking away. When she heard the door open she looked round in a rather scared and desperate manner, and when she saw who it was she jumped to her feet in great confusion.

'Don't get up,' said Herbert, ignoring her confusion. 'I thought I'd bring you something to eat, I don't suppose that you've had any tea.' He put the thermos and the packet on the table in front of her. She had sat down again and was staring at him in a bewildered way. 'If you take my advice,' he continued, 'you'll have a break for a few minutes – rest your eyes – get some food into you – it'll do you all the good in the world. Leave the thermos in Miss Fellowes' room when you've done.' He smiled at her benevolently. She twisted her hands in front of her in an agony of shyness, but she did not manage to speak. Herbert did not wait for any response. He turned and went out of the room in the same matter-of-fact way that he had entered it, as though it was commonplace routine for him to carry refreshments to a junior, and temporary, employee.

When he reached his own room and sat down at his desk he considered what he had just done and found it satisfactory. It was in line with his image of himself as the courteous, considerate employer, unconventionally friendly and relaxed in his relationships with his workers. He could imagine word of what he had done getting about and the workers shaking their heads and confessing that they could not make him out at all. 'There's not many would have done a thing like that – say what you like, he's not a bad sort,' that was the kind of thing he imagined them saying. Precious few other employers would have done it, he knew that, in fact lots of them would have blamed him for the act, considering that he was spoiling his staff and making himself ridiculous. Some, of course, would simply misconstrue his motives and express this by intense sexual innuendo and arch leerings, but Herbert had no dark designs. The girl was a pretty little thing and he felt sorry for her. It had come into his head that it would be rather nice to surprise her, to play the part of the Dickensian philanthropist suddenly conjuring goodies out of thin air. He had not produced a fat goose, with cranberry sauce and brandy, he had merely offered her a packet of sandwiches and a flask of coffee, a cheap enough, innocent enough way of producing a benevolent effect. Probably he would never even see her again, but he reckoned that she would remember him, and with a certain amount of respect and pleasure. For several minutes he contemplated his own good nature with complacency before returning to his work. It was nearly seven o'clock before he heard the door of the outer room open. Evidently she had finished. He paused and listened. He heard her moving about Miss Fellowes' office, no doubt looking for the tray to put the work in. Then there was silence. Then he saw a dim silhouette in the frosted glass of the door of his own room; was she, after all, going to interrupt him? The silhouette passed, then retreated, and he heard the outer door close again.

The following week, on the Wednesday afternoon, Herbert left the works at his usual time, about twenty past five, on the way to the café. He had reached the corner of the street and was waiting to cross the main road when he was aware of a small figure at his elbow.

'Hullo,' he said, 'where did you spring from?' It was little Janet Wilson.

'I – I was waiting for you, Mr Naismith, in the doorway there. I – I wanted to say thank you.'

Her hands were twisting about as usual and, except for a first scared glance, she had not managed to look him in the face.

'Thank you? Whatever for?' Herbert knew very well what it was for but it suited him to act as though he had completely forgotten his kindness of the previous week.

'I didn't say anything. You must have thought me awful. It was so kind of you – the sandwiches and the coffee, I mean.'

'Good heavens, that was nothing at all.'

'I've been waiting every day to see if I could see you.'

Herbert was touched and flattered. He had a vision of her crouched in that dismal shop doorway on the offchance of seeing him.

'I'm afraid I've been away. I only came back yesterday.'

'Yes, I know you did. I saw you yesterday, but I didn't like to speak to you.'

'Oh dear, am I as terrifying as that?'

His teasing seemed to confuse her, but she blushed and stammered a little at this.

'I – I had to see you today, because it's my last day.'

'You're leaving us? I'm sorry about that.'

'The other girl's come back now, so I've got to go.'

She looked young and defenceless. She had a cheap coat on and a synthetic fur hat pulled down over her ears, and that curiously attractive little face peeped out at him from under it. Herbert wished to be kind, it was nice of her to have waited to thank him like this, but he could not think of anything else to say; logically the interview was at an end. Then he had an idea that it would be rather fun to play the fairy godfather again. He was absolutely at a loose end that evening and had more or less resigned himself to a solitary session at the hotel bar.

'I tell you what,' he said, 'I'm just going to have a bite to eat, why not come with me, and then we can have a proper talk instead of standing here like this.'

The proposal brought on a bad attack of shyness, and she murmured something about her landlady.

'We'll go back there first and tell her. How about it? You haven't arranged anything for this evening, have you?'

No, she had nothing at all arranged for that evening, and she allowed herself to be swept into a cab and driven back to her lodgings. She insisted on the taxi waiting in an adjacent street because, as she said, she didn't want to make a fuss, and she was back in an incredibly short time considering that she had, as far as he could see, made a complete change of costume in the interval.

Herbert took her to a rather expensive restaurant where he was not very well known and she was flatteringly overawed by the surroundings. She absolutely refused to take any part in the selection of the dishes, but when they came her appetite was a revelation. Herbert ordered a bottle of wine and pressed a single glass on her. He did not want her to think that he was trying to get her tiddly. He could not have given a clear account of what it was that he did want. It simply amused him to give a girl a totally unexpected treat. After a little encouragement, and when she had warmed up under the influence of the meal, she began telling him about herself and her family. Her mother was a widow who had brought up two children, Janet and an elder brother, single-handed. Her father had been killed in the war, and from the frequency with which she mentioned him Herbert guessed that this had been the most significant event in her life. He had enlisted as soon as the war had broken out and had survived until 1917, when he had been killed at Ypres, a name that she had some difficulty in pronouncing.

'Wipers,' said Herbert, 'all the men call it Wipers, it was easier to say it that way. I was at Wipers myself. What regiment was your father in?'

'He was in the Manchesters.'

'You come from Manchester, don't you?'

She nodded rapidly, she was eating steadily and her mouth was full. Herbert observed that her table manners were good, she had been properly brought up.

'I'm from Manchester, of course,' said Herbert. 'I guessed you were as soon as I heard you speak.'

She blushed a little.

'Do I sound as bad as that?'

'There's nothing wrong with the way Manchester people talk. It's good to hear a voice from home sometimes.'

The fact that Herbert had been at Ypres seemed to fascinate Janet. It was as though she pictured her father and Herbert fighting side by side, sword in hand. He had been killed on the twelth of September 1917. Two months earlier he had been home on leave and they had managed four days together at the seaside. She remembered waving to him as he walked off down the street for the last time, promising to be back for Christmas.

'That was always the worst time,' said Herbert, 'going back after leave.'

She told Herbert how her mother had received the news. 'I came home from school and there she was on the front step. As soon as I saw her face I knew what it was. She had the telegram in her hand and I took it off her and read it.'

Three weeks after her father's death her brother had joined up. 'He's nearly four years older than me. Mum didn't want him to but he said he must.'

'He got through all right, did he?'

'Yes, he was one of the lucky ones.'

Her father had been a commercial artist and her mother had not been trained for any work at all. When her husband had been killed she had had to turn her hand to something which would provide for herself and her two children in some way, so without experience and with no one to help her, she had opened a boarding house in Chorlton. Apparently it had been a hard life, and had cast light on aspects of the drearier side of human nature.

'You wouldn't believe the things some people will do, Mr Naismith. We caught one man at three o'clock in the morning, climbing out of his bedroom window with his cases, just to avoid paying the rent.'

Herbert agreed that it must have been a rather dispiriting experience. Through it all shone Janet's beautiful regard for her family, and her appreciation of what her mother had done.

'I used to help at the weekends and in the holidays, but me mum didn't like me doing too much. She used to say to me, "You're not going to stop in this sort of life, my girl", and she made me keep at my lessons.'

It seemed that she did not care very much for London; the people were not as friendly as those at home. Herbert imagined that she was probably homesick, but was too proud to say so. She said very little about her life in London, she spent most evenings sitting in her lodgings, and she seemed to have made no friends.

'The people here never seem to mean what they say; they're all over you one minute, and then the next they'll hardly speak to you.'

Herbert wondered idly what was behind this remark. Had she suffered some kind of betrayal? She said that she was very fond of sewing, and that she made most of her own clothes, but it was hardly natural for a girl of her age to sit at home every evening stitching.

'We'd better see what we can do to cheer you up,' he said. 'Do you like going to the theatre?'

She regarded this as a theoretical question and said no, she never went. She had only been once in her life to the pantomime in Manchester. She had enjoyed that.

'Would you like to go tonight?'

Herbert thought that he detected on her face an expression of sudden shrewd calculation. He could well imagine what was passing through her mind. A girl brought up in the atmosphere of a boarding house in Chorlton could not be entirely innocent of the ways of the world. No doubt some of those middle-aged bachelors that her mother had entertained had made casual advances to a young and blossoming woman. She again blushed deeply and said that it would be lovely, but she then became silent and rather thoughtful. Herbert smiled to himself. She was quite safe. He had no designs on her. He intended to show her that at least one man was capable of being nice to a girl without expecting payment in kind.

The evening was a great success. Herbert took her to see *The Yeoman of the Guard*, which, he thought, would be a good introduction to the theatre for her. He bought her a box of chocolates and was glad to see that she had the sense not to rustle the paper while the performance was on. Once or twice at first he explained the action to her, but she soon caught the hang of it and then followed it with bated breath. She laughed at the amusing bits, and caught her breath over the fate of Lieutenant Fairfax, and wept at the death of Jack Point. At the end of it all she turned to him with shining eyes and said that it had all been marvellous. They had a single drink in the bar at the interval, and afterwards he took her straight back to her lodgings in a taxi. Once again at her request the cab was stopped a few streets short of where she lived and he walked her the rest of the way. Throughout the evening he had behaved with a grave, almost studied, courtliness, like an uncle entertaining a favourite niece, and now he offered his arm and they strolled together through the night air. When they reached her lodgings they stopped for a few moments on the pavement and she retained her hold of him.

'Well,' she said, 'all good things come to an end.'

'As long as it was a good thing,' said Herbert. 'You enjoyed it?'

'It's been lovely, Mr Naismith, really lovely. I'll never forget it.'

'I'm glad,' said Herbert. They stood for a minute or two in silence and then Herbert gently disengaged his arm.

'Well, I'd better not keep you out here any longer; your landlady will be waiting for you.'

'I don't mind her,' said Janet, 'but you've got to get back, haven't you?'

'Goodbye, Janet,' he said, holding out his hand, 'it's been very pleasant meeting you.'

'Goodbye, Mr Naismith, and thanks ever so much, I've really enjoyed it.' They shook hands and she turned and went up the short flight of steps to the front door. At the top she turned and waved to him and said goodbye once more. He returned the gesture solemnly and waited until she had let herself in – he observed that she had her own key – before turning and walking down the street. As he walked he tried to analyse his motives. His companion had not been particularly clever or witty, certainly she had not been fashionable. Most of his acquaintances would probably have commented that if he had wanted to pick up a girl for the evening, surely he could have done better for himself than that. And yet he felt quite lighthearted and gay. He had been reminded at times of those evenings during the war when he had taken Beatrice out. She too had been impressionable, a little naïve, apt to cling. He had felt young again, as he was in those days, and he had felt the pleasure of an effortless superiority, the admiration and awe of a young girl on his arm. He wondered what Janet had thought. She must have suspected his motives. She must have reckoned that he was counting on a quick kiss and a cuddle, and perhaps a bit more into the bargain. How would she have taken it? Had she wanted him to make advances to her, or would she merely have tolerated them? She seemed to look on him as infinitely old, he had fought in the same war as her father, to her he was a middle-aged man, which was the same as saying that he was an old man. She was a kindly little girl, she had a generous and grateful spirit, and she would probably have put up with him. He thought that once or twice she had been bracing herself to accept his advances, but each time he had refused to make them. He did not want to put himself at her mercy, it suited him to be the giver and not the receiver. He preferred to leave her at the end of the evening thinking about the purity of his action. It was flattering to think that she had been, perhaps, a little disappointed that he had not done anything more, but he had been wise not to test this idea. It would have been so easy for her to rebuff him.

Well, that had been the start of it, and a more innocent start Herbert could not well imagine. In fact it was so innocent that Beatrice would never have believed him if he had told her of it. Come to that, it was the sort of thing that that Winnick fellow would not believe, either. Took her out, wined and dined her, took her to the theatre, and then – not so much as kiss her hand. A likely story. Nobody would credit it. And nobody would believe that the innocent excursion could have given him so much pleasure, but it really had. He remembered it years afterwards, with a tenderness for the self who had been capable of an act of simple, disinterested kindness. When he left Janet he had felt that she would remember him with some warmth, feel grateful, both for his kindness and his forbearance, that she might even be a little piqued by his refusal to take advantage of her.

But he told himself that he never expected to see her again.

18

Herbert could still remember vividly, even after all these years, his surprise when, on turning to pay off the taxi that had taken Janet and him to that hotel, he had seen Beatrice walking towards them. For a second he had refused to believe the evidence that his eyes presented to him. Beatrice was supposed to be some sort of an invalid, she had to be cosseted, if any journeys had to be made then all the arrangements had to be done by somebody else. And now, all of a sudden, out of the blue, here she was, for all the world like one of those private detectives one reads of, racing about, tracking people down, following up clues. It was almost amusing. He felt like putting up his hands and saying it was a fair cop. Instead he bundled Janet back into the taxi and pressed some money into her hand and whispered into her ear the words 'It's the wife, I'll get in touch.' She had gone like a lamb. Then he had turned to meet Beatrice.

Characteristically, this surprise invigorated him, he felt suddenly relaxed and calm, in high spirits, and he took complete control. He stopped Beatrice making an exhibition of herself in the street or in the taxi that he shortly afterwards was able to hail. He managed to keep quite cool, to put the facts before her in an unimpassioned way. He spoke of the strain that he had been under, of the unfairness of expecting a man like himself, an ordinary human being, with the ordinary human being's share of normal appetites, to abstain from sexual activity altogether. He reminded her that he had never set up to be a saint. He said, which was quite true, that Janet meant nothing at all to him really, that she was simply a relaxation, a safety valve. Beatrice seemed to have got it into her head that he must have been carrying on with any number of women and that Janet was one among many. He did not disabuse her. It was more convenient for her to think this and it enabled him to play down the importance of Janet.

'You women make too much of a fuss about these things. You don't suppose that I'm really interested in a girl like that. A man's got to have some sort of release, you know. You didn't marry a Trappist monk. If it hadn't been for those damned letters you wouldn't have known anything about it, and it wouldn't have done you any harm. It doesn't mean that my feelings about you have changed at all.'

Of course she would not have this. She argued that his feelings must have changed, or he could not possibly have treated her like this, but he was speaking the truth. Again and again in this conversation, Herbert had the experience of saying what was exactly and literally true and knowing that Beatrice would not accept that truth because she could not really understand what it was that he said. His feelings had not changed because he had never cared for Beatrice as she had thought he did; he could not very well explain that. And when he said that Janet meant nothing to him, this also was true: she meant nothing at all to him compared with what Florence meant. It was very difficult for Herbert to feel other than detached towards Beatrice and so it was difficult for him to take this conversation as seriously as he ought. It was rather eerie. He tried to be kind, and kindness demanded that he should show some feeling, but he had no real feeling. He paced up and down the hotel bedroom and talked away, trying to convince poor little harmless Bea that he wished her nothing but well. He was genuinely sad that she had found out, and that the discovery had given her pain; if he could have made amends in any way he would have done so, but she wanted love, and he could not give her that, he could not warm to her.

Sitting in an easy chair, rocking gently to and fro, weeping into an absurd pocket handkerchief, Beatrice was an almost contemptible figure. Tears had trickled down her cheeks and made the powder and rouge hideous, her eyes were swollen, her nose looked red and shiny; she was not an object to stir much feeling in Herbert's heart. He could not help wondering how Beatrice would have behaved if she had known the truth and realized that Janet was, in a sense, a red-herring. 'This business with Janet is nothing,' Herbert had said, 'nothing at all.' And he was absolutely right – it was the business with Florence that mattered. What he was up to with Janet was at least normal, but if Beatrice had known about some of the things that he and Florence were doing she would not have considered them normal at all. It was an odd thought, but if she had known about them she would probably have implored him to go back to Janet – Her own sister, playing about with knives and whips. Fortunately she did not know, and so she sat in her chair weeping hopelessly over a minor peccadillo.

Herbert allowed his thoughts to rest on Florence for a few moments. She would have been angry at this. It was a part of Herbert's case with Florence that she was his real love, that it was her fault that they were not married and so had to carry on in this furtive way. She would not take kindly to sharing his favours with a girl like poor little Janet. For Florence had come round at last. Her extended period of standoffishness had come to an end. 'Rose' had suddenly made herself available again. These were the days when Wilfred was 'lecturing' at the technical college. He fancied himself as a scientist and dressed up in a white coat and demonstrated piddling little experiments to groups of earnest ignoramuses. It was laughable but it was convenient. The technical college was some distance away from Herriott Street, and he was never back much before eleven. Again and again Herbert found himself driving Florence back to a house which they both knew was empty.

'Will "Rose" be at home?' he would ask as the car gathered speed down the drive, and usually the answer was that yes, 'Rose' would be. After that it was simply a matter of settling the details of the evening's fantasy.

'I saw this film recently,' Herbert would say, or he would ask, 'Did you get a chance to look at that book I lent you? What did you think of the place I marked? I thought it might interest "Rose", that one.' At this stage Florence was usually non-committal. It was apparently necessary to her own self-esteem that, even on 'Rose's' behalf she should not seem too eager, so she would allow Herbert to take the lead, to outline the scene as he saw it, and to take it beyond the point reached in the film or book.

'He sort of pulled her hair back so that she was looking up at the ceiling and you could see her throat, and he drew the point of the knife down it, but of course, that was as far as they would go in the film, they had to leave the rest to your imagination.'

Herbert's imagination would cope quite satisfactorily with the task of filling in the missing details and occasionally Florence, or 'Rose' as he had to be careful to call her after a certain point in their discussion, would offer an idea of her own. By the time they reached Herriott Street they were nicely worked up, both of them, and would proceed solemnly to enact their little play.

'I think he meant that she was actually tied to the pillar,' Herbert would say, 'with her hands behind her, like this,' and he would take the dressing-gown cord and make an elaborate knot. The knot must be tight, not so tight that it actually hurt but tight enough to secure her properly. It was a pretence that sailed as nearly as they dared to reality. Florence, in the disguise of 'Rose', placed herself absolutely in Herbert's power. His fingers would caress her throat, the blade of a knife would be drawn delicately across her breasts, a cane would cut into a cushion placed inches from her body. It was an exquisite, delicious flirting with danger. Occasionally the roles would be changed, and it would be Herbert who was at the mercy of 'Rose', but in each case the climax was the same.

After it was all over they avoided one another's eyes. This was when the fiction of 'Rose' and 'Sir Charles', which was one of Herbert's favourite names for himself, was particularly useful. They would carefully put everything away, usually without speaking at all, and go downstairs where the gas would have been left on for the benefit of the neighbours. Here they would resume their own identities and chat about ordinary family affairs until Herbert took his leave, or Wilfred returned.

A bout of this sort seemed to satisfy a need in both of them. Immediately afterwards Herbert often felt a revulsion against what he had been doing, and he guessed Florence felt this way also. He would be ashamed and vow not to do it again and, on this wave of self-disgust, for a short time, he would become very virtuous and bury himself in his work and try to make a fuss of Beatrice. But in a few weeks this feeling would slacken and the scene they had enacted would return to his imagination, and he would be reminded of the fierce pleasure he had felt, and then he would long to repeat it. It was another odd thing about this period of his life that, in the weeks when he was disgusted with himself for his behaviour with Florence, he was especially attentive to Janet. Janet was a nice little girl with a very sweet nature. His relationship with her was a kind of reassurance to Herbert because it was so splendidly normal. Pacing about the hotel room, explaining himself to Beatrice, he made this point again and again, 'Lots of chaps do this sort of thing, you know, there's nothing so very exceptional about it.' 'It's a perfectly natural thing to have happen you know.' 'If you're going to blame me for this then you'll blame about three quarters of the men in the world.'

Beatrice had not accepted this as being any sort of excuse and he had hardly expected her to, but he had found a great pleasure, and a consolation, in the fact that it was such a very normal kind of an affair. If only Beatrice had been astute enough to turn a blind eye when she found out about it, all the trouble would have been avoided, he would have retained an essential safety-valve. It was so innocent. He had only met Janet again by sheer chance on the train from Manchester to London. He had noticed her in a third-class compartment when it drew in to Wilmslow Station and, after a certain amount of thought, he had walked along the corridor to find her and persuade her to join him in his own first-class carriage.

'I'll see the ticket collector when he comes,' he said, in answer to an unspoken objection. She had gathered her things together and gone with him without a word.

'It's very nice to see you again,' he said, when they had settled down. 'Have you been home to see your mother?'

She explained that she had been to her brother's wedding, and she spoke about this in some detail. Of course she was glad, for her brother's sake, that he had got married, but she could not help feeling it as something of a loss. She and Tom had been very close, especially after her father's death.

'Your mother will miss him, too. How is your mother?'

Her mother was not so good. She had had rheumatic fever just after the war and it had left her heart weak; and, Janet added gloomily, she tried to do too much.

'I said, why didn't I go home and give her a hand, but she wouldn't have it. She wants me to do better with myself than that.'

'She must try to take things more easily,' said Herbert sagely.

'That's what the doctor says, but she can't. If you're running a boarding house you've got your guests to look after. They won't stop long if you start taking it easy.'

It was an unfair world. Herbert found himself mentally comparing the life of this woman, bravely struggling to make a living against impossible odds, with the life of someone like Beatrice, whose way had always been so smooth. Mrs Wilson had a real illness and refused to give in to it; Beatrice had any number of more or less imaginary illnesses and gave in to all of them, except when there was something that she actually wanted to do. Janet's early reserve, caused probably by her innate shyness, was wearing off and she was speaking quite freely about her family and how things were at home. As Herbert listened he found himself speculating about Janet, a thing he had done once or twice before since that first evening. She had told him then that her father had been a commercial artist and that her mother had been unused to any kind of work and untrained for any profession. This had suggested to Herbert that her background had been genteel, genteel but not well-to-do. The word 'artist' had helped to create an effect in Herbert's mind. He imagined Janet's father to have been a rather mild, ineffectual, kindly man, dressed in a velvet jacket, with secret ambitions to break out of the world of commercial art and to make his mark as a real painter. No doubt Janet's mother had been a cut above him socially, probably they had met at some kind of artistic gathering, a private showing – something like that, and she had fallen in love with his grace, his talent, and his charm. Very likely her family had not been pleased by the match and had turned their backs on her, but she had been happy, they had had children, their marriage had prospered, and then the war had come, and this sweet-natured, talented man had been killed, wasted like so much fine material, on the Western Front, and she had been faced, out of the blue, with the need to fend for herself and her children. And nobly she had done it. Janet would have been too young when it happened to understand the full significance of their loss, but it must have been an agonizing adjustment that her mother had had to make. Gradually her former friends would have dropped her, all the old comforts would have been lost, she would have been overwhelmed by the daily drudgery of her work. And, bravely, she had determined that her children should have something better than this, something more like what their father would have wished for them. The son, Herbert knew, had gone to a technical college and come out with some kind of qualification in engineering – God alone knew what sacrifices she had had to make to bring this about –

and Janet had gone to her secretarial school and attended her evening classes. It was a pathetic story; a lot of it was speculation, but Herbert was prepared to bet that it was not very far from the truth, and it made Janet herself a more interesting and a more explicable figure. Naturally she would feel herself to be a cut above the working girls she found herself mixing with. She and they could have very little in common, and she would have even less to say to the young men she met. Of course she would be lonely, rather intimidated by the world, but inheriting, as she did, her father's sweetness of nature, it was not in her to blame anyone, or to complain about her lot. Now that her brother was married she was more lonely than ever; no wonder that, as she spoke about him, her eyes wrinkled and her face expressed a forlorn, woebegone mood.

Herbert began to feel very protective towards her. She was a nice little kid, the sort who deserved help; it would be good to do something for her. Her face was not strictly pretty, but it was appealing, very gentle and soft, with large brown eyes. She was obviously in awe of him, regarding him as being infinitely superior to herself, and this attitude flattered his self-esteem. She showed a natural, spontaneous pleasure in his company, and Herbert began to understand better why he had behaved as he had done on their last meeting. She had the knack of making him feel pleased with himself, of bringing out his kindly impulses. He said, once again, how pleased he was that they had met again.

'Are you really,' she said, 'you're not just saying it?'

'Indeed I'm not. I thought that little outing of ours was a lot of fun.'

'So did I. I've thought of it ever so often. But I wondered afterwards if I'd done anything wrong.'

'How do you mean, wrong?'

'I just wondered. I'd had a lovely evening and you'd been really lovely to me, and then when you went off like that at the end of it and I didn't see you again, I wondered if it was something I'd done.'

'I see,' said Herbert. 'You wanted to see me again, then?'

'Oh yes, Mr Naismith, I wanted to a lot. I kept thinking about you.'

'I didn't think you'd be all that interested. An old married man like me, old enough to be your father, I daresay.' Herbert said these words in a half humorous tone, eyeing Janet carefully as he spoke.

'Oh, Mr Naismith, you're having me on. I don't think you're old at all. I'm nearly twenty-two; you couldn't be my father now, could you?'

'Well,' admitted Herbert, 'I would have to have started very young, but I'm still a married man. Would you like to go out with a married man?'

Janet turned suddenly serious and directed her gaze out of the window at the dots of light from the houses speeding past in the darkness.

'Do you mind if I say something, Mr Naismith?'

'What is it?'

'I know how difficult things can be at home sometimes. I know it's not always easy for married people to get on together, and I feel sorry for them if they don't.'

'You mean you feel sorry for me?' asked Herbert calmly.

'No, what I'm trying to say is that nobody knows what a married couple go through except them. I've talked about this with my mother and my Auntie Mildred and they've told me that if you're not married then you can't really know anything about it. You being married is your business, it's nothing to do with me. And if you ever asked me to go out with you again, Mr Naismith, I'd go like a shot.'

'Hmm,' said Herbert, 'well, in that case, we'd better think about arranging another meeting; and I think you'd better start calling me Herbert.'

She was a very restful girl was Janet. No doubt if he had seen too much of her he would have found her rather boring, but in small doses she was ideal. She did not make any demands on him, in fact she retained her awe of him for quite a long time, and his word was her law. She had a very sweet, gentle nature, and she was not in the least 'having' or greedy. He enjoyed buying her little gifts, but she would never accept anything at all expensive. He tried to get her to take a brooch once, only a small one, but charming and tasteful, decorated with diamonds and sapphires. She thought it was beautiful, she held it at her throat to see it sparkle, and she tried it against a dress she had just bought and admired the effect, but she would not accept it. 'Oh no, love,' she said, using her favourite term of endearment, 'it's beautiful, it really is, but I can't take it. It might spoil things. Auntie Mildred always says that expensive gifts spoil friendship. You'd start thinking that I was only after you for what I could get out of you, and then it would be all over.'

He protested that this was untrue, that he would not think any such thing, but she would not take the gift.

'It's lovely of you, darling, and I do appreciate it, I really do. You're always so generous and kind to me. I tell you what, I'll take the thought: they always say it's the thought that counts.' So she kissed him and gave him a little hug and a squeeze, and shut the brooch away in its box, and pushed it into his coat pocket. She accepted pretty clothes occasionally, so that he would not feel ashamed of her when he took her out, she said, but that was all.

It was a curious relationship. Herbert felt very tender towards Janet, felt – it was an odd word to use in this context, but it expressed a truth – fatherly, protective. In time, true, he went to bed with her, but this did not happen immediately. They had been friends before it happened for quite long enough, he would have thought, to secure him against a charge of mere lust. When it came it was the natural flowering of their relationship, not, he supposed, that it was reasonable to expect Beatrice to look at it quite in this light. His whole point was that it was not just the sort of casual affair when a man picks up a pretty girl for a dirty weekend together somewhere.

The great irony of it was, as Herbert so often thought later, that Beatrice had found him out on the very last meeting he would have had with Janet in London. Affairs at home had reached such a state, at last, that Janet had been driven to take decisive action. She had sacrificed her own independence, given up her work in London, and insisted on returning home to help her mother. It had not been an easy decision for her to take. Thanks to Herbert she had by now got very comfortably settled and was enjoying life a lot more than she had done at first. And things at home had got worse. She had spoken to Herbert, now and then, of the lodging-house, and it was clear that the prospect of returning to it permanently appalled her, but she had made her decision, given in her notice to her employers and her landlady, packed her bags, said her goodbyes, and she and Herbert had arranged to spend one last evening together; and then Beatrice had popped out of her taxi like the demon king popping up through the trapdoor in a pantomime. If she had come down the following week she would have found nothing, she would have returned home chastened, she would have continued to trust her husband, she would have spared herself a good deal of unhappiness, and Janet would have enjoyed one more evening with him before the horrors of the lodging-house closed over her head. It was a wretched piece of bad luck.

And it was no use presenting Beatrice's discovery as a triumph for morality, or any rot like that. It had been a disaster for everybody, for Beatrice as for anybody else, and no good had come of it at all. It showed perfectly the advisability of leaving things alone, of not poking into things, stirring things up. Beatrice had always been a one for that. This present business with that fellow Winnick was a case in point. She could not resist meddling. It is one of the arts of life to know when to turn a blind eye, when to temper curiosity with caution. It is children who pry into things and take things to pieces and then cry because they no longer work. Beatrice smashed her own life when a bit of common sense would have persuaded her to look the other way. And then she proceeded to make matters a good deal worse. She forbade him to see Janet again, or to have any communication with her, and, later, blamed him bitterly for breaking this foolish and unreasonable order. She insisted that they should move as quickly as possible to London, so that his metropolitan jaunts should be at an end, and this, although it was not so unreasonable, was the worst part of the whole business to Herbert. A hundred and eighty miles is not a distance at which one can casually drop in on Herriott Street on the off-chance of finding Wilfred out. Those cosy drives back from Wilmslow, with the prospect of an exciting romp at the end of them, would become a thing of the past. Without knowing that she was doing it, Beatrice destroyed the one relationship that Herbert really valued. She told Florence about the impending move when she and Wilfred were over at Wilmslow one Sunday afternoon. Of course she said nothing about Janet, she was no more anxious than Herbert to make public the breakdown of their marriage. She and Herbert had decided that their present way of living was too uncomfortable. It was not really fair on Herbert, she said, at which words Florence shot a puzzled and suspicious look at him. They had both of them decided that it would be better if they were to go to live in London. Florence showed no more emotion than was decently accounted for by regret at the prospect of losing her sister's company, but when she and Herbert were alone, she tackled him.

'What's the matter, Herbert? Whatever's happened?'

'It wasn't my decision,' Herbert explained. 'Beatrice suddenly got it into her head that she wanted to go to London to live. I think she was finding it very boring being up here all on her own.'

'She hasn't found out anything, has she?'

'Eh?'

'About us? It seems very odd to me. Beatrice has never had anything to say about London before.'

Herbert had expected this. He had known that it would seem odd to Florence. She was still giving him rather peculiar looks and it was plain that she thought that she had not been told everything.

'She's not as happy in Wilmslow as she used to be. Most of our friends have moved away, I think that had something to do with it.'

It sounded lame, even to Herbert, but it was the best he could think of. His best plan was to confess himself as baffled as Florence was, to put it all on Beatrice, one of her unaccountable whims, that sort of thing.

The four of them had gone for a walk after lunch. It was early spring, a fine day with a watery sun and a suspicion of a nip in the air. When she had been making such a parade of her ill health Beatrice would not have ventured out on such a day, but it was one of the better effects of her London adventure that Herbert had been able to point out to her that she could hardly have been as ill as she had cracked on to be.

'I thought you were supposed to be an invalid,' he said. 'If you want to talk about me pulling myself together, perhaps you'd better do the same. You haven't been much of a companion for a fellow, Bea. You can't really blame me for going off the rails a bit. If you can gad about London like that, playing at detectives, spying on me, it seems to me you could do a bit more at home.'

He had said more in the same vein. He had not taken everything lying down. He had hit back and given, in some respects, as good as he got. Beatrice had taken the hint, and there she was, twenty yards ahead, arm in arm with Wilfred, chatting quite animatedly.

'The fact is, Florence,' he confided, drawing her a little closer to him, 'I've been on at Bea a bit to shake herself up, and she's taken the hint a bit more strongly than I intended, but I can't very easily go back on it now.'

Florence listened carefully but made no sign of assent.

'The trouble now is,' continued Herbert, 'where does it all leave us?'

'What do you mean?'

‘I suppose, really, I should say, where does it all leave “Rose”?’

They must have walked about twenty paces before Florence replied.

‘I suppose it leaves “Rose” out of it. Perhaps it will be better that way. Was that what you wanted me to say?’

‘You know damn well it wasn’t.’

‘I don’t know anything of the kind, Herbert; I don’t know what’s going on. You’ve suddenly decided to go down to London. Well, that’s all right, you’ve got a perfect right to go, if that’s what you want, but you can’t expect everything to be the same up here, can you?’

Herbert tried to say something, but she told him not to interrupt, and went on: ‘I suppose you’ve decided that you’ve had enough of it, is that it? Is it getting a bit boring now? Is this your idea of a gentle hint to me?’

Ahead of them Wilfred and Beatrice had stopped, and Beatrice was looking back and calling them a couple of slow-coaches and telling them to hurry up. Florence smiled and waved cheerily, and continued in a strident undertone.

‘I daresay it’s all for the best anyway. It was all getting a bit much. We were beginning to take fearful risks, sooner or later something would have happened.’

This, Herbert could see, was a typical Florence ploy. She was determined to show that she did not really care whether ‘Rose’ continued in existence or not.

‘There’s no reason why we shouldn’t go on, Florence. We’ll be meeting often enough. I shall have to keep coming back to look after things at this end, you know.’

‘I think it would be better if we dropped the whole thing now,’ said Florence loftily. ‘To tell you the truth, it was getting a bit repetitive. I agree with you, a clean break is the best thing really. Hullo, Beatrice, you are quite your old self again, you nearly walked me off my feet. It must be the prospect of getting to London that has done it.’

She was very careful not to be alone with Herbert during

the rest of the visit but she cleverly conveyed to him a sense of glacial displeasure. He was not really displeased. He knew she would come round. In fact, he was beginning to enjoy a sense of his own real power over her at last.

19

'You were not living in Manchester at the time of the – er – tragedy?'

Winnick was sitting with his clipboard on his knee, his pencil poised ready, determined to make the most of this last chance that he would have with this curiously assorted couple. He had spent the time since his last visit to the Naismiths checking on some of the things he had already been told, and he had made at least two significant discoveries. For instance, he had followed up the story which Beatrice had told him, that Rimmer had been taught the violin by a player in the Hallé orchestra, a man called Grein. Now, Winnick had checked the records very carefully and he had established beyond any doubt that, throughout the Twenties, there had been no player of that name in the orchestra at all. This was odd. There was no reason to doubt the veracity of Mrs Naismith, but was it not possible that Rimmer himself had deceived everybody? Suppose that he had not been taking lessons at all and that the whole story had been concocted by him to account for regular absences from home? For what purpose would a man play such a trick? Obviously only one answer was possible to such a question. *Cherchez la femme*. Winnick could see the words in italics, possibly as the sub-heading to a chapter. Rimmer had had a woman. And if this were once established then everything was explained. Here was a motive, glaring and obvious. Disappointed in his marriage, Wilfred Rimmer had found himself a lady-friend and, as their intimacy deepened, he had tried to find a way of making the liaison permanent. Florence would have to be got rid of somehow. Divorce was presumably out of the question and gradually, as it had done to so many men before and since, murder had offered itself as the only possible solution. He had devised the perfect plan, providing himself with an unshakeable alibi. Clearly he had hoped that his wife's death would be blamed on some mysterious intruder and, after a decent interval, no doubt he had planned to marry this mistress. It was the complete solution and, to cap it all, Winnick was morally certain that he could put a name to this woman.

He was immensely pleased with himself. It was absolutely the touch that his book needed, and it had come to light as the result of painstaking research. Like a latter-day Sherlock Holmes, Winnick would be able to lay before his public every link in the chain of reasoning that had led him to his conclusions. Phrases, even whole sentences, formed themselves in Winnick's head as he pondered his discovery. It only went to show that one should leave nothing to chance, no avenue unexplored, no stone, as the saying is, left unturned. If he had not followed up that name so casually dropped by Beatrice, then he would not have got his first real clue; the rest of it had come by sheer, slogging industry. What he wanted to do now was to check on this theory, but he would have to be careful. It was no use just coming out with it baldly and telling Beatrice that Rimmer had lied about those lessons. If he did this then she would close up directly, dismiss his suspicions as absurd, claim, even, that she must have misremembered the name. She was anxious to defend Rimmer, and she would reject any evidence that went so badly against him. And in doing all this she would be quite sincere. Winnick prided himself on understanding the vagaries of the human mind and he knew that, in her anxiety to think well of her late brother-in-law, she would be able to convince herself that she actually had been mistaken. No, what he must do was to bide his time, ask little, probing questions and see what she let slip. He had this other thing up his sleeve and, when the time was right, he would introduce it casually and just see how they reacted. If he took them properly off their guard they would give themselves away. And so, in the meantime, he asked

Beatrice his question about leaving Manchester, and she replied firmly, 'As a matter of fact I was in hospital when it happened, and Herbert was in Glasgow.'

'Glasgow?'

'He'd gone up there for a business meeting, hadn't you, Herbert? We were living in Wimbledon by then. It was nineteen twenty-nine, the spring of nineteen twenty-nine, when we moved. We neither of us really wanted to leave Manchester. In those days, you know, Manchester thought it was at least as good as London. There was a saying, "What Manchester thinks today, London thinks tomorrow", but all the travelling was getting a bit much for Herbert, so we had to move.'

'And you were in hospital at the time?'

'In a nursing home. I'd had a lot of trouble, we won't go into it in detail, Mr Winnick, women's complaints, you know; so finally I went in to have it all put right. It was lucky in a way, it gave me my last chance of seeing Florence.'

Winnick politely indicated his interest in this and she continued. 'Herbert had to go to Brussels, just before I was due to go in, so Florence came down to keep me company and to see me into the nursing home.'

'So you saw her very shortly before the – er – ?'

'I saw her on the Friday, and it happened on the following Tuesday.' Beatrice's voice was quite firm, she spoke in a very matter-of-fact way.

'And she seemed quite normal, I mean you didn't get the idea that there was anything wrong?'

'She was perfectly normal, there was nothing wrong at all, I'm sure of that.' Beatrice's voice was now very firm indeed.

'How much had you seen of Florence after you left Manchester, Mrs Naismith?' said Winnick. 'The reason I'm asking is that this is the crucial period. If there were any strains between them, then they were most likely to have developed in the months immediately before the – er – tragedy, and this was the very time when you had left.'

Beatrice smiled very sweetly.

'There weren't any strains,' she said. 'I'd have known if there were. Florence would have told me. As a matter of fact we still saw them quite often.'

Beatrice proceeded to make a series of elaborate calculations and then triumphantly told him that she had met Florence six times after going down to live in Wimbledon. Winnick obediently jotted this down, but he reflected privately that it was not the same. Anything could have been going on in Manchester, and Beatrice would have been none the wiser. Winnick brooded a moment, there was something that he did not understand. He consulted his report of the trial to refresh his memory.

'I understand from what Mr Naismith said in court, that he was given the news about the – er – affair in his home on the Wednesday morning.'

'Well?' said Herbert.

'But I thought Mrs Naismith said that you were in Glasgow.'

'I was,' said Herbert. 'I travelled back overnight. I'd only just got in when the police arrived.'

'I see,' said Winnick. He remembered something that Beatrice had said about Wilfred's house, something about being able to see it from the railway. 'The train didn't come through Manchester, did it?'

'Yes,' said Herbert coldly, 'as a matter of fact it did. Why do you ask?'

'It was something that Mrs Naismith said. When she was talking about Wilfred's house she said that you could see it as you passed in the train. I was thinking that you could have been sitting in the train looking out at the house at the very moment when – ' He paused in some confusion. He had a fondness for poetic, ironic juxtapositions, and it had hurried him into an indiscretion. He should have saved the fancy for his book. Evidently it had pained and irritated both these old people.

'I was travelling through considerably later,' said Herbert coldly, 'and in any case, the train was on a different line.'

Winnick shifted hastily back to safer ground and asked Beatrice a series of questions about her last meetings with Florence, and it appeared from her answers that these had indeed been absolutely normal. They had taken holidays together, Florence had visited for occasional shopping sprees, Beatrice had even got up to Herriott Street once.

'You certainly kept in touch,' murmured Winnick.

'Herbert saw them oftener than I did, he was up there nearly every month.'

'Nearly every month?'

'Well,' explained Beatrice, 'he had to go to Manchester, you see, to attend to the business there.'

It struck Winnick that the move to Wimbledon had not markedly reduced the amount of travelling that Herbert did, but it was none of his business, so he merely asked, 'Did he always look Florence and Wilfred up when he was in Manchester?'

'Every single time,' said Beatrice firmly, 'didn't you, Herbert?'

The silent man in the corner nodded sourly. These blasted questions were beginning to get on his nerves. What the devil was the fellow up to? That question about the train had really made him sweat. He wished Beatrice would give up this line. She was treading on delicate ground, and she knew it. His 'looking up' Florence and Wilfred had been a condition of his sentence, so to speak. She had caught him out in London, and she did not intend that he should start playing fast and loose again. Her discovering that Janet had gone back to Manchester had been most unfortunate. Anyway, she had put her foot down and insisted that every time he went there he must pay a visit to Herriott Street. He was only to spend one night in Manchester, anyway, so she was pretty sure that she had spiked his guns. If she had only known. It was like locking a boy up in a sweet-shop as a punishment.

'I suppose, Mr Naismith,' said Winnick, 'you didn't see anything amiss?'

'I don't see what you're after,' Herbert said aggressively.

'I'll be frank with you, Mr Naismith. I'm wondering whether it was possible that Wilfred was having an affair with somebody. I mean, some men do manage to lead double lives for quite long periods of time. Even their own wives may know nothing about it because they are regularly away from home on quite legitimate business.'

Winnick was quite tickled by the reception accorded to this suggestion. Of course, they had been brought up in a different age, and no doubt they were conventional and strait-laced, but they looked positively dumbfounded. When he recovered the power of speech Herbert actually asked him what the devil he meant by that, for all the world like the honest, innocent old squire confronting villainy in some melodrama.

'I'd got the impression from what you said, sir, that Wilfred was quite frequently away from home. I just wondered – perhaps not all these absences were as innocent as they appeared to be.'

'It's nonsense,' said Beatrice, 'Wilfred would never have done such a thing, he wasn't that sort of person.' She stopped abruptly, and Winnick felt a delicious prickle of anticipation. There was something here. She had pulled herself up too sharply as if, in midspeech, she had suddenly remembered something. It was infuriating. These old people had some information which would confirm his suspicions. Winnick was sure of that, and they were determined to keep it to themselves. For a moment Winnick toyed with the idea of firing off his big gun then and there, but he decided against it. He would wait until he was ready to leave and then, with the utmost casualness, drop the name into their ears and see what happened; so he allowed Beatrice to tell him in great detail how perfectly normal all those last meetings had been.

Herbert, watching from his corner, relaxed a little. That had been a most unpleasant moment, and he hoped that Beatrice was satisfied with what she had done. This was the natural consequence of raking up the past, all the unpleasant memories were revived and years of blameless living were wiped out. It had been perpetually on her lips in those days that Wilfred, whatever his shortcomings, however much of a disappointment he might have been, had never erred in the way that he, Herbert, had erred. He had never given Florence a moment's anxiety, etc. etc. Beatrice had been capable of a number of monotonous variations on this dreary theme, and they had all been provoked by her discovery that, in spite of his promise, he had actually met Janet again. What she could not understand was that it had been entirely her own fault. The last Janet had seen of him he was bundling her into a taxi, pressing a couple of pounds into her hand, and saying, 'It's the wife, I'll get in touch.' It needed no very profound knowledge of human nature to tell that Janet would want to find out what had happened. Herbert had tried to be obedient, and the natural consequence was that one morning, over breakfast, reading his mail, he found himself staring at a letter from the girl. She had been very crafty, rather too crafty. She had used an envelope belonging to the firm of solicitors that she had worked for in London, and she had typed the letter. Herbert hoped that he had managed to conceal his surprise, and that Beatrice would think that it was an ordinary business communication, but she was watching him like a hawk. The Manchester post-mark had given them away. When he read his correspondence in the morning he always discarded the envelopes straight away and, under Beatrice's steady gaze, he could not very well retrieve this one. She must have pounced on it as soon as he was out of the room and there, on the back, was the name, address, and telephone number of the firm. She had telephoned the firm, pretending to be his secretary, and casually asked about a Miss Janet Wilson. No, they had said, Miss Wilson had recently left their employ – her address? Yes, if she would hang on for a moment they would find it for her – ah, yes, here it was . . . Beatrice had taken a taxi and cruised past the lodging-house a couple of times that very afternoon while he was actually in the park with Janet. When he had got back she was ready for him.

'Been to see your Janet Wilson, have you?'

It had been a terrific shock to Herbert, but he had managed to remain impassive and to content himself by way of a reply with the monosyllable, 'Yes.'

Then she had really let him have it. She had gone on and on about his lying and deception and untrustworthiness. Two things in particular had shaken her: the first was the realization that Janet had come up to live in Manchester, and the second was a conviction, bred by the business of the letter, that the two of them were accomplished and practised conspirators. It had really been too bad. He had done his best to explain that the meeting had been necessary, and that nothing had occurred except the formalities of a final break between them, but Beatrice refused to listen. And what he said was absolutely true. Herbert felt weary and defeated. He had had a miserable meeting with Janet. They had arranged to meet in the local recreation ground, and he had been ten minutes late, and, he guessed, Janet had been a good few minutes early. It was an unlovely place. It had been a dull grey afternoon and there had been a biting east wind which sent occasional flurries of sleety rain into their faces. He had carefully not taken Janet's arm when they had met, and she had accepted this with a mute, hopeless, dreary resignation and stuck her hands deep into the pockets of her coat. They had tramped side by side along the strips of asphalt, their coat collars turned up against the cold, while he pointed out to her the risks for himself which would be involved in his seeing her. He had explained everything very lucidly and very gently, and she had bitten her lip and nodded, and tried to smile.

'A clean break will be easier for both of us,' he had said, and she had agreed with him.

'It'll be better this way, Janet. I mean, we had already decided that our thing was pretty well over, hadn't we?'

She made a curious noise which he interpreted as assenting to this proposition.

'Quite shortly we'll be going down to London anyway,' and he explained Beatrice's insistence on the move, and told her that they were already negotiating for a house in Wimbledon. There had been some manoeuvring about a packet of money. He had put fifty pounds in an envelope ready and timed everything carefully. They had completed their third circuit of the park and were approaching the entrance, where his car was parked.

'All good things come to an end, eh?' He stopped and she turned and faced him and he put his hands on her shoulders. All of a sudden she was sobbing bitterly in his arms and he was trying to soothe her and calm her down.

'Don't cry, Janet. It's not the end of the world, you know. After all, we both of us knew that it was bound to come, it couldn't have gone on for ever. We had good times.' She was crying like a child who is heartbroken at the end of a party or a day at the seaside, great uncontrolled sobs, a dismaying and ludicrous exhibition of feeling which alienated Herbert and made him feel helpless and foolish. He found a handkerchief and dabbed at her eyes with it and urged her to pull herself together. Then he remembered the envelope and tried to put it in her pocket. This produced a fresh outburst on her part, she protested and tried to push it away, but he made her take it.

'It's just a little something just to remember me by. Buy yourself something nice.' After this storm was over Janet had become passive again. She had rejected the offer of a lift back in his car, preferring to stand on the pavement and watch him out of sight, so he settled himself at the driving seat and beckoned her forward for a last kiss. She had pushed her head through the window and given him a very quick kiss on the lips, then she stood back and watched gravely as he started the engine. He had a last glimpse of her standing stockstill, holding the collar of her coat together at the throat with her right hand and waving slowly with her left, then the car turned the corner. And this terrific act of renunciation was fresh in his memory when Beatrice had pitched into him. Later on he blamed Beatrice for a good deal that had happened. If she had only been a bit more forbearing, if she had made some effort to see his point of view, then he might have been able to make a go of it, but when she treated him like this, then she had only herself to blame if things went wrong again.

Herbert was suddenly aware that Winnick had spoken to him.

'I said, would you mind, sir, telling me about those meetings with Wilfred and Florence? You obviously saw a good deal of them in those last months.'

'Nothing much to tell,' said Herbert, 'they were both of them just as usual.'

'Wilfred was in his normal spirits?'

'He was always the same was Wilfred, full of his schemes.'

Winnick was interested in this and asked about these schemes. What had they been? What about these experiments the newspapers had been so full of?

'They were nothing, nothing at all, just child's things. He did demonstrations at the technical college, that was all, passing steam over iron filings to get hydrogen, that sort of thing.'

Winnick, as he made a note of this, wondered about Herbert's tone, it was so openly contemptuous, he sounded positively hostile, and Winnick wondered why.

'All that about poisons, then, was not true?'

'Poisons. Where would Wilfred have got hold of poisons? He didn't have any qualifications, you know. Besides, what have poisons got to do with it? Florence was not poisoned.'

'Well, the papers – '

But Herbert was terribly insulting about the papers and the men who wrote in them. He produced a sudden explosion of anger which took Winnick by surprise. Herbert had noticed that if Winnick was attacked he drew back into his shell and returned the conversation to neutral topics, and this observation had emboldened him. He did not much like the line that the fellow was taking, and he could see that Beatrice did not like it either, so it was safe for him to take a strong tone about it.

'Those newspaper men got everything wrong. We had a lot of trouble with those people, prying into everything, pushing their noses everywhere they weren't wanted. All they were interested in was stirring up as much muck as possible. I could tell you some of the things they did.'

He shot a venomous look at Winnick as he said this, and was gratified to hear him bleating something about 'disgraceful sensationalism' and the 'gutter press', before he hastily turned to Beatrice again.

Having disposed of this danger Herbert fell to brooding. The less said about his visits to Herriott Street the better. At first both he and Florence had behaved with the utmost propriety. Florence and Wilfred had come down to Wimbledon for a house-warming in July, and he had treated her with absolute correctness. It had been very like the days immediately following his marriage. The first time he had visited Herriott Street Wilfred had been at home and he had had a rather dull evening listening to stories about the technical college and somebody called Dobson, apparently on the staff there, who, in Wilfred's opinion, had not the least idea of the right way to teach his classes. Once or twice, it seemed to Herbert, Florence would look at him rather oddly, as if she was trying to fathom what was going on in his mind. At the end of the evening he shook hands with Wilfred and gave Florence a chaste peck on the cheek and said how pleasant it had been.

'I've enjoyed our little chat,' said Wilfred, 'don't forget to look us up whenever you're over.'

Florence merely asked him to give her love to Beatrice. She looked at him steadily as she spoke, and Herbert thought that he detected a slight smile on her lips. Was she mocking him? Was she enjoying his discomfiture? Or was she daring him to renew his advances? Herbert wondered how long her annoyance over his apparent desertion of her would last. He was certain that she expected him to make a new approach, but he did not know whether she intended to surrender gracefully after a decent show of reluctance, or to snub him and send him away with his tail between his legs. He did not wish to risk a snub, but surely by now she must sometimes wish to resume their affair. Life with Wilfred must be deadly dull for her, and he, Herbert, represented her only escape from that life. For his own part Herbert freely confessed that the old obsession was as strong as ever. He could not drive thoughts of Florence out of his mind. Memories of their affair tantalized him, and the old habit of registering and mentally rehearsing brief scenes, which he encountered in his reading or which suggested themselves to his imagination, grew strong again. On his next visit also, he was unlucky. Wilfred was again at home, busily constructing some weird and wonderful models of the solar system for use with one of his classes at the 'Tech', as he by now nonchalantly called it.

'It's to scale,' he explained proudly. 'This is just our own immediate system, as I shall tell them. And do you know, Herbert, on the same scale as this, whereabouts do you think the nearest star would be? On the same scale as this, mind.'

Herbert had to confess that this was a problem which completely baffled him.

'It's difficult to believe, I know. I'm going to ask them to suggest why it would be difficult to complete the model, and then I'll tell them. On the same scale as this, Herbert, the sun here, the earth here, the moon here, on the same scale, the nearest star would be just beyond Moscow. Isn't that an astonishing thing?'

Herbert resisted the temptation to ask how far beyond Moscow, and dutifully agreed that it was really astonishing. He had no private talk with Florence, but he did manage to leave her a book, with some passages marked.

It had been slow work. On his third visit Wilfred had been out, but Florence had greeted him rather stolidly, and when he addressed her as 'Rose' and began talking about the book he had left, she had sharply told him not to start that old foolishness again. In fact, on this occasion he had unwisely worked himself up into such a pitch of frustrated sexual longing that he had finally stormed out of the house in a fury. That was when he had gone round to the lodging-house to seek out Janet once again. Not only did he need some sort of companionship, but he felt, obscurely, that his going served both Florence and Beatrice right.

It had taken another two visits to bring Florence round fully. It was the old challenge. He was not content to allow her to remain aloof. He had to demonstrate to himself that, if he wished, he could bring her to do as he wanted. He believed that she wished him to continue making his advances to her, and in order to prove this he must go on making them until she yielded. Every rejection increased his determination. In the end Florence gave in quite suddenly. He had begun the evening by behaving quite well, greeting her in a carefully neutral way, showing no emotion when she told him that Wilfred was attending a meeting at the chess club, and answering her questions about Beatrice quite obediently. Then she had looked at him in an odd way and said, out of the blue, that she was expecting a friend of hers round.

'It's somebody you'll be quite glad to see, Herbert.'

Only one meaning could be attached to this.

'Is it my friend Rose?'

'She's been looking at that book you left.'

'What did she think of it?'

'It has possibilities, particularly the second of the scenes you marked.'

'I thought she would like that one, I did myself.'

They had both caught again the light, slightly self-mocking tone of their earlier trips from Wilmslow.

'Mind you,' said Florence, 'she thinks that the girl was a

bit of a fool to behave like that. She should have shown a bit more spirit, she should have given him as good as she got.'

'In that case,' Herbert stared at his boots, 'she would have to expect that Sir Roger would deal with her rather more roughly.'

'I suppose she would,' agreed Florence, and they fell to earnestly discussing the scene and planning a game based on it. Herbert, without actually touching Florence, made a sketch of a possible course of action that Sir Roger might have taken, passing his hands over her cheek, neck and breasts, and she had agreed that his suggestion was natural and effective. Soon they were both on their feet experimentally going through the actions of the scene, laughing over the stupidly melodramatic dialogue that Herbert invented to accompany it, working themselves up to the final performance. In this way they resumed their previous practices and, for a time, Herbert regained his peace of mind.

It had not required all this palaver for Herbert to take up with Janet again. His first appearance at the lodging-house had caused a slight awkwardness because he was not expected, but that had been the only difficulty. He had left Herriott Street, after his row with Florence, in a considerable fury and walked towards the main road without forming any clear idea of what he was going to do with himself. Then he had seen a taxi cruising by, an unexpected sight in that locality, and hailed it on impulse. When the man asked him where he wanted to be taken Herbert gave him the address of the lodging-house. It was quite unplanned, the address just came into his mind and during the short drive Herbert wondered if he had done a wise thing. He paid off the taxi and looked up at the dingy outside of the building. It had 'third-rate' written all over it, and Herbert was half inclined to turn his back on it and return to his hotel, but he slowly climbed the steps to the front door and pulled the bell-chain. There was a tinny clatter inside and then lights began to show through the stained-glass panels in the door. There was a sliding of bolts and turning of keys, and finally the door opened to the extent of a stout chain and a face appeared at him.

'No vacancies,' the face said.

'I'm not looking for lodgings,' said Herbert.

'Not looking for lodgings? I hope you're not visiting at this time of night.'

Herbert began to see better as his eyes adjusted to the light. He saw that the face belonged to a woman who was elderly, rather stout, and that the one eye that was visible glared at him suspiciously.

'I just happened to be in the district,' he began to explain when there was a commotion in the hall behind the stout woman, and he heard Janet's voice.

'It's all right, Mother, I'll attend to it.'

Janet did not immediately have her way. Her mother made protesting, grumbling noises, and Herbert heard Janet's voice urging her to get back to her room and not to worry, and to behave herself. Eventually she drew back from the door and the guard chain was released, and the door was opened to him. Janet stood there staring at him amazedly. Behind her, Herbert could see her mother, singularly unlike the aristocratic figure he had imagined for Janet's parent. She was stout and her face was red, almost purple even, in colour. She was rather shapeless, being swaddled in layers of shawls and wraps, and on her head she wore what Herbert believed, though he had never seen one before, was called a mob-cap. She was lingering by her door wheezing and eyeing her daughter until Janet shooed her inside.

'Go along, Mother, I'll attend to this gentleman, go along.' Her voice was sharp and scolding, it had an edge to it that Herbert had never heard before, and he made a mental note that Janet was not all self-effacing gentleness. When her mother had gone inside she made sure that the door was properly shut before turning to Herbert.

'Well,' she said at last, 'this is a surprise. Why didn't you tell me you were coming? I could have tidied myself up.' Further down the hall another door had opened and a disembodied head was sticking out watching them. 'It's all right, Mr Gentian,' said Janet, 'you can go in now, it's not for you.' The head hung there for a moment longer and was then abruptly withdrawn. 'Nosey old devil,' said Janet. 'Come along, Herbert, we'll go to my room.'

On the right of the hall was a short flight of steps leading to a third door and this was the way Janet took him. Through the door was a further, longer flight leading to Janet's apartment. She carefully locked the door at the foot of the stairs, and she also locked the door of her room when they were inside it.

'It's the only way to get a bit of privacy,' she explained in reply to his questioning gaze. 'When I lock that door at the bottom there I really feel that I've got away from them all. Ma didn't want me to have these rooms, she said we could let them, but I told her I wasn't going to live in that basement, not for anybody. "I've got to have somewhere I can call my own," I said. How do you like it?' She was talking rapidly and nervously. She showed him over her 'suite' as she called it, and Herbert found that it was, in fact, two rooms, because at the far end there was a tiny little cupboard of a place which had been made into a bedroom, and which resembled nothing so much as the cabin of a small boat or caravan. Everything was very neatly arranged and ingenious use had been made of the very limited space available. Herbert was puzzled at first by an odd sense of familiarity, as though he had seen the room before, and then realized that it had been set out in imitation of the flat Janet had had in London, with the same trinkets, many of which he had given her himself, in the same places. He commented on this.

'I did it to remind myself so that I could get up here and pretend that I was back. But I never expected that you'd see it all. Let's have a look at you.'

She was beginning to get over her first nervousness and

she put her hands on his shoulders and held him at arms' length in front of her. As she took stock of him so he took stock of her. She was not looking well. Her face was pale, yellowish almost. There were circles under her eyes and her hair straggled untidily over her shoulders. When he took her in his arms and kissed her he caught the unmistakable smell of stale cooking which clung to her hair and clothes. She pulled away from him rather quickly.

'I wish I'd known you were coming, I'd have made myself look beautiful for you.'

'You do look beautiful, Janet.'

'Oh, what a fibber. I look awful, I know I do, but it's your own fault for not telling me. Where have you come from? I thought you were in London.'

She got his coat off him and sat down and offered him something to eat, but he refused this. He explained that he was back on business and that, of course, he was not supposed to be there.

'I'm disobeying orders,' he said frankly. 'My wife has given me strict instructions not to come here but I wanted to see how you were getting on so I thought I'd risk it.' He went on to explain about Beatrice's instructions that he must spend each evening with his sister-in-law and Wilfred. 'She thinks that'll keep me out of mischief, but I left early and slipped round here. You're not angry with me, are you?'

'Of course I'm not angry with you.' Herbert was occupying the only comfortable chair in the room, but as she said this Janet settled herself on the arm and cradled his head in her arms. 'I'd been wishing that you'd come. I've missed you, Herbert. It's been a year almost.'

'I've missed you, Janet. It's a pity it all had to end like that.'

'Still,' she replied, 'it would have happened anyway, I mean me having to come home like that. Do I look absolutely awful, Herbert?'

'What do you mean?'

'Well, I know I don't look like I did in London. It's this house, it gets me down sometimes. And you should have seen your face when I let you in. I knew exactly what you were thinking.'

'What was I thinking?'

'You were wishing you hadn't come. Isn't that true, Herbert Naismith?'

She looked into his eyes and gave his hair an affectionate tug as she said this. He was startled because it was quite true.

'No, of course not,' he said.

'Oh, yes it is. You're not a good liar, Herbert, your face gives you away.'

Herbert put his arm round her waist and drew her down on to his knee.

'Dear, dear,' he said, 'I must practise then.' He undid the buttons at the throat of her blouse.

'Give me a bit of warning next time and I won't be so much of a fright,' she said.

'You're not a fright, Janet.' He had the blouse open to the waist. 'Let's see if you're the same underneath.'

'But you will let me know next time?'

'Yes, I'll let you know next time.'

'And you are coming again, aren't you?' She peered at him anxiously.

'Yes, I'm coming again.'

'Promise.'

'I promise.'

20

'It was about the trial that I was hoping that you would be able to help me, sir.' As he said this Winnick bent down and drew from his briefcase a sheaf of papers so large that it seemed impossible that he was in need of any help at all. It looked, to Herbert's jaundiced eye, that there was far more in his hand than had ever figured in the trial itself. 'You were present throughout, I believe, sir?'

Herbert nodded, and Beatrice chipped in eagerly.

'He stood by Wilfred the whole time. He was the only friend Wilfred had.' She was pleased to be able to say this. The recent questioning had put Herbert in a very unpleasant position, and she wanted to pay full tribute to his conduct in the hour of crisis.

'It must have been a painful experience for you,' said Winnick.

Again Herbert assented, though the word seemed to him to be weak. Something stronger than 'painful' was needed to do justice to his state of mind through the five days of the trial. He had never expected that Wilfred would be charged with the murder. He had been well out of the way, engaged on his search for Welfield Road East, that was what Herbert had thought. The theory of the wandering intruder, alarmed at his work and lashing out in panic, had been the one Herbert had hoped would gain credence. He had been appalled by the stupidity of the police. They had got one idea lodged in their heads and nothing would alter it. Later, long after the event, he was able to see their point of view better, and to wonder at the astonishing way in which his little bit of plotting had coiled around Wilfred's neck. That telephone call to Wilfred's office just after Wilfred had left the building, it had been sheer chance that the call had been traced. If he had not muffed it and gone through the operator then no one would have known where it came from; but Herbert was used to having his calls dialled for him. It had been suggested that it had been a diabolical plot against Wilfred. The caller was an enemy of Wilfred's who had deliberately drawn attention to the call so that it would be traced. But there had been no plot, just a moment's carelessness, and there it all was, proved in court by a troop of telephone operators, post office engineers, girls from Wilfred's office, members of amateur dramatic societies.

'You say the accused produced a play for you?'

'In nineteen twenty-six, yes.'

'I suppose, in the course of his duties, he demonstrated how some of the parts should be read?'

'Oh, yes.'

'Did you form any opinion as to his powers of impersonation?'

'Er – ' the witness was gravelled.

'His powers as an actor?'

'Oh, yes, he was very good.'

This, in the opinion of the Prosecuting Counsel, was substantial evidence against Wilfred. It proved that Wilfred had been calm enough and skilful enough to disguise his voice so expertly that the girls in his own office, who talked to him nearly every day, would be deceived. It did not trouble this Counsel, nor anybody else apparently, that he also had to suggest that Wilfred had been so agitated that he had muffed the dialling and had to ring the operator. It would be all down there, Herbert supposed, in the bundle of papers Winnick was clutching, all the maddening, trivial details that had occupied so much of the court's time. It would be meat and drink to Winnick. He had the same love of minutiae that the lawyers had shown, and the same casual attitude to the really important matters. The matter of motive, for instance, the judge in his summing up had dismissed that in three or four sentences, and then he had spent a quarter of an hour going over the complicated and difficult evidence given by the expert witnesses about the condition of the lock upon the back door of Wilfred's house. Herbert had sat there in the court day by day, while the police manufactured their case against Wilfred, helpless to do anything about it, not even sure that he wanted to do anything about it because he knew that everything that strengthened the case against Wilfred made his own position safer. And in the meantime Janet was nagging at him, pestering him with questions, refusing to be reassured, dropping alarming hints about going to the police. Herbert had to return from scenes like this to the court room, or to Wilfred's cell, where he had to appear composed and normal. Everybody had commented on Wilfred's fortitude, it was almost a pity that his own had, in the nature of things, had to pass unremarked. 'Painful', no, 'painful' hardly did justice to the case.

'Everybody has suggested that Wilfred seemed to be far too calm in the witness box. Did you think this?' asked Winnick.

'He was calm,' Herbert agreed, 'but then he would have despised himself if he had not been. He always tried to be rational about everything, it was his great pride. To him a trial was like a sort of scientific enquiry, it was an attempt to get at the truth, and emotion was out of place there.'

Winnick stared at Herbert, his hand suspended over his pad.

'You don't seriously mean that he could be as detached as that about his own trial?'

Herbert drew back into his corner again. It was funny. In the early days he had been afraid of speaking the truth about Wilfred, afraid that if people began believing that Wilfred was innocent then they would begin asking who was guilty, but he realized quite soon that those fears were unfounded. Nobody would believe the truth about Wilfred. The prejudice against him was too great, it always had been. At the time of the trial men and women who had no more acquaintance with him than was obtainable from a smudgy newspaper photgraph gathered in the streets to shake their fists at police vans which, they fondly believed, contained him. Stones had been flung with monotonous frequency through the windows of the Herriott Street house, and one or two even, in an excess of zeal, through the windows of the house next door. Whenever he was taken from or to the court a medium-sized party assembled to boo him.

From the newspapers Herbert learned that his brother-in-law was cold, calculating and inhuman in his appearance, that he showed no feeling, that he was crafty and cunning beyond belief and addicted to unnatural pursuits like philosophy, scientific experiment, and chess, all of which made it eminently likely that he was a murderer. It was Wilfred's misfortune that he had always lacked the ability to convey any warmth of personality. Herbert could remember him as a boy, standing on the fringes of groups, not liking to push himself in and never being invited to join the others. If he had felt any disappointment at these rebuffs he had been careful not to show it: he had far too much pride for this. What he had striven for was independence, he had tried to become self-sufficient, he always hated being beholden to anybody. Herbert could remember once, in the days after the war when he was still supposed to be pursuing his accountancy course, he had had to get a form signed by some sponsor. The sponsor committed himself to nothing, it cost him nothing except the effort of scratching his signature on the form, but Wilfred had been astonishingly reluctant.

'I don't see why I should have to go crawling on my hands and knees to old Gatesby to get him to sign this for me.'

'It's no trouble,' Mr Calderwood had urged him, 'it doesn't mean anything.'

'If it doesn't mean anything why do it?'

'Because,' Mr Calderwood had pointed out, 'if you don't, you won't be allowed to take the examination.'

'That's no reason. Why should I have to put myself under an obligation to a pompous old ass like Gatesby before I can take their examination?'

He did not care to be helped, he felt a jagged resentment against those whom he was obliged to approach. He would accept whatever was his due, but he would accept it as a right not as a gift. There had once, Herbert remembered, been something wrong with the accounts at the office. It was not suggested at any time that Wilfred was at fault, but his reaction was characteristic of him. He demanded an interview with the manager, insisted on seeing the accountant and having his own books looked at in the closest detail, and would not rest until he had a statement from them that his accounts were in perfect order. He had told the tale more than once later on. 'I think I taught them a bit of a lesson. I felt entitled, with my record, to see that things were properly done. I said to them, "I have no objection to you looking at my accounts, you have the right, of course. But I think I have the right to see that it is properly and fairly done, and when you find that they are in order I think I have the right to an acknowledgement of that fact." They couldn't answer that one. McGregor could see that he was in the wrong.'

It had probably damaged Wilfred's chances of promotion, but he cared not a straw for that. He was not going to kow-tow to them, touch his forelock, say 'thank you very much for not finding anything out about me'. That, he assured Herbert, was what a lot of the chaps would have done, but it was not his style.

Herbert remembered one conversation with him about this very question of trials. Wilfred had been arguing that the legal profession and the legal system were in some degree contradictory. Barristers claimed to win cases for their clients, and yet it was maintained that a court of law was there to discover the truth, and that innocent men had nothing to fear at the hands of British justice. He mentioned this to Winnick in support of what he had been saying about Wilfred's attitude.

'It was typical of Wilfred,' he said, 'I can remember it very well. He said that if ever he came into court he wouldn't bother with a lawyer at all. "I should just say to the judge," he said, "here I am. You've asked me to come here so that you can decide whether I am guilty or innocent. Ask me any questions you want and I'll answer them as truthfully as I can. Mind you, I don't promise to tell the whole truth, no human being on earth can tell the whole truth about anything whatsoever – " you remember how Wilfred used to talk, Beatrice – "I should tell the judge straight out," he said, "we don't need any lawyers to twist things about." I often thought about that later.'

Winnick scribbled the words down; he was not quite sure how he would be able to use them, but he scribbled them down. He was grateful for this evidence of Herbert's loosening up; the old fellow might turn up trumps after all.

'It shows a certain arrogance on Wilfred's part, doesn't it?'

'He used to talk like that. He always thought that he had the answer to everything, that he knew how everything should be done – that was why a lot of people didn't like him. But my point is that that was how he thought the thing should be done. It actually offended him when they kept bringing emotion into it. He thought the Prosecuting Counsel behaved disgracefully.'

Herbert had not liked the Counsel for the Prosecution himself. His name was Savernant. He was a big bland man with dark, oily hair and a yellowish face. He could look very knowing, and he had cultivated the knack of sharing little confidences with the jury by means of winks and gestures and grimaces interpolated into the proceedings at strategic points. Savernant's treatment of Wilfred had been deadly.

'He kept harping on the blood and the appearance of the body,' said Herbert. Winnick made a little flourish out of finding the place in his transcript and passed it across to Herbert to read, with the comment, 'That was one of the places where, it seemed to me, Wilfred came off very badly.'

Herbert agreed. Wilfred had made up his mind not to lose control of himself in the box, and this decision had lost him the sympathy of the court. Herbert, who knew Wilfred, could see what a strain he was under, but nobody else was likely to because Wilfred betrayed his feelings in such small ways. He would rapidly blink his eyes, the muscles of his neck would tighten, he would caress the edge of his jacket with his left hand. These were the only outward signs of mental disturbance. His voice remained level, almost toneless; his mind had been quite clear. Savernant had badgered him about the body, repeatedly asking him to describe how he had found it, its position, the state of the room. Wilfred had answered meticulously.

'The body was lying across the room, diagonally. The head was near the wall behind the door, the legs were pointing towards the opposite corner.'

'What was the state of the body?'

'It – it had been very savagely attacked.'

'With what kind of instrument?'

'A club, a metal bar, something like that, perhaps.'

'Was there a great deal of blood?'

Wilfred thought carefully before answering.

'There was a great deal of blood, yes.'

The newspapers had described this speech as being delivered 'without a flicker of emotion', but Herbert did not agree. Savernant had directed a significant look towards the jury as much as to say, 'A cold fish, this one', and had then gone on to torment Wilfred with a series of questions.

'There were pools of blood?'

'Yes.'

'Pools of blood on the floor?'

'At one side of the room, yes.'

'Was the blood anywhere else?'

'Splashes – on the walls.'

'Did you examine the body closely?'

'Yes, to see if she was dead.'

'How did you examine it?'

'I knelt down beside it and looked closely.'

'Did you touch it?'

'No.'

'Get any blood on yourself?'

'No.'

'How remarkably careful of you. Pools of blood all over the place, the body soaked with blood, splashes all over the walls, and you don't get a single spot on you.'

'No,' said Wilfred. Savernant shared another of his confidential looks with the jury. Afterwards Wilfred confessed to Herbert, 'It was all I could do to keep a grip on myself. I felt like bursting out at the man.'

Winnick discussed the exchange with Herbert, expressing the opinion that Savernant had made a strong point. Herbert agreed.

'Savernant was a clever chap. Sir Charles they made him later, not because of this case though. But Wilfred could see what his game was. If he'd broken down it would have been just the same, only then Savernant would have said that he'd broken down because he couldn't bear to think of what he had done. He was just working up prejudice against Wilfred.'

Winnick assented politely, but Herbert could see that he was not impressed by this argument, and yet it was true. Savernant had been a great one for getting things both ways. He had spent a lot of time establishing a picture of Wilfred as a man who was inhumanly cold and passionless, and yet his theory of the crime required one to believe that this passionless man had battered his wife to death in a fit of blind fury. It seemed to the lawyer that these two ideas went very logically together.

'It was the same,' continued Herbert, talking more for Beatrice's benefit than Winnick's, 'with the questions about the life Wilfred and Florence had led together. Wilfred said that they had been perfectly happy, and Savernant simply made a mockery of this.'

Winnick had the place in a jiffy, it was wonderful how this man had got his material up, and what a display he made of it. He consulted his dossier with an exaggerated, theatrical flicking back of the pages, a careful pursing of the lips, a pseudo-judicious glance down the length of the page to check that it was the right one, followed by a flick of the head to indicate that he was with you again.

'Here it is. Day Three,' and he held out the page for Herbert to verify. 'This is the passage you mean?'

Herbert read for himself the celebrated exchange.

'You have described matters between your wife and yourself as quite perfect. Now, tell us what you mean by that.'

It was odd, thought Herbert, as he read this, how incomplete the transcript was. Reduced to mere print on the page the words had lost an essential part of their meaning. He could remember Savernant's voice as he had asked the question. Before the words 'quite perfect' he had paused and made an elaborate show of consulting his notes, so that when he spoke them they came out with a sardonic emphasis. Wilfred's reply had been slightly testy and chilly, a rebuke to this insinuation, and his voice had quivered almost imperceptibly as he made it.

'Perfect is a very strong word,' Savernant had continued. 'I have known many married couples myself who got on excellently together, but I don't know that I would say of any of them that they had a "perfect" relationship.'

Wilfred made a tiny gesture with his hands, which conveyed to Herbert, who knew him, that Counsel's judgements on his friends were his own business. Savernant continued the questioning.

'You never quarrelled?'

'Never.'

'Not even a little tiff?'

'No.'

This reply brought more by-play from Savernant's eyebrows in the direction of the jury. Wilfred stood like a stone image, and his answers were given in the kind of voice one might expect a stone image to use, if it had a voice.

'You were out quite a lot, weren't you?'

'Yes.'

'In the evenings, I mean. You had various commitments?'

'Yes.'

'What were they?'

'I was a member of a chess club.' Wilfred stared straight in front of him and spoke as though he was reciting a lesson. He told Herbert later that he could not trust himself to look in the direction of Savernant. 'I played the violin in an amateur orchestra, I did some work at the local institute.'

'So you were out quite a good deal. The house wasn't so perfect that you wanted to stay in it much?'

Wilfred blinked, but he answered in a controlled, neutral tone. 'It was part of the perfection of our relationship that my wife did not grudge me any of my outside interests.'

For several seconds Savernant stared at Wilfred, his yellow face was set in a sneer, his lips curled.

'Really,' he said, and turned his face to give the jury the full benefit of his drollery. He had then gone on to question Wilfred about his other pursuits, making them all sound rather comic and trivial, and had led up to the matter of Wilfred's scientific experiments.

'Where did you conduct these experiments of yours?'

'Upstairs in the back room.'

'That is the room at the top of the stairs, opposite the bathroom?'

'Yes.'

'The room where your wife was bludgeoned to death?'

'Yes.'

It was an unexpected thrust, but Wilfred had not even quivered. He told Herbert, later, that he had decided, as the only means of defiance open to him, to reply merely 'yes' or 'no' whenever this was possible, and not to give Savernant the satisfaction of seeing him wince or flinch, whatever he said. Herbert, sitting in the public gallery, could see what this calm lost him in the eyes of the audience. There had been an audible, involuntary intake of breath, and an instantly suppressed chatter. Savernant had beamed at the members of the jury.

'And you described these – er – experiments at the local Institute, did you say?'

'I lectured at the Institute, yes.'

'I beg your pardon, I should have said "lectured".'

This had got a little laugh. Wilfred said later that it had taken all his self-control not to rise to the calculated impertinence with which Savernant had invested the last word.

'Mind you, it wasn't only Savernant's treatment that infuriated Wilfred,' said Herbert, 'he'd been warned to expect that. It was the whole conduct of the trial, he felt that it was biased and unfair.'

'And was it?' asked Winnick. 'What did you think?'

'The police had no case, no case at all. The direct evidence was very slim, and they did some very queer things. They got that woman to change her evidence, you know.'

Winnick found the place, like a terrier retrieving a bone.

'Mrs Kershaw, the one who spoke to Florence last of all. I wanted to ask you about her.'

It had been a notorious point. Originally she had said that she spoke to Florence Rimmer at twenty-five to seven, but at ten to seven Rimmer himself had been seen climbing on to a tram a quarter of a mile away. Later the lady had discovered that she had been mistaken, and that it was just after six when she had seen her.

'She was got at,' said Herbert, 'everybody knew that she had been got at.'

'But surely,' said Winnick, 'that made her evidence worthless.'

'Of course it did,' said Winnick, 'and that was exactly what the police wanted. I think a lot of people thought that she'd never seen Florence at all, that she made the whole thing up just to get her name into the papers. All that the police wanted was that there would not be anybody, not anybody that the jury would believe, saying that Florence was alive at twenty-five to seven. If she was alive then the whole case against Wilfred simply collapsed.'

Winnick noticed how animated Herbert had suddenly become. He had leaned forward in his chair, he had emphasized his words with his fist in the palm of his hand, his tone expressed a querulous impatience with Winnick's obtuseness. 'By Jove,' Winnick thought, 'the old chap's really worked up about this.'

Herbert leaned back and tried to calm himself. He must be careful not to seem too involved. But it was a point on which he had dwelt frequently and bitterly. When he had first heard of the woman's evidence it had seemed to him to be the perfect answer. She had come forward of her own free will, proud in the knowledge that she had been the last person to see the victim of this notorious murder alive. She had been photographed leaving the police station, she had been interviewed by newspaper reporters, and this taste of publicity had gone to her head. She had been so anxious that nobody else should jump her claim that she had fixed the time of her meeting with Florence Rimmer as late as possible and then, prompted by the police, she realized that she had overreached herself. If her evidence was accepted there would be no trial, she would not be the heroine of a court drama, there would be nothing, whereas, suppose she discovered that her memory had been at fault, it is so easy to make a mistake of that kind, could it have been twenty, twenty-five, even thirty minutes earlier? Her memory had proved conveniently pliable, and Wilfred had hanged. If only she had stuck to her original story everything would have been all right, and Herbert would have been spared much mental agony. Yes, that woman had a lot to answer for. Part, at least, of the reason why Janet had turned against him had been because of Wilfred. Janet's suspicions had only gradually acquired momentum. At first, in fact, she had taken no notice of the crime at all, because the name Rimmer meant nothing to her. When, as he occasionally did, he talked with her about Florence and Wilfred he had never mentioned their surname, nor had he specified the district where they lived. They were only mentioned as the joke couple who, his wife supposed, were keeping an eye on him while he was in Manchester. So when Janet read about this obscure woman who had been battered to death in a seedy part of the city, it never struck her to connect the affair with Herbert. In the weeks after the murder he neglected Janet, his hands were full trying to run a business and look after Wilfred, and it was not until shortly before the trial that he was reminded of her existence. He returned to the Midland Hotel, where he always stayed when he was in Manchester, to be given a message from her asking him to get in touch immediately. He assumed that she wanted to see him about the murder and wondered, rather fearfully, what she was going to say, but the interview took him by surprise. She had only just realized, she said, who it was that had been killed.

'It was when I saw the picture in the paper this morning,' she said. 'It gave me quite a turn.'

A newspaper had published an article about the forthcoming trial, and had illustrated it with a photograph taken a few weeks earlier of Wilfred arriving at the court for the committal proceedings. On the left-hand side of the picture, supporting Wilfred's arm, was Herbert. Janet had recognized the picture and realized, with a shock, her lover's involvement in the case.

'I'm sorry,' he said. 'I should have got in touch.'

'Oh, I didn't mean that. I didn't expect you to think of me at a time like this. It must have been awful for you, your own sister-in-law.' She rattled on in an inconsequential way. As she chattered Herbert realized that she did not have her mind on what she was talking about. She was clearly nervous, but whatever it was she wanted to speak to him about it had nothing to do with the murder.

'It was quite a shock seeing your picture like that,' she said again. 'I'd been wondering how I could get hold of you, and then I saw it. I guessed you'd be staying at the Midland. You always do, don't you?'

'What did you want to see me about, Janet? There isn't anything wrong, is there?'

'I'm not sure,' she said. She could not keep still, she was forever twitching her head about, unable to look at him steadily. 'There may be. The fact is, Herbert, I think I'm pregnant.'

Herbert swore to himself. Outwardly he behaved impeccably, his face expressed the right blend of concern and reassurance, but he swore. It only wanted this. All his other troubles, and now this.

'Have you seen your doctor about it?'

'I couldn't possibly. He'd tell my mother.'

Herbert was perfectly calm, in control, masterful.

'The first thing we must do,' he said, 'is to get you to a doctor. We can't do anything else until we're sure.'

Exactly what he meant by 'anything else' he could not have said. If she was pregnant then, presumably, there were people who would arrange that sort of thing if one was prepared to pay. He did not know if this kind of arrangement was what Janet had in mind, and he did not want to suggest it just at this moment. If she went through with it and had the child it would be a devil of a business, he knew that. One thing was quite certain, Beatrice must not get to know about it. He would pay whatever was necessary, but Beatrice must be protected. Janet must see that secrecy was essential. If a thing like this got out at this time it would be disastrous. The newspapers would pillory him. It would all get mixed up with this Wilfred business, and God knew where it would end. Fortunately Janet was at least as anxious to keep it quiet as he was.

'Oh, I know, it would be awful.'

'Those newspaper men would be on us like flies. You don't know them. I do.'

'I don't want anybody to know, Herbert. It's Mother I'm worried about. With her heart the way it is it would kill her.'

Herbert was soothing immediately.

'Now don't you worry. You'll be all right. I'll see to all that. You go and see a doctor. I'll send you an address. But whatever he says don't you worry. I'll see that you'll be taken care of.'

Herbert did not stay much longer. As he explained, he had to get back to Wilfred.

21

This news which Janet had broken to him was the added burden which Herbert had had to carry through the period of the trial and afterwards. Somehow he had had to find time to visit her regularly, every day if possible. He had had to see that she made arrangements to visit a doctor and be properly examined, he had had to cheer her up while they waited for the results of the tests, and he had had to soften the shock as much as possible when the doctor confirmed that she was pregnant. The news reduced her to a state of abject terror. Whatever would she do if her mother found out? In her state the disgrace would kill her. If she survived she would never forgive her daughter. Janet had no other friends, nobody she could turn to for advice or comfort except Herbert himself.

'You must learn to relax, to calm down. You'll hurt yourself, you'll hurt the child if you go on like this. It's not the end of the world, you know. It's happened before. I'll look after you, you've nothing to be afraid of there. We must try and get you away somewhere, before your condition becomes obvious. We can say the doctor's ordered a rest, or something. You should be able to get help in to look after the lodging-house. We'll think of something.'

The great comforter was money. Herbert had money, and money would take care of most crises. Janet must be calm and quiet, above all quiet. Every so often Herbert told her how important it was that he should in no way be connected with her condition. He reminded her of the press men and pointed out that if they learnt about the affair her picture would be on every breakfast table in the country.

'I have to go through it day after day with Wilfred,' he said, 'and you've no idea what it means. You mustn't let a whisper of this get out, not a whisper.' He never allowed a meeting to pass without reminding her of the importance of this. If this one condition could be fulfilled, if nothing was said to connect him with the child, then everything else would be all right and she had nothing to worry about.

She suggested telling her brother, and, at first, Herbert was very doubtful. 'You don't mean about me, do you?'

'No, no, of course not, love. Just about me having a baby. He's got to know some time. He might be able to help with Mother.'

Herbert was not at all sure. He would want to know who the father was.

'I won't tell him. I'll say that's my business.'

Very reluctantly Herbert agreed, and on the whole, he was glad he had done so. Herbert had not met Tom, Janet's brother, but he seemed to be a decent sort, and he was very fond of his sister, and he behaved very well. He did not storm about the room, or cast Janet off, or insist that his mother should be told immediately. He talked sensibly about the immediate arrangements and comforted her and calmed her down. After the visit Janet was more cheerful than she had been for some time.

Herbert had dropped a few other hints, but these were not well received. 'You wouldn't – I don't know if you've thought about this – but I think I could arrange for you to see a doctor to have it all put right.'

Janet did not understand. She had seen a doctor, what good would it do to see another one? And how could a doctor put this that had happened to her, right?

'It is possible to have a pregnancy terminated. A doctor can bring it to an end.'

Even after this it was a minute or two before the penny dropped, and then she was dismayed, repelled by the idea.

'Oh, no, Herbert, I couldn't do that. You wouldn't want me to do that, would you? It's my own child, it's our child.'

'It's you I'm thinking of, Janet. You've got to think ahead. It's not only having the child you've got to think of, there's all the time afterwards, bringing him up, all that sort of thing.'

But she pressed her lips together and looked mulish and shook her head, and when she could speak, said, 'I don't want that, Herbert, I'd rather anything than that. I didn't think you'd suggest a thing like that.'

Once or twice he spoke of adoption. Janet did not like the idea but she was not as implacably opposed to it as she had been to abortion. 'It seems so dreadful, giving your own child to somebody else like that.'

'The parents are very carefully chosen, and they're supervised. There'd be no danger. Adopted children are usually very happy indeed.' Herbert had never, to the best of his knowledge, met an adopted child, or known anybody who had adopted one, but he felt entitled to speak confidently on the subject because his own judgement told him that this was what ought to be done with this child now. Janet visited her brother again and mentioned adoption to him; when she returned she was thoughtful.

'I think Tom and Eileen would like to take him.' She always spoke of her baby as 'him'. 'They didn't say anything but when I talked about it to them they sort of looked at one another. They've always wanted to have a child and they've never been able to. It's funny, isn't it?'

Herbert agreed that it was very funny. It would have suited him better if total strangers had taken the baby. There seemed to him to be a possible danger in having it adopted by close relatives, but he did not say anything. After all, nothing had been fixed, and a good many things would have to happen before the actual question of adoption arose. He made a comment on her brother's kindness, it always pleased Janet to hear Tom praised, and hoped that the suggestion would make her feel better.

'You see how it is, you don't need to worry, we'll be able to work something out. Everything's going to be all right.'

She was certainly more relaxed, she even smiled and laughed a little; as he said, she was almost her old self again.

This was the state of things when the trial started. Janet had given only perfunctory attention to the murder. Of course it was terrible, and she felt dreadfully sorry for Wilfred, but her own worries were so pressing that she had no time for anyone else's. She asked Herbert to drop in to see her as often as he could, but she said that she would quite understand if he was not able to.

'It must be awful for you. You don't really think anything will happen to him, do you?'

Herbert made a gesture with his hands that implied that he would not like to commit himself. As far as possible he avoided talking about the case with Janet.

'I hope not,' he said. 'We'll have to wait and see. I'll try and look in.'

'You're very good to me, Herbert. I'm sorry to be such a nuisance. I don't know how you put up with me on top of everything else.'

Herbert had his own key to the lodging-house. He could let himself in at the side door without being seen by anybody. Fortunately the pictures in the papers had been very blurred and poor, but he did not wish to take any chances. After the first day of the trial he called round at his usual time, about nine-thirty. By then all the work for the day had been done, most of the 'guests' were in their rooms and he had a chance of an uninterrupted hour with Janet. She was not in her room when he arrived, so he settled himself in the armchair and began to read the account of the trial in the evening paper which she had left on the chair. Five minutes later he heard her steps on the stairs outside the door, and playfully he hid himself behind the curtain so that he could jump out at her and give her a fright. 'Boo' he said, and seized her round the waist. She spun round with a stifled scream and pulled herself away from him.

'It's only me,' he said. 'I was only teasing. Did I startle you? I'm sorry, I should have thought.'

She did not relax. She stood against the wall watching him warily. Her face gave him a shock. She was absolutely white, under her eyes there were dark circles and she was twitching uncontrollably, she stared at him with a hurt, bewildered hostility.

'Whatever is the matter? Has something happened?' he asked.

She did not answer.

'Janet,' he spoke quite sharply, 'is there anything wrong? Has there been some trouble?'

Her reply was puzzling in the extreme.

'I – I didn't know. I hadn't realized.'

'Hadn't realized what?'

'I read it in the paper. I hadn't realized before.'

'For heaven's sake, Janet, pull yourself together. What hadn't you realized?'

'It was that same night. What happened to Florence, it was that same night. It was that night when you came round here. It was the night – '

She was on the verge of hysteria. Herbert tried to take her into his arms, but she pushed him away. When he tried to kiss her she turned her head on one side so that he could not reach her mouth.

'All the time you were here, she was lying there, like that.'

'It doesn't do to think about it.'

'When you and me were – she was lying there all the time.'

'I know, Janet, but you'll make yourself ill if you go on like this. Whatever has happened to you all of a sudden?'

'It was that very night. The date's in that newspaper. Tuesday, February the tenth, it was that very same Tuesday. That was the night it must have happened because it was the only night we did it.'

Herbert's patience was beginning to wear thin. 'Look, Janet, I know it was that Tuesday, of course I know that. I thought you knew it too. I thought you knew all about it. It's been in the papers for quite a long while now.'

'I didn't know,' Janet muttered sulkily. 'I hadn't really taken any notice.'

Herbert looked at her in dismay. This was very awkward.

He had thought that she had known and that the knowledge had not troubled her. He did not ask her what was wrong, why she was getting hysterical about it, because he knew the answer. He sat down in the chair again. Janet remained against the wall for some time, as though she was anxious to keep as much space as possible between herself and him, but finally she too sat down. She had difficulty in looking at him.

'I read all about it,' she told him. Herbert watched her without speaking. Savernant had opened the case against Wilfred by outlining the points which he hoped to prove; if she had read all that then that was quite enough.

'Herbert,' she said, after a long pause, 'you know when you came to me that evening, you hadn't been round there first, had you?'

'Whatever do you mean? Of course I hadn't. Why do you say a thing like that? I told you, I came straight here from the station.' His voice did not ring true in his own ears.

'You were so wet, Herbert, your coat was so wet. I didn't see how you could have got so wet just coming from the station.'

'I told you, I walked to Piccadilly for a bus. I didn't want to get a taxi, too conspicuous.'

It was no good. He could not get his tone to sound convincing. What would an innocent man say, how would he sound? Would he be puzzled, not really understanding what she was getting at, or would he be angry and resentful at the implications of what she said? He was trying to remember what he had been like when he had appeared in Janet's sitting-room that evening. He had thought that he had made a pretty good show, but perhaps he had been more agitated than he had realized. It was his legs that had given him away. He had had no idea that they had been like that. Florence must have kicked out like the very devil. He had been soaking wet, but that had been easy to explain. She had been so pleased to see him, too. It was over six weeks since he had last been there and his appearance was quite unexpected.

'Herbert,' she had said, running to him and putting her

arms about him, 'how lovely to see you. Oooh! you are wet. Oh, Herbert, you're absolutely soaking wet, you must have been in the rain for hours. Wherever have you been?'

'I walked to Piccadilly to get a bus, a taxi was a bit conspicuous.'

'But where've you come from?'

And then he had told her how he had been up to Glasgow for a conference and on the way back he had suddenly been seized by the whim to leave the train in Manchester and pay her a quick visit. It had all been done on an impulse.

'I suddenly realized how near to you I would be. I can't stop long. There's a train at two o'clock in the morning that I must catch. I've got to be at the office first thing.'

And she had fussed him and thanked him, and said how lovely he was, and what a marvellous surprise it all was.

'Here,' she said briskly, 'you must take your things off and I'll dry them in front of the fire. Just lie back, and I'll take them off for you, shall I? Would you like that?'

So she had acted the nurse, and he had helped her discreetly, and she had pulled his wet things off him.

'Oh, Herbert!'

'Whatever's the matter?' He was quite startled by her sharp exclamation.

'Herbert, whatever have you done? Have you had an accident?'

'Accident? What do you mean?'

'Your legs, they're terrible, they're black and blue, haven't you seen them?'

Herbert looked down. It was certainly a shock. His left thigh, both his shins, the right ankle, and the side of his right foot were a blackish purple. In a number of places the skin had been broken and blood had trickled down and congealed. Later on he discovered that his left arm was bruised as well. What was curious was that he had not felt a thing. He had had a vague awareness of Florence calling out, and he seemed to remember getting some kind of a knock, she had beaten at him with her fists, but he had easily quieted her. The shock must have dulled his sensations, he supposed. He had seen it in battle, men running about with the most ghastly wounds, apparently quite unconscious of them. He thought very quickly.

'Good heavens, I didn't know it was as bad as that. I – I slipped on some steps at the station, I came quite a cropper. They were wet with the rain.'

What a fuss she had made of him. How she had praised his bravery in saying nothing about it!

'Poor darling, it must have hurt like anything. You didn't want to worry me, did you?'

She had brought a pile of blankets and arranged them in front of the fire, with her eiderdown on top, and he had lain naked on this pile, like an Eastern Caliph, while she had ministered to him. He had drawn her attention to this.

'I feel as though I was in my harem with my favourite slave girl attending to my every need.'

'As long as I'm your favourite slave girl.'

'Yes, but there's one need you aren't attending to.'

'What's that?'

'Come here.'

It ought to have been like this with Florence. That was what Herbert had planned, but he had spoilt it all by being too eager, by taking things for granted. He had been so busy building up his plan in his own mind that he had forgotten that Florence knew, must know, nothing of it. He had been carefully savouring this moment for many days, but he should have remembered that he came upon Florence unannounced, that she was unprepared. He had expected to be welcomed and made a fuss of, whereas Florence had been cold, hostile almost. Her reception of him had been like a smack in the face and, of course, he could not explain. He could not tell her that he had sent her husband on a wild-goose chase in order to leave the evening free for his own operations. How he would have loved telling her of the cleverness of his plan and the adroitness with which he had carried it out, but he did not dare. Finding the address on the map, that had been clever, if you like. Welfield Road East was such a convincing address, it left so many other Welfield Roads, and Avenues, and Crescents, which any man who approached a task thoroughly, as Wilfred invariably did, would have to explore; the search would keep Wilfred happy for hours. When he had stopped off the train on the way up to Glasgow on Monday, and installed himself in the telephone box opposite Wilfred's place of work, he had felt a thrill of real excitement. It was like concocting a devilish ingenious strategic plan in the war, and then seeing it come off perfectly. As punctually as a figure in a mechanical clock Wilfred had emerged from his office building. He had walked so close to the telephone box that if Herbert had leaned out and put out a hand he could have touched him. He put his hand over his face in case Wilfred glanced to one side and saw him. This, in fact, was part of the reason why Herbert muffed the call and had to get in touch with the operator. He had been so busy watching Wilfred that he had misdialled, but that was the only real mistake that he made.

The next evening, on the way back from Glasgow, he had again stopped off in Manchester, only this time he had taken a tram to the point nearest to Herriott Street and waited in a doorway. And good old Wilfred had not let him down. Good old, reliable, punctual little Wilfred, bless him. Ten to seven it would be, that was what Herbert had calculated, ten to seven when Wilfred caught the tram, and there he was, at twelve minutes to, striding along, his face glistening in the rain, a briefcase tucked under his arm, his spectacles glinting in the light of the street lamps. He broke into a jerky trot when he saw his tram coming round the corner, and even as he climbed on board Herbert saw that he engaged the conductor in animated conversation. Herbert would have bet a good sum that he was asking him where Welfield Road East was. Later on Herbert was to learn that he would have won his bet.

Herbert watched Wilfred's tram disappear round the

bend before he left the shelter of his doorway and set out for Herriott Street. It was an abominable evening. The rain was fine and persistent, the sort that wets you by stealth, and it trickled down his neck, and his sleeves and trouser legs clung to his limbs, but his heart was light. He could see nothing now to interfere with his prospects for the evening. The last time he had visited Florence, Wilfred had been at home, so that had been a washout; the time before, Beatrice had been with him; the time before that, Florence had been in one of her lumpish moods. But these successive frustrations had only made Herbert's obsession stronger. Meeting Florence again had become, not merely desirable, but absolutely necessary. He had become restlessly absorbed in schemes to bring it about and now, it seemed to him, he was on the point of achievement. Even this rain was an advantage. Herriott Street was deserted, and the windows of its houses were blank. Not a soul saw Herbert as he walked up the long pavement and turned into the gateway of Number 29. And he was so excited that he made an error of judgement. Forgetting that he was not expected, he took out of his pocket the key that Florence had given him and let himself in. He heard her working in the kitchen, and then she called out, 'Is that you, Wilfred? Did you forget something?'

'Does Wilfred ever forget anything?' was Herbert's reply. Florence was out in an instant.

'Herbert! Whatever are you doing here? I thought you were in Glasgow. There's nothing wrong with Beatrice, is there?'

Herbert reassured her, Beatrice was fine, everything was all right. He explained that he had stopped off on the way back just to look Florence up. Finding himself so near it had seemed silly not to stop and look in on her. He was standing, large and genial, smiling, his hands, metaphorically, outstretched to embrace her. As she assimilated the fact of his presence Florence drew back a little and surveyed him. Her manner was not welcoming.

'Wilfred's out,' she said.

'What a pity. At the Institute?'

'No, he got called out on some insurance business.' As she spoke she looked at him in a thoughtful way. Herbert was puzzled. She seemed hostile to him, but he could not for the life of him think why.

'You'd better take your coat off.' She took it off him and observed that he was wet through. 'Wherever have you been to get as wet as this?'

'I walked and got the tram. I didn't want to be too conspicuous.'

Again there was that look, watchful, and rather puzzled.

'You broke your journey just to look us up?'

'That's right. It seemed a good opportunity.'

'Did you know that Wilfred was going to be out?'

'How on earth should I?'

'I just wondered why you were so anxious not to be conspicuous. You seemed to be very sure of yourself, opening the door like that. Suppose he'd been in?'

Herbert hesitated a fraction.

'I – I saw him getting on to a tram. I'd just got to the stop when he was getting on it.'

It was a close thing. Florence narrowed her eyes and screwed up her lips and put her head on one side and eyed him. It was a look that she used when she suspected that he was up to something and could not quite put her finger on what it was. Herbert realized that Wilfred must have discussed the telephone call with her. Florence was probably struck by the coincidence that Herbert should arrive on the very night when Wilfred had had this unexpected call, apparently ready for frolics. He stared at her blandly, and she gradually relaxed. He could almost see her working the matter out in her mind, deciding that Herbert could not possibly have had anything to do with the call, that it must be sheer chance that had brought him there. She led the way into the kitchen, and Herbert breathed again; he had been very foolish to burst in like that, but he seemed to have got away with it. He sat down in front of the fire realizing, for the first time, how very cold he was. He talked about Beatrice for a few minutes, describing the operation and how much better she was now that it was all over. As he talked he began to make a plan, and finally he said, 'I say, there isn't any water for a bath, is there? It'd warm me up.'

'The fire's been on all day,' answered Florence indifferently, 'the tank should be full. If you leave your things outside the bathroom I'll bring them down and put them to dry.'

This, if not exactly effusive, was a step in the right direction. Herbert felt that he was establishing a cosy, domestic note, reminiscent of the wartime days in Florence's flat. Getting Florence upstairs would be a great trick; the bath had possibilities, or that little room of Wilfred's opposite. There was no hurry, Wilfred could not even have changed trams yet. Herbert stood up slowly.

'Good,' he said, 'I'll just go up, then. I'll give you a call when I've got my things off.'

He went upstairs and began to run the water for the bath. He took off his jacket and dropped it on the floor outside the bathroom, and then he decided to investigate Wilfred's room. He thought of lighting the gaslight so that he could see it better, but he decided that that would have a premeditated look to Florence, and he was not going to make the same mistake twice. There was enough light from the landing for him to see what he wanted. The floor was clear, that was the main thing. In one corner was a pile of camping equipment, including some old blankets and sleeping bags. He made sure that a number of these could be easily reached and spread on the bare floorboards. The work bench, he noticed, was its usual horrible litter of glass tubes, metal pipes, wooden laths, jars, bottles, copper wire, and bits and pieces of electrical and chemical apparatus. It was strange, mused Herbert, that a man with such a meticulous mind as Wilfred should habitually keep his things in such a mess. Herbert went back to the bathroom and turned off the tap. The water in the bath was piping hot, far too hot for the touch. He did not run any cold in; it would have cooled nicely by the time it was needed. Herbert quickly pulled off the rest of his clothes and added them to the heap outside the door. Then he rubbed himself briskly with one of the towels draped over the back of the chair. The bathroom was warm and cosy, and the friction of the towel had brought the circulation back to Herbert's limbs. He began to feel positively cheerful again.

Florence called up to ask if the clothes were ready and he replied that they were. He pushed the door of the bathroom until it was nearly closed and remained behind it peering out through the gap waiting for Florence to come up the stairs. She did not see him. She was picking up his things when he stepped out quietly and seized her. It was a joke. The whole thing was a joke. It was like the trick he had played on Wilfred, just an amusing practical joke, nothing more. Florence would come round, she would be bound to. She was probably just as keen on another romp as he was himself. Pouncing out at her, naked, like this, was perfectly in the key of their earlier games. Of course she struggled, but that was all part of the game too. There had been a time when Herbert had allowed himself to be too easily discouraged by Florence's pretended reluctance, but he had learned not to be so deferential. Subtly she appreciated a show of manly strength to beat down her resistance. So he laughed, and called himself 'Sir Charles' and said that he had come to ravish his 'Rose', and he nuzzled his face in the curve of her neck, and stroked her breasts through her dress. In truth, as he recognized afterwards, his feelings by now were uncontrollable, and he did not wish even to try to control them. It must have looked an odd scene, himself stark naked, Florence furiously angry; Herbert realized when he looked back on it all that she must have been terribly angry with him. It had been an unreal scene. Years of playing these games together had made caution second nature to both of them, so from sheer force of habit, he supposed, Florence had kept her voice to an undertone, hurling frantic abuse at him in a vehement whisper that would not draw the attention of the neighbours. And through it all Herbert had replied to everything she said in the tones, and character, of 'Sir Charles'.

'A saucy varmint,' he said, 'a right pert wench. Methinks milady needs chastisement.'

He was really too far gone to notice in detail Florence's response. He mouthed his nonsenses, and she screamed *sotto voce*, and thumped unavailingly on his chest with her tiny fists, while he easily lifted her bodily and carried her into Wilfred's den.

'A right firebrand,' he raved, 'a very termagant. A whipping will bring you to your senses.'

Herbert was extremely strong, and Florence's greatest efforts made no impression on him at all. He easily held her with one hand while he explored on Wilfred's bench with the other and found one of the wooden laths he had seen there earlier. He mouthed some nonsense about thrashing and whipping, there was a satisfaction even in speaking the words, and produced a very pleasing effect by swishing the lath in the air close to Florence's body. Once, by mistake, he actually caught her a smart blow on the leg which made her yelp. And all the time he pressed her to him and breathed into her ear the stupid phrases, remembered from a score of bad romantic novels, which had served them so often in these games before. But she was not proving amenable, she was not coming round, she was not beginning to play her part in the piece. She struggled violently, kicking at his legs, and once she kneed him painfully in the groin, and he gasped and momentarily slackened his grip on her. And from the words that filtered through to his consciousness he gradually became aware that Beatrice had betrayed him, that Florence knew all about Janet. Among the abuse that she heaped on him he caught the words, 'common little, cheap tart' and 'shop-girl' and 'vulgar little trollop', which was how Beatrice herself had so often described poor Janet. It was a shock, it helped to explain Florence's mood, and it added to Herbert's bitterness. What did these women expect of him? They were quite happy to string him along themselves, to be coy, to make his pleasure dependent on their whim, and then, when he took the obvious course of providing for himself, they became hurt and angry with him. Herbert continued with the game, he wasn't going to stop this time just to please her. He was gripping her upper arms and shaking her, and as his own mood became more vicious he ceased to do it quite in play, he began to exert something like his full strength, and her voice suddenly took on a note of fear. 'Stop it, Herbert, stop it, you're going too far.'

He began to rave at her in the foolish phrases of his fantasy.

'If Miss wants a lesson, then Miss will have one.'

He seized the lath again and began to apply it in earnest and Florence cried out and beat at him with her hands, and kicked at his legs. In the struggle she pushed him against the bench and he caught his elbow a jarring blow which numbed his arm and made him drop the stick. At the same time she kneed him in the groin again, more purposefully and much more painfully than before. He groped on the bench with his hand and found something heavier. He wanted to hurt her, to hit her, to show her, he wanted to make her regret the way she had treated him. He seized her hair in his left hand. It was a magnificent gesture, a gesture they had rehearsed in the past. He had seen it done on the films; the hero had seized the woman's hair and pulled it sharply back, pulling her face up and exposing the line of her throat. Herbert and Florence had played at this. It did not hurt if it was done carefully, and if Florence did not resist. But now Herbert pulled suddenly and savagely, and Florence cried out again, and he struck at her with the weapon he had just picked up. As he swung it he mouthed the words 'whipping' and 'thrashing' and 'scourging', timing the incantation to the swing of his arm. He struck rhythmically, swaying his body from side to side, striking across and back, hypnotized by the pattern of his movement, down from left to right, down again from right to left, criss-cross, intoning to this rhythm words about whipping her into humility, thrashing her into her senses, beating her until she learnt her lesson. And then he grew tired, and everything was very still, and when he stepped back she slowly slithered forward and fell on to her face on the floor in front of him. He was exhausted and trembling violently, and when he looked at the weapon in his hand he saw that it was an eighteen-inch length of lead piping.

After this his activity had been admirable, cool and precise. He had kept the lead pipe in his hand, he was not quite sure why but he seemed to remember that on these occasions it was a good idea to take the weapon away with you. He had examined his feet carefully and wrapped a rag taken from the bench round them before he stepped across the narrow landing and reached the bathroom. Then he had gone into the bath, still with the lead pipe and washed himself and the pipe clean of all blood. There was a devil of a noise as the water gurgled down the waste pipe but there was nothing he could do about that. He dried himself with the towel he had used earlier, carefully folded the rags he had used to swathe his feet round the lead pipe, and then wrapped it up in the towel. He was not quite sure why he did this, he just had a sense that he ought not to leave anything that he had touched in the house. He got into his wet clothes again, unpleasant this, and made his way downstairs, carefully turning off all the lights as he went. In the little hall he put on his coat and placed the pipe, in its wrapping, at the bottom of his case. Then he turned off the remaining lights and let himself out of the front door, locking it behind him. Later he realized that this was an error. He should have left the front door open, or better still, have splintered it from the outside to suggest forcible entry, but the idea simply never occurred to him at the time. Herriott Street was still dead and dark. His departure was as unmarked as his arrival.

And that was it. That was the perfect crime, the masterpiece of planning that the criminologists had wondered at for all these years. What Herbert had marvelled at later, when he had heard all the details rehearsed by the witnesses and investigators and experts, had been the sheer luck of it all. He had met nobody, either on his way to the house or when he had left it. Nobody had seen him emerge on to the main road at the corner. A tram had come almost immediately and he had jumped on to it. The window, with the black of the night behind it, had made a fair mirror, and he had been able to check his appearance. It seemed to be all right, there was nothing there to attract attention. He looked at his watch, it was nearly half past eight. He could not have been inside the house longer than about an hour altogether. Wilfred would not be back for some time yet. He began to shiver, partly as a reaction, he supposed, and partly because he was wet and was getting chilled to the bone. He began thinking more connectedly about what had just happened. How the devil had Florence heard about Janet? Beatrice must have told her. What a damned thing!

Of course, it explained a few things about Florence's behaviour. She had looked at him very queerly. She had been most unwelcoming. He had put it down to the fact that he had startled her and roused her suspicions, but now he realized that he had been wrong. She had been fuming. He had been carrying on with this little shop-girl behind her back. She must have been seething with resentment, bottling it up, saving it for the right, the effective moment, when she would spring it on him and overwhelm him with reproaches. It was no wonder that she had been so angry when he had sprung on her from behind the door and behaved with all his old freedom. She must have been wild with rage. He could not possibly have chosen a less suitable moment for his attempt. Herbert began to understand the scene much more clearly. He shivered again, his teeth were chattering. He must be careful, people would start looking at him. He could not go all the way to London like this. He needed to dry himself and get warm. It was at this moment that he thought of going to see Janet. That was about the only place in Manchester where he could safely appear, for, he must remember, officially he was travelling between Glasgow and London. Thinking about it all afterwards, Herbert recognized that he had been foolish to go to Janet's, but he could not contemplate the long rail journey in his present condition.

And Janet had greeted him so affectionately, had been so concerned about his wet things, had busied herself about making him comfortable, had expressed true sympathy for the state of his legs. She arranged him naked on her eiderdown.

'There's one thing you aren't attending to,' he said.

'What's that?'

'Come here.'

He pulled her down beside him and busied himself with the buttons on her dress.

22

Winnick was surprised at the animation which Herbert had shown at the mention of the woman who had changed her story.

'Do you really think that she was telling the truth the first time?' he asked.

But at the direct question Herbert seemed to subside. He gazed blankly at Winnick and slowly settled back in his chair again. When he finally spoke, it was in flat, deliberate tones.

'There's no knowing. She told one story and then she told another. You can't believe someone like that. But there's no doubt that the police put a lot of pressure on her – Wilfred thought they had behaved very badly.'

He eyed Winnick defiantly. Winnick could not make out what he was up to. He could have sworn that he was about to proclaim a conviction that Wilfred was innocent, but he had drawn back. He was not prepared to go that far. It must be significant. Winnick wished once again that he could get Herbert on his own. He seemed to be talking as much for Beatrice's benefit as for Winnick's. Whenever he said anything which reflected creditably on Wilfred he shot a look at Beatrice, and she nodded, or tapped his arm approvingly. Like a kind, loyal husband he desperately wanted to please his wife; but there was an inner core of integrity about him which caused him to jib at the lie direct. When Winnick tried to lead him into making a positive statement about Wilfred's innocence this honesty of his asserted itself, and he evaded the question. That, at least, was Winnick's reading of the situation. What he could not quite make out was this: was Herbert actually trying, behind Beatrice's back, as it were, to drop hints about the true story? That defiant stare of his, with his head cocked to one side, staring unblinkingly into Winnick's eyes, was it a challenge: 'Don't swallow all this stuff about Wilfred quite uncritically – I could tell you a tale if I had a mind to.' Was that what he was saying?

But then a minute later he was at it again, labouring at his task of making out a case for Wilfred that would please the old lady sitting at his side.

'The police fed the prejudice against him. There was the business about Wilfred asking all those people the way to that place he was looking for.'

'Welfield Road East?'

'Yes, that's right. Savernant said that that wasn't natural, that nobody would have asked so many people.'

Winnick considered the matter. Rimmer had asked two tram conductors, a policeman, the proprietor of a newsagent's shop and his wife, who had come out to join in the discussion, and the inhabitants of the various houses he had actually called at. It seemed an unusually large number.

'They were all people who could easily be traced and used as witnesses,' said Winnick, 'and that was a bit suspicious.'

'Yes, that was what Savernant said. But I knew Wilfred, and that was exactly the sort of thing that he would do. He was very thorough, was Wilfred, and very persistent. And they were the natural people to ask. Wilfred always used to say that if you wanted directions, if you had any sense, you went to the experts, the police, the shopkeepers, people whose job it was to know addresses. If you asked the casual passer-by you were a damn fool. That was what he used to say, wasn't it, Beatrice?'

She nodded her approval.

'There was another thing,' said Herbert. 'If Wilfred hadn't asked many people, they would have said that it was because he knew that the address didn't exist and was only pretending to look for it. Wilfred said that to me himself. He said, "I can't do a thing right, can I?"' Beatrice patted his arm in commendation.

'It was like that with the business of the motive,' she said. 'Nobody could suggest any reason at all why Wilfred should have done such a terrible thing, so they just said that it didn't matter, that there didn't need to be a reason for it at all.'

'It is, of course, a principle of English law, Mrs Naismith,' said Winnick, 'that it is not necessary to prove a motive.'

'Oh, I know all about that.' Beatrice did not actually add the words 'young man', but they were implied by her tone. 'We were told all that often enough, weren't we, Herbert? But the fact remains that a man doesn't suddenly get up and do a thing like that without having a reason for it. And they never found a reason.'

Winnick thought that he had found a reason. It was a perfect opportunity for him to spring his little surprise, but he resisted the temptation. There were one or two other matters to settle first, so he contented himself by saying, 'Do you mean that if anybody could show that Wilfred had an adequate reason, then you would believe that he was guilty?'

Beatrice was dismayed.

'What a question. I don't believe that he had a reason. What reason could he have had? I don't believe there was anything on earth that would make Wilfred do a thing like that.'

Her voice was agitated, there was a slight tremble in it. Winnick had disturbed her more than he had intended, and he hastened to soothe her, and to murmur that he had just been speaking in a speculative way and had not intended anything further by his remarks. But he thought that her reaction was odd. He noticed that earlier she had said, 'They never found a reason.' She had not said that there was no reason, she had said that they had not found it. These were very small indications, but it was out of them that he would have to construct his case, for he began to see that these old people were not likely to become more frank with him. There was one line he could follow; it would be an awkward point for Herbert to explain away.

'I was rather struck by the evidence of the next-door neighbour, Johnson, the man who was with Wilfred when he found the body. There hadn't been any quarrel between the two of them, had there? He seemed so extremely hostile.'

Johnson had been the source of many of the stories about the callousness of Wilfred. He had described his demeanour when he discovered his wife's body as being 'quite unnaturally calm', according to him Wilfred 'had not seemed at all surprised', he had used the word 'inhuman' in another part of his testimony. It had created a very strong effect. Herbert appeared to find Winnick's question a difficult one and hesitated a long time before answering.

'Wilfred never said there had been any quarrel. As a matter of fact he was surprised by Johnson, he had always thought of him as a well-meaning little chap.'

'Doesn't that mean,' struck in Winnick, 'that we should take his evidence seriously?'

'I always felt,' said Herbert, 'that he had been got at.' Winnick raised his eyebrows at this – surely not all the witnesses had been 'got at'? Herbert went on, 'What he said didn't ring true – saying that Wilfred was "inhuman" for instance. That wasn't a word he would have used naturally, he'd been put up to it.'

'I blame his wife,' said Beatrice unexpectedly. 'She didn't like Wilfred, never had. She thought he was stuck up, and he'd complained about the children more than once.'

'She was a great big woman,' said Herbert, 'Johnson did what he was told.'

All rather thin, thought Winnick as he jotted down a note, a rather desperate attempt to explain away a very damaging piece of testimony.

'How do you account, then,' he asked, 'for that remark which Wilfred made about the blood?'

This was a famous point. Savernant, in his mention of the

Rimmer case in his memoirs, had used it as an example of the small mistake which every criminal makes, which helps to bring him to justice. When Johnson had been about to smash the pane of glass so that he could put his hand through and unlock Rimmer's back door, Wilfred had said, 'Be careful, we don't want any more blood'. Savernant had made effective use of this in his final address to the jury.

'Why,' he had said, 'should the prisoner speak of "any more" blood? As far as he knew, if he was the innocent man he would have you think, there had not been any blood at all that evening. Of course, members of the jury, we know better. We know that there was a room in that house which was positively dripping with blood, stained and soaked in the blood of that poor, innocent woman. If the prisoner knew that also, then well might he say that they didn't want any more blood. No indeed, they already had blood and blood enough; but if the prisoner knew that, members of the jury, then he was guilty.'

'I thought that was very damaging to Wilfred,' said Winnick, 'but he admitted saying it.'

'I told you,' said Herbert, 'he was determined to tell the truth, even when it went against him.' Winnick's eyebrows shot up again, as Herbert had known they would, as any normal person's would. It had been a part of Wilfred's impossible, quixotic, foolish attitude towards worldly matters.

'The real trouble,' went on Herbert, 'was that they wouldn't let him explain why he said it.' Wilfred's counsel had not asked the vital question. Wilfred had tried to give his explanation but he had been stopped; he must not make speeches, he must only answer the questions that were put to him, and the question he had wanted was never put.

'What explanation?' asked Winnick. 'I didn't know that he had one.'

'Wilfred told me,' explained Herbert, 'that Johnson had mentioned that he had once had to smash his own back window to get in, and that he had cut himself rather badly.

Naturally, when he started to smash Wilfred's, Wilfred warned him to be careful and said, "We don't want any more blood". That was Wilfred's explanation.'

'But why ever wasn't he allowed to give it?'

'Because Johnson denied it. He denied having said anything like that, and his wife backed him up. His counsel said that Wilfred would be in the position of calling two ordinary, honest people, who had no axe to grind, liars, and that wouldn't go down at all well with the jury.'

Winnick tried to weigh the value of this. Herbert was simply repeating what he had been told by Wilfred. It was simply Wilfred's word against two other people. It was an ingenious explanation, quite worthy of the man who concocted the whole plot, but obviously Wilfred's own counsel had not been impressed by it. It said, Winnick thought, more about the psychology of Herbert and Beatrice than about Wilfred, or the Johnsons. For years they had been clinging to straws of this kind in their effort to convince themselves of Wilfred's innocence. Perhaps it would be worth a paragraph in his book: a pathetic, proud, lonely couple erecting psychological barriers against believing what was obvious to everyone else. There was something perversely noble about it, perhaps more especially in the case of Herbert. Winnick was convinced that Herbert suspected the truth, that he knew things which he had concealed from Beatrice. In him the effort to believe in Wilfred's innocence was an act of loyalty to his wife. He had stayed by a man he suspected of being a murderer because his wife wished it, and he continued to make a reluctant affirmation of belief in him so as not to cause her pain, there was something admirable in that. Nevertheless, it would be nice to break through Herbert's defences.

'Can you tell me, sir – you were with Wilfred right up to the end – did he ever mention any other person?'

Herbert demanded to know what he was getting at, what 'other persons' he had in mind.

'Did he, for instance, name anybody he thought was

responsible?' That was not, in fact, the only thing that Winnick had been getting at, but it would do to be going on with. He had had a slight hope that he might startle Herbert into a reference to that girl whose name he had so fortunately come across, but Herbert was not a man who was easily startled. The question seemed to make him unhappy. No, he explained, there was nobody whom Wilfred suspected.

'Didn't you find that odd? I mean the plan, the telephone call and everything, must have been made by somebody who knew Wilfred.'

Herbert's unhappiness deepened. No, he did not think that it was odd. Wilfred had believed that the person responsible was a casual intruder caught in the act of robbing the house and lashing out in a blind panic. He added that it would have been quite easy for anybody to have found out about Wilfred's working methods – all that you had to do was to enquire at his office.

Winnick smiled to himself. Herbert was being driven back to the wall. This was the orthodox defence line. Odd that after all these years someone as intelligent as Herbert should still be sticking blindly to that, he must really have run out of ideas. Savernant, in his memoirs, had exploded that one. He had pointed out that Wilfred had been too clever by half:

'He had concocted his elaborate plan of the telephone call, and the search for the bogus address in order to give himself an alibi; but there was not a sufficient motive for anybody else except himself to have gone to all that trouble. A casual criminal, of the kind posited by the defence, does not make tortuous plots involving telephone calls. Rimmer was out more often than he was in. Anybody wishing to rob him could have taken his choice of times to do it. It was an example, in my opinion, a classic example, of the fatal over-elaboration of the criminal mind. Rimmer had a brilliant intellect, he was a first-class chess player, remember, and he delighted in the display of it. I shall always remember his posturings in the witness box, the performance of a man of overwhelming intellectual arrogance. It is my belief that one of the main attractions, to Rimmer, of this murder which he had planned, was the pleasure he took in executing a brilliant scheme and trying to make fools of the police and the authorities. But, like all criminals of his type, he overreached himself and gave himself away.'

Herbert listened grimly as Winnick outlined this argument. He had heard Savernant present it in court, and had sweated with apprehension because he had not then become accustomed to the curiously blinkered way in which lawyers think. Now, here was this writing fellow, an intelligent enough chap in his own way, making exactly the same mistake. Like Savernant, like almost everybody connected with the case, including Wilfred's own lawyers, he had got stuck on one track and if anything was a bit off that track then he could not see it. He had asked a very acute question when he had wondered why Wilfred had not named anybody whom he suspected; but, having asked the question, he quite failed to see its significance. All that he meant was that Wilfred had not named anybody because he knew that he himself was guilty.

Suppose, like Herbert, that one knew that Wilfred was innocent; now the question acquired a much more fascinating dimension. Wilfred must have wondered who had done it. Somebody had plotted against him, deliberately lured him away from his own house and murdered his wife, and all this had been done in such a fiendish way as to cast grave suspicion on himself. It was not in human nature to suppose that Wilfred had not speculated about the identity of the real criminal – why, then, had he kept quiet about it? Herbert had sat with him day after day, dreading the moment when he might broach the question, but he never had. Wilfred's behaviour during those last weeks had been characterized by a self-conscious, stoical gallantry. To Herbert's taste he had been a shade too set on making a fine figure. It was part and parcel of that immense, secret vanity of his, the vanity which had led him to avoid promotion and wilfully seek obscurity. He was conscious of possessing marvellous qualities which the world would never acknowledge because it was incapable of emulating them. His own behaviour had always been immaculate because he owed it to himself that it should be immaculate. So he had refused to act a part to catch the sympathy of the court, even though doing so might have saved his life; he had spoken the truth, even when it had gone against him – lesser men would not have done that. He had been better, finer, more upright than the generality of men, and now he was suffering for it, but even in his sufferings he would show his superiority. He would walk to the gallows with a light step and a smile on his lips. To do him justice he had played the part very well; Herbert had seen too much of that sort of thing in the war to overvalue it, but it was a good performance. He had made his characteristic little jokes. He was visited regularly by the prison doctor, which led him to comment that never before had anybody taken so much care of his health.

'When I was an industrious and useful member of society,' he said, 'I could be as ill as I liked and nobody bothered. Now that they want to hang me they'll go to any lengths to keep me fit and healthy; odd isn't it?'

He played chess with one of the warders, who beat him quite regularly. 'So much for my being the great schemer,' he said. 'If Savernant heard about this fellow I suppose he'd hang him instead of me.' The warder overheard, as he was intended to, and grinned sheepishly.

Sometimes he would speak in a more philosophic vein. 'I was making a list of all my bits and pieces last night. There's not much to a life when you come to think of it. You remember how it was in the war, Herbert, after somebody had got himself killed and you had to collect all his effects. It always seemed so pitiably little. A cigarette case, a watch, some photographs, a wallet, a few letters – a whole life and that was all there was to show for it. There won't be much when I've gone. All things considered I suppose that it's as well we didn't have any children. I used to tell Florence, "this is no world to bring children into", I didn't know how true it was, did I? Now that Florence has gone there's not much for me here anyway. We had a pretty good life together. I think she was in sympathy with what I was trying to do, she was a good pal, was Florence.'

He returned to this more than once, talking to himself more than Herbert. Florence had been a 'good sort', they had been perfectly in sympathy with one another, she had 'taken him as he was'. They were variants on the theme of domestic perfection that he had played to the court. Wilfred had to reassure himself. He dared not believe that there had been anything wrong with his domestic life. He could not face the fact that he had selfishly sacrificed Florence to a peculiarly narrow view of life. He could not admit that he had neglected her, left her at home to her own devices while he pottered about on trivial pursuits. For this reason, Herbert believed, Wilfred had preferred not even to ask himself who had done this murder. Start by asking yourself a question like that and before you know where you are a host of other questions are clamouring for answers. Florence had been left alone in the house, had she, and a perfect stranger had come knocking on the door – why had she let him in? Had it, indeed, been a perfect stranger? On how many occasions before, perhaps, had she let this 'stranger' into the house when he was absent? This 'stranger' had battered Florence to death with dreadful fury. It might be that he had been looking for money and failed to find it, but if you once start to think about a possible relationship between Florence and this man that she had let into her house it was easy to imagine stronger, more plausible reasons why such an attack should have been made. Wilfred must have pushed thoughts like this away, out of his mind. They made nonsense of all that he believed that he had achieved in his life. They were very simple, even obvious, questions; Savernant and the others had not asked them because they were blinkered; Wilfred did not ask them because he dared not. This man who had always prided himself on his fearless logic and strict adherence to the truth had finally achieved a kind of triumph over his own intelligence, deliberately closed his eyes to reality, and prattled on about 'darling Florence' and the perfect life they had led together because he could not face up to the fact that he had been a failure on his own terms.

Herbert had had to sit back and listen while Wilfred struck his attitudes and reflected complacently on his past life.

'All in all, I think I can honestly say that, apart from the war, there are not many things that I've done that I'm ashamed of. Not many men can say that.'

'I never cared much about worldly success. Things of the mind, they were the things I valued – what is it that Matthew Arnold says about the disinterestedness of culture?'

'It always seemed to me that there must be more in life than what most chaps got out of it – you've got to go your own way, you mustn't be one of the herd. I always tried to make myself independent, Herbert.'

Herbert had meekly assented to all these propositions. Wilfred dismissed his being in the condemned cell as an accident.

'It has come on me, it is a misfortune. Some people get struck by blindness or paralysis, I've been struck by this. Now I've got to show that I can bear it properly.'

He said this at their last meeting, and had given an excellent performance of a man confronting an unavoidable calamity with fortitude. He had thanked Herbert for all that he had done in the months after the murder. He had re-affirmed his innocence and asked Herbert to bear witness to that affirmation. He had sent his love to Beatrice. They had shaken hands. Wilfred, with a kind of parody of old-world courtesy, had escorted Herbert to the door of the cell. It had been a pattern ending.

After leaving the prison Herbert had returned straight

away to London. He had no fancy for an early morning ceremony, waiting for a man to post a notice outside the prison gates. He had spent the night after reaching Wimbledon prowling about the house. Beatrice was under heavy sedation in charge of a nurse and, apart from the servants, he was alone. Wilfred was dying by the light of his philosophy, and he, Herbert, was living by the light of his. And if Wilfred could conjure up memories of the trenches to give him fortitude, well, so could he. Many a time he had killed a man to stop the man killing him. One's fate may be spelt out, but there is no harm in helping it a little. God helps those who help themselves. He had shot many a man in the guts and never lost a night's sleep over it.

Herbert had wandered from room to room; every so often he looked at his watch and thought of Wilfred.

Herbert observed, with gratification, that Winnick was about to take his departure. At least, he was fishing about, scooping up papers and stuffing them into his case, folding up his notebook, putting his pencil back into his pocket, all unmistakable signs that the interview was drawing to a close. Beatrice was leaning back in her chair looking gaunt and tired and hopeless. Serve her right. It had been her idea in the first place. He'd warned her all about it, and she had chosen to disregard his advice, and this was the consequence. The fellow was making hee-hawing noises, phrases like 'most grateful' and 'invaluable assistance' and 'first-hand information' fell from him. Beatrice offered him a limp hand, and he shook it cordially. He was standing now, almost ready to go, thank God. Herbert actually went and brought his raincoat from the hall, anxious that nothing should delay him. He put it on and carefully buttoned it up, standing there in the middle of the room. There was something offensive to Herbert about the deliberateness of his movements. He half turned towards the door and paused, holding his briefcase up against his chest while he made a little fuss about closing and locking it, and while he did this he spoke.

'Oh, there was just one other thing.' He fiddled with the lock of the case. 'It was a name I turned up when I was looking through the files of the local newspaper. I don't suppose there's anything in it,' Winnick gave a deprecating laugh, 'but I wondered if you could throw any light on it.' He made a parade of finding and consulting a scrap of paper. Herbert suddenly grew wary. 'It was over a year after the actual – er – murder,' continued Winnick. 'I suppose that is why none of the national papers took it up. It was a girl,' he suddenly looked directly at Herbert and Beatrice. 'She tried to drown herself in the River Mersey, near Stockport.' Herbert stood stockstill. Beatrice looked only mildly interested, puzzled rather than anything else. Winnick continued.

'She was pulled out of the river by a passing workman. He did his best to revive her but by the time the doctor came the shock had killed her. According to the workman, before she died she said something, something about Wilfred Rimmer, something about not having done anything to help him, something about blaming herself. Under cross-examination the workman got very confused and he was not at all sure of the exact words.'

Winnick paused to judge the effect of this. There was no response from Beatrice except bewilderment, but Winnick could have sworn that Herbert had stiffened up, it had meant something to him, and he was determined not to give himself away.

'I never heard anything about that,' said Beatrice. 'Did you, Herbert?'

'Not a thing,' said Herbert.

'You still don't remember any girl who was connected with Wilfred in any way?' Winnick persisted.

'There can't have been anything in it,' said Herbert. 'If there had been the papers would have been on to it like a shot.'

'It was over a year after, the case was pretty dead by then.'

'The workman must have got it wrong, or the girl was wandering in her mind. There were a lot of cranks about, you know. The police were getting about four confessions a week at one time. It doesn't mean anything.'

Winnick privately thought that the gentleman protested a bit too much, but he had to admit that he had not produced the effect he had hoped. Obviously Beatrice knew nothing at all, and Herbert could not honestly be said to have given himself away to any real extent.

'I expect you're right,' he said, mildly. He made another elaborate parade of placing the scrap of paper back amongst his documents, and half turned towards the door. Beatrice was now behind him, but he was still able to keep his eye on Herbert as he chattered away, apparently aimlessly.

'I thought it was worth asking, just in case it happened to ring a bell. Does the girl's name mean anything to you? It was Wilson, Janet Wilson.'

Herbert's face remained carefully expressionless, in fact Winnick noticed the absence of expression as a positive indication of his self-control and determination not to betray anything. If he had been looking at Beatrice he would have been immensely gratified by what he saw, but he had turned away from her and saw nothing. The very slight gasp that she made was covered by Herbert's answer.

'No, no, it doesn't mean a thing.'

Winnick turned to Beatrice.

'It isn't a name that you recognize, Mrs Naismith?'

This was Beatrice's chance. She had invited this man to her home in order to get at the truth about Wilfred and clear his name, and here was a direct question for her to answer.

'No,' she said, 'I don't recognize it.'

'You see my line of thinking,' said Winnick. 'Was there some kind of connection between this girl and Wilfred that, perhaps, provided a motive for the crime?'

'I am quite sure,' said Beatrice, speaking very deliberately, articulating her words with great care, 'that Wilfred had nothing whatever to do with this girl.'

'You will, perhaps, see more clearly what I have in mind,' said Winnick, 'when I tell you that according to evidence given at the inquest, the girl had recently had a baby.'

There was a dead silence about this. It was broken after what seemed a very long time, by Herbert.

'I really do not think that there is anything else that we can tell you, Mr – er – Winnick.'

Winnick took the hint. He had got his coat on, his briefcase was in his hand, these people were not going to tell him anything more, there was nothing to keep him. He thanked them again for all their help, their responses, he noted, were muted, and took his leave. As he walked down the street he felt pretty well satisfied. Of course he had hoped for more. He had hoped that one or other of those old people would have given something away, but they had been very careful, revealingly careful one might say. Still, he was morally certain that that name had meant something to Herbert. He wondered at what point in the case Herbert had got to know about the girl. Had Wilfred confessed her existence? Or had she herself suddenly turned up out of the blue? Winnick preferred this second idea. It fitted in better with what she had said when she was fished out of the river. She must have wanted to help her lover, and certainly, when she had known that she was pregnant, she would have tried to get in touch. Possibly she had even had some romantic notion that if she appeared and pleaded on Wilfred's behalf the court would take a lenient view. There must have been a pretty scene. Winnick could imagine the consternation which her sudden appearance would have caused to Herbert and the lawyers. Their trump card was the absence of anything like a motive, and now here was this girl, pregnant, threatening to occupy the witness box and blazon forth her love for Wilfred. They would have acted to put a stop to that one quickly enough. She would have been bundled away somewhere in secret to have her child, sworn to say nothing to anyone, no doubt, and warned of the consequence if she did. Winnick positively skipped down the road in the excitement of these ideas.

All the weight and worry of this would have fallen on Herbert's shoulders. Winnick thought of that dour figure again. What an extraordinary role his had been! How devotedly he had tried to help a man whom he did not even like! And all in the service of his wife. His one concern had been to save her distress. He must have concealed this particular misdemeanour of Wilfred's from Beatrice all through these years. Probably he had wanted to protect her from this knowledge because he was afraid to hurt her by telling her how completely her sister had been betrayed and misused. From this whole sordid story he was almost the only person who emerged with real credit. Winnick began to see that a minor, but still important, theme of his book would lie just here.

Winnick wished that he had been able to find out something more about the child, or the girl herself, for that matter. The police, he knew, had investigated the story. 'We always investigate such stories, sir,' he had been told with rather heavy emphasis, but they had not been able to find a single link between this girl and the murder, and so they had written her off as a crank. Winnick himself had had no better success. Rimmer had been clever, you had to give him that. Not only had he nearly pulled off the perfect murder, but he had managed to carry on an affair of that kind, probably for a number of years, and not left a single trace. Certainly by the time he had turned his hand to murder, Wilfred Rimmer must already have been an accomplished schemer. It was a pity, Winnick thought, that he had not been able to get in touch with the brother of that girl. He might have had a tale to tell. At the inquest he had given a pretty tight-lipped performance, judging by the account in the newspaper. No, he had known nothing about the baby's father; no, he had never heard his sister speak of Wilfred Rimmer; yes, his sister had been depressed recently; no, she had not confided in him. That was all that the inquest had got out of him. Shortly afterwards he had gone to Australia, and after that the trail had gone cold. Winnick did not even know whether he was still alive. The child was probably still living somewhere; Winnick wondered if it knew anything of its parentage.

Well, it was all a long time ago. He had done pretty well, all things considered, nobody else was likely to do better. At long last he had found a motive – an explanation of the Rimmer case that rang psychologically true. He rolled these words round in his head; they would look well on the dust-jacket. He wondered what the old couple were doing now that he had left. Herbert undoubtedly would have a lot of explaining to do, all the details about Wilfred's having had a lover, and an illegitimate child, would be new and surprising to Beatrice. The old lady would be having a bit of a cry over it. At last she would have to face the fact of Wilfred's guilt. There was one consolation. Her husband's self-sacrificing goodness would no longer be hidden under a bushel. She would be able to recognize exactly what he had done for her over the years and the extent of his loyalty towards Wilfred.

Winnick smiled; he thought that she would find this sufficient consolation.

All these books are available at your local bookshop or newsagent, or can be ordered direct from the publisher.

To order direct from the publisher just tick the titles you want and fill in the form below.

Name ____________________

Address ____________________

____

Send to:
Panther Cash Sales
PO Box 11, Falmouth, Cornwall TR10 9EN.

Please enclose remittance to the value of the cover price plus:

UK 45p for the first book, 20p for the second book plus 14p per copy for each additional book ordered to a maximum charge of £1.63.

BFPO and Eire 45p for the first book, 20p for the second book plus 14p per copy for the next 7 books, thereafter 8p per book.

Overseas 75p for the first book and 21p for each additional book.

Panther Books reserve the right to show new retail prices on covers, which may differ from those previously advertised in the text or elsewhere.